N⊕CTURN

NOCTURN

Book, the First

Book 1 of the Empyrean Cycle

RONALD ANDRÉS MOORE

EMPYREAN
CHAPTERHOUSE

FOREWORD

⊷————◆————⊶

When I sat down to write *The Dark World* series, it seemed natural that it'd be about vampires. Vampires have permeated my world since I was a young girl. The stakes—heh—in vampire novels and movies always excited me more than the conflicts in other monster movies. Vampires, simply, were my focus. It's why I was honored to read Ronald A. Moore's vampire novel, *NOCTURN: Book 1* many a moon ago.

I met Ronnie Moore through Before Sunrise Press where we both were having vampiric works of ours published. Mine, a short story, his, *NOCTURN: Book 1*, the riveting, claustrophobic vampire novel of epic proportions.

NOCTURN: Book 1 gripped me from the very beginning with a setting as intricate and delicately developed as its characters. With vampires—and vampire hunters abound within its pages, *NOCTURN: Book 1* became a novel I would not forget, even as the years pass. His vampires are a fresh take on what I feel vampires have always been at their core: Creations for a purpose beyond themselves. Whether it be to take blood for the sake of surviving, or, in this case, existing to dish out justice to those deserving of it (and sometimes not). At its core *NOCTURN: Book 1* is a riveting tale of that morally gray area we humans always seem to dwell within. It asks the question, "What would happen if we got rid of our criminals and placed them within a town away from the good?" And it answers that question with a roaring romp through darkness, blood, and gore. And now, with this 10th anniversary edition being released, I'm bidden to explore the dark, wonderful town he's created once again. And I hope you will too. It's one hell of a ride.

S.C. Parris, Atlanta, Georgia 2023

PREFACE TO THE 10th ANNIVERSARY EDITION

—◦—

"I must create a system, or be enslaved by another man's.
I will not reason and compare: my business is to create."
— **William Blake**, *Jerusalem:*
The Emanation of the Giant Albion (1820)

Through fiction, we saw the birth
Of futures yet to come.
Yet in fiction lay the bones
Ugly in their nakedness;
Yet under this mortal sun
We cannot hide ourselves.
- **ISIS**, *"In Fiction" Panopticon (2004)*

In May of 2009, I wasn't thinking about writing a novel. I was a house painter working for a property management company. I was an aspiring but subpar singer/songwriter and a worse part-time bartender and barista in North Alabama. My band had just returned from another dismal tour out west where we had lost money and I had no inspiration and little motivation to continue creating. Having lost my mother, grandmother and a younger brother (to breast cancer, complications from cancer and cerebral encephalitis respectively) in the two years prior, death marked my every thought. The sources of light and hope in my life had been extinguished one by one and here I was, an eternal black sheep, a college dropout and toiling handyman, riddled and torn apart by survivor's guilt and depression.

My daily life consisted of running a paint sprayer and staring at blank white walls while blasting music out of a small cd player/boombox and avoiding any inward thought. This became a pretty ham-fisted version of meditation. Around 9:30am, I would put *Panopticon* by Isis on repeat and begin painting to its heavy drone until 5pm. By allowing my mind to wander and pull away from my constant emotional pain, I found an outlet for my creative energy. This would result in a series of vignettes, using different classic tropes: zombies, vampires, post-apocalyptic sword-and-sandal adventures. One of those vignettes intrigued me more than the others. It was a short story about a vampire named Michael. *Monsters in the Age of Man* started as scribbles on a yellow steno pad on an upturned paint bucket and continued to evolve into a 200,000 word behemoth of a Victorian gothic novel called *The Golden Lantern*, which finally became *NOCTURN: Book 1* with a little smart editing by Brenda Errichiello. The content editor was Karolina Manko. It featured artwork by a phenomenal artist from Barcelona named Joel Güell and was published in 2013 by a Boston-based vanity press focusing on transgressive horror called Before Sunrise Press under the direction of Jay Karales.

It was released alongside Charles Ray Hasting Jr's *Tea on the Riviera,* a body horror novel by Karales called *Disorder* and a S.C. Parris short story called *A Night of Frivolity*, which like *NOCTURN: Book 1,* was a vampire horror set in the 19th century and would set the stage for her *The Dark World* series.

Vampire fiction isn't new. From Lord Ruthven to Carmilla, Varney to Count Dracula and from Nosferatu and Barnaby Collins to Lestat and Nandor the Relentless (a personal favorite), the court of vampires has haunted popular culture for a quarter of a millennium. The mysterious vampire went from cursed revenant in 18th century eastern European poetry to horror royalty as a staple of victorian media, popular both on stage and in print. And as its narrative grew, it even became a Hollywood legend. The vampire story has terrified us in every form of storytelling, but I believe the vampire is always most terrifying on the page. It has been drafted for a quarter millennia from simple lines of poetry, weaving its way in and out of folklore into popular narrative and drafted and redrafted. Starting as a rough sketch, he grows and evolves into something more complex— sometimes sympathetic, sometimes aloof, always dangerous.

By 2009, the literary world was still being continually bemused by the success of Twilight. Buffy and Angel had been overshadowed by Bella and Edward and Victorian horror had waned in popularity. Nevertheless, I was still attracted to the landscape of the 19th century and originally the story would be set in the civil war. I remember reading *Fevre Dream* by George R.R. Martin and being entranced with its sense of place. Set along the Antebellum Mississippi river with business-minded, adventurous vampires, it felt like *Dracula* via Mark Twain. Around that time I had also come across *Blindsight* by Peter Watts, whose vampires were so alien and so familiar, both evolved and so primordial. Unfortunately, very little of that weird made it into the writing of *Nocturn: Book 1*.

The path to a novel came in four basic phases. Once I realized that what I was writing each evening was becoming more than a dabbling flirtation with some short fiction and was in fact an obsession to explore the rules of the weird, microcosmic world I was beginning to expand. Each night, I was avoiding friends more and disengaging more socially to escape into the exploration of a dismal nineteenth century town with no real hope of escape. So I began to take it more seriously. Obsessively.

Right off the bat I decided that the tone would be overwhelmingly gothic and likely be a little excessive on the prose. I mean, if you're going to write a book, you should write the one with all your favorite stuff in it, turned all the way up to ten. What if it's the only book you ever get to write? I say go all on in. With *NOCTURN*, that was the compulsion— to write a story, no— to finish a story- yeah and it'll have some weird religious stuff and I'll keep that vampire thing and then I was exploring a world of story that I loved.

On the other hand, the story began to have a sense of urgency; that want to be told. So somewhere between me working as a photo studio technician and the opening of a restaurant, I wrote a story.

I decided that if the story was going to feature vampires, they were going to be scary. I wanted to explore the gothic story and feature the classic villain. I figured that I'd read enough of the classics to start there. The opening scene of the novel is pretty much where I started writing the first draft and that segment pretty well stayed throughout the whole of the drafting process from short story to 200,000 mammoth and back to the more trimmed version that ended up in the original publication and the even more heavily edited *10th Anniversary edition*. The first finished draft of the novel was called "The War Ender."

It was objectively terrible.

Aside from having no real story or objective, it was just dark meanderings for some cardboard characters. The early draft featured a very binary look at heaven and hell and good and evil while not going anywhere. To say the characters were cardboard would have suggested that they had some shape. It did chase down what I found to be an interesting question, "Have we outgrown our own ghosts stories?" or in other words, could the vampire of old, survive my heavy-handed sensibility which had been carved of mostly comic books and MTv and I learned that no, I could not write a truly authentic gothic story. I missed subtlety.

The second draft, now titled *Monsters in the Age of Man*, which still played on the same note of "Man is truly the great evil" trope had a more evolved vampire, which I had stylized Vampyre to mimic Polidori's spelling and even began incorporating classic gothic horror tropes to give structure to my lack of story.

A third take titled, *The Golden Lantern* finally began taking on an organic shape using a broad conspiracy-driven narrative. Michael, the Vampyre would play into a cat-and-mouse narrative featuring opposing factions but the factions kept getting bigger and weirder. What originally began as vampire versus human grew into North versus South in the American Civil War then it became ancient and decadent organizations fighting for mankind.

By the fourth major draft now entitled *NOCTURN*, I had an idea of what my story would look like and I thought I had already written the novel. Ultimately, I went back and picked through each draft until I had something with a structure, a few compelling characters and a sense of place, a fictional Virginia mining town called "Breton," though the name was just a reference to André Breton, a surrealist who I really enjoyed.

With a place and time, I began to let my characters roam free and found, as I carved away at the story, a gnostic thread that tied together a lot of the esoteric pieces of the lore and created a dressing from which I could make choices about relevant tone. So with semi-religious "Vampyres" armed with Victorian pomp set in a conspiracy-laden American Civil War, I finally had an idea of what the story might look like.

That story would undergo twelve major drafts until we arrived at something we thought we could publish.

At the time of the novel's publication, I had already opened and closed a coffee shop and opened a new American bistro with my father. Life had changed. I had changed. The book and the world of that story which I had cultivated took root and began to evolve. The publication of *NOCTURN: Book 1* was the birth of what I now refer to as *The Empyrean*, a pocket universe where all my stories would take place.

Ten years later, that world has continued to evolved into many stories. My father is now gone and I spend more time traveling to *The Empyrean* than ever. My goal with this 10th Anniversary edition is to introduce you, as a reader, to some of those stories. As that world has grown deeper and more real for me as a writer, I have looked back at *NOCTURN: Book 1* and realized that it needed it a little extra editing to adjust for how it would lay the introductory groundwork into *The Empyrean*.

Did I want to go back to a book I had already gotten published? Absolutely not. But as I pulled on the threads of the original narrative, I saw that I could not move forward with the other books without a little more context. That resulted in a slightly more condensed, darker version of Michael's story with a broader view of his world and my own. I have spent the last decade unpacking a lot of my conservative christian upbringing and realized that the dark religious overtones in my writing are expressions of my attempt to dismantle systems of belief that no longer served me in my life. I have found that they continue to make a fantastic framework upon which to hang the horrors of the universe as I see them.

Ronald Andrés Moore, Montpelier, Vermont 2023

CRUX SACRA SIT MIHI LUX
NON DRACO SIT MIHI DUX
VADE RETRO SATANA
NUNQUAM SUADE MIHI VANA
SUNT MALA QUAE LIBAS
IPSE VENENA BIBAS

PROLOGUE

When I was a child, I spake as a child,
I understood as a child, I thought as a child:
but when I became a man, I put away childish things.
For now we see through a glass, darkly;
but then face to face: now I know in part;
but then shall I know even as also I am known.
- I Corinthians 13:11-12 (KJV) (1611)

The seven o'clock summons bell had long rung. Parson Everett Adler muttered curses at the people entering the small wood-hewn church. He was already frustrated and knew things were getting worse. Across the town square, with its benches and looming trees, the Crow's Nest Inn was filling with patrons.

Someone in the small town of Breton had stirred very old, forgotten fears in Adler's calloused heart. He'd had every intention of being a man of the cloth and living a holy life. Instead, he had come to Breton, Virginia with other special people like him hoping to be a man of the people.

Everett Adler was neither.

His nephew, Stephen Smith was down at the general store eating candy, he presumed. The general store was one of many small storefronts that faced the town square. Even though it was only hundreds of feet away, it was far enough away for Stephen.

Adler never let the boy sit in on town meetings. Stephen worked as the church's only deacon but Parson Adler made sure the boy was never put out of the way. He was a beloved son of the parishioners. Though the boy was slow to learn, Stephen was an asset to Parson Adler in the physical things. He placed candles and rang the church bell.

Almost everyone in Breton worked in the local government. Some focused on the chaotic Vampyres. Others tracked the work in the coal mines.

Everett Adler had been a very talented physicist once in a prior life. The entire town of Breton ran on one of his more successful experiments. *But all things have a half-life.* He thought. That experiment was failing. Without that, things were going to get more difficult very soon. Adler had received a letter from the mayor warning that a "Vampyre hunter of some great renown" might be on the way. The parson's outside contacts informed him that the "hunter's" name carried some import. He was dangerous. If he'd been younger, Adler would have given the Vampyre hunter over to the Brethren.

He knew better.

There would be no bargaining with the bloodthirsty Brethren. Those Vampyres would ruin this multi-decade operation. Adler knew deep down, that the Alliance would blame him..

"Was this not a seven o'clock meeting gentlemen?" Adler had grown numb to the death and gore of Breton. It was now a game of numbers and efficiency instead of a fight for the lives of people—his people. Or at the very least, people like him.

The "League", Alliance agents who monitored the town were very talkative that evening. Raymond Warner and Doctor Benedict Brown whispered. A group of huddled monitors gossiped about the upkeep of Desmond Burroughs's home with Mr. J. Gregory Long. "You know, they say, he doesn't even stay there." Others sat waiting. The room was full. Even with weekly meetings and daily reports, it seemed the town was coming unthreaded. Something was working against them from the inside. Parson Adler stood in the doorway of the church eyeing the town for suspicious activity.

Nothing.

From a distance, he could see the new Sheriff approaching, which always meant bad news. Adler cursed. He didn't trust the new Sheriff any more than the old one. He fingered the piece of paper in his pocket, which warned of this man's betrayal. The courier girl always dropped them off, but never knew where they came from. He would have to weed out where the problem was coming from himself.

"Afternoon, parson." The sheriff said, with hat in hand.

"Sheriff Matheson."

"Bad news, I'm afraid," the sheriff said. "Does the name Ruthven mean anything to you?"

Parson Adler cursed under his breath. *Burroughs is going to get us all killed.*

*Whoever battles monsters should see to it that
in the process he does not become a monster himself.
And when you look long into the abyss,
the abyss also looks into you.*
- Friedrich Nietzsche, *Beyond Good and Evil,*
Aphorism 146 (1883)

PART I

Princeps glorioissime caelestis militiae,
sancte Michæl Archangele,
defende nos in proêmio et colluctatione,
quae nobis adversus principes et potestates,
adversus mundi rectores tenebrarum harum,
contra spiritual nequitiae, in caelestibus
-Prayer to Saint Michæl (1890)
As noted in the journal of A.G., Prof. Emérita,
u de Salamanca *(1890)*

ΟΠΕ

I n the days to come, he would call himself Michael.
He woke with a start, his face buried in dirty rags and detritus. Death saturated the air. Lifting himself from the pile of tatters in the darkness, his body agonized down to the bone. His atrophied hands shook, the fingers curling with pain. His head throbbed and swam. *Am I not dead?*

Bile erupted from his mouth in thin red and yellow threads. *No. Not dead.*

Again, he labored against his body, only to feel the weight of his head roll down between his shoulders. He slumped with his head in his trembling hands.

Waves slapped the hull of the ship. They must have crashed ashore. But who were they? *Who am I?* The man whimpered. He rubbed his eyes, the haze of his vision becoming clear in the tenebrous half-light. The floor was splintered and gnarled. The salty and putrid cloths that had made his bed were not rags at all. They were the desiccated corpses of his erstwhile crew mates.

Horror filled him and passed like a dream someone was trying to describe before subsiding into a calm divorced from reality. Eyes were missing, maggots writhing in the burned out sockets. Their faces contorted and frozen in painful richter. Their open mouth playgrounds to flies and vermin. The bodies had been dumped in this place, mummified; skin pulled taut against bone and sinew. The mass grave comprised men still clutching rifles, pistols and knives. All rendered useless. Beyond hammocks, shredded upon their hooks, he saw a shred of daylight. He could

3

escape. The last remnants of the afternoon's orange glow lit stairs from the deck.

Last night, he thought, rubbing his head. *Was it last night?* From the decay of everything around him, days must have passed. *Days?* Crude, indecipherable glyphs covered the walls. Dried blood covered every surface. It smelled good. *Iron and salt.* It smelled sweet. *Honey.* His mouth watered. He examined his hands and arms. His clothes were shredded, caked in black blood but there wasn't a scratch on him. Someone or something had spared him.

He crawled toward the stairs, overwhelmed with a sickening aversion to the glimmering sunlight. It moved like a mirage of a waterfall. His stomach churned.

He reached for the rail. As his hand passed into the light, a flash of unbearable pain struck him. He jerked the flaming appendage back with a hoarse, uncanny shriek. Smoke rolled across his wrist and knuckles. The seared skin bubbled and the hairs on his arm disappeared in flashes of small, bright flame. He pulled it to his chest, collapsing onto the splintered floor. He shook in jaw-clenching agony. He moaned, but his atrophied throat could no longer find a voice. Somewhere in the pain, he could feel unseen eyes watching him.

A presence filled the darkest recess of the hold; a shadow within shadows.

This was Hell.

"Are... you..." He tried. His atrophied throat let out little more than a breathy whisper. *Are you my jailer?*

He clutched his arm, crawling away from the demoniac presence, on the verge of sanity-breaking panic. Whatever it was, he knew, meant to consume him. Nothing moved. He had to remind himself he was alone. He cast glances from one corner of the hold to the other. The presence was always out of sight, but something in the corner of his eye haunted the young man.

He sat still. Time passed.

His panic subsided. He bandaged the wound with a bit of bloodied pant-leg that stuck to the charred, wet flesh. His fingers would not uncurl. Where flesh had been, blackened ligature and sinew reeled.

He hung a hammock in the hold and lay until nightfall with a bare leg hanging from the side, listening to the ocean. The ruined arm lay across his chest and he watched the skin as it continued to bubble with the passing hours. He listened to birds. In his mind, he followed the wind through portholes, listening to the tell-tale sounds around him. The ship's wheel turned, creaking rudderless. A singsong drip echoed in the corner opposite him.

The pain diminished over the hours and panic gave way to frustration and anger. *I will kill whoever did this.* He considered the presence. *I'll kill you too.*

With nightfall, he braved his way outside to find that he was at last free from his cell. His curse would soon feel very little like a curse after all. Though the presence was always nearby, it did not hinder the young man's movements. It moved like a shadow. It felt like a dark reflection.

The night wind was calm. The rain had stopped. The old galleon had been torn in half, sheered down the middle with a great force, splintered and curling. The rear half (including the captain's quarters, the galley and some of the crew quarters) wedged between gargantuan rocks. The rest was gone. The ship's splayed guts hung open toward the rocks. The rear mast jutted out, a splintered bone from the broken hip of the dead ship. He peered over the edge, where enormous crags reached up to him. The rock formations were as skeletal knees rising from the ocean along the fifty foot cliff wall. There was no beach. There was no way to climb the cliff face and the ocean below crashed into the rocks, meaning certain death.

He questioned the elaborate nature of his hell and its jailer. Why go through all the trouble for one man to survive? Again, it seemed that the infernal ship would entrap him.

He looked down at his bare feet. "I guess I'm going to need some shoes." He said aloud, hearing his own voice for the first time. It had a clear and resonant timbre and as he cleared his throat, he found no sign of the hoarseness that had come before.

The deck below his feet was little more than a collection of splinters, yet he felt no pain as he strode across it. Even the angle of the ship, in its precarious position seemed to have little effect on him. Gravity now held less sway over him. He stood perpendicular to the wet, disjointed deck sloping away from him. The last torrents of rain water, ran over the sides of the galleon. He examined his bare foot. *Smooth. Not a single nick.* He looked at his arm, still wrapped in what had been a very bloody pant leg but now saw that it was devoid of blood. He flexed his fingers.

I am a revenant. But to what beguiling devil am I now beholden? Once again, the presence, dark and ever-present came to mind and he searched his mind for it. Whatever it was, gave no outward sign of being aware of him.

He grabbed a rigging knife from the deck and held it in his left hand. He grasped the thing gingerly. The rusty, dull blade wouldn't even do its job, but he slashed the hooked knife hard across his right arm. The heavy-handed incision was ugly but small and healed right before his eyes. *No blood. No scab. No scar.*

5

His shrill laugh echoed out into the vast emptiness beyond the ship and was swallowed up in the sound of the ocean. Though his wrapped hand still agonized, the damages done under the moonlight healed quickly.

He ran to the edge of the ship and looked over again. Jumping off was still an enormous risk. He listened to the sail slapping against the mast and formulated a new plan. The rope tied to the sail was inches out of reach. He jumped, grabbing at the frayed end, but fell to the deck softly as though he'd been flying. Up and down he went, like a child growing giddy, each time touching down on the balls of his bare feet. He put his hands to the mast with a grin and climbed up, barely touching the treated wood.

He pulled out the knot and watched the rope fall, gathering on the floor. *Twenty, twenty-five feet?* Without a second thought, he jumped and landed with the grace of a lion. With a flourish of his hands, he whispered, "Ta-da!" for an invisible audience. The horror of his own monstrosity dissipated in the wonder of his ability.

He ran to the captain's quarters. There was a velvet couch lined with stained oak, a large desk that once held the captain's log and a beautiful bed. Was this the same ship where he'd awoken?. He decided that all the money and true design of the ship was to please one man while all the others toiled in squalor. Had he been one of the one toiling?

The thought enraged him. *I am no slave.*

The contents of the room were scattered. A white silk shirt hung from a bedpost where it had been windswept.

As he rummaged for clothing, or clues to his own identity, he looked up, foolish. In the astonishment of the wonders and horrors put upon his body, he had missed a startling mystery. *How exactly does a galleon end up some thirty feet above the water and crumpled into the rocks?* He couldn't remember. The more he thought about the night of the storm, the sicker he felt. He felt vertigo, as though standing on the precipice of a bottomless pit. It was difficult to think about and soon enough, he gave up on it.

Along the floor, he found a change of clothes and everything he would need to survive. He pocketed some gold and after organizing his provisions in a sack, he sat down on the red velvet couch.

Broken shutters on the rear galley windows allowed a soft white glow. The world around him was dark and beautiful. The reflection of the full moon on the face of the ocean broke up in the waves like a chandelier of infinite shards spreading as far as the eye could see. He wrapped himself in the captain's faded wool bridge coat. *Guess he won't be needing this anymore.* He liked its gold buttons and round epaulette shoulders lined in gold laces. He wriggled his toes in black patent leather, thinking, *Even the shoes fit. Someone out there, some god, devil or otherwise, has given you a second chance—whatever your name is.*

He could hear his name. He knew its sound and shape. Somewhere within the echo of a thought, over the edge of the endless void that was memory, he could hear it.

Then it was gone again.

No point in dwelling on the trauma. He thought.

Within moments, he was back outside and with an eye to the top of the cliff. He wrapped the rope around the base of the mast, then the other end around his ankle. He threw the bag of provisions over his shoulder and climbed down the side of the ship like a spider along a wall. The rest of the way was easy. He leaped from boulder to boulder with increasing ease until he found himself at the face of the cliff.

Upon reaching the top, he stood at the edge of a dark forest. He took the rope, which was still not completely taut, from his ankle and tied it around a nearby tree. He stretched his legs and wandered into the dark with a crooked smile toward the voices of a nearby town.

Unseen and unheard, two Vampyres watched from beyond the trees as the broken man emerged from the cliffside.

What have we done? One asked. *What have* you *done?*

He's beautiful. The other Vampyre answered.

They watched in horror and for the latter, with equal parts glee.

It just wouldn't die. The first couldn't control the thoughts that bubbled to the edge of his mind. *Why wouldn't he die? What is it?*

He *is our future.* The second one said.

It's trouble. The first said. *You'll come to regret this.*

Trouble. The other Vampyre repeated. *Whatever he is, he's one of us now.*

His companion looked away, hiding his thoughts as best he could, but his shame was obvious.

We were once free men. We judged as was right in our hearts. He scoffed. *First Chichen Itza and Tikal, then Roanoke. Now, we're relegated to this?* He gestured at the forest around them. *Corralled. Secreted away. Penned. Satiated to boredom.*

That thing down there is going to be the end of us. The first whispered.

This feels right. He'll come around. We all did. The Vampyre laughed without mirth. *And if he doesn't, so what? What life was this anyway? Endlessness. Immortality. The same song with no end.*

You're going to get us all killed.

So what? The Vampyre grinned. *So what?*

The Crow's Nest Inn was the only real drinking establishment in town but Glenn Lamphere tried not to let it become a doggery. Green wallpaper had faded to gray and peeled along the seams. It was trimmed away and covered with etchings and floral paintings. Only one picture of the owner and his family hung over the bar. A much younger, thinner Glenn Lamphere with a chin of peach fuzz stared grim-faced in the linotype. His young wife Zoya, now long-gone, held a swaddled newborn.

The tavern, which made up the ground floor of the inn was bursting with miners, soldiers and farmhands. The sounds of clapping and singing along with fiddle, jug and banjo filled the room. Men drank whiskey and cider. Ladies tended toward the cider, though no one particularly enjoyed it.

The only person unaffected in the revelry was Ernest Williams. Assistant to Mayor Heath and part-time librarian, the portly Mister Williams sat cramped and dejected, as was his wont, in a corner. Ernest stared into a near empty cup of cider as though an answer would be found in its foul golden eye. "Why will no one pay me heed?"

"Perhaps it's because you often speak to your cider, Mister Williams," answered Marie Sutton. The top-heavy and round-faced barmaid smiled and replaced his empty drink with a full one.

He stared into the "fresh" cup of cider, which smelled more of bread and corn than it did anything of apple or pears. It was apropos of his own feelings. Wasn't there something left in his life? He swigged the rotten stuff. "Nope."

Something was eating at him. Somehow, his life added up to the sum of two fruitless careers. He was a librarian in a town that didn't read and assistant to a Mayor that he rarely saw. Wasn't he better than that? Smarter than that? He finished the drink faster than expected for how little he enjoyed the experience of drinking it. *A small consolation, I suppose.*

His head was swimming. The next day would be as bad as this one, if not worse. He adjusted his spectacles and laid some money on the table next to the empty cup with a shaky hand. He muddled his way to his feet.

"Goodnight." Kat Lamphere, the innkeeper's daughter smiled. "Get home safe." She passed him with a large tray of cups, pulling her aproned dress in to squeeze between tables. "Marie, give me a hand over here!"

He stood outside the door with a head full of rotten apples. He pulled his scarf tight and looked west, toward the residential areas, where his small home hid. It felt like more of a walk than he was prepared to endure. He set his heavy frame down on a small crate; its smell was less than pleasant. It cracked a bit and the thin planks jutted out of the squatting crate.

"Rotten apples." He sighed.

Inside, Kat Lamphere exhaled and pulled her hair back with a ribbon. She picked up the last few mugs of cider, ready for the evening to be over. Her feet ached. Her back and arms ached. She often joked that she was aging before her time, but in reality the town was feeling smaller and the Crow's Nest claustrophobic. It was Ernest Williams who had just recently put the strange thoughts in her head. She'd spent so much of her childhood reading the few novels in Breton's empty library, her heart was full of adventure. She often dreamed of sneaking off with the train in the night. Then she'd see her broad-shouldered father, Glenn working hard and she knew where her loyalty was.

It wasn't a happy feeling.

She looked through the front window out onto the town square. Night had come. Children were still running in the park. Some men stood on the street corner in jovial, raucous discussion . Ernest Williams sat on a now-broken crate out below the streetlamp a few steps down the street.

She shook her head at the poor man.

Young ladies walked through the square away from the church, clutching bibles. No one liked being around the cantankerous old parson, but they all went as often as they could. Men sat in the park lost in languid conversation and pipe smoke. It seemed like the townsfolk forgot to fear the Vampyres until moments after dusk when they went into their homes. Over the last months, more disappeared and more stayed longer drinking at the tavern, drowning fears in liquid bravado.

"Come, Thomas!" The shorter boy cried over his shoulder. *He's sure to wake!* Empty crates and trash lined the street as he made a nimble jump over a box of rotted vegetables where a raccoon dug for its meal.

Thomas was pulling his dirty blonde hair back with a bit of twine he'd stolen, trying to keep up with his cohort. His thin legs overstepped puddles and sidestepped refuse and debris. It had just barely stopped raining and a fungal scent filled the air.

The boys did almost anything they could to avoid returning St. Jerome's Home for the Lost & Found each night. Every evening was an adventure and a test of courage. They stayed out as long as they could before fear gripped them. Then they would hurry down alleys and streets, barreling into the safety of the threshold of the orphanage.

Things were a little different now, as St. Jerome's was now being run by a new headmaster, Mister Smith, an Englishman.

9

Mister Smith read to the children very often. Thomas and his best friend, Edwin, both liked him. He always spoke to them like things were important, like they weren't just kids.

"Wait for me." Thomas retorted with a heavy sigh. *This is quite silly*. The running about each night was not the kind of education he'd expected to receive when he'd been brought to the doorstep of St. Jerome's. It was all wild errands at the insistence of the headmaster or the courier's niece recently. He never really understood it all.

"What are we doing, Ned?"

Edwin pointed down into an alleyway while brushing his thick black hair out of his eyes. "There's the old bummer, Williams." He motioned at a pair of shoes sticking out past a cart beyond the entrance to the Crow's Nest Inn.

Tom and Ned were very funny-looking for boys of twelve and thirteen respectively. Edwin was short and next to Thomas, who was as tall as many adults, he was immensely dwarfed. Thomas always seemed to have his straight blonde hair up in a tail, whereas Edwin could never find the time. He constantly fought with the dirty black mat of hair in his face. They looked feral. Their patent leather shoes were ruined, their pants torn and their sleeves ripped and dotted with blood and mud.

"Wh-what will you do to him?" Thomas stuttered.

"*We*, my friend, *we* are gonna snatch his flask. Let's go!" Edwin whispered and made his way quickly down the dark cobblestone road. Their whispers hardly disturbed the unconscious man.

"Come on, Ned. Just take it and let's go."

"No. We're doing this the right way."

Thomas knew that Edwin would likely return the flask. He was just practicing the skills that he had learned living on the street. The old drunk was never really a target but Edwin insisted on "practice." When Thomas had pressed him about it earlier that day, Edwin had quoted Mister Smith, "Sleep always comes easier on a guilty conscience than an empty stomach." Edwin said that before Mister Smith, the orphans didn't eat as often. The headmaster told him to keep his skills up, if ever times got harder. It was hard for Thomas to believe they could be harder than this, orphaned in a mountain town, plagued with Vampyres.

Edwin called out, "Good evening, Mister Williams."

The man didn't even stir. *And once again, we're roaming the streets when we should be inside.* Thomas thought. He glanced up into unlit windows in nearby abandoned buildings and down the alley. They could be anywhere. "Ned, we should get back to the orphanage." He whispered.

Edwin elbowed Thomas in the ribs. "Good evening, Mister Williams!" Edwin repeated.

Thomas began to worry. "Maybe he's dead," he mumbled.

"Yeah, dead drunk." Edwin kicked him in the foot and the old man started coughing and wheezing. "Good evening, Mister Williams."

"Hullo Edwin. Thomas. How is your Mother, young Thomas?" he asked. The old man started into his standard distant, political tone.

"She's well, thank you," Thomas muttered.

Edwin looked up at Thomas for a moment, confused.

The old man was so drunk he couldn't remember, or he hadn't heard, considering Thomas's new home was the orphanage and it had been for some weeks. Thomas didn't let himself think about it, but Edwin felt a pang of sadness for his friend. Strangely, it seemed commonplace that people forgot things like death around Breton.

"How about you boys help an old man to his feet?" He chuckled. "It would seem I've a brick in my hat."

"Oh, yes sir!" Edwin tried to hide his smile. Each boy grabbed an arm and helped the large man up to his feet. He stumbled before finding his balance. When the boys saw that the man was about to topple over again, they stepped in, one under each arm.

The trio teetered a few steps forward, not noticing the warm light spilling from the inn's open door. A shadow lurked up behind them along the cobblestones.

"Boys," A soft voice asked from somewhere behind them, "what are you doing?"

"Nothing, Kat, just helping Mister Williams home." One of the voices responded from under the old man's arms.

"He's a grown man. He can find his way home, Edwin," she responded.

"Yes, yes boys. Thank you very much, but I think I should be quite alright," said the old man.

Kat Lamphere, the tall barmaid, beckoned them inside, "Come on boys." She snickered, wiping her strong hands on her apron as she watched the old man check his pockets. "Is everything alright, Mister Williams?" The girl had soft features and keen eyes. She was not petite, as many of the other girls around Breton were, in the Victorian fashion. Instead she marked a striking, ominous figure, backlit in the chiaroscuro.

"Ah yes. Well, I seem to have misplaced something."

Kat Lamphere crossed her arms and glared at Edwin, who simply looked away. "Come on, Tom, I have some food inside for you."

"That's as good as caught." Thomas whispered as he walked toward the warm glow of the inn.

Edwin kicked the ground and rolled his eyes. "Mister Williams, I think you dropped this." He pulled the flask from his pocket and handed it to the old man.

"Bless you boy. It is a family heirloom, you know."

He did, having heard the story countless times before. "Goodnight, Mister Williams."

"Goodnight, my boy." The man slurred, oblivious to the prank that had been foiled behind him. He turned up the flask and slumped again onto the strained wooden crate.

Edwin turned from the old man, brushing the dark hair from his eyes once more and ran into the warm light. He found a bowl of pork and beans next to Thomas, who had already started eating.

Ernest opened his eyes in the bright pool of a street lantern's light. The smell hit him and he remembered what happened. "How long..."

"Something like an hour." A voice came from the darkness.

"Oh god." Williams sighed, worked his way up to his feet to face the voice. The truly frightening thing was that the voice was pleasant, almost charming. It had come from somewhere in the dark above him.

"What's he got to do with it?" asked the voice.

"Who?" Earnest asked. "God?"

"Yes." It said. "What has God to do with you sleeping for the last hour?" A low chuckle rippled from the darkness, "Am I the god? Or shall he be making a visit tonight?"

Ernest shielded his eyes with a hand against the lamplight to distinguish what hid in the darkness beyond. He straightened his back. "Word play? From a Vampyre? Are puns the precursor to my end?" He sighed. "Do your deed." He shook his head regretfully. *I should have been home.* Ernest dusted off his matching tweed coat and pants. He straightened his tie and blue waistcoat and looked into the darkness where the monster would emerge.

"Vampyre?" The voice fell silent and then it sounded again, closer. "You seem so certain. Could I not have been a simple thief?"

Ernest Williams choked out a bleak, hoarse laugh, "What thief would come to Breton? Vampyres watch from the dark and destroy the evil man alongside the good."

Vampyre. Vampyre. Vampyre. The word echoed in Ernest's head in the creature's voice.

"Tell me your name." It said quietly. Closer now still.

Ernest swallowed. "Well, it's Mister Williams."

Laughter fell from the dark. "Your name is Mister?"

"No, no... My name is Ernest," he chuckled reflexively, rubbing his fingers against his forehead. "This is not quite what I expected from a Vampyre. What is your name, sir? If I might be so bold as to ask."

Silence stretched out where an answer should have been. He resolved that if he were to die, he should do so as a gentleman. Ernest felt a chill shiver down his spine. He looked out in the dark and exhaled, pulling his flask from his jacket pocket. He knew he could not outrun a Vampyre. He couldn't outrun much anything in his shape.

No one was coming and there was a sense of dread looming over him. He scolded himself. *Falling asleep drunk in the street. It's like you wanted to die.*

"I don't know my name."

Ernest dropped his flask. He looked down at the figure sitting on the crate in an ill-fitted naval officer's bridge coat. His hair was long and pulled back. He was just a boy wearing tattered pants. His eyes were bright amber, as if someone were shining a candle from a distant window. His skin was fair, but not pale. His features could have been carved from stone, angular and well-formed. He looked pathetic, but his curiosity and intelligence was unmistakable.

The Vampyre had caught the flask mid-air and was studying the thing now.

"Vampyre, you say?" the young man asked. He offered the flask to Ernest. "You fear that I will devour you. I can feel that somehow." There was a pause. "Instead, I say we make a trade." The boy kept cutting his eyes to something unseen in the darkness.

Ernest tried to follow his eyes, but nothing was there. "I'm listening."

"I believe that I am consigned, I daresay enslaved to the night, some revenant, yet I do not know to what end. Why? If you help me figure out what I am, if not who am I, or who I was and I will not..." he paused, "eat you?"

"Fair enough, I think." Ernest said. He reached for the flask and hesitantly pulled it to his chest.

Slowly, in trepidatious conversation, they walked away from the warm glow of the Crow's Nest.

The tavern at the foot of the Crow's Nest Inn always appeared to be open, but the Lamphere's closed as early as they could once their patrons were upstairs or out the door. Kat's Father, Glenn, was well-liked and always knew how to handle his patrons. He was a barrel-chested man with thick chestnut brown hair sprinkled with the same blonde as his daughter. His eyebrows and beard were unruly, but never hid his bright brown eyes, or smile. The large man never feared a fight, but things rarely came to that.

When Kat was little, she often impersonated him, carrying empty glasses around and making jokes in a big booming voice. On one occasion she even made a beard out of fleece and wore it until it fell apart. Glenn laughed, saying that there'd never be any denying that she was his daughter.

With no mother to rear her and only the work of the inn to busy her, Kat grew quiet and contemplative. She hid from the other town girls who teased her for being fat, like her father. There she grew to love the old librarian and the stories they found in books. She loved those books. She loved the idea of a world outside of Breton, though she'd never seen anything beyond the forests on the far side of town. Her life would not be one of courting young men like she had read in her books. That was reserved for the pretty and more importantly, petite girls, she thought.

Kat knew she was loved. Her whole life had been filled with love. But she felt so alone. She sat at the one window in the cellar of the Tavern behind the barrels of cider with a copy of "Alice's Adventures in Wonderland," and a small lantern. She listened for the ocean and the quiet bustle of the evening street, knowing that at this time of night, the song would begin.

Kat Lamphere had a secret. She could hear things no one else could. Throughout her childhood, a quiet, loving voice had guided her. Each night, the voice came with a gentle lullaby. People in town had always had bad dreams, but everyone knew that Breton wasn't exactly like other towns. Kat didn't have nightmares. Not like the other people in town at least. The voice was always there.

For years, she had spoken to the voice, but it never answered back — not directly. It somehow always knew what she needed to hear. Overtime, the voice grew quieter and she heard it less often, but her guardian angel always sang to her.

She once asked Miss Allen, the seamstress, a spinster by all accounts, why she heard the voice when no one else could hear it. "It's just your mama's spirit of love watching over you— just a guardian angel." The old lady had told her. But she had encouraged her not to mention it to anyone and to keep it her little secret.

So she did. Miss Allen never looked at her the same way again.

Guardian angel or no, her mother was gone and she held a cold contempt for the Vampyres who took her. What had started as a daily hatred had burned into cold complacency. They had broken her family before she had gotten to be a part of it. This awful little town was no wonderland, but it was all she would ever know. If she got the chance though, she would make every Vampyre regret being born. She chuckled at herself and dabbed her eyes. Alice would have to outsmart the Queen of Hearts tomorrow.

The lullaby had begun far away, haunting and ethereal. It was growing closer, filling her heart with love. She brushed off her dress. A night's rest would do her good. She blew out the lantern; knowing the building as she did, she walked without fear into the dark.

In a previously abandoned office above the train station lobby stood a thin figure, peering out from behind the station's massive clock. Weeks in and the man found himself trapped, in the claustrophobic office-turned-hideout. *Like a squirrel in a hatbox.* Algernon leaned against the rear of the clock with one hand tucked into the pocket of his waistcoat, observing the empty station below through wire-rimmed spectacles on the tip of his nose.

He was a long way from Islington now, in a cursed town that had been eaten inside out. The cobblestone streets were cracked with what suggested seismic activity. Most buildings were abandoned. A gloom hung over the place, despite its bustling streets. Algernon had an inkling as to what kind of evils could orchestrate such a plot with so many moving parts; a North American township that was full of people who didn't seem to live there, while those that did went on as though they weren't being troubled by revenants of every shade.

Breton was a puzzle the Englishman had come to investigate. Vampyres tended to hide away from public knowledge in remote recesses to practice their psionic malfeasance, but Algernon was certain now that there was an even greater threat lurking in this particular place. He had to know what it was.

Algernon heard the frantic, running steps he'd been expecting coming up the stairs. It sounded like a column of rifles firing in succession. Genevieve Moreau burst through the door; a deluge of grass-stained fabrics. The door slammed and she righted herself, holding her arms to her chest. Somewhere beneath the Courier's jacket she wore, she clutched a bundled lump. She leaned back against the door, panting and grinning.

"It would appear you've been up to mischief." Algernon said.

"I have!"

Algernon cleared the small table next to the bed, where she dumped her burden across a rudimentary map of the town, scribbled over, marked and remarked. The debris that now cluttered the table might have interested a naturalist; bits and bobs of metal and stone, covered in dirt.

Genevieve was so proud of her baubles. "I think I cracked it!" She certainly may have. Whatever it was — it was cracked right up the middle. She held up a piece of copper that could have been half of the largest coin he'd ever seen or half of a small metal plate, or a toothless gear. She handed it to him, potted and corroded green, rusted and caked with dirt. Algernon poured the water from a small vase by the bedside that contained a single flower (picked by Genevieve earlier that week) across the copper thing making a small puddle of mud at his feet. Wiping away the remainder of mud and dirt revealed something he knew far too well.

Etched into the copper was half of a symbol; two five pointed stars overlayed and inverted; pentacle over pentagram. *As above, so below.* He thought.

Eagerly, Genevieve held out her next offering. "The more I looked, the more I found these rocks everywhere. They're hidden around town. I think we're really onto something."

"It's not a rock." Algernon said, taking it in his other hand. He held up the medallion alongside it. "It's a crystal." He turned it over. "Quartz, most likely."

"Oh." Her eagerness deflated in a sigh. "Useless then."

"I can't imagine how that would be useless."

"Well," she scratched her head. "Uncle used to say, 'What's a wind chime that doesn't chime?'"

"I don't know." Algernon said.

She just shrugged.

Despite everything, he couldn't take his eyes off of her. He never could. There was something in her feral energy that drew him in. He shook his head. Looking at the crystal again, he could see that it had a small hole from which it could be hung by a string. *Wind chimes.* He thought.

Clearing the debris from the table, he looked at the map again. "You've noticed medallions like this around town, yes?" He asked.

"Yeah. They're all over town."

"And these wind chimes with no chime?"

"Sometimes." She said. "I guess I started noticing them once you told me to look around for anything strange."

He nodded thoughtfully.

Someone knocked on the door.

Algernon rolled up the map and hastily threw it under the bed, sweeping the debris from the floor with a foot. "Come in,

Monsieur Chandler." He said, trying to put on a more casual air though he noted that there had been no footsteps on the stairs.

The door opened and the gray little man entered. In his blue train station attendant's uniform, Monsieur Chandler appeared innocuous, but he made the skin on the back of Algernon's neck stick up. He was diminutive and olive skinned and Algernon would have put him in his fifties. Perhaps Tunisian or some other French-speaking Arab country would have been his home, but his accent was European and polished.

"Good evening, Monsieur." Chandler said with a small nod of his head. "And Mademoiselle." He smiled.

"Bonsoir." She said. Her French was less polished, but Algernon could see that her Uncle Moreau had taught her some.

"I'm closing up the front, Monsieur." He said.

Algernon nodded. "I'll be sure to take platform exit, should I go out." But he knew would not.

"Very good, monsieur." The man smiled wolfishly. Algernon could not tell if he was thinking something untoward about Algernon's company or if the man was simply too intense. Likely the latter.

He began to back out and pull the door closed with it, but stopped with a thoughtful look on his face. "Monsieur, it might be good to know that the town has been having numerous council meetings recently." He looked down at the small trunk at the foot of the bed that Algernon's partner had delivered.

Algernon looked at Genevieve, but she continued to watch the little man. "Thank you, Monsieur Chandler. It would appear that I've arrived at a portentous moment."

Chandler understood. "It would appear you have."

He closed the door and was gone without a sound.

Genevieve cut her eyes at Algernon, "And what was that about?"

As Algernon pulled the map and dirt-encrusted baubles from under the bed, he asked, "How well do you know that man?"

She laughed. "Well, he and Uncle met once a week to commiserate."

"Commiserate?" Algernon asked, his voice still muffled under the bed as debris slid out across the floor.

"Well, they're both French." She said.

Algernon laughed. "Yes, I gathered."

"They used to drink wine together once a week." She got quiet as Algernon popped back up with a handful of bits.

"I think Monsieur Chandler wants me to observe his cleverness."

"What cleverness?"

"He doesn't make any noise he doesn't want heard."

"What does that mean?"

"It means he wants me to know he can watch me, or surprise me with whatever he wants." He spread the map across the small table and placed the pieces on it.

"I'm fairly certain he's just strange."

Algernon laughed, "Well, you know him better than I do."

Genevieve laughed. She was beautiful. Algernon was intrigued by her fierce independence. Part American and part French, she'd inherited her uncle's intense gaze, but thankfully, none of his taciturn brusqueness. The girl's blouse never seemed to fit squarely on her shoulders. Her shoes were always scuffed and covered with dust from running. He'd heard that few men could keep up with her in a foot race. It was thrilling.

"It's quiet out tonight." He said.

"But natural." She said, knowing what he meant. "And a little sneaking might do you some good. I could show you where I found some of this stuff."

She was brave, Algernon had to admit. If he was being honest, he might call that bravery recklessness. From the moment Algernon laid eyes on the American girl, he knew something was different about her. To be fair, the first time he saw her, it was behind a very large revolver that she pointed at his head. Things had gotten off to a rocky start.

Just weeks earlier Algernon had rendezvoused with his partner, who was embedded in the town as a spy. "I say," Algernon complained, as Spencer lifted him up a steep embankment, "I'm beginning to think this entire continent is made of these thorny bushes."

Spencer grunted with effort, lifting his partner until the man could get his hand on the ledge. "Brambles, they call them."

"Like the dessert?" Algernon asked.

"They call it cobbler here."

"That's absurd." Algernon replied, lifting himself to his knees. "Then who repairs shoes?"

"You know," Spencer said, not answering the question, "I've always loved the word 'cordwainer'."

"But cordwainers make new shoes and cobblers repair them." Algernon said.

"Ah, but they do like a smith here." Spencer mused.

"I certainly hope not." Algernon said. "So a boot smith? A tanner?"

"A boot smith?" Spencer asked, incredulously.

"Farrier?"

"Furrier, I'd say." Spenser said.

"Am I?" Algernon asked, scratching the stubble on his face.

"I hope you packed a razor. You look terrible, mate."

"No worse for wear. But I'm ravenous and your talk of desserts is torture on a man that's been hiding in a Vampyre-infested forest for weeks."

"It's a short walk back into town." Spencer said. "Once we get there, we'll get you fed and deal with Moreau."

Both men turned to the ominous click of a large revolver, which emerged from the dark forest. On the less dangerous end of the gun, Algernon saw the most intense black eyes he'd ever seen. If it hadn't been for the gun pointed at him, he might have even noticed the tears running down from those eyes.

"What do you mean *deal* with Moreau?" The young woman asked.

Algernon and Spencer looked at each other.

"Spencer, did you allow this woman to follow you?" Algernon asked.

"It would appear I've done just that, Al."

"Where is my uncle?" She demanded.

Their confused looks only fueled her frustration.

"I knew not to trust you, Smith." She said. Turning the gun on Spencer, she continued. "Tell me where my uncle is."

Spencer gestured broadly toward the young lady. "Algernon, may I introduce the always enchanting Genevieve Moreau."

"I meant deal *with* Moreau, not *deal* with Moreau. I hope your uncle is well and at home, Miss Moreau. Otherwise without him, this mission— *our* mission, our *raison d'etre*, if you'll pardon my French, will inevitably fail. Makes a man feel quite foolish for hiding in this virgin, dare I say primeval forest for weeks."

Genevieve stepped forward with the gun. "A lot of words for a man with no answers."

"I suppose." Algernon replied. "But it's just..." He paused dramatically.

A second menacing click.

Genevieve felt the cold barrel of Spencer's revolver against her temple.

"Enough." Algernon said with a smile.

Genevieve didn't care for the smile and she didn't trust the Englishman behind it.

They never found the Jean-Pierre Moreau. Genevieve presumed that the Vampyres finally captured her uncle. Maybe they had, but either way, Moreau's home would be under surveillance, which forced Algernon to find new lodgings.

Since then, something had begun to flourish between them. Algernon's presence could not be noticed, so he was relegated to sneaking in the night, the most dangerous time and without Moreau, they were left without much of a plan.

He was a conspicuous presence, a liability to his partner and now to Genevieve. He had grown reclusive and indecisive over the weeks he'd spent in the train station office. There were so many moving parts to this strange place that any misstep might see Spencer, or Genevieve killed. Even the more experienced Frenchman, Moreau was bested by this place. And as far as Algernon could ascertain, Moreau was the best there was. Where Algernon and his partner were mere dilettantes employed as investigators of the preternatural, the employer himself was renowned as an expert and some sort of demon hunter. He had looked forward to learning more from this man face to face.

Algernon had to be thoughtful and deliberate. He didn't know what to do in this hellmouth. Any move might expose him, or his partner. Instead, he'd buried himself in academic esoterica, taking to revising his journals and publishing segments in arcane publications, but even the most mundane details of his excursions into the dark corners of the world would be met with disbelief outside of the most devout occult circles, but those people were as easily discredited as his writings were. If anyone had the heart to believe that the world was filled with bogeymen, they might be dismayed to the point of madness.

As for the American girl, she had lived this reality for much longer. Since her uncle had gone missing, she doubled her effort to go unseen, hidden in plain sight. She never showed a moment of grief. People in Breton rarely grieved. They moved stoically forward, always forward. So she did the same.

So the mail never ran late. Even if her uncle was dead. Even if her heart broke with every step, Genevieve rose from the bed and delivered every piece. From Monsieur Chandler to Parson Adler. From Doctor Brown's office on to the mayor in his opulent mansion. From Sheriff Matheson and Mister Burroughs, always at the Crow's Nest. The mail always arrived and always on time. In her uncle's old courier's jacket, with the long sleeves rolled up, she would make her rounds. She had to keep moving forward.

"Just a short walk." Genevieve said.

"What is?" Algernon asked, having lost the thread of the conversation, as a thought eluded him in the back of his mind.

"I mean, come take a walk with me."

"I should." He sighed. "I feel so boxed in." The puzzle came to him. Algernon smiled. "It's a box."

"What?"

"Breton."

"Breton is a box?"

"Well, a grid." Algernon grabbed his jacket from a nail in the wall, where a painting had been. "I'd bet my last copper that if we were to look, we'd find these medallions and chimes with no chime in equidistant locations along the grid." He threw the door open. "Let's go for a short walk."

two

*They who dream by day are cognizant of many things
which escape those who dream only by night.*
-Edgar Allen Poe, *Eleonora (1841)*

*Vampyres issue forth from their graves in the night,
attack people sleeping quietly in their beds, suck out all
their blood from their bodies and destroy them. They
beset men, women and children alike, sparing neither
age nor sex. Those who are under the fatal malignity
of their influence complain of suffocation and a total
deficiency of spirits, after which they soon expire.*
-John Heinrich Zopfius,
Dissertatio de Uampiris Seruiensibus (1733)

Cities burned. The husk of civilization crumbled in his hand.
The dragon called to him. Large, metallic creatures hulked
slowly along the streets. Their bellies were full of fire. Their
billowing black smoke became a black and red sky above. He was
covered in blood.

The demoniac presence was close. He was one with it.

Armies of men with rifles on their shoulders moved along
the horizon. Armies of demoniac, winged creatures destroyed the
path in front of him. The road ahead ran with blood of man and
demon alike. Nations littered the way. Giant worms rose up from
the earth, devouring city blocks at a time. Ancient creatures not
of this world were unchained in the depths of a mountain, hungry
for blood. Thrones sat empty covered in gnarled roots. It was
all laid out in front of him. *Michael, you must return to the Dark
Mountain. Free the Empyreans.*

He woke up exhausted. The dreams that haunted him
dissipated into fragments, until nothing was there. Michael, as
he had begun to call himself, was troubled in his sleep. He lay on

his back, watching the rays of sunlight cut like blades across the Captain's quarters in his makeshift hideaway.

A Vampyre. It sounded so romantic at first. *Such strange powers. Such strange limitations: sunlight means death and the constant craving clouding my mind.* The craving he satiated with the "local cuisine": boar, deer, groundhog and field rat. Raw eggs in the nest he treated like a delicacy. He could taste the differences in their blood. There was a difference in how bitter something was, or how sweet. He could taste their diet in their blood.

He considered what human blood would taste like. In a distinctive, dark moment of calm, he sifted through the idea. *I suppose that's what Mister Williams—Ernest—thought at first. That I was to devour him for my own pleasure. Strange.* The thought was constant, almost nagging. *I am some sort of murderer. At the very least, I am expected to be.*

He and Ernest had spoken until the early hours of the morning, when he was forced to retreat to his dark space. The man had welcomed him into his home. Perhaps out of fear, but still with a warm and friendly countenance.

"Be not inhospitable to strangers, lest they be angels in disguise." Ernest had quoted with the spark of lanterns that filled his home with a welcoming glow. "Yeats, I believe?"

He had poured two drinks with a warm smile.

Michael looked at the liquor in the glass. The thought of drinking it turned his stomach. "No, I think not." He said.

"No?" Ernest asked. "Shakespeare then."

"Hebrews." Michael said.

Ernest laughed and took a sip of the liquor in his cup.

There was something about this old drunkard that Michael liked. While the whole town moved slow and plodding, this man drank with an insatiable anxiety. Something about him was awake. Michael could feel his thoughts pouring out of him.

Ernest spoke endlessly about the War Between the States, but Michael's exploration of the town had revealed little about this "war." What was this town with its dull-eyed denizens? What was this war? Why here? Why him? Who him? What him? Ernest sipped on his corn whiskey and discussed each thing with him, lecturing and rambling.

The Vampyre problem had lasted nearly three decades and its history had run parallel with the construction of the town. Perhaps the mines had gone so deep with the industriousness of war that they, the people of Breton, had awoken the Vampyres. They were an ancient, evil force that had devoured the town for years, slowly at first and recently with more fervor.

Williams had suggested, while contemplating the edge of his glass of straw-colored liquor through wire-framed spectacles, that he suspected there were people in the town who might actually have been agents of these Vampyres. He struggled with how to convey his thoughts to Michael, as his understanding of the situation was foggy. He had been frustrated with the lingering thought that he should have known more about it all. Williams even suspected his own employer.

He talked for hours. Michael listened, sometimes focused and sometimes as though looking around for something he could not see or hear. A cloud of whispering voices grew closer until he sensed the room darkening. Though Ernest was unaware, he did seem to grow more somber. After a few minutes, they were gone.

"Dawn approaches." Michael had told him abruptly.

"Yes, I suppose it is about that time." Williams muttered, surprised at how time had gotten away from him. Ernest, as he'd asked Michael to call him, chuckled as the Vampyre leapt into the dark woods. He called after him, "I should regret not getting any rest today!"

That he did. Hours later Ernest felt as though there wasn't enough coffee in the world to push him through the morning. He yawned and stretched. He fought with sleep. He filed things out of habit. His mind was distracted, filled with dark thoughts about the night before. He straightened up around the Mayor's mansion, which sat further down the same street as the Crow's Nest Inn. He waited on the Vampyre hunter to arrive for an impromptu meeting with the mayor. There was a sense of wonder and excitement that permeated his morning. He had somehow survived; furthermore, he had befriended such a dangerous creature. He was still trying to decipher it all.

The mayor never left his home. He moved his office to the mansion. Most people had never even seen him. Some people even made snide comments around town that the man had long died and that they "knew" what Ernest was up to. Life would have been much easier had that been the case. The old house was a mess of documents and coffee cups. The mayor was not a slob, but a recluse and for the most part, only disorganized. Ernest suspected paranoia was paralyzing him.

Ernest understood why the mayor might not want to work out of the small town hall building. Parson Adler, the Sheriff and those awful bureaucrats seemed to crowd about the place. Once the mayor had gone into seclusion, the old town hall had been all but abandoned. Adler and his cronies took to meeting at the church. At least Ernest saw less of them each day, which was its own silver lining.

The doorbell rang. Even in his hustling it startled him. "Oh no, he's here!" He stashed the papers on the desk in a front room of the mansion and cleared out a space in the messy front dining room.

He opened the door with a broad fake smile. To his surprise it was only Kat bringing luncheon from the inn. "Oh! Hullo lovely child, please come in." He exclaimed with a sigh of relief.

"Expecting someone? It's time for your luncheon." Kat answered, showing him his basket of food. As far back as she could remember she had brought luncheon for the Mayor and Mister Williams. They would have been better off with a maid but Kat knew that Mayor Heath would have only run her off. That little man didn't scare her a bit though.

"Well, yes, I think I should be—we are, I mean. This Mister Gallegos." He stuttered as he closed the door behind him.

"Oh, you shouldn't preoccupy yourself then. He's only beginning to stir at the inn," laughed Kat.

"Wonderful, already looking for Vampyres at night!" Ernest smiled.

"If they're hiding in the bottom of his cider. Otherwise, he is most certainly doing very little hunting." Kat huffed. "In that stead he is keeping me up all night at the inn. He drank all night and told stories to the other patrons."

"Well, we are in dire need of a change. I welcome it. Ironic though…" Ernest's voice trailed off.

"Ironic why?" she asked.

"Oh…" Ernest realized his tired mind had wandered, yet he was so intrigued by his situation he couldn't lie about it. With a sense of nervous euphoria he asked her to sit down.

She put her utensils aside and sat to listen.

"It would be a bold understatement to call it sensitive," he started, "but I too spent all night awake. In conversation with…" He paused, trying to read her face. "With a Vampyre."

"Oh, you silly man!" She exclaimed, "I thought you were being serious!" She stood and began working again at setting the table, but Ernest was insistent.

"I am," he muttered.

The room was silent. "I'd never seen one before…" He began.

She interrupted, "Luncheon is ready, Mister Williams. Have a nice day." She was indignant, if not insulted.

"Please Kat, listen to me. I beg of you."

"That's a very strange thing to tell me, Mister Williams, considering what they've done to the people of our town." she stated without sitting back down.

"Yes, I suppose it is, child. I expected him to kill me. But he had no such intention. He asked *what* he was. Amnesiac, I should say. He had no idea what a Vampyre was. From what I could gather, he has no ideas about aught in Breton and bears no ill-will."

"Did you ever think, Mister Williams, that this thing was trying to pose his charm on you?" Kat said.

"Yes, I suppose so. I was stalling at first but honestly I felt—I don't know. I pitied him. He was more man than beast. Just a boy, really."

"Then perhaps he should be judged so heavily as the people—the children of Breton." She sighed. "I'm sorry, Mister Williams but this is too much."

"No, it's quite alright. I shouldn't have said aught. I just wish I could do more to change our plight. I thought, perhaps I could learn something from the poor..." he trailed off. He noticed Kat looking out the window. Her blue eyes glistened with daylight and she raised an eyebrow. The midday bell was ringing.

"Is Mayor Heath still not awake?" She asked.

"No, I suppose not. It's late even for him." joked Ernest as he stood up at the table, straightening his jacket.

"It's not a problem, I'll go fetch him," offered Kat. She abandoned the conversation and left Ernest to his muddled thoughts.

The scream that came from upstairs rang throughout the mansion. As Ernest hurried up the stairs, he saw Kat collapsed in tears in the doorframe of the Mayor's master bedroom.

"No, it can't be..." he muttered. He ran to pick the young girl up. Ernest lifted her from where she had fallen, consoling her. His mind was racing. While he had been entertaining a Vampyre, someone had murdered the Mayor.

He sat her down on the couch, but Kat immediately forced herself up toward the kitchen, covering her mouth. Ernest followed, but she signaled behind with one hand for him to stay back. He could hear from the couch the sounds of sobbing mixed with her retching. Ernest wrung his hands with worry and slumped down on the couch. "No one is safe," he muttered to himself.

He stood with a new determination and an idea. He walked into the kitchen where Kat was washing her face.

"I'll get some men to come help clean," she mumbled through her hand as she heard Ernest entering the room.

"No," he began. "Kat, I need you to promise me," he swallowed, "that you will not tell anyone what you saw up there." His mind was racing.

"What? Are you crazy?" she exclaimed, turning to see his expression.

He was lost in thought. "No." He said. "For once in my life, I feel like things might be looking up."

"That's terrible. How calloused can you be?" She asked. "I'm aware that Mayor Heath was not very fair with you but—"

"No, child," he interrupted. "This has nothing to do with me, or Heath and I am sorry for what's befallen him, but I need your help now. Please...tell no one. Simply bring luncheon tomorrow as though nothing happened here."

"I cannot believe that even you, Mister Williams, have grown so cold and corrupt."

In the silence, they understood each other. Ernest's eyes fell to the floor. Kat had run the gamut of her senses and was exhausted. She gave in. "Have it your way, Mister Williams."

She walked out with her head down.

Ernest thought as he worked his way upstairs to face his new dilemma.

Thomas was the last to wake in the orphanage the next morning. He wanted to roll over, remember who he was and the good family he had come from. His father was a fur-trapper and trapping was all Thomas had ever known. He was homesick and lonely and he missed his mother.

He sat up. He worked his feet into his worn patent leather shoes and splashed his face with cold water from a basin on the floor. He pulled his suspenders over his shoulders and tucked his shaggy blonde hair behind his ears.

As he found his way downstairs, he saw all the children wrestling to see out of a window in the kitchen. Something outside appeared to be very important. He could see over their heads but still had trouble looking out. Edwin popped out from a hallway and called, "Come on, Thomas!"

They ran into the hallway while Edwin explained, "Some kind of Vampyre killer has come into town!" They found the ladder to the roof. "Edwin, we're not supposed to go up there." Thomas scolded.

"I know."

They climbed the ladder to see they weren't the first. Headmaster Smith was sitting on the edge of the roof looking down at the street. He turned as he heard them, "You're not supposed to be up here, Edwin," he stated, apathetic.

"I know." Edwin answered.

The boys ran to the edge to see grooms leading two horses, one black and the other white away from the ornate wagon. It could have been part of a carnival. From the rooftop, the boys could see the whole town.

Headmaster Smith looked down on the street with his foot on the edge of the flat rooftop, his arms crossed. He seemed both intrigued and worried by the arrival. He was particularly quiet.

"Who is that?" asked Edwin.

Headmaster Smith answered with a strange disdain. "Some Vampyre Hunter they are calling 'The Rectifier.' He's meeting with Mayor Heath today, supposedly."

"Good," spoke Thomas softly. "I'm glad."

"I wouldn't be so sure." Mister Smith replied. "This hornet's nest of a town doesn't need kicking." He turned and kneeled closer to the boys. They looked toward the wagon one last time before they stepped back from the edge to listen to him. "Ned, Tom, I need you to listen to what I am about to tell you." His soft voice rang solemn and filled the boys with a sense of dread. "The world is a very dark and very strange place. It is always changing and it doesn't care for us."

The boys simply looked at each other, puzzled.

"One day, when the time is right, I want you to bring all the other children up here. Let them see the world that you see. The next few days are going to be difficult." The man sighed. "You know, I look at you two and I think about my dear friend, Al." Smith chuckled. "We have had our share of scrapes but we always made it out. Because we always looked out for each other. You two will be fine." He smiled.

The boys shared a confused look, but nodded to the headmaster.

Mister Smith brushed off the dust and pebbles from the knee of his pants. Giving one last glance over the edge where the carriage had been, he finally turned his back to the pair and made his way toward the ladder. His voice lightened up some. "How about I start us some luncheon?"

A large crowd was gathering around the shabby, colorful wagon with its ornate door on the back and collapsible stage on one side. The afternoon was humid and heavy with the promise of rain. Tom and Ned looked down from the ledge of an abandoned tenement building.

"The Vampyre hunter will be out any minute!" Thomas observed.

As they waited, Kat pushed her way through, squeezing into the frantic crowd. Her broad shoulders and golden hair made her easy to spot. "Kat!" Edwin yelled. The boys waved down at the crowd but couldn't be heard over the noise.

"She'll never be able to hear you, boys," Genevieve said from behind them. "Great vantage from up here, though."

Thomas loved Genevieve. He had been an only child and until the day when he met Genevieve, he'd known very little family. Jenny found him stumbling, dehydrated and exhausted. The boy had run down forest and trail from the mountains. She was the one who had taken him to St. Jerome's. The attacks around the woods became more frequent and she kept an eye open for more children.

None came.

Thomas turned toward the crowd as a lanky man emerged. Dressed in all black and whispering incantations, the Vampyre hunter sprinkled salt from a small bag over his makeshift stage. The three of them watched the crowd clamoring to touch him.

"People of Breton!" the thin man cried out. "Let fear take you no longer!" He reached high up and pulled out of thin air a small vial that seemed to fall from the sky with a wisp of smoke. The crowd was awed. "With this ancient herbal treatment, you too can rid yourself of the plague of fear that has cradled your life." His voice boomed with a practiced and professional air. "The Vampyre will have no power in your house! No power in your life!"

The sound of rustling of money in hand turned the man's presentation down a notch, handing out vials from a box. "Thank you sir. Thank you, just remember to say the incantations on the bottle, just as they are written."

"Wow. He must know a lot about Vampyres!" Edwin was amazed.

"I doubt it," responded Genevieve. "Boys," her voice rang low, "get me one of those bottles." She turned to go.

"But Jenny, we ain't got no money..." started Thomas.

"Just get one," she replied over her shoulder.

Edwin reached in his pocket to find a toffee. "Alright!" he exclaimed. Thomas smiled as he found a caramel piece in his pocket. They had learned their tricks from the best.

The cobblestone streets of Breton began to suffer as evening drizzle turned to cold, torrential rain. Muddy currents ran between stones. The square flooded.

Ernest had done his best to smooth things over with his reluctant accomplice, though Kat was still very ill with him. She had, against her better judgment (as she had put it) agreed to help him in his plan.

He walked nervously down the wet street with his coat pulled over his head. The rain beat down on him in violent staccato. His mind was so stirred up that he had forgotten his umbrella. Michael followed behind him with his head up, indifferent to the rain.

Ernest waited, flask in hand, near the place where they had met the night before. The silent visitor startled him again, appearing out of the tenebrous drizzling gray. Michael's curiosity had been piqued and he was beginning to remember things. He could put together the vision of Vampyres attacking the ship. His mind was turning with hundreds of memories from what felt like ten or twenty simultaneous experiences. They were the thoughts of the men that he had found dead in the hold of the ship. Beyond the fragmented memories, everything was still very fuzzy. Ernest was the best chance he had of uncovering the secrets of his own past. So he followed, a shadow within shadows.

Ernest told the young man that he was taking him somewhere warmer and nicer. He could sense mischief, but also a great deal of need. Ernest was his only ally. If everyone reacted like he had to the thought of a Vampyre, he might have some trouble finding more in the future.

Michael paused.

He sensed something dark. It was moving.

There were other Vampyres. Michael took a glance at a carnival wagon across the street and noticed two children lying under it. *Innocent.* The thought ran through him as though it weren't his own and he picked up the pace to catch up with Ernest.

Thomas and Edwin were soaked but neither minded. Each pretended to be soldier, detective, or Vampyre hunter, as the story would play out in each of their imaginative heads. They stayed close to the dark walls, tucking themselves into the spreading night's rainy shadows.

The street lamps would not strike. The street was dark. The boys hid under the Vampyre hunter's wagon. The smell of raw garlic overwhelmed them; the scent almost made their eyes water. At least, under the wagon, it was dry. "How much garlic can one cart hold?" Edwin hissed. He strained to see movement at the end of the street.

It looked like two men were walking down the street in a hurry. One of the men stopped. He was looking toward them. He turned away and ran. They struggled to watch but saw nothing else.

A voice came booming down beneath the wagon. "Hey!" it called.

The boys jumped away from the voice but not quickly enough. Thomas found himself caught by the collar. Edwin, seeing the long arm grabbing his friend, crawled over Thomas and bit down on the arm. It let go and the dark figure fell back onto the ground, "Hey! Stop you little bloodsuckers!"

They never looked back. The voice belonged to the Vampyre Hunter. It boomed like it had when he stood on the stage selling his vials. Thomas was terrified and started running toward the orphanage but Edwin, still thinking, hissed, "Come on, this way!" Rounding the corner, they dove toward a pile of crates and trash. They were both overwhelmed with a sickly, dark feeling. They heard hissing. People were walking by, but never seemed to make a sound, except hissing whispers.

"It's Vamp—" began Edwin, before Thomas covered his mouth. Silently they sat in the shadows. It was too dark to see what they looked like. Only silhouetted forms moved, sinuous and silent. Some cast long shadows. Others were the size of children. Still others could not have been recognized as people at all. The boys watched the procession of shadows pass almost silently in the rain.

As the last Vampyres passed, one stopped. The boys pushed themselves back into the wall as if they could slip through it to be unseen. Its silhouette was less a person, and more an animal on hind-legs. It sniffed. It growled. It went away.

"Why are we not dead, Edwin?" asked Thomas.

"They should have devoured us. "

They were both scared and shivering and kept their faces down for a moment. Neither wanted to let the other know how scared he was.

Thomas had already had enough of Vampyres. *I'm cold*, he thought, trying to convince himself that the shivering had nothing to do with his fear. His heart was racing to the point that he could hear it in his ears. The sound of the rain slowly came back and he looked up into the dark, rainy alley. "Let's go home, Ned." He sighed.

"No," Edwin replied, "we can't. We gotta do this now. The hunter is that way and them Vamps followed, but the Crow's Nest is away from'em." He paused. "We can do this." He wiped his face, turning away from Thomas; a single tear had gathered on his nose. He got up and off they ran into the dark.

Vampyres were in the street. Blood was flowing somewhere and they were on the move. Their presence cast a pall over the whole town. The sudden gloom and uncanny silence suggested *presence* more than the lack thereof. Algernon Elliott had been here before. He had promised Genevieve that he would visit with her, but he knew it could not be this night. He hammered away at his typewriter, guilt-ridden. They had agreed that despite the Vampyres, they would seek some semblance of normalcy. It violated his mission in some way, but he wanted to be around her. Now, he was breaking those promises to her, to protect her from what he knew was out there.

He knew she wouldn't understand. He was feeling something for her and he felt he should protect her. He was angry with himself for allowing those kinds of feelings to betray him. The cold outside the door nipped at his heels and he stood up to stretch his long legs. He moved to the small iron stove and tossed in a limb from the stack of firewood. He crossed his arms and contemplated the fire before returning to his typing again.

The rest of the evening, he sat listening to the rain crashing down on the platform outside, the creaking wood and the whirring and clicking of the clock. He inserted another sheet of paper into his typewriter. He tried not to listen to the far-off footsteps of the Brethren, the dark judges of Breton.

"So what would you have me do, Ernest?" Michael asked. He had found no rest. Something was pulling him. He could feel the other Vampyres. His mind ached to connect with theirs. He felt knotted up.

"Well, truth is, I am in desperate need of your help." Ernest said. He watched out the window onto the storm beating outside the mayor's mansion. "The question is, what would you have me do to keep you around?" Ernest whispered, full of worry.

Michael hesitated. He wasn't putting together the pieces. "I'm not sure what you think I am," he said.

"Well, I know you were once a man with a heart, Michael."

"Yes, I should hope I was." Michael answered softy. *I hope I still am.* "But I am no enforcer for certain. And to be quite frank, I'm not sure what this Vampyre business is really all about, by any measure."

"No Michael. I am not looking for you to enforce anything, but I can keep you safe here—"

Michael interrupted, "I don't exactly need you to keep me safe." He kept sensing the movement of other Vampyres in the street. Their minds reached out to his.

"No, I suppose not." Ernest continued, "But you will have food here, as much as you need and you can help me figure this problem out." He sounded desperate.

Michael's mind began to focus in on Ernest's thoughts. He could feel the man's very presence. Michael could see his thoughts moving around him, his perception of the world. There was much that Ernest wasn't revealing to him. Michael could see the long past of Breton and there was something wrong in the way that Ernest remembered it. It was cloudy, much like Michael's own memories. Focusing further, he could see that Ernest had been brought to Breton against his will. The sense he got of Earnest troubled Michael. It was as if the man's memory had been obscured.

"Ernest," he asked, "what brought you to Breton?"

"Oh." Ernest paused in thought. "Work. I came here when I was a young man to work in the library."

Even as he said it, Michael could see the memory in the man's head. He had been bound and gagged. He had been dragged to this town, but Michael could not sense him lying. Ernest simply remembered the wrong thing. The thought flittered away. Michael listened as new thoughts emerged. In more recent times there was a sense of hurriedness. In Ernest's earlier memories of the day, Michael saw the warm, innocent face of a girl. She was beautiful. He was taken aback at her image. She knew about Michael and her feelings weren't welcoming, but at least she knew of him. He snapped out of Ernest's thoughts. "I don't need food and your problem doesn't interest me," Michael countered.

"No, but if you care to undo your current state, perhaps you might reconsider."

They sat in silence.

"Yes, perhaps you are right."

"What is strange to me," Ernest began, "is that Vampyres are uneasy to enter someone's home unless they are invited. For Mayor Heath to have suffered in such a way, in the privacy of his bedroom..."

"He invited his murderer in."

"Without a doubt." Ernest continued. "I am of the mind that it wasn't the first time either."

"I suppose you're not the first to have a Vampyre friend."

The visitor sat looking at a glass of yeasty cider in front of him on the table. He made everyone in the Crow's Nest uncomfortable. He had pulled his heavy cloak, thinking about his situation. The impostor was in Breton. The man who had stolen his identity had stumbled on more than he had bargained for. He was certain of it.

And me, have I grown so clumsy with age? He had almost mindlessly given up his own identity to the barmaid when he arrived. He had hiked through the forests outside of Breton for two weeks to avoid being spotted. There was something bigger going on. For all that to be lost to some barmaid, who might later have submitted to Alliance torturers, would be unthinkable. *Ponte la cabeza bien, viejo.*

He downed the rest of the glass of sour putrefaction before he headed toward the room he'd rented, observing and recording faces as he went. He forced his body up the stairs. His head ached. He wasn't a young man and he should have been in a university library on the other side of the world. As he made it up

33

the stairs, he saw two little boys run out of a room attempting to pocket a small vial.

The impostor was nearby and he was already being robbed. The old man would have to deal with him soon. *And you have to be subtle this time.*

During the long night before, Ernest had begun snooping, while Michael made easy work of cleaning the Mayor's bedroom. He devoured the spilled entrails and human remains greedily. Ernest started off by investigating the "secret" rooms of the house. Like many houses of the era, the Mayor's lavish home had secret hallways and some small clandestine rooms. One in particular, a room hidden behind a false wall in the upstairs hallway, led to a study that contained records of the entire history of the town. Ernest took a seat behind the small desk in the covert room, amazed at the elaborate lie that had been executed before him.

Breton's involvement in the War Between the States was non-existent. The year eighteen hundred and sixty-five had long come and gone. They were approaching, at least according to the papers in front of him, the turn of the twentieth century. *Thirty years*, he mused.

Their town was a hub for bringing in new "soldiers," who would die and in turn feed the crazed Vampyres. Documents described the Vampyres as "Nephilim" or shortened in often manic script as "Nephs." Other times as "Sons of Pinemé," or "Croatoans." The word Vampyre rarely appeared and only anecdotally.

The mines, the town and everything he knew were simply machinations of some government organization to work with these "Nephilim." As he continued reading, he found out that the Mayor had little to do with any of it aside from his role as a figurehead. Mister Desmond Burroughs, a man he knew well, ran the town. Desmond was rich, but Ernest could have never imagined him as a true figure of authority. A document signed by former President Andrew Johnson named Ernest. He was in the employ of the Federal government. Ernest could barely believe it. He devoured the information. In a storm of new ideas, Ernest began connecting the puzzle pieces. Journals, ledgers and official notices were all laid out with conflicting stories. He began putting together the narrative of Breton, Virginia. The town had never existed.

It seemed that the more Ernest spoke with Michael, the stranger everything about Breton felt. It was like he'd dreamt the events of his life. He was remembering childhood facts and things he'd forgotten altogether, partly because he'd given up his drinking, partly because he was somehow enchanted into his own awakening. But now he was more awake than ever before.

Conspiracy had given birth to Breton and he had been a part of it. There was much more information hidden in the Mayor's mansion; he knew he would have to get to the bottom of it.

After soul searching, he felt compelled to free the others in the same way, though he couldn't pinpoint exactly how, or what had freed his own mind. In the simplest terms he knew that he had to do right by the people, even if that meant death.

Algernon Elliott looked out into the train station the next morning. The few passengers that awaited the train looked at peace. The same ones came every day, just the few of them. It was business as usual. No real terror in their eyes. He could hear the train screeching into the station with a whistle.

What happened? He asked himself, *I know they were here.* He felt like a coward for cancelling his visit with Genevieve last night, but he knew deep down that he very easily could have saved their lives.

I'm going out. He made his way into the bustling street. The fishmongers down the way were yelling at each other as they did that time of the morning; the sun wasn't hot, but it was humid. The puddles that gathered from the night before were beginning to evaporate.

The moving people seemed like sheep, strange and disconnected from reality. He was under the distinct impression that they really were, somehow, divorced from the dark reality that invaded their lives. He hadn't proven exactly how, though.

Miners were walking away, with their eyes toward the inn. The cobblestone streets still had small streams running muddily along the gutter. As he headed down to Genevieve's shanty, Thomas and Edwin passed him in a rush. "Hey, Mister Elliott," the boys nodded quickly and quietly. They moved like they were on a mission. Algernon smiled at the boys, knowing the secret of their collusion.

He could see Genevieve holding a small tube up to the sunlight. He approached, removing his hat to address her, but she gave him a cold glance and began toward the door. "Genevieve," he begged, "please, just a word."

"Your partner will have a word for you this evening, Mister Elliott." Her eyes darted at him.

"I am not worried for Spencer but thank you. The truth is, Genevieve, I regret last night and I am terribly sorry for not coming." He stuttered and then he simply stopped.

"Anything else?" she pried.

"Nothing else."

The silence between them was like a canyon that Algernon could not cross. He cared for her but did not dare risk their lives in this strange town over his feelings. It was certain suicide.

"There are horrors in our world, Mister Elliott," she said, "but you are so busy engaging in it, you cannot see life right in front of you." She wanted to say more, but she bit her tongue. Nervously, she slipped the vial in her hand down into her courier's jacket and ran her fingers through her hair. "There is no end to how much you frustrate me, Mister Elliott."

"I'm quite sure," he responded sheepishly.

"I knew the world was a hard place before you came along. My mother knew it. She taught me. My uncle knew it and he taught me." She breathed, "I am under no delusion that this should be easy. I am more than certain we are to die, Mister Elliott! If one of us were to have disappeared last night, then today we wouldn't be here having this asinine conversation, Mister Elliott. Our plight is bad and only getting worse, so we must begin to live, or we're all we will have to show for it is regret."

Algernon swallowed hard. She was right and the regret was overwhelming. He felt like he was putting her into more danger with every word so he kept it simple, shoving the carefully typed letter back into his pocket. "You're right."

THREE

"In its form of vampir [South Russian upuir, anciently upir], it has been compared with the Lithuanian wempti = to drink, and wempti, wampiti = to growl, to mutter, and it has been derived from a root pi [to drink] with the prefix u = av, va. If this derivation is correct, the characteristic of the vampire is a kind of blood-drunkenness."
-William Ralston Shedden-Ralston, *Songs of the Russian People (1873)*

Smoke billowed in hues of black and white across the battlefields north of Breton. Soldiers sought respite, weary from many days of rain, which had let up only hours earlier. Their blue uniforms had lost their color from mud and rain and everything was a dull brown. The encampments pushed their positions down near the ravines of Breton around the coal mines and into the neighboring countryside. The horrid sounds of the evening after another skirmish were agonizing; some men were left out on the field crying and moaning, waiting to die.

The men were certain that if they were not going to die that day, they would be dead the next. It was just a bloody and everlasting mudslide toward the meat grinder that was death. The shadow of that imminent death hung over the Captain of the Seventh Battalion, the highest-ranking officer left in the all-but-abandoned Union forces in that part of Virginia. A mere nineteen year old boy, Jared Carswell was a tall, broad soldier, who knew that there was no hope in his bleak position. A letter had come down just days earlier from Tecumseh Sherman himself that Grant would not be approving any more reinforcements in their area. Sergeant Cornwall had to read it, for Jared could not read. He realized that his small army would either have to push through their position back west to make a break toward the north, or die, man-by-man, in their current location. There was no room in their orders for retreat and they had their backs to the sea. The word was bleak.

He patted men on the back and nodded to some as he walked along the tents on his way to the mess. In their eyes, he saw empty coffins. Some cleaned their firearms while others sat eyes-down in their meal. Some men stared aimlessly at the hazy late-afternoon sky or at the fires in front of them. He carried his tin cup and a spoon. They might all be damned, but he was still hungry.

It was his night on patrol. Despite his rank, he still stayed in rotation on patrols. He'd never learned any other way. It was just bad luck that he was going to be going back out there injured. He got in line. Even doomed men needed to eat.

Ahead of him, men commiserated.

"It'll be a night for revenants, just you watch." Cornwall grumbled as though cheerfully.

Some men take more pleasure in being right about awful things. Jared thought of his sergeant.

"Just so much gut." The Sergeant Cornwall continued. "They'll be out." He said, looking for anyone to agree.

"Oh shut up, too much rain and mud." Another soldier up the line said to murmurs of ascent.

Cornwall wasn't to be deterred. "What say you, Cap'n?" The old soldier asked as his gaze wandered down Jared's arm to the boy captain's blood soaked sleeve.

"No use thinking on what we can't change." Jared shook his head. "We just gotta get out of these ravines. So get your recruit of strength, maybe we push through tomorrow."

"If we make it that long..." the old soldier grumbled under his breath, sticking his cup out for a ladleful of stew. "If Johnny Reb don't get us, Johnny Revenant'll do the job."

"Sometimes I think them revenants got it easy." Jared grunted a pained laugh, as he eyed the soggy hardtack dropped into the gray stew and salt pork that the cook ladled into his cup. "At least they got a whole soldier to chew on before they find this stuff in his belly."

Genevieve Moreau sat for almost an hour with her head in her hands, waiting. She was not tired like she told Spencer Mayhew, who was getting frustrated with the vial that he held over a Bunsen burner. He stared at the thing with a large magnifying glass that he had fashioned into a headband. He slid a heated metal loop into the liquid, but nothing happened, not so far as he could tell. "Does it smell sweet in here to you?" He asked.

"Sweet?" Genevieve asked.

"Yes, like burnt sugar." Spencer said.

"I haven't noticed anything. Genevieve said.

"Algernon should be doing this," he grumbled. The device he was wearing made his eyeball look disproportionately larger than his face. On any other night that would have made Genevieve laugh, but this evening her mind was elsewhere.

Spencer mumbled to himself, almost inaudibly, "This cannot be."

Genevieve simply grunted.

He didn't answer.

She didn't care.

Spencer Mayhew was not a scientist. Nor was he a headmaster. He was the associate of Algernon Elliott, though they acted, from day to day, as if the two were strangers. Their secretly-exchanged letters were Genevieve's most exciting mission. Consequently, she frequented both their homes, eventually developing the special relationship she shared with Algernon.

Genevieve worried about her Mister Elliott at the same moment as someone knocked quietly at the door. "Algernon?" She muttered, both hopeful and worried.

"Surely not." Spencer replied not looking up.

Genevieve opened the door gingerly to see a broad-shouldered old man draped in a heavy cloak. He looked like a grizzled traveler in a fairy tale.

"Good evening, Miss Moreau. I need to speak to you and your friend Mister Mayhew if you'd allow me a few moments." His accent was thick, some sort of European.

Genevieve was surprised that it was not Algernon but more surprised that the stranger knew Mister Smith's real name. Uselessly, she tried to hide her surprise. "Please," she hesitated. "Come in."

He made his way into the shanty house and Genevieve looked out the door to see if anyone was following him; she saw no one.

"I apologize for my intrusion," he smiled casually. "I can tell you that, for my part, I have done everything in my power to avoid being followed. But in the case of the *Vampiro,* it is often quite difficult to really avoid him.

Spencer turned around fully on his stool. "You're a long way from Spain, friend." He tested the man.

"Yes," the stranger answered. "And you are a long way from London."

Genevieve shut the door and turned quickly. "What are you talking about and who are you?" She didn't hide her impatience.

"Well," he responded. "Perhaps with some warming tea?"

The three looked at each other and after a moment of silence, the Spaniard made his way to the table and sat down.

The further he got from town in his vespertine exploration, the more Michael found the bloodlust rising up inside of him. A predatory instinct had taken over. A Vampyric rage was pulsing inside his head. The smell of blood across a misty battlefield was intoxicating and he was filled with a desire to kill and a need to feed. It rendered him unable to think clearly. Dizzy, he struggled to his feet. He could hear a soldier moving toward him. Each step drummed in his head, sloshing in the muddy earth. It was as if time was slowing.

Jared, captain of the Seventh Battalion, with his long rifle and bayonet, was primed to kill.

How did I get here? Michael asked himself.

Throughout the day, he had thought about investigating the battlefields. With dusk he made his way towards the gunshots and cannon fire out into an expansive foggy meadow among the dead and the wounded. There were decades of death compounded in that place. He heard the captain yelling at him from afar as he stood over the bodies of two patrolmen. He'd killed them both unceremoniously; they were easy prey, riddled with unspoken guilt and murder. He was satisfied with the taste of their sweet blood. Strangely, he could sense things about them in their last flashes of life: fears, memories and hatred. *Guilt.* He thought.

Having baptized himself in the Mayor's remains, he felt fully renewed. And now, his mind awake, he needed answers. Among the aromas of death rising in the fog and the moaning medley of dying soldiers, he would find them.

The soldier was freshly wounded. A bullet to the arm. Michael could smell the charred skin around the wound. He could discern the old blood from the fresh that was soaking the boy's sleeve.

Jared leapt into the air, his bayonet poised for attack. Michael felt like his ears should pop, but they wouldn't. He was no longer dizzy. He was awakening when his rage finally overtook him.

By the time Jared had stabbed his weapon into the ground with the full force of his weight, the Vampyre was nowhere to be found.

Guilt. Where is this man's guilt? Michael thought. Instinctively, he tried to judge the soldier. He knew immediately that the quality of the blood was bound, somehow, to his guilt. Michael could feel a break in the lust, enough to think. *Why?*

An unknown voice swelled in Jared's mind just before he heard the voice aloud behind him. "What are you?" It asked.

Jared was caught in the bloody mess of the mud. He dropped to a knee and he pulled the shaft of the bayonet from the ground. He charged the voice, but it was gone. Jared peered through the smoke and fog, but there was nothing.

Michael felt his lips swelling and tingling. The bloodlust made him rage. His mouth was watering and he wanted nothing more than to kill the wounded soldier, even if he didn't drink the blood. At least he wanted to get close enough to truly smell that blood. He would appear near the soldier.

Jared swung the bayonet into smoke and he jabbed into the dark.

Michael was of two minds. The rage told him to kill the thing. But he questioned it. He would appear nearby, look into the man's eyes, before disappearing into the mist again.

Jared turned in circles, stepping over the dead. He listened for the revenant.

Michael stepped out behind the boy. He could not sense much for thought. The boy was focused like an animal. His thoughts and his instincts were one thing. *A true soldier.* Michael thought. *I could literally cut his throat with my fingernail.* No matter what he did, no matter how much he wanted, he couldn't bring himself to kill the child soldier. *Curious.* He thought.

The Vampyre could sense movement coming toward the battlefield from all sides. It was an avalanche of energy. It was a stampede. "By the pricking of my thumbs." Michael whispered.

Jared turned, swinging his long musket at the Vampyre in a wide arc, nearly catching the Vampyre by the face, as Michael evaded.

Something wicked this way comes. Michael thought.

"Wicked." Jared laughed bitterly. "I will run the wicked through, right here. Right now."

Admirable. Michael said. *But I am not what you should fear.* Michael's chest was heaving and his stomach was wrenching with hunger. He was starving despite having fed on the other men.

Jared could not hear what Michael could; the air vibrated with the slivers and movements of descending Vampyres.

Michael knew that he would have to do something. He needed to know why he couldn't simply control himself, why something else was dictating his senses, what determined who he could or could not kill.

He moved from the curtain of fog, now from in front of the captain and grabbed the musket with a strong and steady hand. Jared had been holding his weapon tight, but it seemed to disappear. The long weapon flew and lay across the body of a dead soldier in the mud. Michael sidestepped the attempted blow from the soldier's now free hands. Wrapping an arm around the boy's throat, Michael lifted him high in the air with a single bound. They landed softly on a branch in a tall tree near the edge of the field. Jared heaved, choking. Michael covered the captain's mouth with one hand and held the other arm around his neck.

The black, empty feeling washed over Jared, as it did every night. He was sure he would be crushed under the weight of the creature's arms, but Michael whispered, "I am no man's enemy yet. Trying to see a way out of this, just as you are." *Be silent.*

So began an orgiastic feast. There were hundreds of them. Vampyres of every size and color flew down on the field like locusts. They landed on hands and knees in the mud like animals. They all moved together. The flowing mass of bodies was eerily quiet. Aside from the physical cracking of men's bones and the distant cry of human fear and agony.

Some of the Vampyres were huge creatures, completely naked and obese, bald with sparse patches of hair growing from their bodies. Their skin was pale and deeply scarred. Their necks were swollen and connected their massive heads to their shoulders like fat webs. They were round like ogres. Their open mouths stretched from one ear to the other and were filled with rows of teeth. Their eyes were voids, black, like they had been burnt from their sockets.

Abominations, Michael thought. Their jaws shifted when they chewed on the bodies of the men. He noticed the scarring around their necks was the same as the scars around their wrists and ankles. *Chained at the neck?* There had to have been twenty or thirty of them.

Others were tall, muscular Vampyres. They looked like soldiers, were built like statues and dressed like vagrants. Their eyes burned red and they tore into the dead bodies with their hands and pulled flesh from bone, separating the denim, wool and cotton uniforms from the flesh before eating it. They would throw the bones, allowing those smaller and more deformed to fight over them.

There were even children among them, hissing, and biting at the other Vampyres to get to their meals. They scrabbled over the lumbering creatures like ants across boulders. They seemed to disappear into the frenzy, tearing into the dead bodies like they were fresh bread, eating everything. They did not simply desire the blood of the men; they were devouring the soldiers whole.

Michael could hear them in his mind, but the battlefield grew quieter by the moment, until only wet sounds and hissing came out of the miasmal black silence. Michael felt no kinship to any of the creatures. His mind filled with their harsh language;

the words less like a human language and more like the sound of sticks breaking or the sound of one's feet rustling and crackling in autumn leaves. There were hisses under it all. Some larger creatures would push the smaller ones out of the way for better pieces as they harvested the field. The smaller ones would fight and bite their way back in. They ground through bone and flesh, leaving nothing but the bloodied mud and scraps of clothes and guns. Some of the Vampyres who were still very human simply reached down, tasting the blood with their fingers as if they were sampling a dessert or delicacy.

Jared had seen war all his life, but what he was encountering was altogether a new thing. He recognized the feeling washing over his body and mind. He was feeling dizzy. He realized it was something he'd grown up feeling. Every night this happened. His body began to go limp and Michael shook him.

"No!" Michael fought the limp body, trying to wake him. "We need to know what this is. I need you to help me find out."

Jared couldn't help it though; he was increasingly faint. The otherworldly, gruesome sight was too much for him. Michael could feel his hostage collapsing in his arms, but he continued to watch. There were some Vampyres who did not engage in the feast, they simply walked through the ranks and watched. The closer he listened to the chanting and crackling of the Vampyre tongue the more he understood one word. *Guilty, guilty, guilty.* It was clear as a bell.

Interesting.

Michael escaped into the dark and left Jared's unconscious body near a tent where a small campfire burned low, still curious about the strange "innocent" man. Before leaving, he left a bottle of some foul-smelling alcohol lying against the man's leg. "Good luck." He whispered.

When Jared came to, he jumped up to hear a few chuckles from his men, "Been drinkin' on patrol, Cap'n?"

"Oh," Jared answered, confused. He looked down to find a bottle in his lap. "Yeah... I s'pose I have." He looked up into the trees and quietly contemplated what he had seen. The Vampyre had every opportunity to kill him but chose not to. Instead, the creature had brought him back to the warmth of the campfire with an alibi. Jared's head ached.

"I bet that arm hurts like hell, Cap'n." A soldier commented from the other side of the campfire.

Jared's thoughts were reeling. He looked down and saw black ooze dripping from his fingertips as he raised the aching appendage. The bullet wound hadn't even crossed his mind. The bottle of gin spilled on the ground in the darkness from his lap as he clumsily rose to his feet. He walked to his tent on the other side of the camp. His stumbling would have easily been confused with his new alibi. In actuality he was intoxicated on the new flood of images, memories and emotions. He recalled the calm people walking among the creatures, the ones who looked like they were in charge. It terrified him. He felt awake for the first time in years. "I guess Cornwall was right about the Vampyres tonight." He sighed.

M ister Mayhew," the old man began.
"Please. Smith." Mister Smith interrupted.
"They do like a Smith here." Genevieve muttered in a faux British accent.

Smith curled his lips in the semblance of a smile.

"*Si, con razón.* Smith. My identity may come as a surprise to you and to you, Miss Genevieve Moreau." He paused and had a sip of the cup of steaming tea in front of him. Genevieve had thought it strange that he pronounced her name *Jon-vi-ev*, the French way, like her uncle had, instead of the American way. His accent was Spanish and thick, unrefined even; the "z" and "s" sounds still maintained a Castilian "th." "My name is Alonzo Gallegos."

"Like the Vampyre hunter?" Genevieve asked, suspicious of the man.

"No, it is my name. This man, who calls himself *Cazavampiros*, he is nothing but an impostor." The old man stopped, "Your uncle never spoke of me?"

Genevieve cut her eyes to Spencer, who just shrugged. "I'm sorry." She said. "Until a few days ago, I'd never heard the name."

The old man grunted ascent. "My name was a curse in your uncle's mouth for years."

"So you were enemies?" She asked.

"No." Gallegos shook his head ruefully, but he smiled. "Friendly rivals. Do you have perhaps honey or a sweetener for the tea?" he asked.

"No honey, I'm sorry." Genevieve said.

The grizzled man laughed. "Well, that sugar water that your Mister Smith has just heated would do just as well."

Genevieve and Smith shared a look of incredulity.

"In the vial?" Smith asked.

"Yes. Of course in the vial." Gallegos replied.

"How could you possibly know what is in that vial?" Smith asked.

"Because I already tested one earlier."

"But how? You just arrived in town." Genevieve said.

"I stole one from a man on the street." Gallegos said. "Then I stuck my finger in it." He indicated with his hands. "And I taste it."

"You could have died." Smith said flatly.

"I did not." Gallegos said with a smile.

Smith handed the still-warm vial to the grizzled old man who immediately dumped its contents into his cup of tea. The old man then stirred the tea with the vial. "Would you happen to have any cookies?

Genevieve raised an eyebrow angrily, but Smith, who was very interested in hearing what he had to say, encouraged it. "Go, go, go!" He commanded, waving her on.

"Miss Moreau," Gallegos added.

Genevieve assumed he'd ask for something else. The man seemed so rough and crude. She turned around with a disappointed look.

"I am terribly sorry to hear about the passing of your uncle."

She looked down, ashamed at her own judgment of the old man.

"Thank you," she said quietly.

"I considered him a confidant. We had a very complicated relationship, but his letters meant very much to me over the years."

As she opened the pantry, distracted, Genevieve's mind flashed to the night her uncle had disappeared into the dark, followed by Vampyres. He had waved her back into the house but she only ran inside long enough to grab a gun. By the time she came out gun leveled, ready to kill any Vampyre she could see, he had been swallowed up in the dark. That was also the night that Mister Smith and Algernon had come into her life at gunpoint as she looked for her uncle in the woods.

Mister Smith looked across the table and asked, "Was there not supposed to be one more in our number?"

"Yes." Gallegos contemplated, stroking his gray beard. "He was to have met me at the inn when I arrived. I've had no word of him."

"Do you know his name?" Smith asked.

"No." Gallegos nodded. "His arrival was to be expected, but information on him was to be kept secret." He looked at them both. "I know nothing of him. Well, that is not true. I know that this man is an expert in both the preternatural and wartime strategy. At first I felt that perhaps our contact met with the other man who carries my name, but I have kept an eye on him and he has kept *contacto mínimo*. The impostor has only spoken in public and he drinks alone." He reconsidered the evidence. "If our contact is as knowledgeable as I am led to believe, then he would have seen through the impostor's rouse."

"Yes." Mister Smith concluded. "Am I to assume you received a letter, as my partner and I had?"

The old Spaniard nodded.

"And a lump sum for expenses?"

Gallegos smiled.

"Experts in the supernatural and strategists," Smith thought aloud. "I'm not much more than a former soldier in British Armed Forces, though my partner has some amateur expertise. In the preternatural."

"Rank?" Gallegos asked.

"Lieutenant Colonel." Smith answered. "But that was long ago."

Gallegos nodded. "But a a man of war will always find a war to fight."

"Are you a military man?" Smith asked.

"No." Gallegos replied. "Never had the constitution."

"Then what is this fight you speak of and what is your role in all of this, Mr. Gallegos?" Smith asked. "Paranormal expert?"

"Just a philosopher." The old man quipped. "Currently I teach at the University of Salamanca."

"And yet you carry yourself like an old general." Smith smiled.

"For some," Gallegos said. He shared a knowing grin with the Englishman. "They are one and the same."

Mister Smith concluded, "It would seem that our benefactors are under the impression that our," he looked around the room, "motley assembly might have the makings of an army." He sighed anxiously. "At very least, they feel someone is going to war."

"Which is why I have been hiding."

Genevieve grabbed some cookies from the pantry and placed them on the table. "Then why is everyone around town talking about you?"

"Any mention of it should be considered stolen, and I shall deal with that matter myself." He picked a cookie from the plate before Genevieve could set it down. Her eyes grew large at his forwardness. "Time is quickly getting away from us, my new *amigos*." He muttered to them with a mouthful of cookie. "Do you have any milk?"

Genevieve just raised an eyebrow in irritation.

The old man, put his hands up in mock surrender and laughed. "My apologies. I have asked much already." The smile that never touched his eyes faded. Gravely, he continued, "But I must ask now for much more."

"What more could we possibly do for you?" Spencer asked.

"I need information. I need to know what exactly you are facing here."

Genevieve laughed ruefully. "Vampires."

"Yes." He agreed. "But why? Why here? Why now? Why like this?"

"What do you mean?" She asked. "Breton has always been infested. Maybe when they built the town, it woke something up."

"Or they found a place ripe for the picking." Spencer added.

"Sufficiently predatory," Gallegos said, "but your little town works like clockwork and it requires many hands to operate. Very complicated. Why?"

Genevieve and Spencer just looked at each other.

"Your little town isn't a hunting ground." Gallegos said gravely. He leaned in. "It is an abattoir and every human is just fodder for slaughtering. But who is turning the meat grinder?"

"Does the 'Alliance' mean anything to you?" Genevieve asked.

The old man turned his head on its side, like an owl eyeing a rodent. "Yes. Very much so. That is a very big 'why'."

Kat rushed along the street toward the Mayor's house. She didn't want to get involved, maybe should could convince Mister Williams that his foolhardy plan would be foiled. But that would be getting involved.

One of the girls who worked for Kat's father hadn't come in and when Kat went by her home no one was there. She knew what it meant and tried not to think about it. The attacks were growing more frequent and even if no one talked about it, everyone knew. Ultimately, it was just more work at the inn for her.

Kat opened the door of the Mayor's house gingerly. "Mister Williams," she called out softly. The house was dark and the only light came from the orange flicker of the street lamps through the windows. "Mister Williams?"

Before she could breathe another word, unseen hands pulled her inside. She tried to scream, but her mouth was already covered. She felt like her neck was being stretched, pulling her head from her shoulders. Whatever was happening was happening fast, wind was whirring and swooshing past her.

Suddenly no one was holding her. She felt herself collapse on a cold, damp floor. She had landed in the pooling of her dress, but her legs were freezing and she pulled herself back quickly.

Then quietly came a voice. "Please, you are safer now than you were."

Silence.

"I," she stammered, "have no need of your protection—whoever you are." *Whatever you are.* She thought.

She stayed quiet, almost holding her breath; she could feel it nearby. She couldn't hear anything else breathing. She felt lonely and terrified, but something inside her told her not to anger it; she had actually planned to survive the night. She covered her mouth and in that pitch-black and cold she closed her eyes tight.

Michael listened in the silence, downstairs from behind the front door to Mayor Heath's large home. Something was coming. It could sense him. He moved along the wall, quietly looking out each window. He couldn't see whatever it was. There was a sinister chill in the air.

Following it with his mind, he was drawn into in a dark forest. He felt as though he had stepped through an open door into another place altogether.It was silent and no breeze blew. He could not smell the blood of nearby animals. The light of the night was turned silvery along the gray leaves of ancient trees that reached high into the heavens. It was familiar, much more so than anything in Breton. Light did not come from above, but instead it glowed deeply inside of everything. The leaves and the ground had their own soft radiance. In the distance, where there should have been forest, there was nothing but fog. It was a strange, yet compelling dream world.

Michael's coat was pristine. His hands were clean and he looked himself over in a beautiful military jacket lined in gold with black-shined shoes.

He could still sense the demoniac presence. He had felt it on the battlefield as he watched the Vampyres devouring the dead soldiers and continued to feel it until he had made it back to the hideout. He had been followed. He looked out across the dreamland and saw a figure moving toward him. He began to grow dizzy.

He's gotten a sniff of you. Michael thought. He shook his head as if to free the thought. He hadn't thought it. It was his voice in his own head, but he knew it wasn't his thought.

Are you going to be hunter or prey, Michael?

Michael was standing at the window again. His own voice echoed in his head with someone else's thoughts. What he had thought to be one thing hunting him, were two entities. One had been with him the whole time, he had seen it in the hull of the ship. He could feel it now, always just outside the periphery.

But the other was hunting him.

Like a storm passing, the otherworldly feeling dissipated. It was gone. He couldn't grasp it all. He returned to the secret room where he had left the girl lying in the dark. He pushed the secret door hidden along the hallway wall to see her sitting haloed in moonlight. Lighting a lantern, he feared for her.

She squinted, shielding her eyes. "What do you plan to do with me, sir?" she asked.

"I have no plan, Miss," he answered quietly. "I came looking for Ernest." He brushed his hair out of his eyes, their ethereal amber reflecting the lantern's light as if they too were lit with flame. "It would seem someone has come looking for me as well."

"Perhaps a Vampyre hunter who might know you're here?" She said quietly.

"Not very likely."

"The Vampyre hunter was to meet with the Mayor today." Kat's voice barely shook.

The Vampyre in front of her just nodded thoughtfully.

"They plan to kill all the Vampyres." She lied, though it seemed as though he was giving it some thought. "The Vampyre hunter even put on a show out by the town square. It's a big to-do. I'd get out of here, if I were you. Otherwise, he's going to kill you."

He just sat there smiling. Infuriatingly, he said nothing.

She stared into his amber eyes, trying not to swallow, trying not to show any fear. They were not unkind eyes. But why was he smiling like that?

Finally, he sighed, "Yes, I will have to go very soon." He cast a glance over his shoulder toward the door.

"The hunter." She said quietly.

"No." He cast his eyes about as though listening to a voice that only he heard. Kat also heard things no one else heard. "The mayor, as I believe we both know, is dead," He shrugged, "and unfortunately, the Vampyre hunter is some sort of huckster."

She blew out a sigh and crossed her arms.

"Ah, so you've met him."

She nodded.

"To be honest, when Mister Williams mentioned him, I thought maybe he could help me with," he gestured at himself, "all of this."

"So you and Mister Williams have been working together." She shuddered.

"So he mentioned talking to me earlier and that I disapproved of his working with someone of your ilk?"

Michael looked abashed. "No miss. He never mentioned you.

"Oh." She paused. So you're here disposing of the evidence." She pointed toward the bedroom, or where she guessed it would be in the house.

He nodded reluctantly.

Kat sighed, "So what? I'm next?"

"Miss!" The Vampyre seemed affronted. "Absolutely not!" Then more quietly, "No." As though convincing himself.

Kat didn't know whether to be afraid of the creature or just frustrated and annoyed. "So people are being kidnapped by Vampyres and though you're not going to kill me— you decide to kidnap me? Is it just a hobby of Vampyres to snatch women up in the night?"

Michael gave her a flat look.

"Yes, I guess it would be part of the whole Vampyre thing." She sighed reluctantly.

"It was not my intention to 'kidnap' you."

"Intention has little to do with it, sir."

"There is *something* out there."

Kat was growing exasperated. "Yes. You."

"No, Miss." He smiled before a flash of worry caused his eyes to darken. "How could I forgive myself if I put you in danger? I brought you up here for your protection. I promise."

Michael set the lantern down on a small table and sat at a chair facing away from the false door. Kat had never been in the room before. She had suspected the mayor's home would have some hidden rooms and passages. Rich people went for that sort of thing.

They were in a small study. She stood and noticed a large desk covered in paperwork. There were all sorts of books in the small room and they were all organized. She had never thought the mayor a reader.

Kat stood, trying to keep her eyes on the creature. She walked around the desk, running her hands across the papers. "I cannot say that I trust your motives, sir," she stated frankly. "Are you not charming Mister Williams into some darker plot of your own?"

Michael thought aloud, "If I were, would I tell you about it?"

"No, I suppose not," she answered. "Well, it's very improper of you to bring a young lady into a dark room like this." Kat offered, though she never really cared for that sentiment. She could fend for herself.

Michael smiled. "Miss Kat, if I had planned to do you harm, I could have accomplished it without very much charm at all."

The color left from her face. "Sir, you said Mister Williams never mentioned me and I'm very sure I never told you my name."

"You're quite right," he answered. "Strange how I came on it." Michael searched his memory. "I cannot say why or how, but it would seem I can stumble onto names, perhaps faces, sometimes entire thoughts while the other person is thinking them. I think it quite rude.

Honestly, I had no intention of stumbling on your name when Mister Williams thought it, it was simply tangled in some strong emotions. This sort of thing, I imagine can bring out a lot of those in a person."

Kat sat down at the large desk with a huff. "Sir Vampyre—"

The word triggered the man. Michael interrupted, "Michael."

She continued, "Alright, yes. Michael. I should feel quite violated, were you to peruse my thoughts like books in a library." Even as she said it she began eyeing the paperwork on the desk in front of her. She leaned forward and her voice trailed off. There were names, lists. She knew them all. She tried to read but before she knew it, the lamps in the room were lit. Even quicker than she could think of it, Michael was sitting back down.

She looked at him. "You didn't just read my thoughts did you?"

"No," he answered, "you were squinting."

"You are quite strange for a Vampyre," she stammered, sympathetically.

For the first time, Kat truly saw his face, the raw fear and anxiety. His voice was quiet "From what I've seen of other Vampyres this evening, I hope I am. I hope I am nothing like them."

"Do you not know other Vampyres?" she asked.

"No, I've no recollection of my life before days ago," he began. "Aside from some vague memories of being on a boat and seeing others, what I think were others, down upon it." He sat quietly looking at his hands. "What I saw of them tonight, though..." His voice trailed off. He looked at her pleadingly.

Kat had served soldiers in the inn all her life. This was the look she sometimes saw; shock, confusion, fear.

"So, before what you saw tonight?" She led, but he remained silent. You didn't know? Maybe you don't remember them? Or maybe you were just a man?"

"I should hope that I am still simply a man," he murmured quietly. "This—" he paused, then continued, "—affliction is quite strange." He looked at his hand. It closed slowly. He looked around again, as though someone else was in the room with them? He listened. He looked like a caged animal.

"Affliction?" She asked.

"I hope this is curable. I hope this isn't just hell."

If it is, surely you're the demon. She thought and she could tell by the way the young man shrank into his seat that if he hadn't just read his mind, he was thinking something similar.

Kat felt pity on him. She sat in the big chair examining the few sheets on the desk. She looked up and caught his eyes. He was something otherworldly, but not like she would have ever thought and she grew warm with seeing him. She instantly hated herself, but she sympathized with him. He looked pathetic in his military jacket, which was obviously fit for another man. He was young and his hair was dark and shaggy. His mouth was slender and made for smiling and his jaw was masculine. His face was almost like that of a child, his mouth curled, worried. He was beautiful. *What? No! What a terribly foolish thought.*

Michael sat up suddenly, but quietly. He sensed something.

"Miss Kat," he sighed. "I beg. Please hide yourself." He listened and his voice betrayed concern. He heard something coming. "Please," he whispered, "Now."

She nodded quietly.

As quickly as he had made the room bright, it went dark again. He was gone and the door was shut behind him.

She felt deep down that the Vampyre was trying to help her. She felt like a fool. Did she just think he was beautiful? Was she so lonely? But he had listened to her. He spoke to her honestly, with frailty and she feared that something might happen to him. The last thing she heard was a crash through the window in the hall as her heart dropped into her stomach.

Ernest had taken his regular seat at the inn and had a large glass of cider. *Just one...to celebrate*, he thought. He had never felt so alive and awake. He could remember things, but sometimes they didn't make sense.

He did notice, however, that the room was quieter than usual. No drinking songs, no fiddles and no jokes. Everyone had their heads down. Something had changed. *Perhaps it's simply my way of perceiving things.* He finished his ale—full bottom's up— and set the mug to the side.

He left money for his drink on the table and quietly made his way out, passing Monsieur Chandler who seemed in quite a rush to get upstairs. Ernest knew Chandler as a man of unending patience and it was odd to see the strange little man in almost a run. He looked determined.

Only the sound of glasses clinking and the low hum of conversation filled the room on the first floor of the inn. He could feel his world shifting around him. He was quickly becoming suspicious of everyone. Who was working with the Vampyres? *Surely not Chandler. Perhaps*, he thought. It made sense.

He heard a commotion; the front door swung open and police officers, whom he had never seen, came running into the tavern. They did not wear badges. Their uniforms were new and pressed and they wore medallions on their chests instead. Their long double-breasted coats were like nothing he'd seen before. They wore helmets and each of them looked very young.

The head of the group spotted Ernest. He didn't make much of an attempt to hide, pushed by a morbid curiosity to find out where they'd come from. The young officer held up a piece of paper.

"Mister Ernest Williams," he began, "you're under arrest."

Ernest chuckled as the officers surrounded him. The situation was terrifying, but he kept a smile.

The patrons of the bar barely noticed.

The officer continued, "For the Murder of Mayor Heath."

C ap'n!" Corporal Vogt, the night patrol called out. "Captain!"
The young soldier panted as he ran to the Captain's tent. He had gaunt features and not even a single thin blond hair grew on his face. He called again, but no one appeared.

Among the nearly four hundred tents that made up the sleeping quarters of the Seventh Battalion, men were going from tent to tent using their bayonets to peer between the pup-tent flaps. "Two bodies, both breathing!"

Horatio Cornwall, a sergeant with a large gray handlebar mustache and thick, curly sideburns, who walked like a potbellied pig, brandished a black polished revolver at his side and walked between them yelling, "Men, if your tent is missing a man, let a guard know!" He continued, "If your tent has a dead man in it, let a guard know!" He yelled in the same tone, "If you and the man who should be in your tent with you are both where you ought be, sit up and be quiet!"

Lanterns and candles came to life. Light was rippling through the sea of tents. A man had woken up that night with night terrors, screaming in his tent. At the sound of the screaming man, another one found that the soldier that should have been with him had gone missing. By that time, they had found that within the last week, that evening included, twenty-three men had gone missing and the one man with night terrors had suddenly contracted amnesia. He didn't know where or who he was, but he knew he needed to be in a town somewhere near.

Revenant charms, thought the large sergeant. "I am beginning to grow more than certain that these Revenants are in collusion with Johnny Reb." He growled aloud.

The guard responded, "Two bodies, both breathing sir."

The search continued for a moment before being interrupted by a corporal who came running down the line. Both guards lifted their rifles at him.

He threw his hands up.

The sergeant spoke, "What is it, Vogt?"

"Sir," the boy swallowed. "The Captain."

"Yes, Corporal?" The sergeant asked.

"Captain Carswell never finished his patrol, sir." The boy said, eyeing the treeline at the edge of the field. "He's not in his tent either."

Fool boy. He replied without emotion. "Twenty-four."

The man that alarmed the entire seventh battalion with his screams was a sallow-skinned vagrant by the name of Garath Lackner. He had murdered a man. He didn't remember that about himself until a strange dream came shrieking into his thoughts. It was calling him to Breton to go to work for a man called Madison because Rodman told him to. Madison was the sheriff. He was in charge. Garath could repay his sins in full if he made it to a place called Breton. Others like him were already there.

He stumbled along in only his nightshirt and only the smoke from old campfires moved against the silhouettes of the trees along the field.

Garath Lackner, the murderer, had to go to Breton to repay the sin of murder to a Sheriff Madison, *No, that doesn't feel right, it's Matheson.* He had to find Matheson— to work for Matheson. The thought was driving him crazy. The guilty memories of killing overwhelmed him, reaching up like hands grabbing at him from the depths of his mind.

Somehow he knew where to go. He knew where he had to be. There was work there. There was peace of mind. He walked into the wood, panicked. *I'm late. I'm late. I'm late.* He had to get to Matheson for peace of mind. He had to repay the sin of murder. *I'm late. I'm late.*

You won't be missed. Came a thought from in the trees.

"What?"

Warm blood gushed down his chest, soaked up by his nightshirt. He gargled and hissed, air passing through a gash in his neck. He clawed at his throat, eyes bulging, unable to see into the darkness. His eyes filled with tears and the blood splashed between his fingertips.

The Vampyres came out of the darkness and devoured Garath Lackner whole.

Guilty, guilty, guilty, they repeated in hisses and whispers. *Guilty, guilty, guilty.*

Thomas chewed on a stale bit of bread from the orphanage's cupboard, as Edwin wandered off ahead of him kicking stones. The moon had turned bright like a mirror in a sunny room. All of Breton was aglow; it was a spiritual night. They turned into the shadows of Abbey Alley, where Thomas could hear muffled yelling coming from inside the old church building. He stopped and listened from the middle of the street. There was more than one voice; it sounded important. Edwin kept walking along, but Thomas remembered Headmaster Smith telling him with a secretive wink to listen if he heard important men speaking.

Edwin turned around and called "TOM—" but before he could finish he realized that his accomplice was listening to something and quickly clasped his mouth with both hands. His eyes were wide; he felt he might have ruined whatever was happening, but Thomas didn't move except to turn his head slightly. His face looked like it could well up with tears. He swallowed hard. Edwin looked around trying to listen at the air but heard nothing. Thomas's eyes jetted left to right like he was thinking frantically, like he was trying to contemplate something very important or lie quickly.

Edwin began tiptoeing toward him, listening to the muffled conversation, but couldn't make out the words; Thomas could recognize one of the voices. It was the sheriff. Thomas had been in enough trouble to know the sound of that voice through a wall. He had sat in the man's office on more than a few occasions.

Thomas looked at Edwin, realizing how close he'd gotten and sighed. He looked around and asked the strangest question, "What is this place exactly?"

FOUR

—————◆—————

There were giants in the earth in those days;
and also after that, when the sons of God came in unto
the daughters of men, and they bare children to them,
*the same became mighty men which were **of old***, men*
of renown.
- *Genesis 6:4 (KJV) (1611)*
- As noted in the journal of A.G., Profesor
Emérita, u de Salamanca *(1858)*
Translated to the English from the Reina Valera
Version *(1602)*
*Anotation: *"of old" significa antigüedad, desde antes*
el Adán?

Michael moved on instinct, darting like a deer from the crashing plate glass that landed all around him. After a quick glance back through the window, he was off and over the wall of the mansion yard. It was on top of the house. Its silhouette loomed high in the moonlight. He had just escaped a feeding frenzy a mere couple of miles away, but whatever he was sensing now was all the scarier. He could only hope that whatever was following him would not sense the girl. He started off slowly, banging through town. He would climb one retaining wall, stop and wait, listen, feel and then continue. He made his way down into the town square, unseen by human eyes, from shadow to silhouette to darkness.

It was coming for him. He began moving more quickly. He breathed in deeply and headed for the edge of town. Whatever it was seemed to be giving him an advantage and a wide berth. Michael knew he'd have to take it. It felt predatory, a lion to Michael's gazelle. Michael seemed to be getting closer to locking in on some of its thoughts. The more he really ran, really opened himself up, the clearer his thinking became. It was a flood of thoughts. They came from all around him, from within the town and throughout the forest. He could hone in on the thought. "TOM—"A name maybe. He didn't focus on it too long, he breathed in again, deeper, cutting through the high grass, his legs barely touching the blades, his feet barely touching the ground. *It would appear you're the prey.* The other Michael seemed to tell him. His own thoughts were betraying him, a disembodied voice, a version of himself taunting him, while yet another more sinister thing moving above him, slinking from the shadow of tree to tree.

He made his way toward the mines, avoiding hunting paths and the muddy cart roads that tied the mines to the town like tangled veins. He flew for miles away from Breton into dark territories. He could feel the life out in the forests, roaming, primeval, unknown and wild.

In his head, he heard the voice of the hunter finally speaking to him. *I am not your enemy. I realize this is difficult to grasp, but you have to trust someone.*

An oppressive feeling was overwhelming him. Michael was struggling to focus his mind. *You will have to find sanctuary before dawn. Allow me to take you in.*

Michael could feel the pressure of the hunter's will. Why not? He could just give in, be taken in by this thing. He cleared his mind. *The hunter has many tricks.* His own disembodied voice came in as a counterpoint. The hunter was right about the sunlight. Without thinking, Michael began a wide turn for the sea.

I will kill you, Michael thought, hoping to communicate to the voice.

Oh, I'm certain you'll try, the hunter chuckled, *but I wouldn't be so sure, considering I've been doing this much longer than you have.*

He began running faster, but the voice stayed close to him. The presence was somewhere in the trees. Indignation began filling him. He'd been running from whatever that thing was, however powerful and it toyed with him like a cat.

Yes. The other Michael said. *Yes, lure him, kill him. How dare this worthless thing challenge you?* Was he thinking it? No. These were not his own thoughts. His blood boiled.

Ah, yes. Anger. Embrace this. The voice called out to him. *There is nothing clearer than rage.*

Michael felt his feet leave the ground, as he flew through the tight brush for miles, healing as quickly as the bramble would cut his flesh, until he pushed through the familiar clearing, having avoided Breton to the south as he moved toward his hideout. In his anger, he found something out. As his feet touched the sandy soil outside of the forest, he realized he could fly.

S*o much for subtlety*, thought Alonzo Gallegos as he left the courier's shanty. Spencer Mayhew, that is "Mister Smith" and Moreau's niece had begun filling in the pieces of the puzzle including the increased attacks around town including the death of Jean-Pierre Moreau. The most troublesome thing was a discovery she shared with Algernon Elliott.

The way Genevieve Moreau spoke about Algernon Elliott, Gallegos got the clear impression that there might be an element of attraction to their recent alliance. The girl had her uncle's singular mind, but it was clouded with the attraction of young love. She was oblivious to it, but each mention of Mister Elliott brought color to her cheeks.

She and the young Englishman had mapped out the entire little town and in turn located what they called "wind chimes" and "medallions." What she didn't know was the purpose of so much copper and quartz. Quartz, he knew, was the universal crystal. In spiritist circles, quartz was ubiquitous. But he knew a more esoteric purpose for the crystal. Alongside the copper plates, obvious conductors of electric energy, the crystals and plates served as conductors of psionic energy.

Vampyres possessed the highest concentrations of psionic talent. Someone was trying to amplify their abilities. He'd seen this sort of thing before. That might explain how they'd kept this place hidden for so long. That multiplied energy would create a haunting effect that would effectively deter most wandering fur trappers or local natives. He could just imagine the mythologies already being built around the forest of revenants, full of angry spirits. The truth was far more terrifying.

Someone was using very ancient means to create a vortex of resonating psionic energy. The prospect terrified him. Before he could think to make a note to research it once he returned to Spain, he felt the hairs along his arms and neck prick up.

The door shut behind him. He saw the shadows dance in the middle distance. Between thirty and forty yards off he could hear the rustle of the wind. The moonlight was with him that night, making long shadows and highlighting the roads and the spaces between the ever-growing shadows. The street lamps flickered their soft amber glow, but for the most part, Breton was full of white moonlight.

Vampyres. *Que tontería.*

He cleared his mind, finding a center place from which to watch his thoughts. They would not find anything in his mind that might attract their attention. He focused on the details in the road, counting each stone. He put his fear for his new friends in the shanty out of his mind. They seemed capable enough. Under Moreau's tutelage, he could only imagine how much so the younger Miss Moreau must be. He noticed that the rocks in the road were cut too large and had been laid unevenly. *This work was rushed.* He focused on the thought and counted each step as he went along, making sure to move more slowly than usual. *Typical Americans.* He thought.

He could feel eyes on him, all around him, a wave of the inevitable.

He stopped to pick up a small stone and examined it and then continued forward. He swung his cane, losing himself in thought. The street lamps along the way flickered. He hummed a song from his childhood before stopping for a moment to admire the stars. *What a small world we live in*, he mused, *with such an expansive universe.*

They were getting closer.

He grunted. As long as he gave them nothing to read, it would make an escape possible. Gallegos passed the Mayor's house, where he saw shattered glass along the road. He set his hand on the small retaining wall where the front gate was and peered into the small yard in front of the extravagant house. It was quiet beyond a rustle of leaves.

He waited and then began away from the house focusing his mind on the idea of vandals. *Perhaps I should alert the local police about this,* he thought for a moment. He slowly made his way down the street toward the inn. He looked across the square to the police station. It was quiet. He stared at it for a moment before silently turning into an alley near the inn.

Vampyres were quietly speaking in thought to each other. At the Mayor's home a few had stayed, climbing the walls and entering the broken window quietly like wisps of smoke. At the square some had run to the police station. With each of the old man's thoughts, the Vampyres were moving. When the final two turned the alley to corner him the old man had vanished.

He's gone. A tall, beautiful Vampyre sighed to his cohorts, appearing in the alley. His eyes shined red like rubies against black velvet, bright with an almost imperceptible light in the darkness. In hidden thoughts that he did not express to the others, he was relieved. *Finally, a real chase. This should be fun.*

Gone? How is that possible? asked a smaller, younger one, baffled from the middle of the square.

He's toying with us. He answered with a smirk. His eyes glowed with delight, but his mouth curled with disappointment.

It seems that the police station is full of new men tonight, came a beautiful female voice belonging to Zoya, a younger Vampyre converted while still a young mother. Beautified eternally, her voice reflected a once-innocent tone, but she was as wicked as any. *Is this part of your precious plan, Ilya?*

Ilya turned a smile that never touched his eyes on her.

An older Vampyre, Letsya, who was watching from the roof of the police station, answered, *Of course it is.*

In the recesses of the quiet of his mind, Ilya thought for a moment, *Oh, so much planning, can't we just have a chase? Doesn't this all just bore them?* He thought about the one they called the "righteous" one and had a twinge of regret, but he hid his emotions and clamped down. He called to the other ones. *Pavl, Rurk, go have some fun. We'll search tomorrow.*

We have something better, said Pavl, from the Mayor's house.

There is no such thing, the tall one answered; he disappeared into a shadow. Two women, unaware of his presence, walked down the street.

The innkeeper's daughter, Ilya. She saw the righteous one, Rurk, Pavl's brother responded.

That does us no good, Ilya, the tall one told them.

What? Zoya asked. *Why? What does she have to do with any of this? Leave her out of it.*

She has very strong feelings for him, Rurk interrupted. *Very pure feelings*.

Well, said Ilya as he made his way up the alley wall, *that's a different matter altogether. Isn't it Zoya?*

Ilya, Zoya tried, *There is no reason to take her.*

Zoya, my dear, the inn is no longer any matter of yours. He replied with a snide tone. *Nor are the little girls in it.*

But she isn't ready. The night of all her nightmares had finally come for Zoya.

Ready? Ilya laughed. *Ready for what? For this? For the life you chose for yourself.*

Zoya had not chosen it. And Ilya knew it. *If your precious Black Council, in their precious mountain, had wanted you, they would have chosen you.* Ilya appeared next to Zoya.

She didn't flinch.

If they were so interested, why would you have been cast down here with the rest of us? You were never meant to be a Sin Eater. Ilya hissed.

And you, Ilya? Zoya asked, *would you be so brave as to say that if you weren't pressed under daddy's thumb?*

Ilya grabbed her blouse. *Maybe I'll have your testimony now, Zoya.* The other Vampyres materialized around her as Ilya lifted her off her feet. *I'll enjoy the taste of the Elder Blood, I'm sure.*

Zoya said nothing.

Isaac won't like this, Letsya stammered.

To hell with him. Ilya growled.

Yes, Ilya, let's see how big you really are, Zoya said. Her feet hit the ground as Ilya let go.

Question me again and I will eat your heart at my father's table. Ilya hissed.

Zoya turned to walk away. She was done with this nonsense. *You hate her because she is like me.*

Ilya laughed.

After a moment, they all laughed as though she had said the funniest thing in the world. It was the empty laugh of toadies.

She stopped. *You hate her because she is more Vampyre even now, than you will ever be.*

The laughing stopped.

Letsya cried out, *No!*

The crack of Ilya's foot against her back was heard before anyone anyone saw him move. Zoya flew across the street, crashing bonelessly into a retaining wall. Dust fell around her as she stood up slowly. The cracking of bones righting themselves echoed down the street.

Ilya walked forward and Pavl appeared next to him with a hand on his chest, *We don't have to do this, Ilya.*

Ilya's eyes burned red. *Unhand me.* He said in a cool tone.

Remember the plan, Pavl said.

Rurk echoed his brother, *This isn't helping.*

Ilya turned his glare on Pavl. *If you don't step aside, I will sever that limb in a way that will never heal.*

Pavl stepped back. He had seen what Ilya had done with that boy's body. He heard the way Ilya had spoken the elder speech of the Black Council. He watched him birth a Vampyre. He had learned the ancient ways. He nor his brother wanted to see more of that.

Letsya, the old fool, always trying to please began pleading, *Let's just go back, and we can discuss...*

No more discussions. Ilya met Zoya as she brushed off her dress. *The elder blood did not save you, nor will it your daughter.* He put a finger to her chest. *You are outcasts just like the rest of us, and in the land of the blind, the one-eyed man is king. In this wasteland, you are nothing. She is nothing.*

Zoya dropped her head. There was nothing she could do. Isaac wouldn't listen to her when it came to Ilya. Rurk, and Pavl were cruel just for the sake of it, and Letsya was a useless sycophant who would do little to slow Ilya's recent rampages. She could only hope that she had done enough to ensure her child's safety. She prayed that Kat would be ready.

Ilya grinned. *I think I'm going to have a word with your daughter.*

Alonzo Gallegos had found a quick way out of his close encounter, but he knew it would not be so easy the next time. He held his breath waiting for the Vampyres to pass outside the window, which was covered by a small crate in the alley.

Nothing came.

He hunched down against the wall on the dirt floor of what he suspected to be the cellar of the Crow's Nest Inn. *Estás demasiado viejo para estarte gateando como un bebe en el piso.* He'd been too old for it for much too long. He sighed.

Behind the barrels of cider and ale, he heard a rustle and a crack. Whatever was behind the barrels was large from the sound of it. Gallegos forced himself up on his cane, pulling a small blade from its handle. He moved unheard, listening to the rattle of a lantern being lit. Gallegos slipped up to the man. The flint struck and a warm glow filled the damp room. He put the dagger to the man's throat. He was solid and young. If there were a fight to be had, *I'll have to work for this*, he thought to himself.

"Evenin', friend," the boy said.

"Good evening."

"Didn't mean to disturb anyone down here." The boy said.

"I am undisturbed, my friend." Gallegos said. "Yet again, I am not the one with a knife to my throat."

"A small knife does as good as a big one." The boy said. "But I'm not exactly shaken by this Arkansas toothpick of yours."

Gallegos instantly liked the boy's bravado. As the light showed him in full, Gallegos could see he was a soldier covered in mud and blood.

He turned around gingerly; the old man let him go and lifted the lantern. "Jared Carswell," he paused. "Captain of the Seventh, United States Army."

"Alonzo Gallegos," the older man said.

The boy's eyes lit up. "I hope I'm not being too imprudent, sir, but why were you hiding in the dark cellar of the inn? You are indeed the man I was looking for."

"You were looking for a man named Gallegos in the inn, yet chose to do it in the cellar? Imprudence might not be the problem." He smiled. "Your town is plagued with Vampyres that seem to have a keen interest in finding me. I am not known here— though my name is on everyone's tongues. There has been a man going by my name, claiming to be a Vampyre killer."

The young man grunted. "These Vampyres...you eluded them?"

"Barely."

"Well then, welcome to Breton, Virgina, Mister Gallegos." Jared grinned, immediately liking the stranger. "Any man that can survive those things is the man I'm seeking."

Gallegos was bemused and unconvinced. "What brings you here, Captain?"

"Shame." Jared's smile washed away from his face. "Perhaps fear for my life. I came looking for this Vampyre hunter." The boy stared at the floor. "Looking for some help."

"In a cellar?"

"I was almost spotted on the street. A lot of commotion out there. Didn't know who to trust."

Gallegos nodded.

Jared sat down on a barrel across from the old man and stretched his left arm. The pain was beginning to trouble him. The men both soaked in the silence of the room, which was only disturbed by the muffled sound coming from upstairs, the shuffling of chairs and susurrous conversation. Gallegos pulled a pouch of tobacco from within his cloak and began the process of rolling a cigarette, which helped me think.

Listening to the footfall upstairs, Jared asked, "Sir, do you know much about these Vampyres?"

Gallegos nodded.

"I encountered one recently." Jared said.

"I see." Gallegos examined his cigarette.

"I cannot fathom why this thing would have let me live," he continued.

"You did not dispense of it?" Gallegos asked.

"Dispense, sir?"

Gallegos looked up at him, "Kill. You are alive, yet you do not kill it?"

"Quite." Jared replied, eyes wide.

Gallegos grunted and lit his cigarette. "And it left you to live." After taking a puff and looking into the smoke, seemingly searching for an answer, he asked, "Did this Vampyre tell you anything? Perhaps a *mensaje*—a message he wanted carried?"

"No. Simply, he stated his neutrality. Said he wasn't anyone's enemy," Jared recounted. "It seemed he had no real intention of killing me, but he did take two of my patrolmen, so I struck first."

"*Que extraño.*" Gallegos observed.

As the young man explained his plight, his reason for leaving the camp, his encounter with the Vampyre and the subsequent visions he was having, Gallegos thought he might have found an ally. He would need as many as he could get.

"The name in the dreams, what was it?"

"Kat," Jared responded. "Just Kat. When I came to town, they pointed me here to a Kat. She's out. I asked for the Vampyre hunter and then some of my men came in, so I hid down here." He sighed, "Not exactly supposed to be gone, but neither were they. Strangely they weren't in uniform." He thought on it again. "How could I reprimand them when I too am here? I noticed them talking to the bartender as though they were very familiar with him. Tonight's apparently nothing new."

"My friend, it would seem that the Vampyre has given you quite a message." Gallegos thought aloud. "This Kat must be quite *importante*." He thought long before standing up. "Would you be interested in a new task, sir?"

"Yes sir, I think I would," Jared answered, standing before his new friend.

"Take my key and hide in my room a while. I will search and by dawn we shall have some new answers," Gallegos instructed.

"No way I could be of service for now?" Jared asked, confused.

"You've done more than you know," Gallegos answered from the window on the other side of the cellar. He opened the window and then paused. "Jared, *amigo*." He looked at him, turning. "Perhaps it should be of some use to know that *el Vampiro* cannot chase you into your home." He smiled. "Welcome home, sir."

His eyes moved from wall to wall and Jared understood.

Gallegos slid some small boxes and crates away from the window and nimbly crawled out before disappearing once again into the darkness.

The moon was bright as the boys turned the corner at the mayor's mansion. Police officers they had never seen ran about in new uniforms, lanterns in hand. A crime scene was still fresh, a shattered glass window spread into the mayor's yard. Men called to each other from within it.

Before the boys could hide again, the sheriff turned to them. "Boys," his voice bellowed, "you should be in St. Jerome's."

"Yes sir," Edwin answered quickly, "but Headmaster Smith sent us on an errand."

"Did he? Bit late for errands," the sheriff grumbled, turning to see his men crunching along the broken glass. The sheriff turned back to the boys. "Perhaps you'd like to see him back at the jail?"

They were gone.

He cursed. "Get a few men after those boys," he commanded to a few officers running into the large house. "They know something."

There was plenty of work to be done that evening. Sheriff Matheson looked over the crime scene. *Williams. Check. Smith. Check.* It seemed their plan was going to play out smoother than he'd previously thought. If only Adler would play his part. The old parson had spent half of his life in Breton, but he acted like the whole thing was gonna come apart in a few days. As far as

Matheson was concerned, the old man had given up, having grown tired of the maintenance of Breton. The Sheriff was already beginning to worry about what might happen if that old man snapped.

Adler was quite stoic for the amount of anger, angst and frustration that ran through him at any one time, but Matheson could see through his facade. They were both equally frustrated that all of that work would be ruined again by the very Vampyres asking to be fed.

Matheson's men struggled with the dead weight of the found man's body, a bag over his head. They found him unconscious at the home of the courier's niece, laid out on the kitchen floor. The young woman was dead on the floor next to the bed, lying in her own blood.

When Mister Smith came to, he couldn't remember what had happened after the old man left, but he was groggy. He didn't move or let the men carrying him know that he was awake. He simply tried to remember what happened. He worried for that old man and poor Jenny. He remembered hearing something on the roof and reaching for his Smith and Wesson pistol and then being grabbed from behind. He'd been had.

Could Jen have done it?

He could feel the toes of his boots dragging against the ground, which had turned from rocky dirt road to cobblestone. They were moving toward the town. He listened to the way the men moved rigidly and in form; they were soldiers. The keys and belts rattling with guns meant they were police officers.

He wondered if Algernon had been found out. Perhaps everything the old man said was a lie.

He listened to them speak while he ran scenarios in his mind.

"Sir," the officer to his right called, "we have the culprit."

Culprit, Spencer thought to himself. *Well, either I'm framed, or it's too late. Either way that's bad news. Too far from any real justice.*

Luckily for Mister Smith, it wasn't the first time he'd found himself in a situation like that. He'd have to get word to his partner soon. Algernon certainly wouldn't like the news.

The boys hid quickly from the Sheriff near the wall of the Mayor's house before making a quick run toward St. Jerome's like Mister Smith taught them in the big games of hide-and-seek. "Don't make your time running," he would say to them. "Remember to be hiding from the time you start. If you have your covert ahead of you, then you can make your move." Which they had; as Thomas and Edwin had spoken to the sheriff, they both scanned the streets for hiding spots until they had time to make a run.

"Stop, Ned," Thomas whispered as they ran.

He didn't.

"We can't go back to the house!" Thomas continued.

Edwin made a turn into an alley and spun around quickly before he poked his head back into the street looking for anyone following them. "Why not?" he asked.

"Don't you realize they'll go looking for us there?" Thomas replied, worried.

"So what, we didn't do aught this time." Edwin pleaded.

"No, but something's wrong." Thomas bit his lip. "You heard the sheriff."

"No, Tom, you did." He turned, making his way deeper into the alley, shaking the hair out of his face.

"Yes I did." Thomas answered, pensively.

"Well, what did he say? Why does it mean we can't go home?" Edwin asked, taking a few steps forward. He listened but didn't hear the shuffle of Thomas's feet and he stopped.

Thomas was truly scared. Edwin turned to him.

"Parson Adler," he stammered. "Adler and the Sheriff. They're working with the Vampyres."

Edwin couldn't believe it. "Now you're just making things up."

"No!" Thomas cried. "They're looking for Mister Smith and the old bummer Williams."

Edwin cursed himself. "And I just told the Sheriff that Mister Smith had us on errand." He sat down and put his head in his hands.

Thomas anxiously chewed on a hangnail. "We're in real trouble."

Algernon Elliott sighed, listening to the portentous clattering of hurried footfalls on cobblestone in the distance. Voices called out.

It has begun.

He made a move toward the trunk at the foot of the bed when he heard a knock at the door. Startled, Algernon reached for the gun that he had strapped out of sight to the bottom of the table, until he heard a familiar voice. He hadn't heard anyone come up the stairs.

"No need for weapons. It's just me," spoke Monsieur Chandler from beyond the door. "We should finally have that talk."

"Please come in," he asked quietly, removing his hand from the gun. It was far too late for visiting and Algernon knew it. He glanced over his shoulder at the trunk next to the bed as the door opened with a squeak. Algernon put his shoes on for company and tried to relax.

The small man entered quietly. He was no longer wearing his neat little uniform and in plain clothes, a well-tailored suit and bowler hat, he looked more like a streettough than an administrator.

"Don't stand." The man said. He stalked over to the chair in the middle of the room and sat removing his hat, placing it on the table.

Algernon raised an eyebrow.

"I've already spoken with the charlatan Vampyre hunter and now I must speak with you, Monsieur Elliott."

"I get the feeling that this is the kind of talk that requires a drink." Algernon said, grabbing two glasses from the night stand and placing them on the table.

"I'd prefer not to imbibe that *déchets.*" Chandler said, pulling a flask from his jacket pocket. "This talk will require a proper drink."

Chandler poured two shots of a of a spirit that smelled of strong licorice.

"Annisette?" Algernon asked.

"Absinthe." Chandler corrected.

Surely they're the same thing. Algernon thought. "No sugar?" He asked with a smile.

The old man rolled his eyes, making his black pupils seem to disappear into his thick eyebrows. "Ah, you English are so garish."

Algernon chuckled. "Well, I certainly welcome a civilized drink in good company."

"One last drink, eh?" Chandler said.

And you French are always so morbid. Algernon thought.

"The powder keg," Chandler said holding his glass in thought, "someone has put fire to her fuse." He sighed. "This is likely the last time we shall speak." Chandler said. "Kaboom."

"And this Vampyre hunter, he's involved in that?" Algernon asked. He took the second glass in hand and held it up.

"He is a harbinger. The name of Gallegos is an ill omen. The Vampyres are restless. The bosses will be coming soon. But as for the circus man who calls himself Gallegos, I had a *talk* with him."

I hate to think of what kind of talk that was. For the first time, Algernon saw what Monsieur Chandler was. The glint in the man's eye confirmed it. There was something sadistic of this little Arabic francophone.

"Is he alive?" Algernon asked.

Chandler raised an eyebrow.

Algernon waited in silence.

The little old man sighed. "He is now on his way to have a word with Parson Adler. If you plan to get out of here on the last train, monsieur, many people are going to have to die." Chandler grunted and lifted a glass, swirling the liquid which caught a light green hue from the candlelight.

Algernon raised his glass to the man. "We could have been the drinking part since I got here."

Chandler smiled ruefully. "*À votre santé.*" He threw back the absinthe almost violently and set the glass down with a clink.

"And to yours." Algernon said, taking the shot. He almost sprayed the liquid into his shirtsleeve. He swallowed it before letting out a hacking cough.

"It doesn't take much." Chandler said. As Algernon wiped his mouth with a handkerchief and attempted to recover, Chandler began. "I have given you refuge where I should not have, Mister Elliott."

"So you're going to poison me with absinthe." Algernon's voice came out hoarse, but he smiled.

"I have given you refuge as a favor to a friend, a compatriot."

"Moreau."

"Yes." Chandler poured two more shots of absinthe. Algernon looked through watery eyes at them, unsure if he could do a second. "The niece was very dear to him. He protected her from all of this. I want to know that, regardless of what happens in this place, you will do what you can to protect her." He lifted his glass again.

"Straight to the point then." Algernon said. "I didn't expect this." He raised his glass to the man.

Chandler did not cheers. He did not drink. He looked Algernon in the eye and continued, "You will repay the favor to my friend Moreau."

Algernon could feel his heart beating in his ears. Yes, he cared for Genevieve. Yes, he was grateful for Chandler's intervention, but was he swearing some sort of oath?

"You will repay the favor." He repeated.

Algernon swallowed. "Yes. I will do my best to protect her."

"*À votre santé.*" Chandler said, throwing back the second shot as easily as the first.

Algernon eyed the liquid, "Cheers then." And sipped the violently burning liquid attempting not to go up in a coughing fit again. He marked a success when he let out a long fiery breath.

The old man was pouring two more.

"Come now." Algernon said raising his hands in surrender, but the dark little man just eyed him.

"Matheson would have found you on the platform on the first night, hiding as you were. He's quite good at that."

"And I'm grateful for what you've done."

"And yet, you came. You and *'Smith'*," Chandler put a disgusted emphasis on the pseudonym. "You came here, to a place that exists on no map."

"Moreau..." Algernon began.

"A fool." Chandler's reply cut off whatever Algernon was going to say. "A dead one at that." The man's jaw sawed back and forth as though he was chewing on his thoughts. "I should have stayed out of all of this."

"But you didn't." Algernon said quietly.

Chandler's look cut have cut through stone. "But I didn't." He visibly tried to gather some internal anger. "Moreau was here simply to observe. He was hidden in plain sight. A lifelong monster hunter - *le grand chasseur*, living among his prey. For what purpose, I do not know. He doesn't tell me, I never ask."

Algernon dreaded the third shot, but he knew it was coming. "So Moreau was *Chasseur de Demon*?"

"He was."

"How long did he live here?"

"Almost nineteen years. Brought the girl with him when she was small."

"Parents?" Algernon asked.

"Not my story to tell." Chandler said.

"So what is?"

"My story is not for you to hear." Chandler said with a smile. "Instead, let us now get down to business as the Americans say."

"Right."

Chandler raised his glass.

"Oh. Right." Algernon reluctantly lifted his.

"*À votre santé.*" Chandler threw back this absinthe and grinned, setting the glass upside down. The man's smile was sharp and dangerous.

Algernon eyed the glass and down the liquid, stifling another cough. He felt lightheaded. "Like being back at university." He gasped.

"*Tré bien.*" Chandler said quietly, "Because it is time to learn. This place was a gamble from the beginning."

Algernon just listened.

The candlelight took on a hazy glow, as the alcohol warmed his body and Chandler's voice took on a musical lilting tone. "The Brotherhood, the covenant of this place, they are anathema to the other surviving covenants; traitors to the Blood. The Blood, they are Anathema by all the other descendants of Cain. The Brotherhood are survivors, some from the Croatoan experiment in Roanoke, some further back, as far back as the Mayans. They have worked for centuries for this thing." The old man laughed and leaned back. "Then it falls apart just a few decades in."

"Falls apart?" Algernon said. He didn't slur, not exactly, but he felt more relaxed than he had in a long time.

"Vampyres have always been secretive and this," he gestured broadly with his arms, "brought too much attention. The Brotherhood cannot survive the failure of Breton. Not after failures among the Mayans. Not after being defeated by Francis Drake."

Algernon's eyebrows rose with surprise, but Chandler motioned him to stay silent.

"Every person who lives in this town is an Alliance agent, whether they know it or not. Every one brainwashed, with new memories — most because of a debt; promised release, but if you can't remember your life as it was, how can you ask to be set free?"

"And their children? Their families?" Algernon asked through the haze of absinthe.

"Fodder." The man scratched his stubbly face. "It is an uncaring world." Chandler pulled a small torn piece of paper from his pocket and placed it on the table. "There is a mining encampment not far from here. You will need all of your wits to get inside."

Algernon reached for the paper, but Chandler placed his hand over it.

"You and I never met."

Algernon nodded ascent and took the paper from the table once the man had lifted his hand.

Chandler continued, "The Brotherhood was already here. The Alliance did the rest. Deals were made. Breton was the last agreement of the Five Great Houses of Cain, which you know as the Nephilim, or Men of Renowned, as I imagine you've read your bible."

Algernon had. He knew of the five families that Chandler called Houses; ancient bloodlines going back to the beginning of mankind. They were a lurking cancer.

"That agreement must be abolished."

"This is politics for you?" Algernon slurred again.

"No." Chandler stood.

Algernon's head had grown heavy and his eyelids the heaviest part. "So what are we to do?"

"We?" Chandler asked as he strode to the door. "Do not confuse me with your crusade." His voice faded into the black of sleep as Algernon thought, *He dosed me.*

"I am not one of your good guys." The voice dissipated into the black of sleep. "Call me an independent operator. Don't miss the last train, *monsieur*!"

Algernon awoke and pulled his head into his hands. He hadn't been poisoned! He was just drunk. He looked at the giant clock behind him. Only a few minutes had passed. He would have to find Spencer and let him know that he would be continuing the mission alone, preferably once he sobered up. He scrambled to an abandoned cold cup of coffee and swigged it down. He would finally uncover the mystery of Breton and hopefully be out in time to catch what Chandler called "the last train."

He opened his steamer trunk. *Finally!*

I t was the silence, not the darkness in that secreted room that troubled Kat. She heard nothing and she worried for Michael, who had made an obvious attempt to protect her from whatever was happening outside. She put her head against the wall and stretched her legs.

She chided herself. She could not fathom how she could possibly be worrying about that Michael was a Vampyre, but there it was: a genuine worry for that poor creature. Was there any way that Mister Williams could have been right? Perhaps Michael had nothing to do with the ones who had menaced the town for so long.

She inched through the room with her hands, completely blind, back to the desk in the center of the room. She reached for the lamp sitting on the desk. Its glass body was smooth. She knew that if that room were like any other in the house (which she had cleaned for most of her life) it would be impossible to find any matches.

She moved around the desk, finding the rotating chair with her hand and sat down using her hands as eyes. She pulled the desk drawer and sighed to herself. It was locked. She continued feeling around and found that the key to the desk was actually still in its lock.

The key turned with a small click and she opened the drawer. She felt around for a moment before finding a long slender box that she recognized. *Matches.* She sighed at how fortuitous her discovery had been and shook the box just to be sure. It was full.

She lit the lamp and the room filled with a warm light. It was fully-furnished and organized. This must have been where the mayor did his real work. By contrast, the downstairs office was always in disarray and looked incomplete. She wondered if Mister Williams knew anything about this secret space.

She started looking at the files on the desk and absorbing as much as she could.

Mayor Heath had been working for the Vampyres through something called the Alliance. A man named "A." was in charge of very much, including the mayor. She could only assume that "A." was Parson Adler. She never trusted him anyway. He was in charge of "the alignment of minds." In another folder, she read about a system of pendants, charms and medallions that were being used to enhance this alignment. They kept the wearer's mind in a haze. That department was under the care of "D.B.": obviously Desmond Burroughs. He was supposed to keep a large inventory of the pendants and medallions. She'd never worn hers because, when she was young, her mother told her it was too pretty for the kind of work they did in the inn.

She guessed that, over time, the "alignment" had stopped working on her. She continued reading. "Avoid contact with Vampyres. Realignment will be required."

Kat recalled one night, when she was much younger. She had talked little on it, but, the encounter would change her life.

A ragged and emaciated child sat hunched over a piece of raw meat, away from the light of the doorway at the inn, where Kat was tossing a bucket of mop water across the cobblestones. She called out to the half-naked pitiable thing, thinking he, or she may have been a stray orphan. The child would not answer but instead turned quickly on her. It was no orphan at all. Kat fell back into the alleyway with the creature screeching at her. The small creature was full of rage and its eyes glowed bright yellow.

It jumped at her, but swatted away by a dark-robed Vampyre, who never showed her its face.

According to what she had read, contact with a Vampyre of any sort would undo the charm on the pendants that each person was required to wear, but other charms and wards were placed throughout the town. It was an inescapable loop of

The next revelation was even more ominous: a folder stamped with the federal seal of the United States, dated eighteen sixty-five. All the other files, the newer ones, were dated upward until eighteen ninety-seven. The only education that Kat had ever had was the reading that she and Genevieve had received from Mister Williams when they were younger, back when he spent more time at the library. It had never troubled her until then that no one ever mentioned the date beyond what day of the week it was. It would seem no one actually knew. The haze was so bad that everyone had stopped caring.

"The best ale is from eighteen fifty-nine," They would say. Kat's stomach dropped. *What would happen to all those people?* she wondered. She would have to find Mister Williams or anyone who might know what was actually going on.

Something has to be done.

The world was made new in her eyes. She read through the files on Mayor Heath's desk for only a few minutes and realized her entire life had been a parody, a hoax. It was bittersweet. She felt both betrayed and liberated. She realized that Michael and Mister Williams were on to the truth. She grabbed a pen and started scribbling what she could on a sheet of paper in front of her. She would have to get the knowledge out to people to free them from their complacent imprisonment.

Suddenly she heard the crackle of glass in the hallway. No one knew about the room where she hidden, but that wasn't enough. She blew out the lamp and crawled under the desk as quietly as she could.

Michael? Kat thought to herself. The door opened with a sigh.

A dark chuckle followed. *No, darling. Michael won't be coming tonight.*

They carried his body to the police station and although Mister Smith was tiring of the position they had him in, he acted as if he were still unconscious. He had put it together in his head finally. It must have been the old man Gallegos, who may have been seen arriving at or leaving the shanty. That would have tipped someone off. He was surprised at hearing footsteps on the roof and could only guess that they belonged to Vampyres. He didn't get his gun turned on the thing in time and the last thing he heard was Jenny getting carried away, screaming.

The people in town really were working with the Vampyres. Miss Allen was right after all. They walked, heavy-footed, into the police station and dropped his body in a cell. He made sure not to move while he listened. He heard a man tell them, "Wait on Burroughs, or Adler. We'll be done with this yet."

After the commotion behind him settled and he heard the bolt click in the lock, he rustled himself up a bit.

In the next cell sat a man who could not have been more thankful to see him dropped there. He heard a quiet voice. "Mister Smith? Are you alright?"

He made his way up onto his elbows and put his back against the wall. His legs had gone quite numb and were all pins and needles. "I suppose that depends on how one looks at alright." He responded, a bit coy.

"I'm glad to see you, Mister Smith."

"Well, most unfortunate for the circumstances, Mister Williams."

"Call me Ernest. What do they have you here for, Mister Smith?" he asked quietly.

"Murder." He responded. "You?"

"Not sure yet, but I'm certain it will be just as ghastly."

Ernest waited for a moment before answering. "Would I be wrong to guess that you were a military man in your time?"

"Quite a good guess, Ernest. Fought the Boers in Transvaal." He raised an eyebrow. "Why do you ask?"

Ernest answered quietly, "Because I'm afraid the walls have ears, my good man."

Even as he spoke, Ernest moved his bench to the wall that he shared with Mister Smith and began tapping out his thoughts in Morse code. It went slowly. He waited a moment before he heard a similar noise from the other bench being moved.

Ernest had found an ally. And just in time.

When the boys arrived at Jenny's shanty, the door was cracked and a lantern was lit. That was not a good sign. Edwin snuck up to the wall of the house while Thomas waited, watching out for the sheriff's men. He could see one walking around in the street nearby, but told Edwin he would give a birdcall if he began approaching. They had gone altogether unnoticed.

Edwin brushed the hair out of his face and peered into the window to see a shadowed man sitting at a chair looking down with his legs crossed. It was Mister Elliott, who always came looking for Jenny. When Edwin looked further, he saw a body lying on the ground just beyond him.

Immediately Edwin panicked. He ducked down on the grass and covered his mouth, trying not to breathe. His eyes filled with water at the thought of Jenny being killed by that man. He feared it had something to do with their conversation earlier.

He could hear Mister Smith's voice in his head. It echoed: "The smallest details are the most important." He thought back on what he had just seen and realized that the girl in the dress that lay on the floor was not Jenny at all. Jenny always had short hair, but that girl was not as thin like her and she had long hair. *But why?*

He heard a birdcall and a rustle, which was the sign that the Sheriff's man was coming. He made a quick look into the house. No one was there, so he darted in the door. He had to find somewhere to hide. He looked and could not see anyone. *Where could he be?* he asked himself.

Edwin made a quick move and dove under the bed. He listened to the officer walking toward the door; it creaked slowly. The man made a round through the shanty and walked to the counter to pour himself something to drink. *How rude!* Edwin thought. The officer obviously hadn't seen Mister Elliott either.

Then there was a moment of quiet.

Suddenly he heard a *crack!* From where Edwin lay under the bed he could see another set of feet come out of the dark and the policeman falling with a thud face-first, eyes open, staring right at him. He jumped back and away further into the dark under the bed.

"You can come out now, my little friend," came a warm, British voice. It was Mister Elliott.

Edwin made his way out from under the bed slowly and shook off the dust. He looked up to see Mister Elliott dressed in a very peculiar way. He wore goggles like the blacksmith, a long coat and patent leather boots buckled up to his knees. He wore a gun under his arm on a holster and had a bandana tucked into his white shirt like an ascot. He looked like an adventurer, not the quiet bookworm writer that Jenny had described to them.

"Perhaps you should signal your friend to come in for a moment. We shan't have much time at all." Algernon stated softly, trying to drag the body of the police officer out of the way.

Edwin went to the door and gave a birdcall.

Thomas heard it, but was terribly confused. He had seen the policeman go inside, but no one came back out. He could only fear that Edwin was acting like everything was going as planned when it wasn't. He sighed to himself, realizing that Edwin was his only real friend. If he were in trouble, they should at least take care of it together. He rose out of the woods reluctantly to go to his friend.

By the time Thomas had made it to the door, Edwin was sitting at the table and Algernon was getting some cookies. Algernon turned and gave a soft smile.

"Wow, Mister Elliott!" Thomas exclaimed. "I'm so glad it's you!"

"Sit down, Thomas," Algernon said in his soft way. "Let's have a snack before we get to work. I'm terribly glad you both arrived here. I have something I need you to pass on to Mister Smith from me."

Thomas looked around the room. The dead body of one of the girls from the Crow's Nest lay strewn across the floor. The policeman lay face down, possibly also dead. Thomas sat down to listen to Mister Elliott and began to eat from the cookies on the table.

Michael jumped across from the cliff's edge down onto the ship among the rocks. "Come and get me, you bastard."

He saw the silhouette grow against the full moon atop the cliff above the wreck of the ship, coat flapping in the sea breeze. The figure looked down at him, analyzing. Michael gritted his teeth and straightened his shoulder blades out. He wanted nothing more than to jump, or fly up to it and dispose of it, but he waited. *I'm no prey.* Michael told the voice in his head. It felt satisfied.

I want to help you. It replied.

Lies. The other Michael hissed.

"You lie." Michael said.

The figure up on the cliffs said nothing, thought nothing.

"Are you predator or prey?" Michael asked. His voice echoed off the cliffs.

The figure backed away, if only inches from the edge, but said nothing.

Michael walked slowly across the deck, removed his coat and hung it from a splintered rod hanging from the mast. *I'm ready*, he told the figure above him.

The figure launched itself from the cliff. A cloud of splintering wood exploded. It had caught Michael in his moment of overconfidence and now crashed into him with both fists. Michael's body dug into the planks. He could feel a knee in his spine. Something was breaking. His fists came down like a blacksmith's hammer, blows reigned down on his skull, each a lightning bolt of pain, blurring his vision.

You are quite strong, it said, *much stronger than you appear*.

Michael's thoughts were gone: gone too were his humanity, logic and reasoning. He smelled blood in the air. He felt the darkness. Rage filled him, He shifted his shoulders, shaking the body from him like a cloak. It rolled across the deck and he turned around to see a man standing up before him. His eyes were translucent amber, but they shined like some distant lantern. Broken bones cracked loudly along his ribs and spine and he stretched his neck.

You are one of our kindred now, Michael, child of Pinemé, the man in front him gestured. *You are of the blood.*

Michael remembered the massacre he'd witnessed earlier. "I am nothing like you." He threw himself at the figure. His feet dug into the wood and it exploded from underneath him. The dark figure disappeared again. Michael crashed into the ship's railing with his forearm. The pain was gone. The wood splintered and rained down around him.

Anger can only push you so far, my brother. The creature stood behind Michael with a snide smile curling on his face. *There is a darkness beyond anger that you have not yet known.*

"I am darkness." Michael whispered.

The smile slipped into confusion.

Again, Michael sprang from one end of the deck with his full force, watching the man. He could sense what he was and where he would move. Michael knew that wherever the nameless Vampyre was going to be, he would be there first. His rage fueled every movement. His body fed on his anger and heat emanated from his skin.

The man dodged again, his footfalls landing softly along the deck, but not quickly enough. Michael caught its rib with a shoulder, lifting it high into the air. The Vampyre clawed into his back, shredding through fabric and flesh. Michael only let out a grunt.

Midair, they were now face to face. Though he fought with all of his strength, the surprised Vampyre watched, as Michael's eyes lost their amber glow, deepening into the bright burning red of a fiery coal.

The creature turned its body in the air and Michael struck it with a body blow that sent it back down toward the deck, exploding through the deck. The smell of blood from within the hull of the ship was released. Michael had sealed the deck days earlier in order to think more clearly, as the smell of the blood always clouded his mind. He could sense surprise in the creature. He stood above on the deck, leaving the Vampyre in the crater of shattered planks. The Vampyre's body lay in the center; the splintered fragments of fractured wood came down around him like snow and the cavity looked like the great wings of a snow angel. The Vampyre looked up at him and its eyes glistened bright yellow.

It was confused. It was dazed. It was angry.

There were no words between them. No thoughts. The creature forced itself up slowly, up to one knee with its knuckles pressed into the fragmented, damaged deck, never taking its eyes off of Michael.

It grunted and clambered out of the hole slowly toward him.

Michael wanted to ask, *Who am I? What am I?*

The Vampyre stood up before him like pieces of statue putting itself back together, realigning. It cracked a dislodged shoulder back into place. It watched Michael, who never moved.

Michael could feel the sunrise coming soon and he waited.

Darkness, Michael thought, *there is comfort in darkness*. He hid his thoughts in a distant recess in his mind, seeing them compartmentalize. He did not speak, or think toward the strange Vampyre. The calm inside Michael was troubling to both of them.

Darkness was not comforting for him. If there were no answers for him here, he would be forced to destroy them both.

The stranger showed his teeth. He brushed off the dust from his cloak and with a shriek exploded into Michael, baring sharp teeth and claws.

Michael fought back the barrage of fang and talon. He punched, at its head and its ribs. He kicked at its knees. The creature was unrelenting. The Vampyre finally tackled and lifted him with a preternatural roll, pulling Michael's body over a shoulder and jumped into the air away from the ship. The air whipped past them and he threw a flurry of clawed fists into Michael's chest, crushing his sternum and ribs, puncturing his heart. They crashed into the deck again.

The creature lifted Michael's body and hurled it with all of its strength east, toward the empty sea, toward the breaking light of the sun.

Michael was paralyzed, falling toward the water. Beyond the ringing in his ears, he heard nothing but the roar of the air. He flailed downward, still flying further away from the safety of the ship. He was unable to take control of his body. For hours, he'd run faster than he fell, he'd even flown, but in that moment, he could not turn himself. He fell to the ocean, flailing across the surface of the water until he was swallowed up into the cold darkness and silence.

The Vampyre could hear the man crashing violently into the ocean in the distance. He looked around at the ship. It had been dropped in that mysterious location, nearly hidden from view among the rocks. It was a large ship, broken in half: an old brig whose quarters were carried there. It wasn't natural. Someone powerful did it and if not, it took a number of people to do it.

He smelled around and knew the putrid and satisfying smell. He worked his way through the wreckage and rubble down to the sealed door at the entrance into the hull of the ship and he found his way into the small room that had once housed a very grim group of sailors. Their bodies still lay there in a very familiar pile. Only Vampyres knew how to create it. He studied the walls, reading the ancient texts written in human blood, carved with a fingernail into the wooden hull. He had written those very same life-giving texts in his life. They were the words of Mother Pinemé, Mother of all Vampyres, written in the ancient Enochian language of his people.

He put his hands to the wall. Someone was trying to destroy the covenant. *Did the Blood do this? Or was it someone within the Brethren?* Someone had created a Vampyre that was somehow more and different than any other. It spoke with the audible voice of a man. No Vampyre kept its human voice. That poor, confused man, for as powerful as he was, had surely come from within the hull of the ship. The blood was no more than a week old. Some betrayer did the deed. Someone close.

It occurred to him: there was no guilt in Michael at all. He'd overlooked the first clue. Any man of his age would have some spot of guilt that he would have carried with him into his Vampyric afterlife. As he had looked into Michael's blank mind, he should have found guilt, or darkness, malice, or deceit—but nothing was there. No goodness either. It had all been burned away. Anything that man had been before was gone. More terrifyingly, the man spoke with his physical voice. No Vampyre had voice, save for the claim of guilt. Physiologically, they could not speak, using their minds as their voice, the psionic gift of Pinemé.

And he could fly. Vampyres were agile, but that man left the ground as though it could not hold him. He was more than a Vampyre. The most grim thoughts entered his mind. He would surely not die out there.

There was genuine fear in Isaac Constantine's heart when he headed to the covenant's sanctuaries below Breton. The old Vampyre put a hand to his chest, full of regret for what he'd done.

Dawn was approaching. He could only hope for mercy on the poor soul.

PART II

Who trusted God was love indeed
And love Creation's final law
Tho' Nature, red in tooth and claw
With ravine, shriek'd against his creed
-Alfred, Lord Tennyson, *In Memorium A.H.H.*
(1850)

ΟΠΕ

The Devil pulls the strings which make us dance;
We find delight in the most loathsome things;
Some furtherance of Hell each new day brings,
And yet we feel no horror in that rank advance.
- **Charles Baudelaire**, *Au Lecteur (1857)*

Michael felt his crippled body sinking into the black water. That thing had left him in so much pain he could barely move his arms. The ice cold water pulsed through him, shocking then numbing. He could taste the blood in the water and he knew it was his own.

He had no idea how long it had been since he hit the water. He couldn't tell if he'd been unconscious. He didn't remember falling or from how high. Nothing was right. Suddenly he felt that familiar burning like days ago on his arm. His entire body was burning; he was steaming in the murky sea. It took all of his energy just to move his fingers and he closed his fists, gritted his teeth and opened his eyes. He was only a few feet under the water and he could see from the green tint that dawn was beginning to break.

He turned, looking for the galleon that had been his makeshift home, but it was too far away. With the sun coming up, there was no way to get there. He was going to drown. The frigid waters would be his grave.

Then it dawned on him. He hadn't been breathing, nor did he have to. He could feel the pressure on his ears and his aching body. He looked down into the water and started making his way into the dark of the sea.

Hours passed and Michael lay unmoving at the sea floor. He could see the light far above him getting brighter and beyond his sight, he could see the fish swimming around him. The burning had subsided and he watched the quiet world below. At first he could sense large fish coming to the blood, presumably sharks, but they hadn't bothered him for a while.

Michael lay in the murky weeds trapped in thought. He had come to terms with the fact that his name had once been Michael. He remembered bits and pieces of being on the ship and having an overwhelming feeling of his very important mission but couldn't remember much of the ship. He'd been a stowaway. *Important mission. Stowaway. Spy?*

This place is strange and full of darkness. Indignation filled his chest. The voice that was both him and yet not him whispered now in the silence of revenge.

He began to formulate a plan. He looked over his memories of Breton and could remember a great deal. Planning came second nature to him. He could see the very schematics of the town laid out in front of him. Maps unraveled in his mind. He thought of the people he sensed he could trust. He would destroy the Vampyres, even if the act necessitated his own destruction, which he assumed would be the case. Regardless of the price, he would take care of them. He scratched at his itching shoulder blades and waited for the evening to come.

Once again, Edwin was up before Thomas. He stood near the edge of the orphanage roof, where he'd been with Mister Smith before, unseen by the people below.

His legs and arms were still sore. The boys had watched Algernon Elliott disappear into the night after they had told him about Mister Smith and explained what little they had heard. Edwin looked down into his hand and examined the package that Algernon had given him, suspecting that Mister Smith would be in trouble. He had attached a note while the boys ate cookies and tried not to focus on the dead bodies or worry about Jenny, who Mister Algernon Elliott said would be fine.

Algernon told them that his friend, Mister Smith, was actually never a headmaster and that he was helping him in a venture to rid the town of the Vampyres. Edwin didn't care about all that. Mister Smith was the only person that had ever treated him like more than a kid. Mister Smith was the closest thing that Edwin ever had to a Father.

He and Thomas agreed that they would risk going back to the orphanage and hiding up on the roof. Edwin looked back at his friend who was still lying under the blanket that they had hung for a makeshift tent. He was contemplating if what they had done would make a difference.

The night before, Thomas stopped him in the orphanage, realizing that the pendants and medallions, the charms that Mister Elliott had spoken of, were everywhere. There was one on the wall and one on everyone's shirts or jackets.

They spent the rest of their evening getting rid of them, throwing them in the fire one by one. They watched the silk burn and small tin char and curl. They were being as destructive as ever, but they felt good about what they were doing.

Edwin could hear Thomas rustling around, putting his shoes on. He looked down on the street. *Today is not going to be any fun.* One thing that Mister Smith had always told Edwin was "No matter what the trouble or danger, no matter the boredom, life is a game. Find the fun in it." He would have to look harder.

"So what's next?" asked Thomas, squinting at the morning sun with a weak smile. Thomas was never quick to smile and he wasn't a morning person, but Edwin could see that he was coming to life with all the mischief.

Edwin turned to him. "I don't know. I guess we wreck this old town."

"What do we do after that?" Thomas asked.

"Does it matter?" Edwin ventured, his contemplation falling on the town.

Thomas smiled, "No, I suppose not."

When Thomas and Edwin made their way down onto the second floor of St. Jerome's, the quiet games they had grown accustomed to had given way to a much more comfortable thing. It was strange to both of them. The children in the orphanage were running around. The room was full of organic life. Some were cooking. Some children were playing tag. They were all laughing.

The boys had grown used to a quiet orphanage. The children of St. Jerome's were docile creatures like most of the people in Breton. Edwin was silent. Thomas simply smiled. They looked at each other, unable to comprehend the fullness of the situation, but they stumbled forward.

"Hey Tommy," called out James McLaughlin, the twelve-year-old, redheaded boy that normally listened quietly to Mister Smith's storytelling each night. "Come play with us!"

Thomas thought on it. *Tommy?* No one had ever called him Tommy. His stomach sank. His sense of dread was awful. *What have we done?*

Edwin quietly turned to him, "Well, we can't exactly pull those things out of the fire." Thomas clenched his teeth. Edwin continued in a whisper, "Might as well..."

Thomas interrupted him. "If all of the people in this town are bad people and they're going to kill us all, then we're going to make it difficult. Very difficult."

Edwin's eyes opened with surprise and then he laughed.

"Hey James," Thomas responded, "Would you round everyone up please?" Deep down he didn't want to do it.

Everyone around them was so happy for the first time ever. He'd never thought about it, but he always felt like an adult, so this moment was no different. He looked down and Edwin sat on a bunk next to him. "I have some really terrible news."

The man who called himself Gallegos, born Jasper Markov, a failed circus ringleader and successful thief of some very important documents, had a new task at hand. That, a bruised rib and a cut above his eyebrow. *I should have skipped town once I had the money. Instead I decided, 'just one more night.'*

He wanted to stay long enough to find the kids that bit him. Then the train station manager, of all people, barged into his room, and assaulted him. The crazy little french man packed a wallop.

Jasper Markov always works independent. We just have a loose contract. So he did what the lunatic told him to do and headed toward the ancient-looking church building to meet with a man called "Adler." Chandler advised him it would be a wise thing to do. He even memorized what Chandler told him to say so as to not allow the monstrous man to kill him. If everything went well, he might have been up for quite a sum of money, but if Chandler were wrong, the young man might very well have been walking into a trap.

What Chandler didn't tell him was that on his way out of the Crow's Nest he looked at the register and noted that one of the rooms was rented to a "Miguel de Morillo." Chandler was quite aware of the nature of that name. Markov would not have very much time to get away with his plan before the real Gallegos would swoop down on him. Chandler would not want to be around when Gallegos, the torturer, got a hold of that young man. He obviously had no idea whom he had stolen from.

Markov made his way across the square, saying quiet prayers to himself, hoping all would go well. *Why am I praying?* He thought. *I'm going to talk to a priest. He's already got God on his side.*

Spencer Mayhew and Ernest Williams tapped secret messages to each other through the wall of the jail. The night progressed and it seemed they were both in quite a bit more trouble than either had bargained for. Ernest was under the impression that they would be hanged publicly though Spencer couldn't see why at first.

With some deliberate thought, Spencer realized that so much of how Breton worked came from the "alignment of the minds," a teaching he'd heard about from Algernon. Vampyres had a bizarre expertise in the field of telepathy and much of their philosophy, or even their religion—if they could have religion—had come from the idea that minds could be aligned to create more powerful meaning. That was why they lived in covenants. Unfortunately, in the case of the people of Breton, it simply meant living for decades as brainwashed sheep in a herd disguised as a town. He gritted his teeth at the thought. He'd really started to care for the boys in the orphanage. He wanted to figure out a way to help them all escape from the wretched town.

He'd have to get himself out first.

Ernest had advised him that it would take another day or so before they'd be hanged and that was only slightly promising. Spencer could only hope that Algernon could come free them before then, but Ernest didn't have as much hope. He knew he had nowhere to go. He never imagined he'd die that way. The awakening was liberating though. He was sober and happy for the first time since he could recall. He hoped that Kat might visit him. He thought that perhaps she might even bring him food. He took comfort in that thought.

Both men sat listening to the police officers that went back and forth discussing the rest of "the plan."

"Could a couple of gentlemen get some water in here?" asked Ernest politely.

The police officers stopped mid-conversation and laughed.

They'll not have begun their torture yet, Algernon thought. He could only see that Genevieve had been taken for assisting him. He had already planned to explore the mines near Breton, but he would have to do more than that. He was weeks early, but he was going to go in and create hell for those living in the mines. Whether it was the ancient Druid people that he'd been researching or the evil Vampyres, it would not be pleasant for anyone with the exception of Algernon, whose morbid interests might be satisfied.

H e sat in the grove's tall grass outside the mouth of the mines watching and listening. He was about fifty yards from the entrance examining the mouth and any possible traps. *Nothing. Someone inside seems confident that no one's coming.*

His first encounters with Vampyres were in dealing with strays in Whitechapel and Mile End, which led to some strange, upper-class Vampyres in Kensington. He abhorred their good looks and felt that they used their charm only for evil purposes.

Algernon had lost much in pursuing his interests in the paranormal. Disowned by his family while at Oxford, he paid for his education secretly, out of his pocket. Quietly ridding small towns of monsters paid impressively. He joked that the English did not fear their own monsters but rather feared the monsters of opinion. He met his partner while studying there, a rambunctious young man named Spencer Mayhew who had very little interest in the paranormal but lived for adventure.

Spencer would go on to quit Oxford to join the Army and then go to South Africa during the first Anglo-Boer War, returning without a scratch and with more stories than anyone cared to hear. Algernon encouraged him to write his tales down, but Spencer enjoyed telling stories more than writing them.

Breton was proving to be the strangest trip yet, considering what they'd seen already as young men. It had been difficult enough trying to convince Spencer to come, but once adventure came into it, Spencer had lead the way from London to Breton. He'd even convinced the real Mister Neville Smith at the train station that the position was no longer available while Algernon cleaned his pockets.

The Vampyres did not scare Algernon as much as they intrigued him. He did quite well when it came down to it. He knew he was physically weaker, but research had revealed numerous weaknesses that a man of science could exploit. He carried a satchel full of vials of blessed water, which contained unknown metaphysical properties that were quite damaging.

He had changed clothes from his proper gentleman's attire to what Spencer had called "adventurer's gear," which included spectral goggles that he wore on his head and a Remington 44-40 six-shooter, holstered under his arm. He had acquired most of his utilities through less-than-honest means. He wore a dark waistcoat and a long "duster" jacket. His attire was as dark as his mood and he blended into his surroundings. He carried a small pouch under the back of his vest that unrolled for thief's tools (and doubled as a make-shift pillow) and a few vials of his own concoction. He was ready.

As a child Algernon had had a sense for the magical and unknown. As an adult he saw the world differently. There was no magic, only a world that extended beyond the physical. In the Earth, there were layers toward the core. He theorized that, metaphysically, the rest of the world would function in much the same way. The power that those monsters were capable of harnessing simply came from a dimension or layer deeper than the one to which humans were accustomed.

He pulled the spectral goggles down and rotated the small knobs to adjust for time of the evening. He lifted one lens to reveal another, peering through purple then red glass. There had been movement recently. There was a lot of metaphysical movement near the coordinates given to him by Monsieur Chandler. There were residual traces moving in different directions. The colors were vibrant. They looked like lamp oil sitting in water reflecting the sunlight. It was beautiful and liquid. There were also traces of smoke. Algernon took note.

He pushed the goggles back up his forehead, pushing his hair up in a dark, spiky mess. Had Genevieve seen him, she'd have found him a beautiful, disheveled disaster. Aside from his distinctly British sense of social faux pas, he was never very good at evaluating his own looks.

He ducked back down into the tall grass as he considered the implications from his notes. *There are traces of humans in there, more than one. And recent. That's quite odd*. He observed. *According to any of the numerous applicable metrics, there should be virtually no human traces in this vicinity. Why so many?*

Jared had changed out of his uniform into some better clothes. Gallegos didn't mention where he'd gotten them and Jared didn't care. It felt strange to wear something other than a military uniform; it felt even stranger to touch his own face. He had trimmed his thick and matted beard into something manageable and clean. He looked like a different person. He looked virile and appropriately handsome for a young man his age.

Gallegos had spent the prior evening exploring Breton in a tactical way. He kept the Vampyres in mind. He looked at things with blood; he looked at houses and dark spaces. He noticed the pig farms out away from town and the horse ranches. Everything spoke to him. The entire town could easily be converted into a nightmare for the Vampyres.

As luck would have it, just before dawn, Gallegos observed one of the creatures running at an incredible speed through the woods. Vampyres never allowed themselves to be seen, so he could only guess that the coming sunlight was enough of a threat for the thing to run without cover. He watched the limping creature jump down a well. *How lucky am I today?*

Standing in the alley behind the inn, he related some of those thoughts to Jared. Between the two of them, they could figure something out.

There was also a part of Jared that simply wanted to walk around the town. He hadn't been in Breton in five or six years at his best guess. The night his family disappeared, he had been forgotten. When he walked out the next morning, no one noticed that they were gone and the soldiers were going out, so he followed them. He never gave fighting with them a second thought despite the fact that some of the men had been opposed to it. He ran water to them for some time, until one day—while under the pressure of the opposing army—he picked up a rifle and took his place as a soldier. It was natural to him.

In that moment his entire life flashed before him and he boiled it down to one question for his new ally. "Is it strange that a war has been going on for years and somehow when I walked away from the battlefield, I found myself running back to my childhood home?" He couldn't gather his thoughts fully, but he was sure he'd been moving in circles the entire time.

"Well, my friend," began Gallegos, "you act on the assumption that a war has been going on."

"But..." Jared tried. They walked on into the square.

"No," Gallegos interrupted, "there has been no war. "I can assume that you are quite efficient at your job, can I not?"

"Efficient, sir?"

"You are quite good at killing. Yes?"

Jared thought about it. "Yes, I have done my part."

"Well, then you have spent the last years of your life doing your part to feed an army of Vampyres." Gallegos continued nonchalantly.

"That cannot be." Jared stated quietly.

"Think about what you saw last night. The war that you feel you have been fighting was over long before you were born. Grant became president. He died a few years ago. The uniform that you wore so proudly has not been in use in twenty or thirty years." Gallegos answered. "The American War Between the States, the North versus the South and all that, has been over since eighteen sixty-five."

The statement left another gap in Jared's thinking, but Gallegos was quick to answer. "My friend, the year is eighteen hundred and ninety-nine." Jared's face was pale. "Welcome to reality. This place—your home—is a harvesting ground. The Vampyres have grown lazy, in my opinion."

Breton had acted as a front. Its fields were "battlefields," where brainwashed criminals were dumped with the thought that they were soldiers. They killed each other off only to be fed to the Vampyres. Similar efforts had been attempted before, according to his research on Vampyre history. The "lost" colony at Roanoke, modern-day North Carolina, had been harvested completely by the Vampyres while their leadership, including Sir Walter Raleigh, was in England. It was not the first time either, but Gallegos focused on the task at hand instead of wandering off in thought.

"I take it you will not be the kind of man that will succumb to his emotion over this revelation?" Gallegos asked the young man.

Jared's eyes were distant but it seemed that anger was replacing any other emotion. Whatever he wanted to think would have to be suppressed. It was the soldier in him. "No." It flashed throughout his mind that had it not been for the Vampyres, he'd been born a different man with a different life. He was ready to destroy them all. "I am not that man."

"Good." Gallegos said before standing up, lighting a cigarette and walking away. "I will return momentarily with word on our friend Kat."

As he sat on a park bench waiting for Gallegos to return, Jared saw a few police officers coming his way. He knew them by name. A larger officer, Dan, had fought next to him for at least the last six months before his disappearance on the battlefield. He had not expected to find him in that clean, pressed police officer's uniform.

It seemed that their plan was quite intricate, with costumes and roles for everyone. It made him sick. War was all he'd ever known, but in that moment, it was like the battles had never existed—and indeed they hadn't. Jared could only imagine the horrible things people had gone through and how Breton was the epicenter for all of those crimes, all that loss. He looked at the children again, running. Their lives too were a lie. His ears were getting hot and he clenched his fists; his anger was too much. He turned his head so the men wouldn't see him and saw Gallegos coming across the way from the inn.

Gallegos sat down quietly next to him.

"No good?" asked Jared.

"No." Gallegos responded. He looked down at Jared's white knuckles and waited before continuing. "I did not ask for her, but I did listen in the inn's tavern. She has disappeared." He looked down. "I may have done something terrible, *amigo mio*."

Jared looked at him squarely.

"The girl's father," he explained, "the innkeeper—he came by me with drinks. I snatched off that pendant he was wearing—the one they all wear." He held the small brass pendant in his hand, a trinket with a five pointed star, over an upside down five pointed star. It was small and innocuous. "Pentacle over pentagram makes the star of ten points." He pocketed the small thing. "The innkeeper should have noticed, but alas he did not." He sighed, "He dismissed his daughter's disappearance so easily. It troubled me. There is no greater tragedy than a parent outliving their child."

"So you have now woken him up for the torture of it," interrupted Jared, coldly.

"No." Gallegos continued. "You make the incorrect assumption that because someone has a hazy mind that they are also without feeling." Gallegos reached in his pocket and pulled out the pouch with his cigarettes and then deftly began rolling one. "That girl might not be dead yet. We don't know. I feel her father should have the opportunity to do something about it. Even if that something is to simply grieve." He paused pensively and licked the edge of the cigarette. "We all have that right." He lit the cigarette as they turned to listen to the sounds in the inn.

Glenn, the innkeeper, had come to life.

Jared sighed.

"You are quite young yet, my friend." Gallegos answered. There was even a dark smile in it.

As they continued conversing, they watched.

"There is a great opportunity for us here," he started.

They heard the sound of the man screaming at his patrons and tables being overturned.

"I was asked to come to this strange place to meet someone: a man who never came. He would have quite special knowledge about Vampyres and other—let's say *otherworldly* folk." He paused to relight his cigarette.

The innkeeper was sobbing as he opened the door. Glenn walked across the square and paused to breathe. He swallowed hard and spit.

Gallegos wondered aloud through a puff of smoke. "They had quite strong ways of persuading me when they found me at la Universidad de Salamanca, where I was working on some research."

"This isn't right," stated Jared. He pitied the man.

"It is bigger than this," said Gallegos. "This Kat, presumably the daughter of that man right there, is important, according to your dream and sir, I do not play with the notion of dreams. So we do what we can to find her."

They both listened to the pause.

"Do not allow your emotions or sense of empathy to impede your sense of duty." Gallegos instructed quietly.

Jared's eyes fell to the ground before he nodded in agreement.

They could hear Glenn from a distance. The man was in full rage as he entered the station, screaming at the police officers. "What do you mean, calm down?" he screamed. From where they sat, they could hear the sound of a desk sliding. The children running in the square slowed to a walk. They craned their necks to listen. "I will not be spoken to like a child!" he cried out. "No, she will not be fine! No one ever simply comes back from disappearing in this town!"

Gallegos gritted his teeth. *Not exactly what I wanted to hear.*

Jared cursed aloud.

The two police officers that had walked by were running toward the station. The children had stopped altogether and were listening to the sounds.

Gallegos scratched his head. He heard the heavy door to the orphanage shutting as some little boys had quickly gone that way. The police officers pulled out their batons. "You will do something!" the man yelled, weeping openly. His grief was fueling his rage. Before the sheriff could even get to the front of the building, one of the officers came breaking through the wooden window. His body was limp before he'd hit the ground. In two quick steps, the sheriff was inside and then there was quiet.

Glenn walked out with the sheriff, speaking quietly like two men who had been friends a long time. Gallegos couldn't figure it out, but it wasn't right. He could hear the old innkeeper thanking the man and then they parted ways. The look on Jared's face was equally puzzled. *That's something you don't see every day,* he thought. The innkeeper was as docile as a lamb. The sheriff, in only seconds, had brought him down from a rage of righteous indignation. Jared had seen many men filled with rage and none had ever been cured of it so quickly except by a bullet. It wasn't right. That sheriff had something up his sleeve. He was sure of it.

Gallegos didn't speak. Neither he nor Jared had been paying attention and an older lady had approached them. "Hello." She grinned politely. Jared jumped. "Well, that does tell me quite a bit about you both." She smiled. "Could I invite you both to a cup of tea at my home?"

Gallegos turned to her very methodically, "Absolutely ma'am." He looked at Jared. "Tea would be quite nice right now."

"I am the town's tailor." The old woman smiled. "I do hope you'll come enjoy some company for a bit. My name is Bernadette Allen, but Miss Allen is just fine for either of you." She smiled knowingly.

Gallegos stood to introduce himself. "Miguel de Morillo." He smiled. Even as he looked over her shoulder, Parson Adler was leaving the police station. *Yes. That explains the docile innkeeper.* "This is my associate, Allan Pope," he remarked, looking at Jared.

"Well, Mister de Morillo and Mister Pope. Just follow me."

Allan Pope? Jared thought as he stretched his arm. *This is getting quite silly.*

The door of the orphanage slammed heavily. The young twins, Henry and Archie, shaggy and always sad-looking, turned and put their backs to the door as though they were holding out some kind of evil. Their freckled faces were pale.

"They're fighting out there." The one to the left stuttered. No one could tell the difference between the two, but it was Archibald who, had anyone cared to notice, had a small scar under his left eye.

Before that morning the twins were quiet and complacent, but they woke up and went straight to the square to play tag. They were energetic and growing full of nervousness.

Everyone looked up from what they were doing. "Who?" one boy asked.

It was Henry that responded. "The police."

Thomas and Edwin had spent the night before lying on their backs, hiding on the roof and discussing whether or not they could tell everyone what was happening. But it seemed the others were becoming aware of it. They didn't realize that the difference would have been so obvious. Thomas had regretted it immediately, but Edwin knew they had done the right thing.

Edwin suggested that everyone might be safe in St. Jerome's for a while, but Thomas realized that nothing was safe, especially since Mister Smith was gone. All the good people were disappearing and the bad ones were walking around. They were in charge. He didn't know what they could do about it, but like Mister Smith always said, "Something must be done."

The twins stood, almost frozen, looking for someone to say something. A few of the boys ran to the window to look, but the police station was too far out of sight. They strained and stood over each other anyway, hoping to see something.

Edwin sighed.

Thomas thought it through. He fingered the envelope in his pocket. He knew that without Mister Smith, they were all going to be in trouble. "Ned," he sighed, "tell them." Then he walked up to the twins. "Edwin has something to tell everyone. Go to the kitchen." He was sure of himself and he herded them with his open palms against their backs. As the boys moved away from the door, things felt quiet outside.

Something would have to be done.

Miss Allen welcomed the two strangers into her shop. There was a chill in the midday air and it seemed another storm might be brewing. Gallegos entered first, leaning heavily on his cane. Jared, the much larger man, entered the warm room where a small fire glowed in a corner. The blinds were ornate but the fabric was plain and covered little of the window. The midday light spread the through room where the winter was cut by light and fire.

"Please," Miss Allen spoke, "make yourselves at home." She smiled and sat down in a rocking chair next to a large table that was covered in rolls of plain fabrics. Gallegos immediately recognized their texture. Even the apron that hung neatly around his host's waist was cut from that cloth. An identical twin was hanging from the wall next to a row of scissors in numerous sizes.

As the men settled into the room, her voice was a near-whisper. "Can I offer you nice young men anything to drink?"

Jared shook his head.

"It's really no trouble at all," she responded.

"Well, Mistress ..." began Gallegos.

"Miss," she interrupted. "Miss Bernadette Allen."

"Right, you said that earlier." Gallegos smiled, "I apologize. I did say some tea would be quiet nice."

She seemed giddy, more so than they could have expected. Miss Allen got up and began boiling water over her small fire. She smiled like a little girl getting ready for an imaginary tea party.

Gallegos thought quietly for a moment, Allen, yes. I knew that name. From listening in on the conversations of the town, he'd heard gossip about the crazy old spinster. He held in a laugh, realizing his mistake. Morillo was one of many pseudonyms he used for himself, but he'd never thought to prepare any for a partner. *I had been reading a Mister Poe's notes on the behavior in his own house cat.* Instinct Vs. Reason, he recalled. *Perhaps I recalled her name "Allen" alongside Jared's name, a close anagram of Edgar and arrived at Allan Pope.*

Miss Allen simply hummed a tune for a moment while she removed the pot from the fire. "I hope you boys like your tea with a bit of sweetness," she mentioned.

"I've never had it prepared so," Gallegos answered, with his eyes on Jared before poking him with his cane.

"Oh," Jared seemed to come back to life, "no ma'am. Neither have I."

"My grandfather was a wealthy farmer in South Carolina when I was a child. The French came and taught them how to plant tea and we make it a little sweet since we already had sugar cane crop. It's the Southern way." She smiled.

Gallegos could tell she was very glad to have company. She seemed like she'd been very alone all that time. He could tell that she was very lonely deep down.

"Before coming to Breton, which feels like forever ago, I was a married woman living on quite an inheritance," she recounted. Jared listened. Gallegos could see the woman who had aged so strangely in the town, preserved by her madness. He visualized her and thought she must have been quite beautiful. Even in her resilient hardness she seemed quite beautiful. Her hands looked wrinkled and hard and there was a certain toughness around her wrinkled eyes like she'd been straining to see for many years. He noticed a pair of old reading glasses on the mantle. They had gathered dust. It had been many years since they were last used.

"But my family, though powerful, was not very good at making friends," she remarked. Her tone was quite cheerful, but Gallegos could tell that there was a great sadness in her words and that her story had waited a very long time to be told.

"Well, one thing led to another," she continued. She spoke, skipping many chapters in a book and landed toward a strange resolution. "These people who were enemies of my family, they had my poor Edward killed and I ended up here."

She turned, smiling, with teacups steaming on a tray in her hands.

Gallegos smiled back instinctively.

Jared's face didn't change. He simply watched, nearly horrified at the woman's behavior. Would she pull out a gun? Would she begin crying? He could not understand her.

She placed the tray on a small side table and sat down.

Jared did not move, but Gallegos, a much more civilized man, took one cup of tea and handed it to him. "Thank you," Jared mumbled. Gallegos' eyes shifted quietly to the old lady and Jared read his thought. "Thank you, Miss Allen," he corrected himself, "for your hospitality."

Miss Allen took a teacup from Gallegos. "Oh no, Mister Pope. It is more than my pleasure." She smiled, the cup of tea held to her face, the aroma and warmth enveloping her for a short moment. Gallegos, grabbing the third teacup, watched her, sad for her. When she opened her eyes there was a quiet life in them that had been missing before. She leaned in toward the men. She was ready to talk. "Gentlemen," she mused, still quiet, "I hope you will find that my home is a place where you can be honest."

Gallegos smiled.

She continued, "I have told you how I landed here in hell." Her eyes shifted softly between them. "I'll pray that you have the courtesy to do the same."

"Yes, quite right," Gallegos responded. "There is no reason that we cannot all be frank." He took a sip from his cup. "I am not from here, as you can tell." He smiled. "I am from Spain, Salamanca to be exact and I have come to investigate the problem with the *Vampiros*." He turned to Jared, who had not taken even a sip of the tea, simply holding the cup. "My friend here was unfortunate enough to have an encounter with one of them very recently on the battlefield." Jared looked at him and Gallegos continued, "but luck should have it that we met here at the inn."

"Neither of you struck me as their kind," she said, referring coldly to some unknown people. "But as I walked by, I noticed that your shirt was stained with blood, Mister Pope."

"Oh," Jared noted. His shoulder had not been healing properly. He looked down to see that the shirt was indeed moist with blood. He pulled the sticky fabric from his aching arm.

Gallegos looked at him but dismissed it. They were in good company now. "Their kind?" Gallegos asked, changing the subject.

Miss Allen stood gingerly and walked over to her sewing table and found some light gauze. "Oh yes, Mister Morillo." She returned and handed it to Jared, who took it quietly with a thankful smile. "This entire village is run by the Vampyres and if my memory, which has failed me many times, now serves me in this moment, there are even greater evils than the Vampyres. That is why I am here."

"The Vampyres. They brought you here?" Gallegos tried.

"Oh lord, no," she replied. She took a sip of her tea. "Their lords." She was quiet for a moment but both men listened. "The Vampyres can hardly be tamed. They need people to run things for them. They are much like children. They come running at the smell of dinner."

Gallegos contemplated her words. *And we're dinner.*

The cannons fired, coughing large plumes of dark smoke. The blasts were deafening and the smoke blinding. The cannonballs crashed in large explosions, throwing clouds of dirt, along with bodies and a mist of blood into the air. The armies fired into each other as soldiers stepped over the dead, reloading their rifles and muskets. The mud sloshed between their boots and the suctioning sound of their feet trapped in the mixture of blood and dirt was only heard intermittently as the sound of rifle fire rested.

The world was a haze to every soldier. The life they shared on the battlefield was the only life they had come to know. What had come before did not matter. The important thing was to survive the haze that spit cannonballs and enemies with bayonets and to suppress the constant fear of the revenants in the darkness.

Their pasts were no longer hazy, simply forgotten.

Horatio Cornwall, once the strongman for an organization specializing in insurance frauds now only knew that he had to push the Seventh Battalion forward before sundown. He fired his revolver and winged a rifleman that was reloading across the field.

He laughed, "Johnny Rev gonna chew on Johnny Reb tonight!"

As far as Sergeant Cornwall was concerned, they'd all be Vampyre chow, but not tonight. Tonight, let them find more grays than blues.

two

Midway upon the journey of our life
I found myself within a forest dark,
For the straightforward pathway had been lost.
-**Dante Alighieri, *Inferno, Canto I (1314)***

A lgernon sat in a small cove in the woods, analyzing the spectral traces and ectoplasmic markers that denoted otherworldly energies. According to the information, there was a lot of movement at the mouth of the cave, more than he'd ever seen in London. He winced a bit. He could feel his nervousness in his heartbeat. He focused his mind, sure that he would not let his own emotionality get the better of him. Clenching his teeth, he listened. It was silent beyond the breeze.

The cave was warm and damp and there was a bit of a swirl of wind. It reminded him of his own childhood, when he, the dark-haired son of a bank manager, would leave the front door open on his way out in the mornings before school. He'd run to the gate and turn around to watch the door slam itself shut behind him. He knew that would only happen if the maids left the rear door open while they began their morning chores in the rear garden.

He was a clever boy and he had grown into a dangerous man. He hoped there would be no doors shutting him into the cave. He would wait for sundown. If there really were Druids down there, they would probably be wandering around during the day and he'd rather take his chances with the Vampyres. At least he knew how to deal with them.

There is a rear entrance, he calculated.

There wouldn't be much time. He sat down preparing for his meditation. The meditation would be useful to keep his thoughts clear and his reactions quick. One powerful tool employed by the Vampyres would be their psychic charm. They would look into his mind and the closer he got the more they would see. The meditations would keep them from seeing very deeply.

They would already have known him, which played as an advantage for him. Algernon knew that they'd made a mistake taking Genevieve. She knew so much about him. Her voice, her thoughts about him, would act as a cover for Algernon to hide under for as long as he could. Had he been a stranger walking into the cave, they'd sense the change of energy. They'd sniff him out, blood and thought.

There came the crackle of footfall and a rustle in the grass and Algernon knew better than to rise up and look. It was still too early to be a Vampyre so he could only assume it would be an animal or some form of Shifter. He presumed there would be plenty of Shifters running the colony and reporting back to whatever hierarchy they abided by, but he hadn't expected to bump into any that evening. He craned his neck to look but whatever it was had gone.

He knew better than to wait too long and dusk would be perfect. His logic would have seemed strange to Spencer, but he knew it had to work. By day he'd be much too visible and by night there'd be too much activity. Algernon needed to be inside before anyone knew.

With a quiet genuflection, he moved to his feet, thinking and watching; it would be his greatest adventure yet. He wished Spencer were coming with him, but he was alone. Algernon Elliott looked around and put his goggles back on his forehead. The time had come. He stood in the tall grass outside Breton looking at the mouth of the cave and considering that it could be the end of his life, but the rush was overwhelming and he walked forward quietly with a strange smile curling on his lips.

He made his move toward the entrance.

The Vampyre called Isaac Constantine lay on his back, staring at the shallow ceiling of his room. His room was claustrophobic, little more than a closet. Isaac was not comfortable with open space and was much more at home in confined quarters.

No one knew about Isaac's past, which predated the Byzantine Empire. In the year eighteen ninety-nine, Isaac would have been sixteen-hundred-and-seventy-six-years old—had he been keeping count. He was the oldest of the Vampyres in the "Brethren," the covenant of Vampyres that lived deep under the town of Breton, by far. As a matter of fact, Isaac Constantine was the mastermind behind the entire idea of building a human feeding system over a covenant hideout—though the benefactors would have claimed that it was their doing. He didn't need to be known for it and would happily pass the recognition on to others.

He focused on the confused man that he'd met the evening before. In all his life he'd never met something so powerful. Isaac recognized the confused, angry eyes, uncontrollable bloodlust and sheer anger that he saw in the man named Michael. Someone had done that to him. Someone had given him that horrible burden. He hoped Michael was dead. He hoped he'd never see the burning red eyes of Michael's anger, but he feared that somehow, in his strength, Michael would have survived.

For the first time in over a hundred years, Isaac thought back on the day when he was transformed into the creature that lay there that afternoon. He was a child, in the burning ruins of a small village, crying over the limp corpse of his mother. The Viking slaughterers ravaging their lands did not carry her off, unlike many other women. She had fought them alongside his father. Everyone fought and those that were not carried off for their vile desires were killed. Isaac did not die, though. A young Viking had laughed hysterically as the child cried over his mother's body. They left him there, having spit on him.

He lived for weeks, unable to hunt or feed himself, much too young and weak. He only had the energy to burn the bodies of his mother and father where they lay and hope that whatever gods or devils came would take the spirits of his parents and leave him to die alone. The rest of the corpses lay strewn throughout the rubble, cold and rotting.

Isaac rolled over on his side with thoughts of that ancient time.

No gods came that day; instead, two men in animal skins and long, dark cloaks came to him and surveyed the village quietly. The boy stood by the fire, holding a stick lit at the end from his small, smoldering flame.

When they sat down, the child brought them water. The men that came were like angels; they called themselves Sons of Pinemé. They never spoke aloud but instead spoke through thoughts. They called him the "innocent."

He asked to go with them as their servant.

They did not want to take him.

Instead, they offered him his revenge.

He woke up days later in a pile of cinder and bones, the only remains of those who had been killed around him. The men had gone and he existed for the first days cycling through his family's memories and those of his neighbors. Through the transformation, they had become part of him. Like Michael, he had been confused and angry, swelling with bloodlust. The child Isaac would have his revenge—and if Michael survived, he would seek his own as well.

Isaac would end much of the Viking rule and later work with the Varangian Guard protecting the emperors of the Byzantine era though once his own people discovered his true strength and secrets, they rejected him as a devil. Since they could not kill him, he found himself locked in a room for over one hundred and twenty years with nothing to feed on, withering to nothing. That room was much like the one where he lay. His entire life, he had moved from one cell to the next, from physical cells to a mental prison of a dreamless eternity and with time, with each kill, each innocent death and the increasing bloodlust, came the final prison of the darkness.

He had watched the passing of empires, the fall of kings and countries, always an outcast. Even in that moment, he lay in a beautifully furnished room alone. As he lay in the dark, approaching the turn of the twentieth century, Isaac was well aware that he was not immortal. No Vampyre was. Nearly seventeen centuries of life and he had only aged some thirty years or so. At that rate, he might have lived another three thousand years. Vampyres, the children of Pinemé, had longevity on their side, but their corrupting desires seemed to get them into very fatal predicaments. Despite Isaac's attempts to create a society for his kindred, he sensed that the others might get themselves killed as many before them had. He could hear the psionic chatter coming from other rooms. *One of them had to have created that foil,* he thought. *One, or maybe all of them, with their love of mischief, had to have spoken the words of the Mother to create the man.* Michael was an innocent. He was pure. He was righteous. In the language of the Vampyre, all those things were sacred. There was no part of his soul or his memories that any Vampyre could feed on. None of them would have been strong enough to destroy him. They would have had to convert him.

He couldn't wrap his mind around it.

Only a few Vampyres would have the will to create another without the help of the Sin Eaters and they wouldn't know how. Isaac thought. Once, he would immediately suspected Ilya. But the boy's secretive expulsion as attaché to the Sin Eaters, the highest among Vampyres, changed something in him. *My boy will never have the power he once had.* He thought.

He went one by one and counted who could have turned the man into a Vampyre, if any of them could. He drew a blank.

Isaac's spine tensed; he sensed the hidden thing. It sat in an air duct, a faceless, shapeless creature. Despite not needing oxygen themselves, the Vampyres found the fresh air comforting. An intricate system of air ducts had been devised particularly for that purpose.

"Your debt is not yet paid." The voice resonated, solemnly. The ritual had once again begun.

What am I to do? Isaac asked the thing. He pulled his gaze from an old book he'd read hundreds of times. It was the poetry of a Lord Byron, a man he'd met only a hundred years earlier but whose words were so bright and so full of anguish and life that it made Isaac's hardened heart rush. The inside of the title page was signed:

"The wretches of this world will never understand monsters, they simply fear. What monsters there are in this world will never compare in their terrifying magnitude as those in the human heart."

He set the book on the table in front of him. The candlelight flickered as the thing breathed some unearthly wind down the air duct.

"A horrible act," the voice replied. "An act of murder."

Isaac rolled his eyes. *Horrible?* He laughed.

"An innocent."

Isaac turned and looked up into the duct. *Have one of the hungrier ones do it.*

They said you.

Why? he asked. He did not hide his anger.

Because we're evil men, Isaac.

You don't believe that, he replied.

"No one cares what I believe, I'm afraid." The disembodied voice said in the vent. *You are the judge. How easily would your scales come crashing with their verdict on me? How harshly would you judge yourself?*

There's no judgment left for us. We're no longer men. We're already punished. Isaac said.

"Ours not to make reply. Ours not to reason why." The voice said, mock solemn.

Tennyson? Isaac asked. *I didn't take you for a reader.*

"I'm not. I just appreciate the ironic wordplay."

The 'Light Brigade' part?

"Yeah, I suppose you all were the original 'Light Brigade'."

Ours but to do and die.

"Ours but to do and die."

Tell me the target. Isaac replied, defeated. He reached down and found a piece of scrap parchment and folded it.

The voice began again in a solemn tone. *Upon reading this name, you swear your allegiance to the Lords and obedience to their greater will.*

Isaac knew there was nothing he could do. The dark process in which he participated was the most difficult part of everything he was. They would ask him to kill and become darker still. The very need for the feeding in Breton, the shipping of criminals to a place to be devoured, was to undo, if possible, the thousands of transgressions committed against mankind.

The Lords knew that.

And there he sat, knowing he was submitting to their will again.

Each innocent kill would drive the Vampyre closer to pure darkness and uncontrollable madness; each righteous kill could offset that progression, even if by only the smallest measure. Their very purpose and meaning in the world had once been to be righteous weapons and restore balance on Earth. That had gone horribly wrong.

Do you swear? the voice asked.

Isaac looked at the clean parchment and knew they'd find someone else, someone weaker, to do it if he didn't. For as young and foolish as the other Vampyres were, the darkness would drive them mad. He didn't want that for them.

"I swear."

Fear ran through his body as he saw the parchment filling with ink. He unfolded it and recognized the face associated to it.

The angry scream could be heard throughout the hallways of the complex as Isaac threw the desk across the room, smashing it into pieces. The candle that had lit the small room lay across the book of poetry. The page burned a low amber flame, the ink turning green, where the word "monsters" showed itself to Isaac as angry tears welled in his eyes.

After the twins delivered the news of what was going on outside, Thomas had waited for Mister Lamphere, the large innkeeper, to return to the Crow's Nest where he could speak to him. The man had been distraught. Kat had gone missing. Thomas wept quiet tears but told the man, "We can do something."

The man was surprised by Thomas's bravado. Glenn told the boy that he would quietly support whatever endeavor to find and help Kat. She was all he had.

Thomas had returned to find that Edwin had gathered the children in the kitchen. The ragged group stood in a semi-circle around him, waiting impatiently to hear what the two would announce. It took some energy just to get them all together; for the first time, they were all engulfed in their own games and activities.

Newton Bullington, twelve, the largest in girth of all the children, sat nervously. He quietly scolded Oliver Whipple, eleven, for sticking his finger in the stew. "Mister Smith don't like when we do that."

Ollie retorted, "Well, he ain't here is he, Newt?"

No, Newton thought, *he's not*. Which only made him more nervous.

Penny and Emily Hughes, sisters, ages eleven and fourteen, respectively, talked quietly, gossiping where no one listened. In reality, they had never spoken to the boys or remembered doing so. They were the only girls in the orphanage.

Many girls, when orphaned, would go work in the town for a fishmonger or in the inn. That had not been the case for Emily and her younger sister, Penny. Mister Smith had gone out of his way to make sure they came to St. Jerome's. No one knew why.

In that moment, all the children in the orphanage were strangers to each other.

Patrick Foster, fifteen and the oldest of all the children in the orphanage, stood in the doorframe of the kitchen waiting to hear the bad news. Most of what was happening had not set in and it hadn't even occurred to him that Mister Smith gone. He had a very uneasy feeling and his stomach was turning.

Edwin found Thomas, alone and thinking, in the common room. "Come on!" he whispered. "Everyone's waiting in the kitchen."

Alexander Shaw and Albert Perry, both twelve and unrelated, had been very aware of Mister Smith's absence. They stood shoulder-to-shoulder, ready to hear whatever "bad news" Thomas had.

Thomas and Edwin walked into the room quietly arguing how they would tell everyone. Everyone's attention turned to them. Edwin pushed his accomplice forward. "Tell them."

Thomas was quiet at first. He struggled with any words. He was speaking to strangers with whom he'd spent the last months of his life. Suddenly, for the first time, he noticed that one of the sisters—Emily, the elder, was beautiful. Her hair was sandy, darker than his blonde. Her eyes were hazel and gray like the color of the sky on a rainy day. He forgot what he was about to say. Edwin nudged him and all the children giggled a bit. Emily, who also noticed Thomas staring, was flattered. She blushed quietly, whispering with her younger sister.

"Go on," pushed Edwin.

"Right," Thomas replied. "What Henry and Archie saw outside is part of something very..." He struggled to find the word.

"Sinister," whispered Edwin. "Something very sinister."

Thomas continued. His voice was weak and he was scared. He'd never thought about having to speak in front of everyone and they were all staring at him. He swallowed. "It has to do with the uhm..." He turned to Edwin, whose eyes told him to continue. "It has to do with the Vampyres."

All the children gasped.

"Until last night, you were all—"

Knowing what he was going to say Edwin quickly corrected Thomas. "We."

Thomas acknowledged the correction. "Yes, until last night, *we* were all under a spell from the Vampyres."

Ollie Whipple, who'd had enough, interrupted. "Oh come, Thomas!" Ollie sucked stew off his finger. "You're a liar."

Thomas quickly understood that he was not going to like Ollie and one thing he wasn't going to tolerate was being called a liar.

Edwin replied quickly, "Oh shut up, Ollie. And keep your hands out the stew."

Thomas fumed quietly for a moment before continuing. "The Vampyres. Did they not kill the people you loved?" That being the one thing they all had in common, they agreed. "And are they not out there every night, walking around our town like they own it?" They got quiet. "It's because they do." He walked through the door of the kitchen past Patrick Foster, who moved quickly to see where he was going. Thomas continued talking. "Edwin and I came last night after seeing and hearing horrible things." His blood was boiling and he was nervous. He walked to the fireplace in the common room. "We threw all the medallions and pendants in here." He pointed at the charred tin.

Patrick was the first in the room and the first to notice that the large seal on the wall had been taken down. He put his hand on his jacket where a pendant had always been. It made sense to him. "Wow." He mumbled. His head ached to remember days before the pendant had been there. *I don't remember coming here.*

Thomas was adamant. "I listened to the Preacher, Adler. I heard him say he was working with the Vampyres. He called them idiots. He said they could be destroyed." Thomas was trying not to cry.

As the other children came into the room and looked, they felt for the pendant or medallion as Patrick had done. Emily and Penny sat on their knees looking through the ash in the fireplace.

Archie, the braver of the twins asked, "I believe you, Thomas. But what does that have to do with the terrible ruckus that happened out there?" His brother Henry just nodded.

Thomas's reply was calm, "The sheriff. He was the man that the parson was talking to. He arrested Mister Smith." The air seemed to leave the room; everyone gasped.

Edwin walked over to Thomas and spoke solemnly. "Mister Smith isn't even his name."

"Then who is he?" Albert Perry asked, his voice as small as that of a mouse.

"Was he a spy for the Vampyres?" continued his friend, Alexander Shaw.

"No." Edwin responded flatly. "He came with another man, Mister Elliott, to kill the Vampyres."

"So," Patrick asked, "they threw him in jail?"

Thomas answered, "Yes, we think so."

Ollie walked into the center of the bunch. "This is all silly." He nodded. "They're just teasing us. Mister Smith is probably just doing late shopping and he'll be back soon."

Alexander and Albert breathed a sigh of relief.

"Shut up, Ollie." Newton Bullington commanded. Newton was short but a stocky and strong boy. He'd helped Mister Smith with rebuilding bunks and he was shy but did not fear anything. His memories were clear. He'd seen the Vampyres kill with his own eyes. "You just shut up." He pointed his finger at Oliver's nose. "You always have to be contrary."

Oliver responded quickly. "I do not!"

"See?" Newton replied.

The children all sighed. Penny giggled.

Newton was clever and honest. "You always eat extras and blame me because I'm fat and I never say nothin' cause I know you're hungry and it ain't nice to tattle." He spoke calmly. "But Ollie, you called Thomas a liar and now you're telling all of us that even though we've seen our families killed, that they're silly for thinking the worst?" He paused. His anger came out a little in his red cheeks, "Well, Oliver Whipple, I think you're the worst."

Oliver's face was turning red and everyone was staring at him. Emily looked at the door, hoping that Oliver was right, that Mister Smith would walk through it calmly and stop the bickering, but he didn't.

Ollie gritted his teeth. His eyes darted from face to face and before he knew it, he'd jumped on Newt, punching and kicking as hard as he could. Newton didn't fight back; he simply fell on the ground. Edwin and Patrick pulled the smaller boy off as the tears ran down his face. He kicked and clawed, but Patrick was much too strong and big for it to have mattered.

Newton just lay on his side sniffling. Thomas leaned over to help him up and little Penny rushed over to his side. "Newt, are you alright?" she asked, but he was silent. The room had exploded with energy. Everyone was talking and a panic began to fill the space.

Patrick Foster tried to speak to Ollie, but in the noise and commotion, the little boy wiggled out and ran to the door. Patrick watched and he let him go. *He should go,* he thought.

No one else saw where he went.

Edwin tried to get everyone quiet, but it was Emily Hughes who whistled so loudly that Thomas had to cover his ears. The room rang with the whistle before growing silent.

Everyone stared at her. She waited a moment before she realized what she should do or say. "If Mister Smith is in trouble," she continued quietly, "we should help him." She turned to Patrick Foster, who stood over everyone at the moment, the tallest and oldest in the orphanage. "Don't you think?"

Patrick was quiet, but Edwin nudged him. "What do you think?"

"We've got no family but this one now." He thought. *Family.* The idea was giving him a queasy feeling, but he continued. "Gotta do what we can to keep it together, right?" He seemed confused. "Yeah, we should," he corrected. "We should."

The early afternoon sun was to Jasper Markov's back. He had hesitated like a child at the thought of going to see this Adler at the behest of Monsieur Chandler and had been sitting in one spot for almost two hours. He watched from across the square as the large innkeeper threw the police officer through the window of the police station. He watched the parson deal with him like a scolded son. Adler controlled the police and the sheriff. From what Jasper could see, the religious man controlled everything and everyone.

Across the square, the sheriff stood on the front steps of the station and watched intently. It gave Jasper goose bumps. He felt like the man could see right through him. He couldn't just sit there anymore. He knew the man was staring at him. He moved himself from the bench, dreading what he was doing. He had to go; he was compelled to get out of the gaze of the man who stood cross-armed and seemed to tower over him. Jasper moved toward the small church as casually as he could, but he felt like he was shrinking under the stare.

He approached the church with his final thoughts before pushing the door open. The door moaned and Jasper poked his head in looking for the man they called Adler. He could smell pipe tobacco burning. There was no one there. He entered quietly and the door creaked behind him.

Jasper turned and jumped like a child to see a man sitting on the last pew next to the door in a small, thin cloud of pipe smoke. He was staring right at him.

"Parson Adler?" Jasper asked, his voice shaking from the scare.

"Ah yes," the man said calmly. "The Vampyre hunter."

"Yes sir," Jasper replied, unable to hide his nerves.

"Who sold all the silly holy water vials to the residents of our town?" Adler asked.

"Yes sir," Jasper began. "I am of the opinion—"

Adler interrupted him flatly. "I am in no mood to listen to your opinion." Adler stood up and Jasper saw that the man was very small. He seemed quite frail and he moved slowly. The old man continued. "What's more is that this town has a delicate balance—an ecosystem of sorts. Your little transactions around town, your vials, they were unnecessary." Adler moved up the middle aisle between the old oak pews.

It had taken him some time to measure out how to speak to the man, but Jasper was beginning to understand what Chandler had told him. He felt a bit more confident. Jasper Markov was a brilliant salesman and a charming man. There was no reason he couldn't sell the idea to the stubborn old Parson.

"Sir, perhaps I have not properly communicated my intentions," Jasper pleaded.

The old man turned around, eyebrow arched. "Your intentions mean nothing." He paused. "Your mere presence in this town will result in the deaths of the people you lied to."

"Lied? I have not—"

"Do you think two ounces of water is going to kill a Vampyre, turn one away?"

"I came here to make money." The young man replied quietly. "But now, I see there is a true need. And no, I do not know how to kill a Vampyre, but they are a nuisance to you and those who work so hard to maintain this 'eco-system.' I am quite capable..." he recited what Chandler had told him, "of controlling them."

The old man reached in his pocket for a match, which he struck on the pew. Adler's eyes glared as he lit his pipe. "You have no idea what those words even mean. There are two men being prepared to be hanged right now. I could make sure it was three. That would make my life a little easier." He locked eyes with Jasper, as he gathered the pipe smoke in his mouth. "No one, nothing can control Vampyres." He breathed out a small cloud. "This I can say with certainty. You see, my dear boy, these Vampyres have been in my care for quite some time. You are some sort of actor who obviously came to my town on the rumors of bloodthirsty monsters." He laughed. "I do appreciate, however that you would come to me," Adler continued. "I will consider your employ. We can always use some fresh blood."

Jasper wasn't exactly sure what the man meant. "Yes sir, thank you very much."

"Stay in the inn and don't leave tonight. They will be out this evening." The old man turned and walked away.

Jasper had no idea exactly what had just happened and after a moment he let himself out of the building. "That went fairly well," he convinced himself. *Yeah, I'm one of the good guys now.*

Ollie ran as quickly as he could, the tears streaming down his face. He began running toward the police station but stopped cold in the middle of the street, which was busy with people. No one noticed him. He stared at the police station. He could see the busted window. Everything the twins had said was real. He couldn't go there. *What if Mister Smith really is in there?*

Ollie swallowed hard.

He walked into an alley and sat behind a barrel, sobbing. He shouldn't have hit Newt but Newt shouldn't have embarrassed him like that. He sat with his head between his knees and his face in his hands. He couldn't feel any more sorry for himself.

I still don't believe Thomas.

Ollie forced himself up and wiped his eyes with his sleeve. He was braver than that. He would go to the police station and see what was going on himself.

"You're the worst, Newton Bullington. You are!" Ollie spoke into the empty air and then emerged back on the street unnoticed.

He was only half a block from the police station and headed straightway to the building where a police officer stood, looking out into the bustling street.

"Good afternoon, sir." Ollie looked up at the tall man in uniform.

"Run along, little boy," the officer replied, looking straight ahead.

"But is Mister Smith inside there?" Ollie asked, pointing at the door to the station.

The officer looked down at him. "Yes. Headmaster Smith is inside there."

Ollie's blood went cold.

His jaw shook. His whole body shook. "Thank you," he stammered, ready to return to the St. Jerome's full of apologies and news. The thin boy felt all the smaller in that moment. With his first step back, he stepped on someone's foot. His shoulders thudded against a large man behind him. He turned around on his heel. "I'm so sorry, sir," he stuttered.

The large man reached down and grabbed Oliver by the shoulder. Ollie felt the gloved hand as he tried to run. His legs got away from him, but he was going nowhere.

Ollie swallowed nervously.

The man came down on one knee.

"Hello, young man," he said with a smile.

It was the sheriff.

"Hello, Sheriff." Ollie replied, anxiously.

The sheriff smiled sympathetically. "I just noticed you talking to the officer and was wondering if I could help you."

"No sir, I am quite fine." Oliver answered. "The officer was very helpful." He smiled.

"Yes. Well, that there is the problem, little brother." The sheriff smirked. "Why would anyone think that the Headmaster was in that building right there?"

Oliver's eyes grew large. "I don't know." His stammering words slipped out on scared breath.

"Where are the two other rats?" The sheriff growled. "Or are they not even smart enough to hide?" He smiled.

Oliver's eyes gave him away. He looked at the orphanage, fearing for them and himself.

"No, no." The sheriff smiled. "We're doing this my way," he said aloud, despite the fact that the boy could hear him.

Ollie was confused and realized he'd been wrong.

"What is your name, little boy?" The sheriff asked, still on one knee.

Oliver did not want to help him. He realized the boys were right. It meant trouble. The sheriff did not wait for an answer. He grabbed the little boy by the arm and squeezed. "Tell me your name."

The tears burst from the boy. "Ollie. I'm Ollie Whipple."

"Very good," the sheriff replied. "Now look at me, Ollie."

The little boy looked up at the man's face. Where there should have been a pair of eyes, Ollie saw nothing but translucent black smoke.

They walked along together quietly toward the orphanage. No one noticed them.

The door to St. Jerome's was unlocked when the Sheriff pushed it open. Oliver Whipple walked ahead of him quietly. As he entered the large common area that had some bunk beds and cots, he could see into the kitchen where two young girls were preparing a communal dinner.

A boy with a round face mended a pair of pants with a string and needle and one taller, older boy swept the floor in a hallway behind the bunks.

The sheriff wasn't going to play the charade. He called out, "Thomas, Edwin. Come out. We need to have a talk." No one looked up. They continued doing their chores. He walked into the room and said "Ollie, show me where their belongings are." Ollie raised his arm without moving and pointed at a bunk. The sheriff went and began opening trinket boxes and suitcases.

He realized that the orphanage had nothing. There were no resources. It was more of a boarding house than a genuine orphanage.

Thomas and Edwin's clothing was missing. Their beds were made. There was every indication that they hadn't returned, but the Sheriff couldn't figure out how the little boy would have so quickly guessed that the headmaster was in the jail and not dead. He sat on his knees between the bunks and looked at Ollie again; his blank stare was more familiar than the panicked one from earlier. It wouldn't last long—he didn't have the power that the Vampyres did.

The sheriff stood up and dusted off his pants. "Someone in this room needs to tell me where Thomas and Edwin went," he scolded.

"They went out," said the boy mending his pants.

"Out," the sheriff replied as he moved closer to the boy. "Out, when?"

"Yesterday," the boy replied. "Thomas and Edwin went out yesterday." He then continued sewing.

The sheriff could not believe him, but it made sense. The taller boy walked by with the broom. He was older and built like he could have been a fighter. "You, boy." The sheriff said to him.

"Yes sir?" the boy asked quietly.

"What do you know about the two boys, Thomas and Edwin?" the sheriff asked.

"Quite a bit, sir," he replied.

"When was the last time you saw them?"

"Yesterday afternoon. They had gone to run an errand for Headmaster Smith but neither of them ever returned."

The Sheriff was obviously frustrated. "What errand?"

"I do not know. They left early yesterday afternoon but did not return."

The Sheriff walked past the boy and looked into the short corridor that led to another room. He pushed the door open to see twin boys with red hair cleaning the room out.

Newton, who sat near the fireplace pretending to mend pants, which he did not know how to do, looked up at Ollie and whispered "Oliver, what are you doing?"

Ollie turned, but his look was blank; there was no life in his eyes.

"Ollie. You've got to snap out of it." Newton whispered, "You're not really the worst."

The boy's blank stare give Newton the chills, but he only sat there looking.

In the headmaster's bedroom, there were boxes with the man's personal belongings and the bed was neatly made.

"What are you doing?" The sheriff shouted.

The twin on the left, which was Henry, replied, "Preparing for the next headmaster."

The sheriff laughed. He looked under the bed and around the room; there were books of fiction, letters and all manner of personal effects but nothing he could use. He walked back to the door. "There will be no more headmasters." He smiled.

The large man walked into the common room again and spoke very loudly so as to be heard by everyone. "Mister Smith is to be hanged tomorrow for murder." There was a small gasp from the kitchen. He smiled. "You will all go to work at the mines after that."

He walked toward the door. "Have a pleasant evening."

Oliver followed after him quietly.

I lya Constantine was as close to restless as Pavl had ever known him to be. Pavl stood at the door to Ilya's chamber but did not enter. Ilya paced slowly from one corner to the other and back. His energy pulsed through the walls. Pavl could sense it, a figure eight pattern, meandering back and forth; a wolf in a trap or a moth at a flame. Ilya was far more troubled than he would let on, but they were all suffering the anxiety of uncertainty. None of them, with the exception of Letsya—that old slob—and perhaps Isaac, had slept at all. Isaac lived in his own world, and if he could not longer feel the anxiety of the covenant, then maybe he wasn't really their leader anymore. *No,* he thought, *I can't think of him like that. Isaac saved us. He gave us a home.* But Isaac lived in his head now. Walking the halls, thinking. He spent most of his days alone. Since Ilya had returned from Cairo, working for the magistrate, Isaac avoided him. *Something went wrong. It's all gone wrong.* The long hallways of the underground complex that housed the Brethren were much like the tunnels of an anthill. They were burrowed long ago by other kinds of creatures. The work of burrowing anthills was not for Vampyres.

Even before the Crusades and the Spanish Inquisition, Vampyres had started becoming frail. Their strength was superhuman, but the Vampyres could easily be destroyed by the tools of the very Church that they had served for centuries: holy water, the symbolic cross and the incantations and prayers of exorcism could take the life of immortal creatures, many of whom had been sworn to the church. Centuries later, they lay in catacombs and tunnels, caverns and tombs throughout the world, seeking refuge in darkness. Vampyres, once men of renown, were now the abandoned detritus of decadent ages now past. They were relegated to this so-called life of subservience to the Alliance. The Magistrate of the Black Court was a toothless entity. No Vampyre had been raised to the High Seat of the Light Bringer in thousands of years. The Sin Eaters had all been hunted down and executed by the church. And that man, Gallegos, followed them throughout the ages. His name was beginning to come up in delvings each night. Yes, something was wrong below Breton.

The complex that sprawled under the town of Breton was the newest and most intricate in design. No light entered and it would take a great deal of force to penetrate its depths from outside. The complex was large, carved out by creatures much older than the Vampyres themselves, creatures that the Vampyres had once controlled. Once called Builders, the Druids were horrible, banal little people who solely existed to manipulate the elements. All they ever talked about was "nature this" and "Gaia that." But didn't they know that they too had been thrown on the midden heap? How was the earth going to save them? The world had already betrayed them. But still they worked, as if their prayers would soon be answered, as if they weren't forsaken too, forgotten revenants of another time.

The Vampyres didn't care about the work anymore. The decay had been slow, the centuries unkind and unforgiving. In years, Vampyres went from high courts and sunlight to exile in the dark places: the catacombs of Paris, the labyrinth under the Vatican, the immense sewers of London. The High Seat itself, sat abandoned in Cairo with other antiquities apparently in the "care" of the Library of Alexandria. In the far East, there were still some refuges in the mountains, some said, but even that had grown into myth. In this new land across the ocean, wickedness reigned. And that meant a meal from time to time and darkness for those who could find rest.

Do you sleep, Ilya? Pavl asked quietly.

Not in thirty years, Pavl. He answered quietly.

It is done. Pavl said.

Do not tell me where she is hidden. Simply take her home when the time comes, he told Pavl. Ilya lay on his back with his hands behind his head, staring at the ceiling. The chandelier in his room danced very slowly as the air from outside had moved it.

Pavl stood in the doorway but did not leave. Ilya sighed. *What is it, Pavl?*

What about the other girl? The courier's niece. Pavl asked.

She's inconsequential now, we were just delving her for information. The lips of his perfect mouth curled with anger. *In her mind, I saw Algernon Elliott and other demon hunters. I saw the Rosicrucian himself, the wizard really is here. But it doesn't matter.*

Finally he smiled. *The innkeeper's daughter, Pavl. She is ours. And in her mind, I hear echoes of the song.*

But Ilya, Pavl said, *that's just a story.*

Ilya's anger dissipated with Pavl's words, why would he take the time to explain himself to the idiot? *Of course, it's just a story.* wasn't clear on what that would be. He closed the door and was quickly surprised by Zoya, the darkest and most beautiful of all the Vampyres. She stood there listening.

So Pavl, what's the plan? she asked.

Go away, Zoya, he replied. *If Ilya wanted you to know, he would tell you.* Pavl turned to walk away, but she followed.

Well, since you don't know... She watched him cross his arms as he walked. *Maybe I could just ask him myself.*

Then suddenly and quietly, Pavl started, *I do know the plan!*

She grinned at him.

But I do! he retorted.

Pavl, she smiled, *I don't have to be inside your head to know when you're lying.*

He stopped walking and turned to her. *It's about the innkeeper's daughter and...*

Pavl! A voice came from down the hall.

Zoya narrowed her eyes. The look she gave Pavl could have curdled blood.

Pavl's brother Rurk, the least intelligent but most loyal of the Brethren, stopped him from talking. *We do not discuss the plan*, Rurk thought. *Ever.*

Zoya spoke up, *But...*

Rurk had no problem scolding her, shoulder-to-shoulder with his brother. *I will tell Ilya.*

Zoya exposed her sharp fangs. *I'll tell Isaac.*

Rurk grabbed his brother by the shoulder before addressing her again, *There's work to be done and no need to discuss it.*

Zoya knew that she would not tell Isaac. She could tell no one.

Darkness was setting across the face of the ocean. Michael had spent the longest day of his life, at least that he could remember, at the bottom of the sea hiding from the light of the sun. He had found rubble and stones to cover himself with. He passed the day healing from the Vampyre's bite and the powerful blow against his chest. Michael began seeing things very differently while he made himself comfortable at the ocean's floor.

Throughout the day, he could sense fish and all sorts of animals smelling and coming down the current toward him, but none of them approached him. There was fear in them. He could sense it through the water. Even the large dark bodies, the sharks and whales out in the cold water, left him in peace.

He swam to the surface, pushing through the sheet of water and forced himself up onto it as though climbing through a hole in the floor. He had seen the Vampyre levitating and over the last hours at the bottom of the sea, he had figured out how to make himself do the same. Up then down without swimming. It was easier than he thought.

Michael kept his eyes on the ship that had once been his home. It was probably three-quarters of a mile away and at any point he could have swam toward it at the bottom, but his anger kept him still at the seafloor. He was also tired of being in the water. He was full of rage, but it had cauterized into a bitter calm. He was a new creature as he steered himself in the direction of the ship. The hours in the darkness had presented him with numerous ideas. His resolve to destroy the Vampyres of Breton had only been solidified. He was going to talk to Mister Williams and he was going to break Breton from the clench of whatever tyranny was stifling it. With time, if he couldn't find out who he was or how he'd become the monster that he failed to see in mirrors, he would destroy himself as well.

Michael had imagined Breton across a grid. He could see each alley and dead-end. He could see every door and window. He visualized the war that was happening on the outskirts of the town, the farce of battle that fed the Vampyre clan. His otherworldly powers were growing and his anger honed his vision into a clear plan.

He would shift things around for the Vampyres. The planning was a second nature. He couldn't remember what he'd done before, but it may have had something to do with strategies. He didn't care anymore.

First he would find Mister Williams and then he'd speak to the righteous soldier and Kat and once they were of one accord, he'd set his plan into motion.

He was walking inches above the water, organizing his thoughts. It was only a few moments before Michael flew up to the bow of the ship where he landed softly to retrieve his coat off the peg where he'd left it.

Much better. He pulled his arms through the sleeves of the small coat. *Perhaps I'll get something a little smarter in town tonight, though.*

THREE

Satan: I will have Human blood, and not the blood of bulls or goats,
And no Atonement, O Jehovah! The Elohim live on Sacrifice
of Men: hence I am God of Men! Thou human, O Jehovah!
By the rock and oak of the Druid, creeping mistletoe, and thorn,
Cain's city built with human blood, not blood of bulls and goats,
Thou shalt Thyself be sacrificed to Me, thy God! on Calvary.
- **William Blake,** *The Ghost of Abel (1822)*

Corporal Vogt was caught on a branch. He'd heard a man crying out for help. There was a young, red-haired soldier, who was shot in the leg, praying with rosary in hand. The shadows of dusk were giving way in the half-light to night. Vogt had dragged the man as far as he could and it had caused him to get caught in the brambles. The young soldier did everything he could to stand up, but he was losing a lot of blood.

"Come on!" He dragged the man backwards through the brambles until he got himself caught. He pulled at the branch that had hooked into his skin. With another step to the left, Vogt found himself caught in another bush. He began to panic, "Help me, man! Help me!"

The soldier just lay there, crying and bleeding. Vogt had found himself in a predicament. "Always trying to be a hero, Corporal Vogt," he scolded himself. He couldn't get the branch out of his shirt and he could feel the trickle of blood running down his back and his shoulder.

Then he calmed down. He knew time was precious. "Give me your gun, soldier." He reached for the man on the ground.

The weeping soldier looked up to Vogt and collapsed.

"Your gun!"

The young man trembled as he reached to his belt and removed the gun. He was losing a lot of blood and his freckled skin was beginning to go pale.

Vogt snatched the gun from him. He quickly turned and, against his better judgment, fired a bullet into the branch, freeing him of the snag.

It reminded him of something: his surroundings, the smell of the air and the weight of the gun. He couldn't shake the déjà vu. There was something in him that smelled of a murderous streak.

Guilty. Guilty. Guilty. He heard them coming from a distance. He had a few hundred yards before he could reach the safety of the encampment. If he didn't make it, he knew what would come next.

"No Vampyre chow tonight. Not me," he replied to the sound that came. They were getting closer. It felt like an oppressive weight on Vogt's mind.

Guilty.

He looked down at the soldier, who could hear it too. "Please help me!"

Vogt didn't hesitate. He raised the gun and fired a bullet into the young man's head. He could hear them. A depression washed over them.

Guilty. Guilty.

I know. He made his run toward the encampment. Campfires flickered and the soldiers reflected on their day, glad to be alive. There were bizarre thoughts among them. Weren't reinforcements supposed to be coming? Who was in charge? Why could no one remember his life or home before the war? There was a peculiar mumbling around the campfires. Many men did not eat.

Corporal Vogt looked at the gun in his hand. He could feel something inside him coming to life. "I killed a man," he mumbled at the gun as he walked back to the mess. Memories flashed before his eyes.

Sergeant Cornwall played with his mustache as he watched the fire. "We all have." The fire crackled and he looked across to see Vogt distressed. "It's just part of it."

"No, Sergeant," Vogt replied. "In cold blood." He obsessed over the gun. He remembered the weight of it in his hand and the way it was too hot once it had been fired. The way he had been careful with it after shooting it. He couldn't remember the rest.

Sergeant Cornwall sat up. "Vogt, you just did what you had to do. That man was a goner. I don't know why you went back for him anyway."

Vogt's eyes were cold. He looked across the fire and leaned in. "No. Before all of this, I killed someone." He looked around. It seemed surreal. He was certain he was in some purgatory. "I killed someone and that's why I'm here." Cornwall just listened as something dark started growing inside of him. "That's why we're all here, Sergeant." The murmur among the men was increasing.

"That's not all." Vogt reached down and put a hand to his chest. There was a wicked gleam in his eye.

"Every man here is guilty of something, I'm sure," Cornwall admitted, trying not to let his contemplation get out of hand.

"Not all of us are men, Sarge." Vogt replied. His wicked, crystalline blue eyes shined with evil. "I killed my husband."

"Husband, Vogt?" Cornwall stood up. "You're shaken up from your ordeal." The corporal was beginning to make him nervous. "Why don't you go back to your tent, get some rest?"

Vogt undid the top button of the heavy uniform shirt to reveal cotton bandages tied across his chest. "I remember now. I dressed as a man to avoid being arrested for my husband's death. I joined the army. Then I woke up here."

Cornwall just listened to the whisper of the Vampyres in the distance. "Guilty. Guilty," they hissed.

"Welcome to hell, sarge." Vogt said.

You're disappointing people," came the nasal voice of Desmond Burroughs. Desmond was the leader of Breton's "League" and Breton's only judge. His face was skeletal and what had once been dark brown eyes sat atop bags. The skin of his face was saggy and he was balding—his remaining grayed hair slicked back. His clothes were stylish and new, unlike most people in town.

Parson Adler sat back in the chair behind the pulpit of the small church building. He rolled his eyes. He hated few things as much as he hated Desmond. Breton had made Desmond a very wealthy man and he lived a very comfortable life. He was one of a few people that lived comfortably. Like most, Parson Adler did not.

"I realize that you've grown..." Burroughs paused, "less than motivated about our objectives, Adler but..."

"Save the contrived speech, Desmond," the parson interrupted. "I'm well aware of what you're going to try on me and I don't care." He stretched. "I have spent nearly thirty years in this place with diminishing returns and awful living quarters and a pack of bloodthirsty fools to ruin everything we do for them." He watched the man's face. "*I* am disappointed, Desmond."

Burroughs waited quietly, his mouth curled with displeasure; it wasn't the first time they'd had that conversation, but Desmond knew this would certainly be the last.

"What are they going to do? Torture me like the train station manager? Brainwash me? Desmond, it doesn't matter now. I've run this experiment of theirs' as effectively as anyone could. It's the Vampyres who should be tortured."

"That's not my department," Burroughs responded. "Nor do I care."

"Then let's get this over with." Parson Adler stood up and walked over to a file that lay on a small table. The pages had shifted out of it and were dangerously close to where the candles dripping on the table would run across them. The parson didn't notice.

"Yes," Desmond replied, "I have a carriage waiting for me." He walked to where an inkwell sat undisturbed, surrounded by obvious ink stains. He was beginning to hate the conversation.

Parson Adler laid the paperwork out for him. "Two. To be hanged on the third day." He iterated, despondent and indifferent. "Ernest Williams to be hanged for the murder of the mayor." The Parson tried not to show his disgust over the matter, knowing. He turned the page as Desmond signed. Guilty. "And Neville Smith, the orphanage's headmaster, for the murder of the courier girl, Genevieve Moreau."

Desmond signed both of their death warrants as he had signed thousands before. "Very clever about the Mister Smith. Wasn't he hired?"

"Yes," Parson Adler replied. "You hired him."

"Unfortunate how those things work out sometimes."

"Unfortunate." He answered without veiling his sarcasm.

Desmond just smiled at him. After a moment he replied, "Have a good night, Parson."

Adler sat silently as he pulled out his pipe and matches.

Desmond laughed, "I'll let myself out." He grabbed his hat and coat that lay across the back of one of the pews. "Oh." Desmond said, "I've always meant to ask." He turned to the Parson with a sardonic smile. "Is it not strange to smoke in your condition?" After a long silence, he let out a big and awkward laugh. "Or is it comforting?" His dark eyes squinted with laughter.

"Get out," Adler replied quietly.

"Good night," he replied.

He's up to something, Adler thought. But then again, Desmond was always up to something. He was the worst kind of man, the indifferent bureaucrat that would trade the life of anyone to clean off the paperwork on his desk.

He was singular in his greed and people, aside from the League, did not like being around him. His first wife had died young, which Adler had presumed was less accidental than it had seemed. His second wife had gone mad and was locked up somewhere. It made sense. *Who could stand to be near such a person?*

As the despicable bureaucrat left the church, the parson let out a sigh. Hate was not his function.

Desmond turned to the tall man in the blue uniform off in the shadows as he walked out the door. "You know what to do."

"Yes sir." The sheriff stepped forward out of the darkness. "Are you sure this is the best way?"

Desmond did not turn toward him as he stepped up into the carriage. "You will not question me." He left the door to be closed. "Unless you want an ashy grave tomorrow, you terrible idiot."

The sheriff did not speak. He closed the carriage door and tapped on its side. It pulled away with the clop of the horses' footfall.

We're all dead now, the sheriff thought as he disappeared into the darkness.

M ichael made his way into Breton, listening for voices he might recognize. He could hear the thoughts of so many people. He could hear the voices of children, the repetitive droning of songs and laughter in the inn and the chatter of townsfolk. The one common note was unrelenting fear.

He walked along unnoticed.

Some police officers came running down the street and he disappeared into a shadow. He could read their thoughts. They sounded like echoes. Their thoughts were hollow and he was sure they were not theirs at all. They were like the echoes of something told to them. They weren't officers at all. They were weapons.

He could smell the guilt on them. He could sense that they had both done terrible things in their lives. They had committed crimes worthy of death. *These are the officers of the law in this place? I don't think I want to know what the law is.*

In the drone of thoughts he could hear a voice he knew counting out letters, spelling.

V-e-r-y s-o-o-n

Very soon? Michael repeated.

T-h-e-y and then he waited *h-a-n-g* and another pause *u-s.*

Very soon, they hang us. Michael went over it again. *It's Ernest!*

Michael panicked. The only friend he had was in trouble. He climbed to the top of a short building with a rusted, slanting roof and looked over the town. He felt for Ernest. *East.* Two streets over and across the square he could see the police station. Michael quickly jumped across to another building then leapt across the street looking over the town square. Immediately south was where he had met Ernest for the first time. He could hear the quiet thoughts of the general store shopkeeper and his wife speaking in hushed whispers. There were no voices in any of the other buildings. To the north he could feel something strong, not human, supernatural and very calm. Whatever it was, it was evil.

He closed in on the police station. *Three guards. Two outside, one inside.*

He wouldn't risk the battle; instead he would learn the nature of the problem. Quickly, Michael climbed up a small tree and jumped across to another. He quietly jumped from the large branch across to a tall office building.

He didn't make a sound. He climbed on the roof of the building and then hopped down onto roof of the police station, which wasn't more than a shanty itself. He came down gracefully right behind the building where he could sense the heat of the presence of two men.

They had been communicating. Morse code. *Accomplices.* Instinctively Michael knew he would have to trust the other man, whoever he was.

Ernest. Michael thought.

There was a silence, but Michael could sense paranoia from the cell.

Ernest, it is I, Michael, your friend. He paused. *I am outside the cell. I heard you say that they are to hang you tomorrow.*

There was laughter that came from the cell.

You can read my thinking, Michael? came Ernest's voice.

I have learned much about myself recently, he answered.

Very good, Ernest replied. *It would seem so have I. That is to say, I've learned much about myself, not you.* Even in thought, Ernest was long-winded. *How have you fared?*

Michael chuckled. *You're in jail and ask how I am doing?*

Well, Ernest thought, *I worry.*

I've survived so far. Going to have a word with some people in charge soon though, I think.

Ah good. Maybe you can talk some sense into someone.

Should I break you from this place, Ernest? Michael asked. He could hear the man sigh from inside the cell.

No. Ernest answered. *There are bigger things afoot and I'm afraid my escape would not help much.* He waited a moment. *And I am quite afraid I'd not know where to hide myself in any case. Not much of a vigilante, my lad.*

We have to do something, Michael argued. He could feel Ernest's resignation through the wall.

Oh yes, Ernest agreed, *there is much to be done.* Michael listened. *There are many people in this town that will be of service to you if you let them know your intentions.* Ernest paused. *The sheriff brought in a young boy from the orphanage; he is under some spell of sorts, I would think. I think they might do the same to others. You must find help; there have to be people who are willing to fight. I don't know how you will find them, but I promise, now that I've had some sober thinking, I think this town is quite ready for a revolution. Don't you?*

I do. Tell me what to do, Ernest. How can I be of some service to you?

Well, it is a surprise that you're here, to be honest, Ernest replied.

You're my friend.

Silence.

Michael, you've already saved my life once. No, you have given me my life. I owe you the greatest debt of gratitude. I looked up this morning and felt the sun on my face, and I was myself. My thoughts were clear. Today, I went to work. Today, I had a small life. You gave me today. I'm no longer their prisoner. Ernest grew solemn. *Find Kat, she'll know what to do. People around town believe she's crazy, but she's not. There are children in this town. These police officers come in and out like they're preparing for war. There is soon to be much bloodshed here. Maybe she can help save them. Michael, if you should need a place to hide, you can go to my home. No one should be there for a day or two. You need not be Caliban. You are your own master.* Ernest could sense the Vampyre was gone.

We are our own masters, Michael. Go do what I can't.

W hat are we going to do?" Newton Bullington asked Patrick Foster, who ignored him completely. Patrick ran into the corridor and pushed boxes out of the way to access the ladder. There was a padlock on the door and they'd left Thomas and Edwin upstairs on the roof with a box of Headmaster Smith's personal belongings and their own boxes and suitcases thrown up there haphazardly. They'd hid the things in an attempt to outsmart the sheriff but, with the coast cleared, it was time to bring the belongings back inside.

Thomas had been organizing their belongings anxiously since they could do nothing but wait. Edwin simply perused Mister Smith's things.

"Mister Elliott was right." In the large box, Edwin saw a revolver, which Mister Smith would have explained was a Webley revolver, his standard-issue sidearm that he'd trusted with his life for almost ten years. "A Headmaster of an orphanage would not need a gun, would he?"

Thomas heard the padlock rattling on the roof's access door. "The last headmaster got killed in the street by Vampyres while buying groceries and this one is in jail for a murder done by the police." He sighed. "This has to be the only town that would need it."

"How do we know the police did the murdering though?" Edwin replied.

"Well, I don't, to be honest." Thomas remarked. "It just made sense in my head."

The hatch opened slowly and Patrick stuck his head through. "It worked!"

Thomas and Edwin smiled at each other over their first successful mission.

"But the sheriff has Ollie," he continued.

"Let's get to work then," Edwin replied.

"That's two people we need back," Thomas said quietly. He handed the organized boxes to Edwin, who began handing them to Patrick.

"Newt, Henry, Archie, come help." Patrick called down the ladder and the boys could hear rustling downstairs. They passed the boxes back.

Taking a box from Edwin, Patrick asked, "How did you know that the sheriff would come looking for you?"

Edwin didn't answer, but Thomas answered, passing the last box down to him, "Because he said so. Also, Mister Elliott, who is Mister Smith's friend, said that they would stop at nothing." He paused.

Edwin continued for him. "We don't know anything but we can't take any chances."

The boxes were shuffled back into St. Jerome's and left at the foot of the stairs. The boys climbed down one at a time until Thomas closed the hatch.

They all went back to the common room, but Thomas stopped in the corridor. There was candlelight coming from Headmaster Smith's room. He wasn't there. Edwin could feel the emptiness where he had once been. He returned and blew the candle out as he looked over the empty room and shut the door. *We're going to save you, Mister Smith. I promise.*

As the boys filed into the room, Newton was preparing bowls of the stew that had been cooking. The girls were cleaning up. Alexander and Albert had made a poor attempt at hiding in a cupboard. Had the sheriff searched St. Jerome's, they would have been easily found, but that was all right. It would have posed more questions for the sheriff and, consequently, diverted his attention away from Thomas and Edwin.

They all talked in hushed voices and Newton brought the stew out to them. It had troubled him deeply to see Ollie that way with a blank stare like the people outside. He couldn't remember having been that way but, until earlier that day, he was sure he had looked very much the same.

Alexander was the first to begin eating. "Have you ever been so hungry in all your life?" He shoveled the stew into his mouth, holding the bowl up under his chin.

Patrick realized that he too was quite hungry but couldn't understand why. Patrick had been running the spoon along the edge of the bowl thinking. "I have a sense of you and Thomas, Edwin," he said, looking up. "But it feels like trying to remember a dream. I just," he struggled with the words, "I just feel like I knew you were there."

Albert agreed, "Mister Smith too."

Everyone agreed. The twins were especially vocal.

"This is an awful curse they made us live under," said Emily.

Penny added, "Is it not strange to all of you to miss a person who you don't remember meeting?"

"Yes. It is, Penny." Patrick replied. "But I know deep down that Mister Smith took care of us. I don't have to remember it to know that I know it."

Thomas and Edwin had never considered the feelings of the other orphans before. They had always just felt that they were the strange ones. There was a terrible guilt in knowing that the others had all been prisoners inside their own minds.

Thomas looked toward the corridor where the boxes sat. "Tomorrow we get to the plan." He thought about the letter that Mister Elliott had given him. He thought about the weight of it and the round thing inside of the envelope. He thought about the words that Mister Elliott had told him before handing the envelope and letter to him.

"This letter is the only thing that can save Spencer's life." He told them. He clarified that Mister Smith was indeed Spencer Mayhew and that he was a good man. To Thomas, he was still Mister Smith, the best man he'd ever known. He would get the letter to him somehow. He would save his life.

The carriage had been parked in front of the Crow's Nest Inn for about twenty minutes when Desmond decided to emerge from within. A young officer came to his side to inform him that the deed had been done.

"Good," the man replied. "I don't want to lose any sleep over it."

The officer opened the door and Desmond walked inside. There were numerous unknown faces, but the room got quiet when he entered. The police presence did not bother them, but everyone knew who the well-dressed man was. They did not know how much power he had, but he rode his carriage in and around the town at night without any fear. Everyone respected that the Vampyres did not attack him.

The tavern turned into a hush as though a teacher had entered a classroom of rowdy students.

The barman, Glenn, was wiping down a table. He turned around to see Desmond standing in the doorway.

"Innkeep," he called sarcastically, "I'd like my room prepared."

Glenn threw the rag down and clenched his jaw. He looked like a dog right before it bites into its prey. The young police officer pulled out his baton and stood in front of the old bureaucrat. The young man watched Glenn cross the room. His misery, rage and grief were boiling and could be seen in the red around his eyes. Desmond simply arched an eyebrow.

"Halt." The police officer commanded.

"After what you've done?" Glenn asked through his teeth. "You have some nerve." His voice bubbled with anger. The bearded man was menacingly large and towered over the officer and Desmond.

"Do I have some quarrel with you, innkeeper?" Desmond asked nonchalantly. His face curled like he smelled something awful, but it was really his simple disdain for that kind of confrontation. It was below him to be yelled at and even more so to ever feel like he should yell. He took his hat off.

Glenn swallowed. He knew what that man was and represented. "My wife. Now my daughter," he replied.

There was no way that the police officer would be able to stop Glenn if he wanted to crush the two men, but he stood there. The room became silent.

"Aw, yes." The frail man replied to the giant in front of him. "The sheriff reported to me that your daughter seems to have gone missing." He ignored the accusation.

"Seems?" the large man asked. "I know what you do, Burroughs," he continued. "I know who you are. No one disappears in this town without your consent."

The small man smiled. "Yes, I suppose it works that way. Very effective language. I appreciate that. Not an easy thing—running a town and what not—but in this circumstance it would seem that I have no idea about the whereabouts of your daughter."

Glenn did not know why but he believed the man.

"As I said before, I do not remember having any quarrel with you, Innkeeper and if you want to continue running your..." he looked around, "quaint establishment, you will not seek to have such a quarrel with me."

Glenn got quiet quickly and looked down at his shoes. "Someone will have your bags up in a moment."

"Thank you, Innkeeper." The old man smiled.

Desmond walked by and made his way up the stairs with the young police officer behind him.

Glenn felt his shoulders collapsing in. He stood there with his head hanging and his chin against his chest. He dragged his feet to close the door feeling useless, impotent and stupid, as though no one could help him.

The room began to move again and the conversation and sound of laughter resumed. Glenn was utterly alone.

He collapsed in a chair in the kitchen.

He couldn't stop thinking about Kat. She was beautiful like her mother had been. She was smart and funny. His mind flashed between thoughts of who she was with what was happening to her.

As his memories cleared of the curse, he began remembering the Vampyres and remembering Kat's mother, what she had done to them and how Desmond came and took her away. His memory was blank beyond that.

Kat wasn't like her Mother, though; she didn't have that same dark sadness in her heart. He knew Kat couldn't be charmed by the Vampyres the same way and that she didn't sympathize with them like her mother had done so many years ago.

He experienced the sharp betrayal all over again. He didn't even want to think his wife's name. Kat was so much stronger and if the Vampyres had her, they would resort to violence and horrible things. He tried not to think about it.

She doesn't deserve that, he thought. He felt the life leaving him. He would be an empty shell without her. She was his life force. He would trade his own life in that instant to see her happy and breathing again.

But she was dead. He knew it.

How could they have lived in such a horrid place for so long? He couldn't remember anything except the sudden image of his wife in his mind, smiling. His head was foggy and the grieving just made it worse.

He held in his tears. He was so weak. He just wanted to cry.

Night had fallen on all of Breton. Stephen Adler smiled at the ceiling. He always tried to fall asleep before his uncle but instead his mind wandered from shade to shadow, from flick of light to silhouette that might give way to the wind. Stephen was fifteen years old, but he had the mind of a child. He had always been that way. The people of Breton loved him. He was something pure.

He was innocent, but he was sad. Something felt wrong inside his mind.

His uncle tossed in his bed across the room, restlessly. That was his way. Stephen had never worried because it had always been that way. His uncle seemed to wrestle in his dreams. He lay on his side with his back to Stephen, who reached toward the ceiling, making shadows against the wall.

The light of the moon entered through a small window. The room glowed a soft blue in the darkness and there was an eerie quiet.

Stephen sat up quietly with his arms to his side.

He cast his legs off the bed, stood up and then walked slowly outside. The wind seemed to stop blowing. A figure stood in the shadow. There wasn't a sound in the world. Only silence. Stephen's strange urge was like that of a fish on a line.

Confused, he wandered into the dark.

FOUR

Birth is not the beginning of life - only of an individual
awareness. Change into another state is not death -
only the ending of this awareness.
— Hermes Trismegistus, *Corpus Hermeticum*
(148 AD)

The next day, the morning bell was half an hour late. Albert Perry stood dressed neatly on the corner of the street just a few feet from the door of the orphanage. He eyed the bustling street; there were people going in every direction. He signaled to Newton, who sat on a park bench in the middle of the town square.

Newton's feet didn't touch the floor and they swung in rhythm, nervously, as he signaled across the square. Everyone was ready.

Two guards stood at the door of the small police station. Inside, Mister Smith and Mister Williams sat quietly, awaiting the unknown. Thomas and Edwin approached the front of the building. Edwin called out, "Hey! Tell the old sheriff that the errand boys are out here!" One guard ran down on the steps and stopped, hesitating, waiting for orders. The boys waited. The second guard ran inside to find the sheriff, who screamed from inside, "Get them!"

The guards exploded through the door.

The boys cut through people in the crowded street, elbowing and ducking between them. The first guard, yards ahead of the second, ran and pushed to catch the boys who split up in the crowd.

The sheriff came outside to see where they'd gone. The orphans were playing a trick on him. Were they trying to break the Headmaster out? He looked inside and there the man sat quietly. *What are you doing?*

The first guard continued running through the park and reached for the shorter boy. He crashed into Emily and Penny Hughes, whom he didn't recognize. "I'm so sorry for my clumsiness, ladies," he apologized, keeping his eye on the boy who, by then, was rounding the corner at the inn. He made a dash away from the girls and turned the corner to see the little boy sitting next to the work entrance to the inn. He sat there eating a loaf of old bread.

"Don't run," the officer demanded. "I will shoot you."

The boy looked up, but it wasn't the same one who had called out earlier.

"What?" the little boy asked, terrified at the threat.

"Where's the boy?" the officer asked, confused.

"Boy?" the child replied.

"Where's the boy that came running through here?"

"No one has come this way, sir," the boy answered quietly, intimidated.

The officer walked away and Alexander Shaw sat, a smile cracking across his face. He chewed on the stale bread. *Edwin was right. They are idiots!*

Just inside the inn, Edwin hid under the bar next to Glenn's leg. The boys had found a new ally in the old innkeeper. He watched the police officer walking away through the window, confused. "Looks like you boys are on to something," he thought aloud as he cleaned out a glass with a bar rag.

The second police officer, followed by two other officers, clambered along the street. They watched the taller boy disappear behind a horse and carriage near the church.

The boy passed Parson Adler, running, who barely noticed. As the officers came running by, he asked, "Have any of you men seen my nephew?"

The last of the three officers answered, "No sir. Not this morning." And he ran on.

They finally closed in on the tall boy and tackled him. "I got you, you cretin!" The man who led the race toward the boy turned him over and immediately hit him, blacking his eye.

The boy grabbed his face. He was on the verge of tears. There was a sense of victory inside of him, though. He hid his smile in his hands. The other guards came and picked him up to drag him back.

The very first officer, who had found Alexander at the inn, approached the others as they dragged the tall boy back. Another officer asked him, "What happened to the other boy?"

Winded and confused, he answered, "He got away."

"Well, we got the other one at least." The leader replied.

The officers carried the kicking boy up the stairs as he complained, "What did I do? I do not deserve to be chased and punched."

The first officer responded by throwing a large fist into his ribs and the boy coughed in pain.

"I suppose you shouldn't have made us all work so much then," the officer grimaced sarcastically.

They carried him inside and the boy looked across the room into the cell where Mister Smith sat. Deep down the boy smiled.

Spencer looked up and recognized the boy. "Patrick!" he called out.

The sheriff sat up from his desk. "What is this?" he asked.

The officer answered. "Sir, we found one of the boys from the incident."

"Incident?" the sheriff asked.

"Yes sir," he replied. "One of the two orphans. The 'errand boys.'"

"Orphan, yes," the sheriff answered. "Wrong orphan."

Patrick looked at Spencer. "Mister Smith, Why are you in here?"

"Patrick, my boy—"

The sheriff interrupted. "Get that scum out of here." Then he turned to Spencer. "You. Shut your mouth."

The sheriff eyed the boy with a grin. "Why don't you go back to the orphanage? I'm sure you're needed there." He paused. "What was it Patrick? Or Marcus?"

Spencer watched quietly as they let the boy go, pushing him with a heavy hand out the door.

"Go on, get out of here." One of the officers yelled at Patrick, who lingered on the porch long enough to give Mister Smith an assuring nod. A moment later, he had a very dark sensation. He had been in that jail before.

Spencer smiled and sat down. *They did it!* he thought. He looked up at Oliver, who had fallen asleep late in the night hours and lay on his side. *You'll be free soon too, Ollie.*

"Hey!" The soldier who had punched Patrick in the face stood up and called out. "Where's my gun?"

Ernest Williams let out a laugh from the other cell and Spencer looked up at the sheriff, who turned, betrayed. He glared at Spencer, who shrugged innocently.

The officer headed out to look for the thief who had pulled the gun from his holster when they'd wrestled him to the ground.

The sheriff spoke to the rest of the officers. "Let him go alone. If they have something else planned, I would rather you all be here until tomorrow. Nothing gets between us and the heart." He turned to Spencer. "Maybe your children will come out for the hanging tomorrow, Mister Smith."

Spencer's eyes dropped to the floor.

After a silent moment, Ernest called out from the other cell, "Sheriff, had you considered hiring real police officers?"

The sheriff turned to his desk.

"No?" Ernest laughed.

Patrick poked the skin under his eye with a fingertip. It hurt more than anything had ever hurt. He smiled. He was alive and he had stolen that guard's gun right off of him while they carried him. He did it with precision and skill, but he didn't know how or why.

Edwin was right. He laughed to himself. *Marcus?* the boy thought. *Why did the Sheriff call me Marcus?*

He walked between the buildings, staying out of sight. They would not join up again at the orphanage if they could avoid it, so he walked through the alleys to the meeting point. He felt like a spy. He was a spy. Like something from one of Headmaster Smith's adventure stories.

He was beginning to remember things from his own painful past; he remembered the sounds of his family's screams and the police officers carrying him into town. *What had happened?* He remembered his "induction" into the orphanage and then the bland, gray dullness that came after. But mostly he remembered Headmaster Smith.

He paused at the street where he saw Albert Perry, who was being questioned by a police officer. *Just walk away*, Patrick thought, *don't tell them nothing, Albert*.

Thomas had thought it best to take different roads and paths to get out to a grove where he often went. That would be the next meeting spot. Edwin had warned everyone, "If you get spotted or approached by anyone," he told them, "don't lead them to the next place. Just don't come. Go to the inn instead."

The reality was that the man had stopped Albert to ask if he'd seen the parson's nephew, Stephen Adler. But he had not. No one had seen him that morning.

At first, Edwin and Thomas had been strange spies, but it was very natural to everyone to go along with what they said. Their memories came back slowly; the adventures that Headmaster Smith had told them night after night gave them a sense of purpose. Breton was their adventure.

After coming out of the sewers, Mister Elliott and Mister Smith spent an entire evening going from pub to pub until sunrise so the Vampyres wouldn't locate their hideout.

According to legend, that night Algernon Elliott had been spotted breaking into the home of a very rich family in an attempt to elude the Vampyres. While the man of the house, Sir Matthew White Ridley, had a gun to his chest, Elliott quickly took to convincing him to invest his money in other assets. It was one of Headmaster Smith's favorite stories to tell. As a result the rich man had funded many of their adventures after that. Elliott's charm had paid off.

Patrick thought about Headmaster Smith and his stories. *They weren't stories after all,* he thought. He had been telling them all how to survive.

Jared made good on his deal with the Vampyre, though he couldn't figure out what he was gaining from it. Michael had come to him in the cellar, where the young soldier felt more comfortable than in Gallegos' room. It was a terrifying thing, but Jared had an instinct to trust the Vampyre. He even clambered out the cellar window to finally see the Vampyre face to face. Michael was looking for Kat. He trusted her. To Jared's surprise, the telepathic Vampyre had not known of her disappearance. He could see a change in his eyes: a sense of guilt and confusion. Jared felt terrible, being the man who revealed it to him. He told Michael everything he knew: the curse, the old man helping him, the old lady.

Michael was determined. "Tell the girl's father what you know." Pensive, he continued. "I also have another task for you." Jared felt he couldn't turn the Vampyre down. He had saved his life, as miserable as it was. He looked forward to having something to do. Somehow Michael had recognized that Jared was a good man and did not kill him, though in Jared's mind it shouldn't have been a challenge. The first task would be the hardest, but he had gone straight to the door of the inn and spoken to the innkeeper. Would he think him crazy? In his grief, would the innkeeper fight him? He was a big man, and any man that didn't see him as a threat, didn't value his own life. But no, the bearded brute had listened calmly and nodded, arms crossed. Jared rambled on. First about the sham war, then about the Vampyre that had saved him. He talked about Gallegos and Miss Allen. And the man had just nodded.

When Jared had finally finished, the man simply stood up and uttered three words, "Then we fight."

The morning had come and Jared had not slept. He stood on the street, loaded with bundles of tools, including a pickaxe wrapped in canvas. Multiple bags hung from his aching shoulder. He would make his way out into the woods where he could prepare for whatever fight was coming to Breton. Police officers were on every corner, scouring the streets; armed to a man, every one a threat. Jared kept his eyes down as he walked.

Gallegos was not pleased with Jared's decision. Originally they had decided to work together, but Jared felt the need to see it through with the Vampyre. The old man, however, felt that he should make himself less visible, which if Jared gave it any thought, he could could understand. The heat was on. The disagreement left them parting ways amicably in the alley by the Crow's Nest.

"Don't die." The old man told him before walking off in a cloud of cigarette smoke. Gallegos would keep spying. To what end, Jared could not understand. The time to kill Vampyres had come as far as he was concerned. He was sure that would be the last he saw of the old man. He'd only made it onto the street when the old parson, whom Gallegos had called "Adler," grabbed Jared by the arm. It startled him.

The pitiful man looked like he'd lost his mind. His hair was disheveled and his shirt unbuttoned. He smelled of acrid smoke and alcohol. Adler had also not been to bed. "Young man," the crazed old preacher asked. "Have you seen a boy of about fifteen come this way? Dark hair. You'd know him. He's a good boy but he's not real smart. About yay tall?" He demonstrated with a flat hand.

Jared replied softly, "I have not, sir. If I do, sir, is there somewhere I should send him?"

The man's eyes glazed. "No. It is too late now." Adler said solemnly as he walked away, still scanning the street. The man slumped, resigning himself to the worst.

Jared was terrified for him. He looked around at the awful town. Vampyres were respecters of no man, even a man of the cloth it seemed. Perhaps he was their enemy, as a man of God. *That poor man.* He thought. He shook it out of his mind and continued walking. The tailor's shop was only a block away. He'd go by there first. Jared walked along the bustling street trying to avoid the gaze of the officers. He wore some old clothes that Mister Lamphere, the innkeeper, had found for him from articles forgotten at the Crow's Nest. Jared looked like a miner. A very tall one. One who had bathed but it would have to do. With tools in hand, he walked along the crowded avenue until he stood at the seamstress's home.

She waved at him through the window and disappeared momentarily. "Mister Pope." She said, smiling as she stepped through the front door. She held a cup of tea in one hand over a saucer held in the other. "I hadn't fancied you a miner."

"No ma'am," he replied. He looked up and down the street. "Would it be rude to ask to come inside?"

She looked a bit surprised. "Not at all. Come right in my boy."

The tailor's shop had not moved. Even the chair where Jared had sat the first time was turned just as it had been when he left last. He held the wrap of tools on his forearms like it was a sleeping child.

"Oh," she noticed, "You could have left those outside." She laughed between sips of tea. The boy looked burdened.

"Ma'am. My name is not Pope." He stared at the ground. "I must apologize for my associate lying to you. My name is Jared Carswell." He looked up. "You said you had hoped that this could be a place of honesty."

"Honesty is good." Miss Allen said. "But in my experience, men are prone to lying."

"Well, that ain't right, ma'am."

"No." She replied, "I suppose it's not."

Jared walked across the room to the woman's sowing table and put the tools down. He unrolled the wrap to reveal that the pickaxe was the only miner's tool. A scattergun and a carbine rifle lay wrapped tightly.

"I have known little if aught in my life but war," he told the little lady, whose surprise was evident. "I know when war is coming." He pulled out the scattergun and set it out on the table. "There is no reason you should feel impotent again. You should be allowed to protect yourself, ma'am. This is your fight too, and its coming soon."

"Fight?" Miss Allen asked.

"Yes ma'am," he replied. "It's us or no one."

"Well, ain't that the saddest affair." She said.

"It's not great, ma'am."

Miss Allen smiled. "Thank you, Jared. It has been many years since young men brought me such lovely gifts." Miss Allen's manners held strong, but it was evident that her demeanor had changed. She was filled with purpose and resolve. "Would you like a cup of tea before you leave?" she added, smiling.

The boy grunted and then smirked, "Might as well, reckoning its the end of the world."

Glenn Lamphere, the innkeeper, was on the verge of tears again. No one could see his jaw tensing behind his beard, his nostrils flared as he held back the flood of sorrow. He clenched a fist around the neck of the broom and swept the floor.

The side door opened. Albert Perry slumped in. He looked disappointed.

Glenn relaxed. He couldn't help but smile. "Sit down, Albert."

The small boy pulled himself up on the bar and then hunched on it as if to say "get me some of the good stuff, barkeep," but instead he just stared at the scratches on the bar.

Glenn just looked at him for a moment. "Are you going to tell me what's wrong or are you going to make me trade a glass of milk for it?"

The boy looked up and smiled at the man with twinkling eyes who was as large as a bear. He inspired happiness in people. Albert let out a sigh. "I got spotted by one of the sheriff's men," he complained. "They said if we got spotted that we should come here to the inn."

"Right," Glenn answered. "And a good idea that is too. You children are really on to something," he continued. "I don't know what it is but that sheriff, old Parson Adler and mean Mister Burroughs, they're up to somethin' and it seems to me you might be on to finding out what." He sat a glass of milk down on the bar for the boy. "I'll keep an eye out for anyone else. You rest a while, then head out through the window down there in the cellar and get back to the others."

The inn was empty; the morning risers had already gone on their way around town and luncheon was not yet ready. Glenn experienced a twinge of hope in the early hours of the night before. A young man had come to him with strange news regarding Kat—the only news since her disappearance. The soldier, who called himself Jared Carswell, spoke of a Vampyre who had given him a dream and a name. He came looking for "Kat," whom he had envisioned as a beautiful blonde girl. The Vampyre was also troubled by her disappearance. The Vampyre seemed to think Ernest Williams could help. Glenn knew Ernest very well. He was a good patron but a good patron for a guy who sold mostly alcohol, your best patrons weren't always exactly trustworthy. But Ernest was a good man, harmless even. What could he have to do with Kat or Vampyres? Maybe he loaned them a book and wanted it back. Ernest the drunken librarian and the children's headmaster were now in jail, apparently criminal masterminds according to the sheriff's men. And now, the orphans were running a covert military movement against the Vampyres, with the help of one no less than a army sergeant and one of the Vampyres themselves.

He watched as the little boy, this spy drank his milk. *My Katarina is gone. You, my boy will likely be dead soon. We probably all will. How are we supposed to fight Vampyres?* The two waited for other children to come. They never did. Albert and Glenn worked in the inn together, keeping each other company until the afternoon.

Ernest Williams's home was small. It was downright modest. As the dawn approached, Michael took the blankets from the neatly made bed and quickly hung them over the windows to block out the sunlight. He closed the door into the bedroom. The small living space had a wood stove and seating area. He took Ernest's pressed shirts, quilts and sheets and lined the gaps under the front door and the door to the bedroom. Michael knew he would not sleep. He would just be trapped in this small wooden box until night. The little bit of light that came in created a dusky glow throughout the room. Michael sat in a large chair, lost in contemplation as he scratched his young face. He was still perplexed by his own identity, his true purpose for being in Breton.

The town was full of voices. It was enough to drive him mad. They all echoed each other. There was a strange reverberation in the voices as though chanting. They were taking commands: very simple orders. *Today is Tuesday, the 17th. It is a lovely day outside.* A few minutes later, multiple voices would ring out: *It really is a lovely day.* While others would reverberate: *Oh, I was just thinking how lovely it was.* Each thought was an echo of the first.

Michael didn't want to hear people's thoughts. He didn't want inside anyone's heads. He wanted to figure out his own. The commanding voice was apathetic and cold. Someone was controlling the minds of the people around the town. It was some elaborate form of puppetry.

He sat with his face in his hands. *Isaac.* He focused. *The creature's name was Isaac.* Isaac looked to have been in his late forties, but Michael sensed that he was an ageless creature. *Isaac. Isaac.* He repeated the name until it sounded odd in his thoughts. *Isaac.* Michael was regaining control of his own thoughts. It was a relief. Michael thought about Jared and then his mind wandered and he considered the kindness that Ernest had shown him. He grabbed the decanter of wine that he and Ernest had drunk from when they first met and he set two glasses on the table.

He poured two glasses of wine.

This one is for you, friend, he thought, staring at the second glass. As he stood there, he noticed a small flat box on the table.

The small note on it simply said "Michael."

He set the decanter down and opened the box. Folded within it was a beautiful white shirt with a high imperial collar and a black tie. Folded also were a pair of dark charcoal trousers that matched a frockcoat that hung on the chair at the table; at the bottom of the box, there lay a vest made of beautiful red silk with a golden inlay.

Michael felt the fabric. His shoulders collapsed and he sighed. His heart wrenched. As he held the vest to his chest, caressing the fabric with his thumb, a small dark stain showed up on the fabric. Michael touched the stain and then his face. He was crying.

He looked at himself in the captain's clothing and realized for the first time what Ernest had seen under the candlelight. He looked pathetic and his hair was matted. He looked like a little boy in his father's clothing.

He's right, Michael thought, *Vampyre or no, this is no way for a gentleman to dress*. He set to changing his appearance and spent the rest of the afternoon thinking on how to free his only friend in the world.

J ared followed Glenn's directions into the shallow wood north of the town. The path lead on west, according to Glenn, to a large mining site a few miles further, but that wasn't the concern. Jared turned right off of the path at a tree where a piece of string had been tied to a branch. The hide wrap in his arms made a clanking sound with each step.

Even as he approached the small clearing in the woods, he heard the crackle of footsteps in the soft grass. He knew when someone was hiding behind the trees.

He walked into the middle of the grove where a small tree had fallen and laid his tools down. He sat down on the grass with his back against the tree and waited. It was only a few moments later that two young boys appeared from the woods, silently. He didn't hear a footstep from either of them.

They introduced themselves as Thomas and Edwin. They looked every bit of poor orphan. But then again, so did Jared.

Despite his beard and large shoulders, Jared was still very young and still remembered the night his parents disappeared. When he stumbled into Breton eight years earlier, he had not found the orphanage or town's officials but rather soldiers walking into the dusk light, saying, "One day, we'll get those Vampyres."

That's all it took for Jared to decide that he needed to follow them. Unfortunately his desire for revenge was never squelched. Jared fought and survived battle after battle until, as a captain, he took command of the Seventh Battalion.

The man dwarfed the young boys as he stood up. Thomas, who was the taller of the two, only stood at the man's sternum. Jared's voice was quite deep when he introduced himself. When the boys were comfortable, they gave a signal and the rest of a small group of orphans came out of the woods.

Including Thomas and Edwin, ten children appeared. Jared noticed aside from the two leaders, there came six boys and two girls. "Is this everyone?" he asked.

They all looked around and it was Patrick, a tall, quiet boy and obviously the oldest, who spoke up. "I saw Albert. A police officer was speaking to him."

"So, he's back at the inn?" Thomas asked.

"Yes. That's where he was headed when I came here."

"And Ollie," Edwin reminded.

There was a moment of silence, like a sigh.

"Ollie?" Jared asked.

Patrick replied again, "When the police had me, looking for Tom and Ned, I saw Ollie in the station next to Mister Smith's cell."

"Captured?" asked Jared in surprise.

"No," replied Patrick. "He was just sitting there."

Jared looked for answers. The children sat down around him. The air was cold, but the light shined down in the small grove and it was comfortable.

They explained to him that they had learned of a spell that kept everyone from thinking clearly. They struggled with the words to explain it but Miss Allen had already done that for him. He understood.

Jared spoke. "Our goal is to rescue Mister Ernest Williams, Mister Smith and your friend. My source has told me that he senses that there will be some bit of chaos in the coming days. Our plan is to make sure that it does not go well for our enemies. Chaos is essential for us. We are saboteurs."

The idea of a shared enemy had never occurred to most of the children. They had never thought of themselves as being at war. Jared had never thought of himself as being anything else. Jared had never found anyone else like him. Men who didn't talk about their pasts and always claimed to not remember what had come before had always surrounded him, but in that moment he was one of them, a member in a company of orphans.

It didn't take them long to outline a plan. As long as they had daylight on their side, they could do what needed to be done to prepare. They would not treat the orphanage as home anymore. Edwin had already scouted ahead and found some abandoned stables where they would set up camp. Five of them—Jared, the girls, Alexander and James—would go ahead and go to the stables. The other boys—Patrick, Newt, Thomas, Edwin and the twins— would go find food and listen to what was being said about the following day.

Parson Adler's eyes were red from crying. He knew what was next. He expected silence and the dullness of the town. No one would be bringing consolation except the League, those fools. He'd been betrayed. They would follow Desmond into a flaming house. That bureaucratic idiot would destroy the town if it was in his paperwork.

Maybe I'll just do it before he gets the chance to look. He thought. It had been fifteen years since the skirmishes came close enough to see cannonballs crashing into Breton. Of course that misdirection had been Burroughs's fault as well. While Burroughs had taken credit for Adler's work, somehow Adler had in turn received the blame for Burroughs's failures. What Desmond Burroughs did better than Adler was place blame. That would change.

He sat in his small bedroom in the rectory, imagining the return of his nephew, the child he'd raised since birth. The other bed was empty and Stephen's clothes and shoes still lay strewn, kicked off in the manner of teenage boys. The evidence was right in front of him but he could just feel that the boy would come back. He hoped against hope that this was a mistake. Of all of the people to hurt like this, why him? He'd been faithful. He'd given his life to those impetuous Vampyres. He'd given the Alliance the greatest weapon mankind had ever known. Adler was aware that he deserved a lot of things. There was a lot of evil in the world because of him, but no one deserved *this*. He had to laugh at himself for thinking that way. How many times over the years had madness driven someone awake in town and grief driven them to come to him, praying for a lost child?

It had always been just a job.

He was as evil as Desmond Burroughs and deep down he knew it but he didn't make the same kinds of mistakes as Desmond. *First the mayor? Mistake. Now this? If—* he swallowed hard. Tears were filling his eyes again. He wiped them away with a sleeve. *If he did. It'll be the last mistake he ever makes.*

He heard a knock on the door. It was too soft. He bit his lip and prayed, more of a guttural utterance than any real oration, then cleared his throat, sniffed and cleaned up his appearance. He didn't want anyone to see him falling apart. The door opened quietly before he could get to it. It was the sheriff.

"Bad news, I'm afraid, Parson" he began.

Adler let out a breath and sat down on his bed, defeated.

The sheriff waited a moment. Then, looking down, he stated quietly, "I've brought his body inside."

Newton Bullington had seen the sheriff carrying a body on his horse. He ran to tell the boys. He found James, but before he could tell anyone else, they saw the twins, who were at the general store listening. From across the way, Patrick sat with Albert and Glenn in the Crow's Nest, watching out the front window, from a window above peeked Jasper Markov. Alexander was walking with Jared when they heard two women come walking away and sobbing down the street past the orphanage.

Word was spreading quickly: the Vampyres had gotten Stephen Adler.

FĪVE

Just so is life from limb thus rent,
Just so is soul of æther torn;
But then of blood made whole again,
But then of darkness are we born.
-Quatern verse fragment, Song of the Sin-Eaters (1561)

It was a quarter mile walk from the road to the stables where the orphans had taken up camp. Perhaps years ago, there had been more use for horses, but now the stables were in disrepair. Despite other possible hideouts, the stables weren't visible from the road, so the lamplight would be shielded if anyone were to pass in the night. They had set up posts along the edge of the wood to watch if anyone was coming.

As James McLaughlin sat at his post, hidden among some trees up ahead of the old abandoned mansion, he saw people coming and going. Their conversations were surprising and lively. Not like those of the people in town. They talked about Vampyres; they talked about politics and the world outside.

The quieter post was near the grove, where Newton sat. He watched like a hawk. No one would catch him by surprise. The woods stayed quiet as the night approached. Once darkness came, they would all come back to the hideout. Night was coming on quickly.

Henry, one of the twins, was on the third post. He sat about a hundred yards further at a bend in the road, giving him a better view of the road toward the mines. To his amazement, some of the people walking toward the mines would disappear as if into smoke or thin air. He watched with wide eyes and held his breath. It all would have scared him much more if it hadn't been for Mister Smith's stories. "Not all people are people," he would laugh. "Some are demons and others daemons and some are angels and some are just downright devils!"

The children spent much of their time around the campfire, talking through everything they were learning. Penny Hughes posited that maybe they were trapped in a dream world: some land between two other worlds. Emily, her sister, thought maybe it was purgatory. Alexander joked that it was hell. No one laughed.

Perhaps they weren't allowed to think because bad people were taking all their thoughts and memories and giving them to other children. Maybe they were in some mysterious land that no one knew about—but that wouldn't explain the war going on outside.

Jared sat in the woods allowing his eyes to adjust to the darkness, but when he heard a crack in the silence, he turned his gun on the sound, seeing nothing.

"There's no need for the gun, Jared." The voice came from behind a tree. It was Michael. "We don't want another run in the mud, now do we?" he asked with a smile in his voice.

"You should give a little more warning." Jared lowered the barrel of the gun.

"That was the warning." Michael said. "I think it's time to introduce me to your army," Michael stated.

"Army?" Jared asked.

"I'd expect no less from the Captain of the Seventh Battalion."

Jared laughed. *Michael is quite charming*, he thought and *he looks much better in his gray suit*. He looked like a man, not like some horrid sea creature or like something spit up by a sea creature. The same could have been said about his own change in appearance.

As they approached the stable, Thomas saw them from a distance. Everyone was accounted for. *Why is there someone with him?* He ran inside. By the time Jared made it to the threshold of the stable, the fire had been covered and there was darkness inside the building. Everyone was hidden.

"No need to worry, everyone. I have a friend with me." He turned into the darkness.

Michael only stood at the door. He did not come inside.

"Well, come on in, Michael." Jared turned.

Immediately Michael had a sense of relief. The last time he'd felt that sensation, he almost lost his hand. He stepped inside cautiously but nothing happened.

Jared realized what Gallegos had meant. "Could you not have entered without my welcome?"

Michael felt like that was as good an answer as any. "I believe that's the case."

"I was told that. Good thing I remembered." He smiled. Jared leaned over and put a small log on the fire and Thomas came out to meet him. In his hand, he held a gun that seemed too large for the boy to hold. It shook with its own weight. It was Smith's revolver.

Michael said nothing.

"Thomas," Jared said, "this is the man who brought me to you all."

"Jared," Thomas replied, "is this a trick? Is this a trap?" He looked at the man, whose eyes glowed like distant lanterns. He was tall and handsome with black hair combed from his face. "This is a Vampyre."

"Yes. He is a Vampyre. But he is a friend. He is the reason I came to Breton." Jared spoke to everyone in the room. "You don't have to trust. But you should listen."

Even as he said it, heads started popping up from behind the posts and old bales and stacks of wood. Everyone was armed. Newton held a scythe and the twins had knives. Alexander, Albert and the girls were also armed with an assortment of sharp objects. Edwin came out from behind a cart with a pitchfork and Patrick held a revolver in his hand.

Michael smiled. "I love a good army."

The campfire smoldered. There was food for everyone. Newton had made a stew with the assistance of Penny and some of the children ate quietly. They had trouble relaxing around the Vampyre, as beautiful as he was, but they put their weapons down.

Edwin was pensive; it had been days since he'd seen Stephen. Everyone was devastated at the loss. Even worse, they would not be able to attend the funeral the next morning. They had all become fugitives. They'd angered the sheriff and it was not safe in town.

Michael could sense a sadness in them all, but he needed to win their trust and time was against them. He sat, very gentlemanly, on a large bucket with one leg crossed. Jared, Thomas and Alexander listened and spoke to him. Penny had already fallen asleep from eating and Newton was cleaning. The other children were just talking quietly and Emily listened.

"I was not always as you see me now," Michael told them, looking around the stable. "I don't remember who I was. There are times when I remember some things. You see, I remember I was coming from Europe—somewhere in Europe— for a very special purpose, but I don't remember what. The old ship, a pirate's ship, was attacked by Vampyres. I don't know them. I can see their faces in my mind but I have no recollection about them. They had a terrible interest in me though." He paused.

"Please, Michael, go on." Jared nodded. The children listened intently.

It was difficult for Michael to speak because he was listening to their thoughts. He didn't want to read their minds. His intention was different. He could remember hearing a voice in town, the same echoing voice that was in everyone's head. Something like that was happening all around him.

"I have since found that I have terrible powers." *I have the power to communicate using only my thoughts.* Everyone heard what he was saying though his lips were not moving. "I have the power to walk on the air, some beyond-human strength. But this all comes with some sacrifice. I can no longer see the light of day," he reflected sadly, "and I cannot, as I have just sensed, enter any home without invitation."

"Wow." Thomas spoke the simple thought that floated throughout the room.

"Yes. I feel all Vampyres might be restricted in the same way." He continued, "I have no idea what I look like, in puddles or a mirror or windows—my face—my reflection does not appear."

Emily Hughes thought he looked quite handsome. His eyes had glimpses of yellow and brown ,and his hair was black and it was combed neatly behind his ears. His face would not betray his age; he looked like a man in his late twenties or a very sad old man.

"Imagine that," Michael said with a sad smile, "waking up to not know who you are and not even knowing what you might look like."

As Michael spoke and listened, he heard in conversation a name, "Mister Smith," that continued to resonate. It felt like each mention of the imprisoned man echoed in the heads of the children.

That was the voice. It was Smith's voice. Michael smiled. The adventurer had left an imprint on the children, leaving them brave and adventurous, willing to give their lives to save him; the only friend they'd known. Whatever curse had befallen the town had opened their minds to him. Smith was their caretaker; he spoke kindly to them every day and told them stories of bravery, heroics and adventure every night. Michael would say nothing. The children smiled, growing more comfortable with him.

He discussed the plan with Jared and they plotted out the next day's work.

P erhaps you're feeling a bit stir-crazy." Desmond flipped through pieces of paper as he spoke to Chandler, who sat across the table in the train station office. His voice was nasal, bored and grating.

"I don't know what you're talking about," stated Chandler.

"Well, Monsieur Chandler, I realize work has been slow and we've allowed you your visitor, perhaps to keep your mind at ease," Desmond continued.

Incredulous, Chandler didn't move.

"I know about your Englishman: the spy." Burroughs laughed. "As we speak, my men are going through his things upstairs right now." Burroughs lifted his monocle on its chain and polished the silver ring around the glass. "He is simply a kook and he stands no chance in this town. The Vampyres will have devoured him by now," he said confidently. "He should have left things to the professionals."

Chandler was well aware that Desmond and his men would have been coming and he had rearranged the room to that end.

"I also know about your visit with the Vampyre hunter." Desmond always talked like he was in control. Perhaps he was. Perhaps he was just American. They had a way of seeing the world as if it were property.

"That's what we're calling a Vampyre hunter these days?" Chandler scoffed. He had not been harboring a spy. He had been harboring a Vampyre hunter, if young and inexperienced. The Vampyre hunter, whom he'd treated like a spy, was a fraud. Desmond didn't see it. He'd already lost. Chandler imagined the grid of Breton, with its crystals and copper resonances laid out. He could see it with a bird's eye like a big chess board. How could Desmond not see that he was losing? The germans called that point in the game "zugzwang." It was a foregone conclusion. Everyone just had to make their moves until it ended. At is age, Chandler could always see the ending.

"Charlatan or no, he came here threatening our livelihood." Desmond said, eyeing a receipt through his monocle. "I can't have you running away right now," Desmond continued, "though Mister Hastings in Washington was reluctant to allow it, we will be exchanging the lanterns this week."

Chandler's caterpillar eyebrows jumped with surprise. He looked around the office. There was so much evidence, so much incriminating paperwork: false stamps, backdated logs and passports. If Desmond knew what he was looking for, they would have already been torturing him. They were already torturing Jasper Markov somewhere near the inn. The dogs were on the wrong trail and for that Chandler was thankful.

"What if I don't want to participate? Torture me? Put your Vampyre dogs on me?"

"Let's hope it does not come to that, Chandler. You'll be fine."

Zwischenzug. Chandler thought. Desmond had feinted. *Maybe he wins this then.* If what he said was true, Desmond would have the upper hand and it would mean a lot of pain for Chandler. He had only been observing Desmond's tête-à-ête, but if he didn't get involved, he would be experiencing a lot of pain soon.

Chandler laughed. "*Oui, mon ami.* We'll be fine." His heart sank into his stomach. Over the years, he'd been reminded of what the heartless little bureaucrat could do. Chandler could leave town, but it wouldn't matter, they would bring him back and make him pay for it. He knew that he was imprisoned just like everyone else.

"Is that sulfur I smell?" Desmond grinned. "Demons abound, Monsieur Chandler and unlike you, they feel no pain."

Chandler could faintly make out screaming through the office window. It was Jasper Markov. He knew it. Desmond's men had Jasper Markov spread across an alley floor with his face in the mud. His left arm was stretched out with the heel of an unknown man crushing his open hand. Bones broke. Jasper screamed.

Desmond could hear it too. He smiled. The smile never reached his cold eyes. He tapped the floor twice with his cane. "I pray that you will not fail to accomplish your task without event." His eyes were cold and emotionless.

A moment later a guard entered the office. "There is nothing upstairs, sir. It's clean, sir."

Desmond grunted. "I hate being lied to, Chandler." Chandler hated putting all of those beautiful things, including Mister Elliott's typewriter, under the platform outside.

Outside, Chandler could hear Markov's sobbing become a gurgle and then quiet.

Desmond left quietly, "You know what to do, Chandler."

Chandler did not wait for Desmond's carriage to pull away from the train station. He closed and bolted the door, ran to the office, blew out the candles and quickly made his way outside through the platform exit. He knew he would be followed but it was too late to worry with it. He was beyond the point of no return. *Zugzwang.* He thought again. *And I'm losing.*

Desmond was making rash decisions on behalf of the Alliance. The Brethren were panicking. They had kidnapped Genevieve Moreau. They had kidnapped Kat Lamphere. They might have just been collateral damage but he knew now that Breton was at war. Chandler tried not to run down the street, but he walked quickly, watching for Desmond's men. He would need Jasper Markov's help.

He turned the corner, scanning the square. The orphanage looked abandoned now. One of two things had happened, either the sheriff had put an end to Smith's dream, or the children had finally gotten out of the town. The night was setting in, but the sheriff's men were finishing the platform where Smith and Williams would be hanged. Across the square, the lights in the church were on. It was full. With the Adler boy's body being found, the members of the church would be there to pray. No one would have noticed Jasper being beaten in an alley.

Desmond's men were still across the street busying themselves with ransacking Markov's brightly colored carriage. No one even looked at where the man lay. It was impossible to distinguish what was blood and what was mud. Jasper Markov's mangled body laid submerged in a darkening puddle.

Chandler fell on his knees, lifting the man by the shoulders and pulling him against his chest.

"What did you tell them?" Chandler demanded.

The man gurgled then violently coughed up stringy dark blood down his chest.

"You're not going to die tonight. Not until you tell me what they got out of you." he grunted. "But *wallah* if you told them aught tonight, you'll wish they'd have killed you here."

H is feet fell silent in the grass. Algernon did not breathe. He moved with scientific precision and care. His gloved hands stayed out ahead of him, caressing the bark of trees as they moved past him. He was as quiet as the breeze. He gazed into the mouth of the cave and closed the gap from one hundred yards to one hundred feet when he felt the cold wind from the mouth of the cavern.

He stopped cold.

Over a short but successful career in the field of paranormal investigation, he had developed a keen sense of timing for strange occurrences.

He noticed a short blast of warmth pass across his face. It wasn't natural. He noticed what looked like smoke from the corner of his eye.

Shifters.

Algernon's study of "Shifters" had been purely theoretical. The ancient race of half-demon shape-shifters was as elusive as their natural "talents" allowed them to be. Unlike the Vampyres, the Shifters had no desire to participate in modern society and they avoided people when possible.

Not tonight, Algernon observed. *Tonight, we research.*

Even as the thought crossed his mind, the cold steel of a long blade passed under his nose then disappeared in a quick cloud of smoke that tickled his chin.

Lucky for me they're so confident.

The reality was that had the blade appeared behind him, he'd already have been dead. That was not the case and a small smile curled at the ends of his lips. As he collapsed to his knees, feigning his fear for the creature that had just flashed in front of him, Algernon thought on a poem:

"Death be not proud, though some have called thee / Mighty and dreadfull, for, thou art not soe."

Thomas Campion, was it? he asked himself.

He had studied the poem at Oxford.

Irony, I feel, that it should be pride that leads this poor beast to its death.

He rolled over onto his back with both hands working, one in his satchel and the other pulling out his revolver.

They hovered above him, the wisps of smoke dancing and solidifying into cloth or flesh as they looked down on him. *Two of them.*

They solidified on either side of him as he rose to his feet.

To his right, a towering man with a squared chin and a thin shroud of a beard crossed his arms laughing. Algernon furrowed his brow to see a boy becoming soluble.

Interesting, Algernon thought. "Good afternoon."

"Aye," the tall man said, "I suppose it should be."

The boy just snickered into his hands.

"Should be?" Algernon asked.

"Would be, if I were not having to make with killing of you." The tall man spoke awkwardly. He put his sentences together like a man laying brick and the boy just snickered.

Was it Sir Walter Raleigh that wrote that poem? thought Algernon to himself as he felt around in his bag with his left hand. His mind was working out the situation.

"Well, I should hope there would be no reason to do any killing, sir." Algernon half-smiled in his polite British manner.

The tall man just grinned. A long blade solidified in his hand.

"I see." Algernon commented quietly. *No, definitely not Raleigh and it's certainly not a Shakespearean sonnet.*

"So, I suppose I'll be on my way."

The boy let out a hoarse laugh and Algernon turned to look at him. His eyes weren't like that of a child—or even human at all. They were hazy and as the boy laughed, the inside of his mouth did not appear with a tongue but rather looked like a pipe filled with smoke, empty and charred.

Algernon simply noted it. He found what he thought he might need.

"You are a long way from home," the man observed, commenting on Algernon's accent.

"Oh, no, no," Algernon corrected. "Home is, as they say, where the heart is and what not." Then he turned with a smile to face the man. "But I suppose that is only for those with hearts to know about."

Even as the words left his mouth, the Shifter lunged past him and Algernon dodged the blade by an inch. He turned the gun on the two of them but did not remove his hand from the bag.

"What do you plan to do with that?" The tall man asked and the boy chuckled, echoing him.

"Kill you." Algernon stated plainly. He knew that firing the heavy revolver would give away his position, so his brain worked to keep him from having to pull the trigger. It would do little good anyway, he figured, since the creature turned to smoke anyway. There would be no use in it.

The man let out a loud laugh.

Campion, Raleigh, Shakespeare... What Elizabethan am I forgetting? Algernon asked himself.

The man raised the blade again and Algernon feigned a smile. Then he lunged at the two Shifters with the gun ahead of him. They disappeared into tongues of smoke and Algernon noted that the man disappeared many seconds before his smaller counterpart.

"When I was a child," Algernon related, "my father took me one day to the bank where he worked." There was silence. "I can't imagine him doing that with me if his work were so dangerous as yours."

Suddenly Algernon felt the man behind him. "You will speak not of mine." There was a silence and then with a breath, "Son."

And within a moment, the child appeared ahead of Algernon, quiet and not snickering at all. There was a green edge around his eyes and an emptiness that Algernon could not fathom. It was alien to him. They disappeared again. Algernon noted that the boy seemed to disappear a moment more quickly than the last.

"Outstanding trickery," he suggested. "You'd make for a fine magician.

"Magic," the tall man observed, "does not. Exist."

Algernon reached out, revealing a small vile in his left hand. He caught a wisp of smoke and capped the vial with his thumb.

Then there was silence.

Algernon held the gun out, watching everything in his periphery. He had to have caught part of the smoke that came from the voice.

"NO!" The man cried out as the boy appeared, holding his stomach, sick and in pain.

Algernon made his move. He ran toward the boy and pointed the gun directly at his head.

"Not so snide now, are we?" he asked the man. Algernon's guess was right. Instead of catching the man, he'd caught some segment of the son in the vial. The last thing Algernon wanted was to kill the man's son, but he knew that either of the savages would kill him in an instant.

"I will. Cut you up. Millions of pieces," the Shifter threatened. "Take hand."

"That is fair," Algernon assessed, "but it won't bring your boy back once he's dead." He put the vial to his lips to inhale the boy's smoke. The essence around the vial and his hand smelled of burning rosewood. As the seconds passed, Algernon realized that the boy was getting sicker. His skin pulsed with green and gray flashes and the veins under his skin appeared then disappeared, rippling with energy.

The boy let out a moan.

"Let. Let. Let him. Go," the Shifter stuttered. "He not. Changes back."

"Go," the boy mimicked. "Changes."

"That can be arranged," Algernon answered gently. "Give me your word."

"It is. Given." He solidified in front of him, showing Algernon his hands.

"Alright." Algernon removed his thumb from the vial. He watched the boy breathe in the dark wisp of smoke. "Then we are done here?" he asked.

"Done," the boy mimicked with a soft and confused smile.

John Donne! Algernon thought to himself. *John Donne wrote that infernal poem!*

He sat and gathered himself for minutes. His sense of guilt slowly lifted like a shroud that was stuck to his skin with morning dew. Algernon felt sick at having put his gun to the head of the Shifter's offspring. They had dissipated, leaving a genuine sense of fear in the square-jawed man. He knew the demon-boy's empty eyes would trouble him later on. It would wake him from his sleep if he ever slept again.

He quietly made his way down into the large mouth of the cave. *What sort of fortress would only be guarded by a Shifter and his son?* thought Algernon. He looked forward to finding some time with his typewriter to write down those exploits. That would have to wait. The ground was shifting.

"Oh," he mumbled. *Now, that's more like it.*

He turned to see what was coming, but it was too late. He felt the crushing blow against his rib cage as the cracking sound of stone grinding on stone filled the cavern. The cave was collapsing on him and the force had knocked him back. He crashed against the wall of the cave and fell with the rattle of his bag. His gun slid across the floor. He opened his eyes to see the world in a blur and some rock figure crumbling on him.

Quickly, Algernon realized that it wasn't the cave falling in on him; some species of rock creature had hit him in the chest: a Golem. He wheezed, trying to regain his composure. He fingered the floor around him while trying to gain his breath. The gun was just out of reach. Algernon unbuttoned the duster and heaved one big breath.

The creature was coming for him.

Algernon lunged out of the way as its fist crashed into the rock wall. Rocks and pebbles fell on Algernon through the cloud of dust.

He cursed under his breath. He had dodged away from his gun; it was even further away than it had been before.

This makes more sense to me, thought Algernon, *as far as security systems are concerned. First, a creature of properties insoluble then a creature of unwavering solubility.*

Brilliant!

He wanted to take note on the creature's dimensions, but as its large hands came down on him, sweeping him off the ground, he thought that it would be easier to gather that information if it were no longer moving so much.

So he got back to work.

The monster was large and shaped like a man of approximately ninety inches. Its muscular shape indicated that it was male, but it had no genitals of any sort. Its naked body towered over him. The creature had a human face with the inscription "תמא" on its forehead.

"Truth," Algernon translated.

The creature grunted as it lifted him up. Algernon's goggles fell around his neck. He was thrown up in its hands like a small child. His mind continued to calculate and work. The rock Golem, which he deduced from the Hebrew inscription on its forehead, was surprisingly nimble for its size, but it was not as powerful as it looked; it did not squeeze him. He further deduced, squeezing his arm up to fit his goggles on his face, that the real strength of the beast was in its absolute hardness.

He planted his feet on the thing's chest and pushed hard. The Golem groaned as though it were in extreme pain and Algernon fell flat on his back. He adjusted the goggles quickly and then reached for his gun.

When he looked back up to see the creature through the goggles, he saw a human figure where the monumental beast should have been. The man's face was in agony. The symbol was there on his forehead flaming in red through the vision of the spectral goggles. The red tongues of flame burned and danced around the moving man.

Then the small man opened his eyes and his pain dissolved into rage.

Algernon watched the little human figure running toward him. He removed the goggles to confirm his strange suspicion; there was no human, rather it was the monster who was moving in on him again.

Algernon cursed aloud and tried to dodge its heavy fists. But upon crashing down, the fists caught Algernon's long coat and he scrambled on the ground trying to get away. It let out a hoarse and pained laugh. Algernon reached for his gun. His fingers skimmed the butt of the weapon, but he was pulled away.

"Emet" is Hebrew for "truth," and if my understanding of Hebrew teachings is correct, he contemplated, reaching again for the gun, *then removing Aleph from the word changes it to "met."* As the creature let go for a moment, lifting its body to lumber above Algernon again, he grabbed the pistol. *And "met" means something important.* The Golem reached above its head to pound Algernon into the rocky ground.

Algernon turned around on his back, revealing the gun. *"Met" means...* The fists came down as he fired a shot at the creature's head.

"Death."

In the echoing of the shot fired, the creature grabbed its face as it stumbled backward. Algernon grabbed his ears. The cavern echoed with the loud noise of the pistol. Algernon's shot had been true. Where the inscription had been, a white light flashed, with a haze, from its face. The creature began to crumble. The white light began to grow as the rocks fell away from its skin. A small man collapsed on his back, falling away from Algernon.

"Most intriguing." Algernon mumbled. He looked down into the corridor that led into the cavern. No one was coming yet. He stood up and pointed the gun at the small man, who was bleeding from the head.

Algernon approached him with caution, covered in dust and gravel.

"Freedom." The man quietly smiled at Algernon.

"Freedom from what?" Algernon asked him.

"Destruction," the man said calmly. "The night ones." The man's eyes were in a haze.

Algernon regretted not getting a better estimate of the size of the Golem before he deactivated it. It occurred to him that he'd never faced a Golem of any sort; it was only in theory that he knew what to do. His studies in Alchemic Homunculus never suggested that a human could be used to create a Golem, only inanimate objects. There should not have been the man lying before him but rather a pile of stones. The man was bleeding and a bit of skull was exposed.

Algernon bent over to help him, but the man stopped him. "No. Freedom now." The man sounded foreign, presumably Jewish. He grabbed Algernon's hand. Blood ran down across his black eyebrows. He looked at Algernon and pointed into the cavern. "Freedom."

Algernon began to ask him for clarification when he saw that the light in the man's eyes had left. There was nothing but an empty stare.

Freedom, he repeated. The cursed man's word rang in his head. *Genevieve is still down there.*

The mouth of the cavern funneled down into a maze of corridors. What began as a typical cave expanded quickly into an intricate network of dark, damp tunnels. Algernon moved through the tunnels effortlessly, comforted that they did not have the horrific, stale smell of the dead that emanated from the tunnels of Paris or the even more horrendous smell from the sewers of London. There was always something pulsing under cities.

The smell was organic, but that bored Algernon. He was always interested in the preternatural and supernatural things he could find and explore. From the walking dead of Nepal to Oxford's own aristocratic Vampyres, the clan of one Lord Ruthven, Algernon always found an interest in what he called the "queer realities of an otherwise boring world."

He sat down on a cold rock in what could barely be called a hallway, assuming he'd made a wrong turn, though he trusted the trails of spectral energies that his goggles helped him detect.

He was getting close to something.

He reached in his bag and fingered around for a moment before finding a box of *Bryant & Mays* non-phosphorous matches. The flash of striking the match emitted a small yellow glow that sparkled and the light was reflected in the droplets of water all over the tunnel.

Once his sense of claustrophobia subsided, he blew the match out and let his eyes readjust to the darkness while he contemplated what the Golem said about freedom. He adjusted himself in the small hallway. He thought about Genevieve and what they might be preparing to do to her. There was the possibility that she was already dead.

He shivered at the thought. It was difficult to admit it to himself, but he'd fallen in love with her. He didn't want to see a world where they couldn't be together. One way or another, he'd have to find her.

Death was not an option.

The words troubled him. He thought about what the Golem had said. *Why did he point into the cave when he said freedom? Are there others? Perhaps under a spell or even physically incarcerated below? Perhaps the Vampyres and the Shifters have herds of people to feed on.*

He didn't know.

The empty echo of the drip-drip that came down the hallway suddenly settled into another sound. It was in his head.

You clumsy ape! You'll drop her, a young voice whispered.

As Algernon climbed further into the tunnel, he found that it fed into a larger corridor. He was looking down over an ornately carved hallway. The stalagmites that had naturally formed throughout the cavern were cut into columns or doorways. Small lanterns hung along the walls, casting a constant but ebbing light throughout the hallway, where beautiful rugs and paintings adorned every direction he could see.

It was not a cavern at all anymore; it was an underground complex.

Lay her on the gurney, you oaf, the young man demanded quietly. Then he let out a chuckle. *It would seem that our other captive is dreaming about her suitor, Mister Elliott.* He closed his eyes and tried to focus on what he was sensing. *Oh, it's no use. As long as those branch-bearded Druids are holed up in here, there's no real clear thinking.*

Algernon knew that the young man was speaking about him. He focused on the painting in front of him. It was scenery, a castle raised up in a marsh. It reminded him of his trips to the South Coast of Britain with his family. His mind was blank except for generic images of the lands.

Apparently he's going to come and save her. The young voice laughed. There was a disarming and child-like softness trapped in the Vampyre's voice. It was charming. *She must think he's close. I can sense the thought pulsing.* The Vampyre sighed. *It's like he's right here with us.*

Algernon noted that somehow the Druids interfered with the natural telepathy of the Vampyres. *What a curious thought. Perhaps the Druids have a grounding effect. Ground. Root. Yes.* He stored the information away for later study.

His thoughts on the painting had worked, distracting the Vampyre from getting too much further into his mind. His theory was correct—since they had probed Genevieve's mind, they already had a sense for him and the young Vampyre could not distinguish his presence from her memory, quite probably aided by whatever disruption came from the Druids.

The young man instructed the large Golem that stood with him there. It looked much like the one that Algernon had already killed.

Freedom. Freedom. Freedom.

There were others.

The large creature laid the girl down on a gurney with a squeaking wheel and they began to move down the way. The hefty woman looked nearly dead. Life had been pulled from her.

This is genius, Ilya. The young-looking Vampyre said, obviously speaking to himself. *As long as she looks like one of the prisoners, this plan will come together just fine.*

Kat's long blonde hair flowed down like golden waterfalls. Her muscular arms swung freely and the young man went to each of her limbs and tucked them up as his large creature pushed the squeaky gurney down the hallway. He laid her arms across her chest and tucked her hair up around her shoulders. She looked peaceful.

There we go, sleeping beauty. Ilya laughed. *Beauty.* He mocked her. *I don't know what he sees in you, well, there's plenty to see.*

From the way her body moved against the gurney as it rolled along, Algernon observed that she was not dead yet. From the tone of the young man's voice, he could deduce that he didn't have any intention of killing her.

He was very charming though. Most Vampyres were.

The complex seemed to go on forever. It was a city. The columned archways reached up further and further, leaving the ceiling higher and higher as the floor sloped in the slightest manner to a darker place. The lanterns were lit and the whole place had an eerie, ethereal glow. The ceilings grew so tall and dark that they disappeared, becoming a night sky. One could almost forget that they were underground. Out beyond Algernon were small neighborhoods, even a market space. By all accounts, it was not what he had expected. It was beautiful.

Algernon peered around a wall to see streets expanding between buildings and he ducked from one alley to the next. Street lamps replaced the columns. The lamps burned green with wisps and sparks of pink and blue. He heard the loud shuffle of dragging footsteps in unison and could see a Golem pulling a chain-lead at the wrists of a line of men. Algernon looked through his spectral goggles again to see the Golem's real shape and saw what he found to be the most peculiar thing. Through the lenses, Algernon saw a little girl with a red glowing hand. It glowed with the same symbols as were on the forehead of the other Golem. She was pulling the lead of monstrous beasts. They looked like superhuman creatures chiseled from stone, all seven feet or taller. They hung their heads.

Fiends, he observed. *The very same from the book of Mark. "My name is Legion. For we are many." Demoniac warriors. Cast out by Jesus Christ into pigs, only cursed to return over the millennia.* He sighed. He could hear Spencer telling him to shut up. He worried for Spencer. He could already be dead. Something about the whole excursion felt like a mistake. He catalogued the demons for a moment to avoid allowing his own emotions to take over.

This can't be right. Fiends being led by a Golem? Fiends were rare. According to his research, Fiends were soldiers that, according to some texts, came from the lineage of a fallen angel called Gaderél. These were the same "men of renown" found in Genesis chapter six. *A shameful fall from Grace.* Algernon thought. Born with a biological imperative that predestined them to combat, they were doomed to suffer psychosis in times of peace. They were the anointed of war, but cursed otherwise. With the faux-battles staged by the Vampyre covenant and their Lords for feasting, the Fiends would be attracted. They would work their way into the picture and if they did not, they would be the adventuring types that got caught and brought there.

What intrigued Algernon even more than the Fiends was the Golem, who he did not expect to see at all. For all the oddities that he had seen, there were still others that he felt were things of myth only. Golems should have only been a thing of broken, ancient mythology, but he was wrong. *Anything you can think of is true.*

The Hebrew mythology of the Golem puzzled him and he thought as he eyed the little girl inside the rock creature. He had expected to find the ever-elusive Druids, who were children of the elements. As he leaned in on the perfectly carved rock wall, he put the puzzle pieces together.

The Golems ARE Druids!

SIX

━━━◆━━━

We know nothing in reality; for truth lies in an abyss.
- **Democritus**, *Fragment 117, (423BCE)*

Jared leaned on the bar and whispered to Glenn. "The Vampyre and the children: it's working. Seems we have an uprising on our hands."

Glenn Lamphere's anger had flared and waned since the disappearance of his daughter but the low-burning fire was undying. Barmaids cleaned up the tables and the patrons drank and sang. "I never thought those songs would grate my nerve so." They shared a knowing look. The air was thick with drink and dull merriment. Glenn looked at the medallions and the pendants everywhere, every one a reminder of the controlling hand of the alliance and the Brethren. The room seemed empty without Kat. Desmond would pay for it. Everyone would.

"We're going to free the headmaster and the mayor's assistant," Jared nodded quietly.

"Why?" Glenn asked.

"Well, there are reasons." Jared smiled. "But more than anything else, they're the enemies of your enemy, are they not?"

Glenn stared into the darkness through the window. "That they are."

The door swung open and there stood the old man, Chandler, carrying a body. Blood ran down his arms to his fingers. His face was unrecognizable. "It was Desmond," Chandler said as he looked across the bar. The man was dwarfed carrying the large body.

"I suppose that makes this man a friend," Glenn chuckled darkly to Jared, who moved to take the burden of the man's weight off of Chandler. "That's the Vampyre hunter, get him to his room and I'll have the girls bring up some water and ointment for him."

Jared and Chandler carried the man up to his room and laid him on the bed.

"The book," Jasper moaned quietly.

"Book?" Chandler asked.

"What book?" Jared asked. Why would anyone want that useless man beaten unless he had something quite powerful? "You're the man that stole Gallegos's book."

"How do you know that name?" Chandler interrupted coldly.

Jared raised an eyebrow. "He's a friend. He is quite interested in seeing it returned."

"Not anymore. Not if Desmond has it," Chandler said.

Jared sensed the edge in Chandler's voice. He grunted and looked down on what he was beginning to think of as a corpse. He had seen his share of war wounds. "You should make him comfortable. I don't suppose anyone should be alone for their last hours like this." He left the old man Frenchman standing over the younger one, bleeding. The dingy sheets grew dark with his blood. The man deserved to die as far as Jared was concerned and probably would from the blood loss alone. As he walked down the hallway, two girls came with a pan of water and rags. He stepped aside as they ran past. When he returned downstairs, Glenn was watching the door. No one had followed. "Tell the old Spaniard with the beard that 'the book is gone.' He'll know what you mean," he told Glenn. "I have to return to the kids now."

"Would you like me to send you anything?" Glenn asked.

"No. Let's not attract unwanted attention." He walked out. Jared was growing more worried. Gallegos could handle Vampyres and he could go without being seen, but that book of his, it sounded like more of a weapon than it did a piece of fiction. When he got out of the lamplight in the street, he pulled his coat down and made a run into the woods.

Ernest's stomach dropped. He had told Michael not to rescue him. He was such a fool. With the sunrise, they would have him hanged for killing a man. The mayor was so awful anyway. He was the only person that Ernest could imagine being worse than Desmond, or at least as apathetic.

He felt alone. He was completely engulfed in his fear. He was going to die and there was an eerie silence in the cells. The officers had stopped coming and going. They were building the platform outside for the hanging. The sheriff had not appeared almost all day. Spencer had not moved or made a noise for quite some time and Oliver Whipple, the little boy whom the sheriff had pulled in nights before, was lying silently on a pallet near the door.

He wasn't going anywhere.

The night was bright and gray. The woods were a monochrome of moonlight and shadows. Michael walked slowly along the main road toward Breton in his charcoal gray suit. He no longer felt any reason to hide and if Isaac wanted to find him, he could. He sensed a shift on the wind and sensed fear. It was akin to a sharp and acrid smell. Isaac was nearby. He'd already engaged with Isaac. He had a better sense of the creature now. Michael walked. He could see the edge of the dilapidated town in the distance. The road was like a long hallway with a wall of trees on either side. The tall evergreens reached straight up like graying pillars in the moonlight.

I promise to make things more interesting, Isaac, he thought, smiling. Michael turned to look into the dark woods. Even the wind on the grass was visible to him; each breath moved. He could see the Vampyre standing in the distance.

Pain only strengthens you, Michael. It came as a surprise to him that Michael had arrived at his name.

Before pain, I knew nothing. I woke up a monster and there was only pain, Michael replied. *I have you to thank for that.*

No, Michael, Isaac answered. *I have no idea how you came to be here.* He sounded sincere. *Whatever happened to you aboard that boat is beyond me.*

Michael's eyes flashed. *Is that why you toyed with me and nearly killed me? Couldn't figure out the riddle?*

No, Isaac replied. *I regret that now.*

Not yet you don't. Michael smiled.

Michael, Isaac pleaded, *you don't have to do this.*

There was both guilt and hope in his voice. Michael sensed an overwhelming darkness in Isaac that had not been there before. Isaac feared. He knew he couldn't fight forever.

"Yes I do." Michael said. Once again, he sensed Isaac's fear rising.

You are not like us, Michael.

Michael laughed.

You are a Vampyre but there's something else. Isaac hid in a dense copse of trees. He could see the young man's aura from a distance. Red psionic energy flowed around Michael and haloed around his head and his eyes. Tongues of flame rose within the aura from Michael's arms and his shoulders like expansive wings. Behind him stood something larger. Behind Michael, there was darkness where there should have been shadow. There was an emptiness. Out of the corner of his eye, Isaac could almost make it out. It was a silhouette, almost identical to Michael himself but almost twice his size.

Michael, you have to listen to me.

"No. I don't. I'm going to instead enjoy the silence once I kill you." He stopped walking. "I'm going to kill every last Vampyre among you. I am going to show you what a predator is."

Yes, I attacked you. You could have been from another covenant. You could have been a spy. We have many enemies. It was a mistake.

"A mistake that will cost you."

We Vampyres fight. It is in our nature.

"And since I'm not like you, I shouldn't fight you?"

No. Isaac sighed. *Vampyres don't have voices. We don't fly. We are fast, yes. We are strong. But your feet barely touch the ground. And you speak with the voice of man.*

Michael said nothing. He clenched his fists until the knuckles cracked. *He's lying,* the voice in his head told him. *He knows you will win. He's buying time, he's waiting on reinforcements.*

Come back with me, Michael. We can work together. Isn't this what you want?

"It was what I wanted."

Was?

"I have seen the desolation of this place." Michael said. "I have seen your work."

But you don't understand... Isaac began.

Michael jumped forward: the predator toward his prey. He sensed the voice and located it, flying along the grass, weaving between trees.

"Understand this."

Isaac dodged as quickly as he could, but the force of Michael's fist in his sternum knocked him to the ground. He picked himself up, barely able to ward off the powerful creature. There was no escape that he could see.

Michael lunged at Isaac again, catching him by his throat. He would have no problem killing him.

He grabbed Michael's hand with both of his own. Immediately, he knew that was a mistake. He could feel his life leaving his body even through the palms of his hands, absorbed by Michael.

The power of the Vampyres was in the regeneration of their energy; they were faster than humans and had a capacity of healing greater than any other creature. It was a mystical force not understood by anyone (even Isaac, one of the oldest living Vampyres), but Michael had suddenly tapped into it for the first time. He was pulling Isaac's life force directly from within him.

Isaac wouldn't die yet; he fought at Michael and pushed. Isaac closed his eyes and clenched his teeth, engulfing both Vampyres in a flash of light.

When Michael opened his eyes, the Vampyre was gone. He stood alone in the mysterious dark wood again. He could sense the light in the place. The cold hard ground was illuminated with flowing energy. Unlike the first time he'd been there, when he stood in the mansion, he could now see the apparitions. They were men, women and children walking along the road. They watched him, turning heads and crooking necks with eyes focused on him.

Michael asked them, "The Vampyre. Where did he go?" But they did not respond. Michael ran to a man in all white with a trimmed beard and asked again, "Isaac, the Vampyre. Where is he?" His voice rang out like a lion's roar. The man, caught by his lapel, responded slowly and quietly but Michael couldn't understand what he was saying at all.

He was frustrated. He pushed the man away. He could sense Isaac was somewhere nearby.

Michael, the voice gasped inside his head, *you must listen to me*. But Michael only looked through the faces in the crowd and turned back to the forest ahead of him through the ancient trees. *Please understand; I can help you. I can help you figure out what you are. You mustn't kill me. No matter what your instinct tells you—I can help you*. Michael walked toward the voice and saw Isaac lying limp against a tree. The light that shined around and throughout them had been drained from Isaac's body. The illumination was dim around him. His eyes did not glow and he held up a hand. He'd only bought himself a few moments.

Say something. Isaac gasped, but Michael stood above him quietly. Isaac had seemed so strong and powerful—before, he had been the hunter. Michael had run from him full of fear and confusion.

Michael reached down and picked up the weak man by his lapel. He tried once again to drain the creature's energy, but before he knew it, Isaac had vanished once again. Michael stood in the dark, empty-handed and fuming.

You will be mine, Vampyre.

Stephen's wake had gone well into the evening. Parson Adler had to get away from it all and made his way across the square.

As Adler opened the door to the inn, he listened at the quiet room. "God, this whole town is dead." He muttered.

Lamphere, the innkeeper, crossed the room to him, "Can I help you, parson?" His voice was a calculated balance of professional courtesy and his own mitigated rage.

"I came to visit a patron of yours, sir."

"Well, I hope it's that idiot Vampyre hunter," he replied sarcastically.

"It is, in fact." Adler was abrupt. "Is something the matter?"

"Boy's bleeding out." Glenn seemed neither surprised nor concerned. "Brown's up there now. Not much hope."

Adler moved toward the stairs. "Brown. Wonderful."

Glenn turned to him and then paused. He looked down. "Parson." He seemed to have trouble with his words. "Quite sorry for your nephew." He could barely look at the man and his eyes were drawn outside through a window as he spoke.

Adler stopped. He could tell the innkeeper was sincere. The parson held back a rush of emotions that he felt would burst out of him in tears. "And I am sorry about your daughter." For the first time in many years, he meant it. In the back of his mind, it gave him pleasure to see Glenn and Bart hurting for his nephew. It meant that Desmond would have more work to do.

He made his way up the stairs to the hallway quietly as a young girl with a handful of bloodied rags came hurrying by. He stepped out of her way. There was a dead quiet in the inn except for the shuffle in the young man's room.

Adler stood in the doorway. Doctor Brown listened at the young man's chest with a stethoscope and Chandler sat in a chair across from the bed. He was covered in blood. One of the girls that worked in the inn, a shapely and humorous barmaid named Marie Sutton, stood watching the Doctor with her hands to her mouth.

"No use," the Doctor sighed. He looked toward the door. "He'll be dead soon." He stopped. "It's this devilish lifestyle. Drinking and philandering gets men in these situations. Blood in his lung." The doctor was both cold and judgmental. "I don't see why you've troubled me to come see a dying man. There's no hope for him."

Chandler just watched him coldly. He crossed his arms and watched the man from under his dark, thick brow, burrowing his chin into his chest. He clenched his jaw. He could have ground his own teeth into dust.

"You should have called a priest." The doctor yawned.

Chandler looked up to see Parson Adler standing there.

"Yes," Adler replied. "I will take over, Doctor Brown."

The doctor was surprised to see the man there. "Oh, Parson," he stuttered. "I am so sorry about..."

"I know," Adler answered. "Why don't you go on home, Doctor Brown? Perhaps you're out of your depth now," he growled, knowing that the doctor, a member of the League, would not have troubled himself with Jasper's life.

"Sir," the Doctor replied. "I am the finest physician in a hundred miles!"

"Oh, there's no doubt about that." Adler smiled as he entered the room. "I am more than certain that the Alliance would have it no other way, considering you're the *only* physician for a hundred miles."

The man glared at him.

"Goodnight, Doctor Brown." Adler remarked sarcastically. The doctor pushed his way past Adler.

Chandler stood up. "To what do we owe this rare pleasure?"

"I had an agreement with this man." Adler pulled up a chair next to the bed. "Young lady, would you mind fetching me some tea, please?"

The barmaid, Marie, hesitated.

"I promise to make sure he is fine," Adler assured her with a strange and uncomfortable smile. She got the feeling that he had forgotten what it was like to deal with people.

Marie left quietly.

"I know about your agreement..." Chandler admitted. "My idea."

Chandler leaned forward with his elbows on his knees, while Adler crossed his leg and leaned back to listen. The room glowed dark by the lamplight. Jasper's body looked awful and his face was bruised. He was not the same handsome, charming young man he had been earlier. They'd placed a cold rag on his forehead to offset the fever. He coughed. The sound sloshed around.

Parson Adler said nothing. There was a silence between the men, interrupted only by the sound of the wheezing and coughing.

Chandler continued. "Truth is, Adler, you and I know how this works. I want out and this young man would have helped buy me some time in that endeavor."

The sentiment angered Adler, but he listened. His perspective was changing quickly.

"Time's up for us," Chandler mused, "yet, we continue doing their bidding."

"I suppose you're right there," Adler replied coldly.

"They took your nephew, Adler," he pushed. "They took your life. I know you. Don't treat me like a fool."

Adler sighed and contemplated the man's thoughts. He did not take Chandler's words lightly. Adler was one of very few people who knew Chandler's true identity. It was top secret.

"What do you submit?" the parson asked.

"That we end the charade," Chandler said, leaning forward. "That we go find out what is in this world, why we are whatever we are. We dismantle Isaac's dream. We run through Desmond. We take back what they've taken from us."

"I'll never have my nephew back, Khalil," Adler replied.

"No. No, you cannot. But you can have revenge at the very least." He grinned. "And at very least, you owe me that. You owe me my revenge."

Adler stared past him, through the window into the darkness and he scratched his face. "Very well," he replied. "Let us begin."

What a glorious, however disconcerting, contrast, he mused. From Tibet to Paris, I swear these must be the most wonderful living conditions for any Vampyre I've ever seen. Algernon examined the paintings. They were ancient and beautiful; they were as well-preserved as anything in a museum. Truth be known, he continued, these may be the finest living conditions for any person of any sort. He considered the squalid living conditions for the citizens of Breton and shook his head shamefully. He thought about the beautiful, young Genevieve and the shanty where she lived. Every thought about her disheartened him.

He'd lowered himself into the large corridor and decided to go in the direction heading away from the charming young Vampyre and his Golem. They had extracted that girl's body from somewhere in that direction. He would investigate there first.

The corridors expanded even further, carved directly out of the stone in the earth. At his best estimation, Algernon guessed that he was only thirty or forty feet under the ground. The cavern's slope was a gradual one. He was moving back in the direction that he had come from. He deduced that it was an ongoing excavation, an immense undertaking, comparable to the work put into the pyramids at Giza.

He snuck from shadow to crevice, watching and listening. He moved through dark rooms, empty catacomb-like sleeping chambers and then into a small library. The bindings on some of the books suggested that they could have been upwards of four hundred years old. It would have been a treasure trove of knowledge and history if it weren't sitting wasted in the hands of destructive, anti-social monsters.

The door opened and Algernon quickly rolled under a long table and held his breath, meditating. He watched two very nice pairs of shoes stop in the middle of the room.

No, Rurk, one voice explained. This is not for you, my brother.

But Ilya asked me... An identical voice answered.

Ilya doesn't know what he wants, much less what we all want, the first replied. These are not orders and we're not soldiers. This is sabotage, plain and simple. They began walking again and Algernon sat unnoticed. What we did to that strange man is irreparable, but Ilya's right—it puts everything in play for everyone.

Ruthven or Isaac—it doesn't matter. We no longer need leaders who don't listen to us; we used to be free.

They spoke in broken English to each other. Algernon deduced that they were brothers of Russian descent.

Even as we remembered who we once were, this man too will remember, the first brother said again. *And with the 'presentation' of his blonde lover,* he smiled, *he may very well welcome the chaotic way of the Vampyre.*

And Isaac? the more doubtful brother asked.

Isaac knows nothing. Isaac will know nothing until it is too late for him.

Algernon opened his eyes and looked across the room to see a painting of a pyramid much like the ones at Giza. *Interesting.*

The men continued their walk and went out the door that had brought Algernon into the room.

Algernon crawled out from under the table to look at the painting. A small gold plaque below read, "Death descends on Tikal." Upon closer inspection, the real focus was not on the pyramid structure at all but on the people below it engaged in a bloody war; the natives were being overtaken by powerful Vampyres in full daylight.

"Terrible," he observed. "I suppose this story has many a chapter yet to be told."

Chandler contemplated stopping for a slug of whatever foul spirit Lamphere would pour him. He was covered in Markov's blood. He couldn't stop now. He had to be on the move. He'd left the boy in the Crow's Nest with wicked-hearted Adler, who had also just lost his own nephew.

The street ebbed like a quiet lake. The flow of people was slow. He never trusted anyone that lived in Breton; there were monitors and spies everywhere. He often felt lulled by the illusion of Breton being a town, but in the three decades he'd spent there, he'd been tortured and pushed to the edge of insanity dozens of times. The first and last thought during those times was, *I'll find out who turned me in this time.* The middle thoughts he chose not to recall anymore.

The only friend he'd ever made was Jean-Pierre Moreau, though even that was mistrusting. He hated that he'd kept the Frenchman at arm's length. He was surely dead by now. That would be same fate for the man's niece and her English suitor. The fool fellow had run off to save her from inevitable destruction. Vampyres would devour them both. Chandler pulled the collar of his frock coat up around his ears and walked with his head down.

"Is there some reason that Vampyres have not killed you yet?" There came a man's voice from the darkness. "Riddled as you are with blame and guilt."

Chandler did not stop walking. He kept a calm pace. He did not fear the voice.

"A friend told me that, in this place, the Vampyre consumes good and evil alike. And you see," the voice continued, "I have not studied the hearts of men for long, but I see that you are deeply troubled. Why is that?"

"I'm sure I'd be delectable, sir Vampyre."

"Yet here you stand."

"Here I am."

"Why is that?"

Chandler laughed. "Maybe someone told them to leave an old man alone."

"From what I can tell, no one tells these Vampyres what to do."

"That's an understatement. They didn't warn you about this old man?"

"No. It would appear they haven't had the chance."

"That's a shame."

Chandler stopped walking. He could sense the blood in his ears. This was becoming a nuisance. "Why are you toying with me?"

"Toying?"

"Yes, toying." He looked at himself, covered in blood. The voice was too calm to have been poisoned with bloodlust. He had stopped directly in front of a dark alley where the voice came from and whispered, "Do you think for one minute that you are capable of killing me?" *It would be a blessing.* "Do you think that you, fool, will be able to do aught with me?" He scoffed. His eyes searched the darkness calmly. "I, Vampyre, am the face of death." He pulled a weapon out from his pocket and casually unfolded a brass six-barrel pepperbox pistol. The handle was a brass knuckleduster. A small dagger folded out of the front. It was a dirty little thing.

"What is a gun going to do to a Vampyre?" the voice asked.

At that moment, he realized that the Vampyre didn't know. "This is my Apache. The reason Breton exists. It is Hell on Earth for Vampyres like you."

He searched the darkness. "It stopped Ruthven. It stopped Betancourt."

He turned around but saw nothing. "So, you do fear me."

The Vampyre spoke. "I don't." Chandler watched a pair of eyes like dim lanterns appear in the darkness. "You're responsible for this purgatorial dwelling? For the slaughtering in the woods of those poor, grave men? You are the reason for the orphans?" The voice paused. "This is the face...of Death?"

A young man stepped into sight. His dark suit seemed to spread into the haze as though he were stepping from a dream.

"I am not acquainted with your Ruthven, nor your Betancourt. Nor do I know the hell of your Apache. All I see here is a man who is eaten with the cancer of guilt."

"Whose time is being wasted." Chandler said. "For however interesting it is to hear a Vampyre speak with is own voice, I have more pressing matters."

"I can't imagine how that could be true."

Chandler began to grit his teeth with anger. "Shouldn't you be speaking to Isaac about all this?"

"No. I don't have anything else to say to him."

Chandler smirked and raised his caterpillar eyebrows. *Impressive.*

"Why, then, old man, should I not kill you?" Michael asked.

"You could most certainly set yourself to it, Michael the Vampyre, but it'll be of little use." Chandler anticipated the Vampyre's move and pulled the trigger of the pepperbox pistol, but Michael had caught him by the wrist, sending the explosive shot into the wall of the building. The flash was blinding and the sound rung out between the brick walls. Chandler was immobilized. His feet weren't touching the ground. The Vampyre lifted him by his coat.

"You're asking the wrong question," he wheezed.

"What?"

"Correct." He wheezed again.

Someone was running toward them. They could both hear the footsteps.

The correct question is 'why?' Chandler thought. *Why would someone so attractive to Vampyres still be untouched?*

Michael snorted with derision. He twisted the man's wrist. Police were rounding the corner of the alley. Michael lifted the man farther until his own feet were not touching the ground.

Levitating in the shadow, Michael peered into the man's cold black eyes and he felt himself being sucked into his thoughts as if through a doorway into a large house with countless rooms. The old man's voice rang out from every room, *Bismillāh, nothing is true; everything is permitted.* The voice was thousands of voices. Some were ancient, while others were the voices of children. Michael could sense though that they were each incarnations of this same man. *For every life I have taken, I have died a hundred times.* The voices grew more quiet. *For every day I have stolen, I am given a thousand more.* The rooms twisted into one another and Michael ceased to sense his own body. He was a cool desert breeze blowing through a North African village distant in both time and space. At the center of this universe of thought was an ugly child with black hair and olive skin. They eyebrows were the same. The desert breeze followed the ugly child through the abandonment of a father as a hardened boy became a man, violent and psychotic. The rooms of the house twisted and the colors of time, space and their memory became a kaleidoscope of amalgamations, hatred and anger then tempered by a calculating murderous drive; the murderer becomes soldier going to fight skirmish after battle after war, hungering for the gunpowder death of his enemies. War upon war became hate upon hate. Khalil Sayid, killer, Algerian bastard son of Egyptian ambassador and French slave, hungered for death.

In the swirl of time and memory, the satisfied crunch of a grasshopper in between a child's fingers becomes a knife in the belly of a lover and blooms into petals of death upon death. A spray of blood rises in the cool desert breeze.

The assassin is born a francophone dog turned on the Spanish and the French. By knife, by gun and by bare hand, Khalil Sayid killed. The grief and solitude poisoned his mind to insanity and then to suicide—a knife to his own throat and the prayer he gurgled to Allah, not for forgiveness, but for silence. As the light faded in the cold man's eyes, a final thought: *Bismillāh, nothing is true; everything is permitted.* He saw the red pool and the steam rise from the sand where he had killed himself. It should have ended there but the cool desert breeze blew on around this moment. In the warping house of his memories, Khalil Sayid felt his throat the morning after, waking up in a pool of blood with a perfect scar across his neck in confusion. The cool desert breeze blew down a final corridor where life existed with no end, only pain but not joy.

Decades of wandering.

No death. No silence. No peace.

In an instant, Michael was washed over with countless lifetimes. The anguish of a life, amplified. Then nothing. Over and over. Michael's mind was flooded with experiences and emotions and in the middle of it all was a window in the man's memory. This gaping hole of existence that would be death. Khalil Sayid, now Monsieur Ives-Henri Chandler, could not be killed. There was no death for him. He felt the torture of eighty years, never aging: governments, national powers and religious leaders came and went. He couldn't continue looking inside him.

Michael came crashing back into his own body, still hovering above the scuffle below them; the police were looking for whatever the shot had been and after a few moments, they went running through the alley to the other street searching.

Chandler had stopped kicking. His glazed eyes held on Michael.

Michael could see the scar just above his white knuckles, gripping the man's coat.

I don't know why either, Chandler thought. The fire in his eyes was gone. The old man just looked resigned.

Michael lowered the man to the ground and gave him some space. Chandler swallowed hard and grabbed at his neck. He breathed heavily, watching for anyone passing by. "What covenant sent you?"

"No covenant."

"Well, who cursed you into the dark?"

"Don't know."

Chandler nodded. "Start with what you do know." He straightened his long frock coat.

"I will never be what they are." He stepped closer to the man. "Even if I am cursed to forget day and death and peace, I will never be as they are."

"I respect your resolve, young Vampyre." Chandler said. "But never is a long time."

Michael sighed.

"But I'll give you this: you are not what they are."

"What does that mean?"

Chandler shook his head. "You're a wolf among dogs."

"No." Michael closed his eyes. "No. I don't feel anything akin to them."

Chandler let out a rueful chuckle. "No, I suppose you're more of a lion in wolves's clothing."

"I won't be judged by you." Michael said.

"A killer recognizes a killer." Chandler said. He adjusted his frock coat. "There is and will always be blood on my hands." He showed his palms, exposing the weapon in his hand. "But tonight, I'm trying to be on the side of the angels. If you're not helping the Brethren, will you help me?"

Michael nodded. *I'll keep an eye on the children.*

The old man smiled. "That's all I ask. They shouldn't be in this mess. The rest of us will have to sort it out, monsieur." Michael turned away, but Chandler spoke up again, "When my judgment day comes, Michael," Michael stopped to listen, "I hope that it's you that finds me."

I do not know if you are a religious man, Mister Markov, but I can tell you that I am not." Parson Adler spoke with quiet concern. He held his unlit pipe in one hand. "I do not know if you believe in 'miracles' or if you have a mind for the scientific, but I can tell you that in some way both science and religion have failed."

The young man lay in the single bed, its sheets soaked with blood and sweat. His bruised eyes were swollen shut and he passed in and out of consciousness with fever.

He was dying.

"Doctor Brown would probably have tried a little harder if he were not in league with Desmond, as I have been for almost twenty-five years. But the difference," Adler played with his pipe, "is that unlike them, I have no reason to believe in religious texts."

He put the pipe back in his pocket.

"So it is ironic that they should put me, a man of science, to act as a man of the cloth for so long." His tone changed a bit. "You see, Jasper, I am not a man at all. Humans, or that is to say, full-blooded humans, have reserved that name for themselves. Since I am of another blood, as the Vampyres are, we are cast out of your societies and we are used as weapons, but we are not allowed to live as civilized men. I can save you, Mister Markov, but I need you to know that *man* did nothing but hurt you."

The young man coughed and Adler wiped the blood from his bubbling mouth.

"I am one of very few of my kind and I may not survive what happens in the next moment. My nephew was human, mostly I think and I loved him. And I know he loved me. I need someone to know that."

Adler stood and took off his coat and laid it across the chair. He leaned over the young man and put his hand to the wound on his side and then reached across with the other and supported himself above the boy, face to face with him.

After a moment the man's hand began to disintegrate into smoke and penetrate the wound. He opened his mouth as if to say a prayer and smoke billowed from within him, smelling like pipe tobacco, not burned but sweet. The boy breathed in, slipping into a dream where he was falling through suffocating, endless fire.

Adler's hand became wisps of smoke and he began disappearing into the boy, a body of haze. The boy coughed, choking, but then he would relax again in his sleep. The bed grew warm and blood dried into dark crusty stains.

The young man breathed heavily and heaved. The process was slow and painful for both of them.

When the sun came up with morning, the old man sat in the chair, unconscious, with a trickle of blood from the nose and the young man awoke in pain but still very much alive. The bruising was going down and the fever was gone. It had all felt like a very strange dream, but the fear of dying resonated in him.

Adler lay back in the seat. He snored and moaned with pain and he was covered in blood.

As Markov felt his bruised ribs, he felt the scar on his right side.

"I do believe in miracles."

The morning's humidity clung to Chandler's clothes. The morning train had already run and he sat in his office with his sleeves rolled up. His tie and coat sat on the desk and the loosened shirt showed his scar. He rarely gave it much thought anymore. Years ago, he had made sure to have his wardrobe tailored with taller collars. Good thing for him that sort of thing was "in."

The night before was troubling him. That thing that had found him with the burning, righteous eyes; there was no condescendence or self-valued judgment in him. There was something pure. He was unlike other Vampyres.

It put Chandler off.

A righteous Vampyre. That was rich.

It did change the equation, however. Perhaps things could work out for the best. Perhaps there was a chance for his silence. What the Vampyre had said really shook him, though the pain of falling forty feet could have woken him a bit. "Even if I am cursed to forget day and death and peace, I will never be as they are."

Then there was the matter of his old partner Everett Adler, "Parson Adler," he scoffed. The lifelong Alliance lackey was suddenly running in and saving people and he was definitely on Desmond's list now. But the Vampyre, that soldier, Gallegos and Adler were all angry with Desmond— not to mention Algernon Elliott like Jonah down in the belly of the whale. Things were about to change. He was ready for change.

He grabbed his tie and jacket and his way to the door, he had a funeral to get to.

With dawn came mourners. Word had gotten out. Parson Adler looked up at the bell tower with disdain and sadness. Arrangements had been rushed, but they were beautiful. The women of the town had gathered flowers for Stephen. Some folks spoke. Adler heard little.

He leaned on a cane, feeling he'd aged decades in one night. The quiet speeches had given way to a short walk outside to the courtyard. Many people were shaking hands and patting each other on the back. The coffin sat next to the hole in the graveyard outside the church and a young lady was organizing flowers next to it. Adler watched the crowd intently.

Sheriff Matheson stood by closely and held his hat under his arm. Matheson stepped forward, watching the two orphans, the troublemakers standing in the back, hidden with hats.

"Are you going somewhere, Sheriff?" asked Adler with distrust.

"No." He replied through his teeth. The sheriff nodded to two officers on the edge of the crowd, who moved around to follow, but by the time he looked back, the boys were gone.

Adler looked for familiar faces that would not be there: Headmaster Smith was missing (and jailed) and all his orphans gone. The two mischievous boys, Ned and Tom, were the only friends poor Stephen had. He felt it wrong that they not be given time to mourn properly. Ernest Williams was also jailed— that idiot man had always been painfully patient with the boy. Glenn Lamphere, the innkeeper had watched from across the square but returned quietly and painfully to his tavern. All those people who truly saw how special his boy was were the very ones being snuffed out by the Alliance's cronies throughout the town. Those very cronies were building a platform across the square to hang the very men who had shown kindness and taught children to show kindness to his boy. The irony would not be lost on Everett Adler. The crowd of people who spoke in hushed tones in respect to the life of his nephew would be crying for out for the deaths of two men before the noon bell rang.

As for Desmond, he was nearby and, from the courtyard of the church, as people were gathering to lay the body in the ground, Adler could see his horses and carriage parked rudely in front of the inn instead of in a stable. He knew that he had something to do with Stephen's death.

His rage was full, but he stayed quiet. There were only moments left before he would be freed from his three-decade-long charade with those people. He would show the only true love of his life, his own blood, a proper burial. For the first time that morning, tears swelled in the old man's eyes and he leaned heavily on his cane, full of aching and pain. He pulled a kerchief from his pocket and dabbed his wet eyes. Jasper came quietly. "Are you alright?"

"I'll be fine," he answered. It was the most human and weak he'd ever felt. He would be vulnerable for only a few moments more.

Jasper took his seat.

The only people seated were Jasper Markov and one of the young ladies that had helped make the arrangements for the funeral. Adler hadn't sat down all morning.

He stepped forward to where the coffin sat at the edge of the hole. The shovel had made fresh scars into the layered soil until it reached the dark brown. His shadow was cast into the hole as he leaned on the cane over the boy in the box.

There was a hush in the crowd as he prepared to speak.

"Thank you for coming today to help me say goodbye to my nephew. There's no name for the bereavement one feels at the loss of a child." For the first time, his heart truly went out to Glenn. "If a child loses their parent, they are orphaned, as Stephen was. The terrible days of war that have beleaguered us for so long saw to that. But for fifteen sweet years in my life, I had the opportunity to raise and love him as my own."

There was a silence among the people. Some wept quietly and the gentle breeze moved through the fabrics of their clothing. Then his tone changed; there was no more a sadness but a bitterness that took hold.

"There is no name for the man who loses a child. We are not widowed. We are not orphaned. We are robbed our task and our will. We—I—am nothing."

Sheriff Matheson straightened his spine but he, more than anyone, could sense the poison in Adler's words. He sensed dread. It had all gone wrong. Desmond was wrong.

"We have all lost something to the Vampyres," Adler continued. "We have all been robbed our peace and our lives." There was a quiet agreement. "We will no longer..." Adler stopped himself. He looked around. He found Matheson's eyes.

"I," he told the crowd, "vow today to end the plague of night." There was a moment of applause that came divorced from the crowd; some didn't want to believe. The power of the curse was weak and Adler knew it. He knew Desmond had a plan to renew it and he knew that it was his moment to strike. "I pledge to you now, not as citizens of this town but simply as people who want peace: The reign of the Vampyre comes to an end in Breton."

Silence.

"And with that, you will all be free."

Edwin and Thomas ran quickly away from the funeral. They had been spotted—again. Thomas was a few steps ahead of Edwin. They had to get back to the plan. They had to save Mister Smith and Mister Williams. Everyone else was getting into position.

Emily and Penny had been at the funeral but hid themselves in the crowd well. They would not have been spotted. Thomas was slowing down. They needed to be making a getaway before they could get into position for the noonday plan.

"No Thomas!" Edwin exclaimed. "They are right behind us."

But Thomas couldn't push himself to run. His heart was breaking in that moment. He had been making himself strong for everyone, for the orphans, for Emily, for Edwin his friend, for Mister Smith, but his heart was coming apart. He hadn't mourned Stephen.

"Why did they kill him, Edwin?" His final steps sputtered into a slow walk on the street.

"Thomas, we can't do this now!" Edwin tried to encourage his friend as he looked past him to see if they were being followed. They were. The police were only blocks away, walking briskly around the corner.

Thomas had no tears. There was no sadness. There was just a pain that he couldn't express in words. All he could feel was that Stephen Adler, the simpleton, didn't deserve to die. Mom and Dad didn't deserve to die. He felt like he should have died and they should have been let to live. It didn't make sense.

Edwin grabbed him by the arm and dragged him, but even his feet didn't want to work. "Thomas, please."

"I'm just a thief, Ned," Thomas pleaded. "Why didn't the Vampyres kill me? Why did they take Stephen and Kat and Jenny and my mama and my dad?"

It hit Edwin. The sensation was awful. He had been in denial. They had been playing heroes, but he hadn't realized that the game was so deadly. It had only begun to sink in.

He kept pulling Thomas. "I don't know. I don't know, but we have to go."

"They are going to kill Mister Smith today too." Thomas was despondent.

Edwin stopped. "NO, THEY ARE NOT." His voice strained. There was a weak, childish anger in him. "We are going to stop them today, Thomas."

"But what if we fail?"

Of the two boys, Thomas was of a much stronger character. His resolve was powerful and his faith was large, but the largest hearts are often the most easily broken. Thomas was lucky to have a friend like Edwin who rallied him.

"Do you think Mister Smith and Jenny taught us to pick pockets, to hide and to survive just so we could be thieves, Thomas? Do you think they want us to live the lives of the bad people? Mister Smith is good and Jenny loved—loves us." The police had spotted them. He grabbed Thomas's sleeve. "No, they taught us to live in the night—where the Vampyres live—because someone has to fight them." He swallowed.

"So..." Thomas answered.

Edwin looked worried. He started to step away and run.

"So we fight." Thomas gritted his teeth. The police were running toward them. Thomas turned toward the alley. "This way." His heart swelled with goodness. His legs felt renewed. He ran past Edwin and turned into the alley. He would fight for Stephen, who was innocent and Kat, who was smart and Jenny, who was full of love.

Edwin followed on his heels.

They were only children. But they were born into a world where death did not discriminate.

As the police entered the alley, they saw no one. They ran on through to the next street. A cellar window closed noiselessly as the boys disappeared into a home—into the dark.

SEVEN

---◆---

*He who makes war his profession cannot be otherwise
than vicious. War makes thieves, and peace brings
them to the gallows.*
- **Niccolo Machiavelli**, *Art of War*, *(1521)*

The platform was set high. Two nooses were thrown over the
gallows. Officers toyed with the mechanism that released
the raised footing on the platform. It would drop the
criminals to a painful death. The men worked tirelessly. They did
not joke or speak.

A crowd had begun to gather around the new platform.
There had never been any need for hangings in Breton. Most
people feared punishment enough to simply disappear in the
night. Fear made people behave, but there was an undercurrent
of rebellion in the air and Desmond Burroughs was going to make
sure that fear resonated in the minds of people as his new plan
took shape.

Desmond had not been seen. He had not left his room in
the inn. Sheriff Matheson walked the square, watching for the
rebellious orphans. There should have been no reason to fear,
but he knew from his own experiences that people did strange,
extraneous things when faced with their own death. Would it be
the ever-charming Smith or the fearful Williams that would make
his day difficult?

There was still talk of the morning's funeral service. There
were very few people buried in the church's front cemetery,
which was usually reserved for town elders, but no one disagreed
that Stephen deserved to be there. He was a deacon. He worked
his whole life in service of the church. A pity, some women said,
for the Vampyres to have found him so young. It made many
people question their motives. There was some gossip that Adler
may have had something to do with it himself, having crossed the
Vampyres. Some people were sure he was in league with them.

Sheriff Matheson smiled at the gossip. It was the little
shred of hope that whatever bit of integrity Adler had tried to

build would be a failure. As long as people didn't believe in him or the other rebels that came along, Desmond would feel his plan was coming together.

Matheson had an ear to the ground in ways that Desmond did not and he knew that Adler had decided to turn against Desmond.

Morbidly, the crowd of people lingered around the platform, ready for the strange spectacle. They were voyeurs, allowed to watch a strange ritual. *There is no need for this*, thought the sheriff, but he would let Desmond play his game. He just needed everyone gathered.

From a distance, Jasper Markov watched from outside the church.

"Come, my boy." Adler beckoned from inside. "We have much work to do."

There was gossip in the air and the police stood at a perimeter. Hundreds of people were gathering. People had come in on horseback. The word had been sent out to every corner of Breton that the mayor's assistant was to be hanged.

The whisper in the crowd indicated they were only a few minutes from bringing him and another man out. There was an electricity in the air. In some towns, that energy would have dulled down some after a few criminal hangings, but Breton had not seen one in many years. In fact, it had been fifteen years. The last man to be hanged was one General Boniface Donald for treason to the US forces, which had led the Southern armies to destroy parts of Breton.

Two officers, brandishing shining deputy badges, led the two men up onto the platform by a makeshift staircase. They stood, hooded, with their hands tied in front of them like they were praying. Ernest Williams was.

The officers arranged the men under the nooses and removed their hoods. "It was a pleasure getting a sober conversation with you." Ernest said. His eyes were red from silent crying in the cell. He didn't deserve to die in such a degrading manner. There was nothing gentlemanly about crying and being hanged for someone else's crimes. He readjusted his shoulders and raised his chin. He pulled his shirt down and arranged himself properly; he would face death as a gentleman, despite the unfortunate circumstance.

"It was my pleasure to know you," Spencer replied somberly.

One of the deputies shouted, "Quiet, you!" He stepped in and punched Spencer in the stomach. The man doubled over in pain, but the deputy erected him immediately. He coughed with spittle on his lip. The deputy laughed and the crowd jeered at the man. As Spencer was raised back up, he spit in the man's face.

The man grunted at him. He touched the saliva on his face with his fingertip and, enraged, raised a fist to strike him.

"Hold your hand," the sheriff demanded. "His time is soon enough." He came up the stairs, his heavy boots thumping on each plank. The man held his fist and Spencer smiled. It made the officer uncomfortable. Somewhere near the stairs stood a very quiet and listless Ollie Whipple. He did not speak.

"Restrain yourself, man!" the sheriff commanded again through his teeth as he loomed over the two of them.

The deputy backed away, but Spencer quipped, "Looks like you've a little something on your face there, mate." He smiled big again. The man charged him and struck him across the face, knocking him over onto the platform. The officer stood over him and watched the man writhe on the platform with his hands to his face.

"Get yourself up, Smith," the sheriff muttered. "If you have any dignity at all, you'll stand yourself up and face your death like a man."

Ernest watched with wet eyes as the man stood up quietly, face bruised around the left eye, which was watering.

"Citizens of Breton," the sheriff called loudly, quieting the crowd. "Today is a sad day, indeed." He raised two sheets of paper in the air. "What I hold here are the guilty verdicts for these two men, Ernest Williams and Neville J. Smith." There were boos coming from the crowd.

"The first man, Ernest Williams, is guilty of colluding with the Vampyres!" The crowd jeered. "And he has been found guilty of the murder of Mayor Lawrence Heath."

"And this evil-doer..." the sheriff began. "Mister Neville Smith. For collusion with the Vampyres, which led him to murder poor Stephen Adler!"

The crowd exploded in an uproar of anger and tears. No one had even asked how it had happened; they simply assumed "the Vampyres had gotten that poor child." They yelled in anger. They cursed Spencer.

Thomas looked down. He knew it wasn't possible. Mister Smith had been held in the cell since before Stephen's murder. He tried to blend into the crowd as well as he could. "At the strike of the noon day bell, these men will hang by the neck until dead for their crimes against humanity." At that moment, Sheriff Matheson looked at his pocket watch, which indicated that the bell should be rung at any moment. The crowd jeered and screamed.

The bell did not ring.

In the bell tower, the body of one officer lay bleeding from a strike on the head. Newton Bullington stood over the body with a fence post whose handle he whittled to fit his small hands. He had hidden there during the funeral. He knew that, without the noonday bell, they wouldn't hang the prisoners.

As time passed and people grew restless, the sheriff nodded to a deputy. "Go ring that bell!"

Spencer smirked.

By the time the deputy had arrived at the bell tower, there was no body left. His boots stuck in a puddle below the rope. It was blood.

Enough time had passed; everyone was in place.

The deputies slid the nooses over the necks of the fugitive men and the moment approached.

People awaited the bell almost reverently, while others still yelled profanities at the men.

Emily Hughes stood far off behind the platform, watching Oliver. If the plan were to go right, she could snatch him away, but it would be difficult.

Edwin, Thomas and Albert sat throughout the crowd. Albert saw Newton from a distance and he was cleaning his hands as he came around a corner, having left the unconscious guard somewhere. He would only have a moment to get into position.

The sheriff stared up at the old tower as though he could will it to ring. Ernest looked out over the crowd, looking for friendly faces, but he saw none. His only friends were a Vampyre, a missing young girl and orphaned children.

He felt terribly alone.

Spencer looked into the crowd and caught a pair of eyes with his glance: it was Edwin. The boy looked horrified. Spencer smiled at him reassuringly, like a father, to say "It'll be fine," but Edwin swallowed and held back tears. He was anxious. Spencer winked at him and gave him a nod.

Edwin didn't know what to make of it.

Then it happened. The large bell rang out over the town. Everyone held his or her breath in anticipation. Sheriff Matheson raised his arm and with a smile, dropped it.

The false floor dropped.

The men dropped.

The rope pulled tight.

Michael crashed onto the small sofa in Ernest's home. The anxiety was getting to him; he was flashing in and out of the limbo, some purgatorial dimension with Isaac and the conversation with that strange man—the one who could not die— it was all too much.

Ernest could be dead at any moment and probably would be. He tried to focus in on Ernest's thoughts but couldn't. All of the voices were filling his head in unison. Ernest was lost in a sea of thoughts. He mourned his friend. All of the things in his home would be meaningless. Michael undid his tie and unbuttoned his shirt.

He regretted not getting an opportunity to talk to Ernest again, but the evening had not played out as he'd expected and the night had raised more questions than it gave him answers.

He sat up. "I won't be had again." He'd had enough of Isaac's tricks and Isaac knew that Michael would finish him eventually. He would figure out what the strange transference that Isaac did was. How did he simply snap into the other world?

He sat for minutes concentrating and then straining, to no avail. It was useless. He would try in intervals until his mind was tired; he laid back down until he thought about being there, remembering it. He thought about simply going there, not as if it were a muscle that he could mentally flex, but rather as location he could arrive to.

Then, like the night before, he arrived in another place. He opened his eyes in the twilight and saw the apparitions milling aimlessly, though some seemed to be moving toward what he imagined would have been the center of Breton.

He took two steps and stopped. He flashed again and found himself on Ernest's sofa. The last thing he needed was to bring himself out of twilight into an inferno of his own skin, but instead he found out that he could go, only to return to the place where he had started. It was a strange disconnect.

As he entered the new dimension, he looked around and tried to take it all in. The place seemed to be filled with light but not like anything he could remember; strangely he felt like he knew the place. Where there had been buildings there were beautiful trees, but he sensed no life in them. The ethereal place seemed like a memory more than something that actually existed. It felt strange.

He walked through the unusual forest and followed what seemed to be hundreds of the apparitions forward. They were moving toward the center of town. When he saw them gathering there, it seemed that there was an opening of a strange vision. The more of them that gathered, the more it seemed he could see into the other realm. He was right in the middle of town.

It dawned on Michael that perhaps the actual dimension was only an extension of the apparitions, souls, or ghosts, or whatever they were. Collectively they grew stronger when they stood together. The large group was intently watching the scene that was taking place before them. It was the hanging.

He watched as a deputy ran by toward the church. Apparently Newton had successfully kept the bell from ringing. Michael smiled. He called out through the window but no one replied. No one could hear him.

The window kept growing and it phased with otherworldly energies. There were more apparitions gathering. Michael stood near the window and its blue and purple flames and took a risk. He would stick his arm through and see if anything happened. It simply disappeared. He stuck his face into the window and opened his eyes to see the interior of Ernest's home.

It was useless; he would only be a spectator, but it seemed things were unfolding quite quickly.

"Ernest," he whispered, "I wish you knew."

The bodies dropped hard and pulled against the nooses. The wood creaked with their weight. There was a moment of surprise and anguish on Ernest's face as he grasped for the rope. Spencer did nothing.

The crowd gasped as the stage swung open and the men's legs could be seen from below the platform, kicking.

The strange and palpable silence that hung on the inhaled gasps of the crowd was broken with gunfire. The sound of a rifle shot came from the rear of the crowd. People fell to the ground with fear, but even as the Sheriff and his men turned their attention and their guns on the crowd looking for the shooter, they heard the sound of a rope cracking.

Jared reloaded his rifle, preparing for another shot.

People scurried with fear under a rain of gunfire that came down in their direction. The men's pistols could not seem to find the man that was buried in the crowd at thirty yards away.

Sheriff Matheson fumed.

In the confusion, Emily ran toward the platform. She grabbed the despondent Oliver by the sleeve and pulled him. In only moments, they disappeared, engulfed in the chaotic flow of the crowd.

The moving crowd pushed Thomas away from the gunshots and toward the platform. He quickly crawled under the stage where legs were still kicking when he heard a second shot fired from a distance. He pulled Mister Smith's gun from inside his coat and held it with two hands.

To Thomas's relief, he saw Mister Williams fall through the platform onto the ground with a thud, his hands clutching the noose at his throat. The man fell limp to the ground. *Jared'll get the second shot soon. He must!* But the rope did not unravel and even as splinters rained from above him, he could not see any movement from Mister Smith. He looked up at the man through the hole in the platform and waited.

Is it too late?

Ernest rose up on the ground to see Thomas standing there with the gun. He realized what was going on around them. There was gunfire coming from other places. Patrick had started taking shots from within the crowd as well to cover Jared's escape. He stood in a cloud of smoke and blood. Patrick turned the gun into the crowd and fired shots, killing a man and a woman. His eyes were cold. The panic spread in the crowd and he disappeared with a few steps.

But why did Jared leave? Thomas thought. *It's not over! He hasn't fallen!*

Ernest found his footing and crawled quickly to the boy. Sheriff Matheson looked over his shoulder and saw one of the bodies was gone. He laughed sardonically and yelled to his men, "Don't let them get away!" before stepping off the platform. He eyed his new prey as he waded into the crowd. The shooter was running.

"Thomas!" Ernest whispered.

Thomas did not respond. He aimed the gun up above Mister Smith's head at the rope above him. Ernest looked up and instinctively grabbed the gun from the boy.

"No!" Thomas cried. "We have to save him!"

Ernest turned and saw two guards crawling under the platform as Thomas ran and grabbed Smith's legs. He tried to lift him but could do nothing. The body just swung around in a circle, plumbing like a pendulum above the boy.

Ernest turned the gun in his hands, still bound, at the officers raising their guns. He fired a shot near them that exploded in the dirt below their knees. Both men dodged the explosion in the ground with surprise.

As they jumped away, Ernest grabbed Thomas and fired another shot at the officers, plugging one of the men in the leg. The man screamed in agony.

"NO!" Thomas yelled, "It's not too late!" but Ernest's panicked hands were much too strong for him, dragging him out from under the platform. Ernest looked around amidst the chaos of people and gunfire. He knew he would be a target. He was too fat and old to be running, but he had to save the child.

"Thomas! Run!" Ernest pointed into the crowd. The boy began to move, but he looked back yelling, "Headmaster Smith!"

The officers fired from under the platform and the bullets whizzed past them. Ernest pressed himself into the crowd with Thomas in front of him. A plume of blood exploded from the chest of a miner standing next to Ernest. The soot-covered miner collapsed onto the people in front of him.

Ernest turned and shot toward the smoke of the revolvers and rifles that fired toward them before disappearing into the crowd.

Michael watched the plank under the feet of the two convicted men swing open. They fell hard and within a split second he watched as the look of genuine terror came across their faces. As the rope caught them from their fall a strange thing happened. The strange, lightless blue that phased in and out around the window of energy flickered and flashed and the silhouettes of two figures appeared near him. Michael looked again at the men hanging and realized that something deeper was happening.

He heard the gunfire and looked again through the window; Ernest had disappeared through the hole in the platform floor. The silhouette that resembled him had also gone but the other one, the one that had to be Spencer Mayhew was there, still hanging in the balance. It phased and pulsed like his breathing and his blood flow: clear and solid. Michael could see a series of veins, like tributaries that made up the body, flashing. Then there was gunfire again and a few yards further down in the ethereal forest, there stood a new apparition altogether.

Am I in Purgatory?

Michael turned around, but the window was closing as the apparitions moved away from the place where they had been standing. There were multiple new apparitions milling around aimlessly, but Spencer had disappeared.

The men who remained to stand guard at the platform lowered the body from the noose and laid it in the back of a cart pulled by a single horse. The undertaker had one of the men place the body in a rough-hewn pine box that could barely be called a casket before riding off.

Jasper Markov and Parson Adler walked side-by-side nearby, watching.

"There is a small rebellion already brewing, Mister Adler," Jasper commented.

"So it would seem," Adler replied, "but I would never underestimate the strength of Burroughs's resolve. The man did send people to have you beaten or killed while sitting only a few floors away from your room in the inn." He thought for a moment. "There must be a reason he is so confident."

Adler knew much more than he was telling the young man, but thought it better to keep him out of the know.

He thought about the ringing of the bell, something that he and his poor nephew had done for years. He had gone with the young man earlier, before the hanging and had the boy light a lantern. The whole town ran on that bell. They walked to a small shed behind the church where old belongings had stayed hidden.

He had opened a chest full of old books and notebooks.

"What is this?" Markov had asked.

"Chemistry, my boy. It's what makes the world turn here in Breton."

Walking through the square, only half an hour later, Jasper asked, "With all that commotion, do you think there will be a market to shop in?"

"I am more than certain of it."

The undertaker pulled his cart across the square to collect the other bodies.

People were talking to each other as though the events had never transpired. There was no fear and they laughed quietly or talked about politics or flirted. He looked at the police who did not look up paranoid or keep guard; they simply cleaned up the platform.

It looked just like it had the day before.

Algernon Elliott had not slept. The worst thing that could have happened to him would have been allowing himself to dream. He did not want his thoughts to betray him and announce his presence to the telepaths. He watched them come and go and he snuck closer to where the Druid child was leading the Fiends. He had meditated quietly on what the Golem he had shot meant by "Freedom." It seemed that he had been very troubled by his state and was relieved to be freed. It occurred to Algernon that they were imprisoned much like the Fiends.

It led him to contemplate a new plan.

If the elemental Druids, children of an "Earth God" or the fallen Angel Asbél, depending on the mythology he read, were brought to that place, then the work of carving out an entire haven for demons underground would have been their work.

Algernon knew that the elemental creatures lost their human form when exposed to any singular element for too long, which explained the idea of mermen, centaurs, talking trees and many other ancient cultural mythologies. He speculated that the time against the rocks under Breton would have converted them into rock creatures. That meant that the inanimate parts of the rock Druids would be available to any powerful magician to convert rock into a rock Golem.

It was sick.

They were trapped inside of the large and lumbering creatures. It was also intriguing. He would write about it later. His only goal was to free Genevieve at whatever cost. He forced himself up to his feet; he had been sitting still for hours. It was time to make his move.

The pathway was quiet and stifling. It reminded him how far underground he was. There would be no escaping. Algernon began to feel claustrophobic. He knew enough about Vampyres to know that he could barter with them, but it wouldn't get far. He'd have very few chances to get Genevieve freed from them and took it for granted that they weren't both going to leave.

Algernon guessed that it was near midday. The stifling feeling would not go away, but some of the Vampyres would be resting so it was time to go. His nerves were on edge and he was fatigued. The hours had eaten away at him. Each time a Vampyre came by he sat quietly, trying not to fall asleep, keeping his mind focused on the scenery. He knew that Vampyres sensed, but they were not intrinsic mind readers. As long as his thoughts were basic ones, it would go into the white noise of their thoughts.

He tried not to sweat when a Vampyre almost kicked him, walking by, smelling around for the scent of fresh blood. *Too many slaves...too many prisoners...* it commented, mumbling.

The path was clear. There was an obvious cycle to their movement. Vampyres treated the sun much like farmers treated the moon; it reminded them of what was on the other side. They avoided it and they watched its movement with solemn reverence.

The hieroglyph of the watching eye, also known as the Eye of Horus and, by other interpretations, the eye of Egyptian sun god Ra, was on most of the doors.

Algernon flipped the lenses on his goggles, but he couldn't get a clear focus on the energies in the cavern. It frustrated him. He removed them and they dangled around his neck.

He looked around. Passages led everywhere. Some hallways were open, like alleyways. Others became corridors at the mouths of buildings. He felt like a roach in an anthill. Spencer had told him of South African ants that could tear down entire buildings within the span of only a few days. It made him miss Spencer. Earlier, he'd laughed at himself because he'd thought of Charles Dickens, who Spencer loved so much. He'd thought to reference the title of a very dense piece of fiction by Mister Dickens in his next article. He would call it "A Strange Tale of Two Cities." He would then open it with a great line: "It was the worst of times, it was the worst of times."

That was before he realized that he probably wouldn't live long enough to write that article. He tightened his vest and holster and moved forward. He was getting close.

The room opened up into a large meeting hall; the corridors, alleys and hallways all broke off into separate directions. It was all chance as far as he was concerned. One corridor closed in and the dirt floor became marble. He imagined that, much like the first area with the beautiful lanterns and library, it would turn up nothing but more Vampyres.

The dirt road had much more tread going into one particular hallway and there were no lanterns there. It was dark and many heavy things had been carried in that direction. He imagined people. He could see the presumably enslaved Druids or Golems carrying those men or Fiends, whatever they were, back and forth. He could imagine the dead bodies and all the feeding that the Vampyres did there.

It made his stomach turn. That's where they would be.

He descended into the darkness of the hallway with a hand on his gun. Suddenly, he had a very bad feeling about it all. His bad feelings had saved his life more than once, though. Without him, Spencer would have been devoured by a mummy looking for a host-soul, caught in a temporal web by an ancient inter-dimensional spider, or had his brain eaten by cannibals in an unnamed country in the Orient.

But then again, without Spencer, Algernon would have been shot in London, shot in Paris, beheaded in Paris and then shot in Paris again on a separate and much stranger occasion. Not to mention the time that he had actually been shot in Boston by Spencer.

He missed his closest friend dearly. It flashed inside of his chest for only a moment there in the darkness, but the last months of being separated from Spencer, who kept his thoughts in line with a simple "shut up," had been difficult.

He dodged.

Algernon had felt a change in the air; something was near him in the corridor and whatever it was came down on him fast. He stepped out of the way again. The walls seemed to move away from him and he felt like he was in a large chamber. It was very dark. Though quick on its feet, whatever was moving was as blind as he was. He knew his goggles would do him no good. The thickness of the spectral energies clouded his vision.

He heard a growl that churned into a deafening, thunderous voice. In an unknown language, it cried out. The voice echoed through the chamber and lanterns flickered green and blue in the hands of large Golems, presumably Druids, that lined the walls. All around them, prison cells lay in the shadows. The corridor was not a hallway at all. They were the shoulders of the guardian Golems that then began attacking him.

He cursed under his breath and rolled his eyes. He had stepped right into it. *At least*, he thought, *I'm in the right place.*

The shooter was only a quarter of a mile ahead of Sheriff Matheson as he turned the corner out of town. *Adler's people?* His gray mare had her nose down as he pushed to catch the man. He was closing in on the mysterious figure, but the long straightaway, heading south, would turn into treacherous territory quickly. *Too many outsiders. Hard to tell who you work for.* It didn't worry the sheriff.

He closed in on the man, young and bearded, who looked over his shoulder, riding a large brown steed as hard as it would run. The sheriff looked closely at what was just a boy and then he reined his horse to a stop, braking in a cloud of dust.

He pulled his revolver from his hip and fired. The man ducked his head but kept riding.

"No." The sheriff smiled. He fired a second shot, landing a hit.

The horse began to collapse with a horrible noise, a plume of blood sprayed from its hind leg and it released a whinny as one of its legs gave way, throwing the rider far off the road into the grass. The fall could very easily have killed him.

The sheriff held his gun out and smiled, looking at the dying horse through the spiral of smoke. He chuckled. The horse rolled over and neighed in agony, but the rider didn't seem to move at all. He waited, but there was no movement. He fired another round in the air but the man's body did not flinch. He looked dead enough.

He considered going back but instead he would make sure. He hadn't recognized him, so it wouldn't have mattered. There was no one to show; the bell had already been rung. Curiosity had him and a smirk curled on his face as he rode up to see the body.

He lay just fifty yards away when the sheriff heard the man's rifle fire. A bullet buried itself in the weeds near him. He ducked and in that split second, the man rolled over and ran into the woods. The Sheriff fired two more rounds into the forest before clicking through empty chambers repeatedly, frustrated by the rouse. He stopped the horse and reloaded his long-barreled revolver. *He's clever.*

Jared ran, rifle in hand, just as he had so many times before. He looked over his shoulder and he could see the gray horse, but the man that had been mounted on it was gone. He had hoped to get further away from town before facing any trouble. He bounded through the trees and jumped over bushes with the rifle at his chest. He covered a quarter of a mile of forest before he began to slow down. Only a minute had passed. He listened for the familiar sound of an enemy's footfall in the grass, or the scraping of twigs and leaves, or the cracking of branches.

There was nothing but the breath of the wind.

Instinctively, Jared dropped to the ground. It was just in time. A bullet exploded into the bark of a tree behind him. He aimed at the plume of smoke but the man was not there at all. He did not shoot. The reload time on his rifle would be longer than that of a pistol, so he didn't want to put himself in that situation with the man so close.

He forced himself to his feet and began running again. The shots seemed to rain down around him. It felt as if he were running from an army of men. Jared could not imagine how he was staying so silent. It seemed to Jared that the sheriff had not taken a step into the woods. There was no sound other than the echoes of the gunshot and the ringing in his ears.

Jared flinched when he saw the man's face and part of his shoulder just behind him and he put his head down to run. He was out of luck.

The reality was that the sheriff was getting quite frustrated with the young man. He hadn't been able to land a shot, as if the boy could sense how and when he was going to shoot. He ran with grace, like a spooked deer; he was comfortable in the woods. *Too clever.*

Jared looked ahead and saw a break in the woods; he could smell the ocean air. He was running out of forest cover. As he broke through the clearing, he slowed to a stop. There was nowhere to run.

The sea was below him. The clearing ended at a cliff and the jagged rocks below reached up like skeletal fingers from the crashing waves. He was cornered. The sun was beating down on him and it was only a little past noon. He had his back to the east and Jared was squinting. He held the rifle out ahead of him. He had to make his shot count.

"I don't know who you are." The sheriff's voice came from behind a tree. Jared turned on it. Then from behind another tree, "Or what your goal is." Jared turned the gun again toward where the voice came from. "But it ends now."

Out of the corner of his eye, Jared saw a movement of dust or smoke around the base of the trees. "What in the?" Before he could ask, the sheriff appeared in front of him from a cloud of smoke.

The sheriff held his pistol in front of him. Jared turned the rifle on him, firing a shot into his belly.

The sheriff exclaimed as he doubled over. Then there was a breath of smoke where blood should have been and he chuckled. He coughed up smoke. He erected himself with a wicked grin and presented a hand in a small smoldering cloud. When he opened it, there sat the bullet from the rifle, still steaming. "You lost something," he commented sarcastically.

Jared showed less surprise than the sheriff expected. His mind was working on how to alleviate his situation and before the sheriff could see what had happened, Jared threw the rifle to him, which floated through his chest in a cloud of smoke. The boy jumped off the cliff. He was gone without a sound.

The sheriff looked over the edge, where he could see the waves crashing hard against the cliff.

The boy was dead.

EIGHT

"But first, on earth as vampyre sent,
Thy corse shall from its tomb be rent:
Then ghastly haunt thy native place,
And suck the blood of all thy race;"
-Lord Byron, *The Giaour*
[Unquenched, Unquenchable] (1813)

A dler was right. The market was full of people. They bustled and moved about fluidly. The smell of fish and fresh vegetables filled the air. The vegetables were brought in each morning on the train, but the fishmongers did their own work. It had been that way for years.

Parson Adler stood at a booth and looked beyond the groceries. He focused his eyes in on a red door across the street. He instructed that Jasper watch as well. The parson reached down and felt a piece of fruit and then smiled a forced smile at the merchant. He was biding his time. "There are things a man needs," he told Jasper, without turning his gaze from the door.

Adler had lived in the clockwork town long enough to know when things should happen. He knew when they would happen. The door came open and two older men, two of his very own monitors, came out talking, wearing their top hats and canes. The sign above the door read "Breton Apothecary," and Doctor Brown, the proprietor, was one of the men talking. *Good*, thought Adler.

He turned to Jasper and whispered, "If those men return, keep them—stall them. Be loud."

Jasper nodded.

"It won't take much." Adler stated. "They both think you should be dead. You'll have plenty to catching up to do." The old man walked inside, limping and Jasper did his best to act like he was shopping or ready to purchase something. He grinned awkwardly at the merchants and busied his hands with fruits and vegetables, keeping his eyes open and watching over his shoulder for the men.

A merchant asked him, "Sir, have you interest in these wares?"

Jasper hesitated and filled the air with his inability to answer. The merchant had an odd, familiar accent.

"*Por supuesto*, let me show you something."

The young man looked down and it was simply a cart full of fruit. There was nothing to be seen, but before he knew what was happening, the man had rounded the table and grabbed him by the shirt. Jasper didn't want to scream, but a loud gasp escaped his open mouth. He silenced himself. He didn't want to alert Adler.

The merchant pulled Jasper, who was fighting as well as he could, into the alleyway behind the table. Jasper heard the slip— the unsheathing of a blade—and felt its cold edge pressed against his throat. Jasper closed his eyes with the shock of being thrown into the wall. When he opened his eyes, he was faced with both memory and regret.

"It looks, *amigo*, as though this place has had its way with you before I could."

Jasper glanced into the dark eyes of the old man, Gallegos. It was the second time in the same week that an old man had held him at knifepoint. He remembered the man's face. He thought back on the smiling man that smoked his rolled cigarettes over cards at an inn in Maine. The man he saw in front of him was different; he was distant, maddened and terrifying. Chandler's words rang through him; he knew Gallegos would be coming. Chandler had warned him.

"Where's the book?" The man hissed.

There was a flash in Jasper; he felt sorry for himself. It seemed he couldn't keep from getting himself killed.

"Where is my book?" Gallegos's voice shook Jasper and the old man's knuckles and fingertips dug into the boy's skin, the blade against his throat. Jasper could feel the warm trickle running down his throat to his shirt.

"It would seem I've gone and made a mess in cutting you." Gallegos grinned. "*Debería matarte*." He looked at the pathetic boy and noticed that there was a glow of something else on him. The old man gritted his teeth with a look of resignation, though still terrifying and large. *It would seem you've found your way into something* mucho más grande, he thought.

"Find me the book."

It occurred to Jasper that he hadn't mentioned the disappearance of the book. He looked down and put his hand to his neck.

Gallegos looked either way down the alley and put his hand to the young man's chest. A trickle of blood rolled down the wrinkle of his dark shirt and wet the tip of the old man's calloused fingers. "I am just a man." His bearded jaw shifted with thought. "I am not a killer." There was guilt in his eyes. "Do not." He paused. "Do not make me kill you."

Jasper looked down with shame and wiped the blood from his throat. The man was gone in the shadows. He jumped; Adler needed him.

He turned to the mouth of the alley where he looked to the red door. It was open and there were men standing in the doorway, some were officers and some just well-dressed men, obviously very important ones.

"No, no, no, no!" Jasper mouthed under his breath, panicking. He ran toward them as quickly as he could. He thought on his feet.

"Sirs! Officers!" He cried out.

The men turned to see him, confused.

"A man just attacked me!"

The officers seemed complacent. He showed them the blood on his hands and, realizing they didn't care, changed the story.

"I think it was the one that got away from the hanging."

Their eyes lit up and their eyebrows arched.

"The fat man!"

As the officers ran off, one of the important-looking men came through the door. "Perhaps it was Mister Williams then that broke in here as well, wouldn't you think, Mister Vampyre Hunter?"

It was Doctor Brown.

"Yes, perhaps, it was," Jasper lied. "The man seemed wild."

"Ah, yes. He is mad."

The Doctor went to lock the door, but it was smashed. He shook his head and left Jasper standing, looking at the door. He turned around with a puzzled look. "You look quite well, sir." The Doctor seemed nonchalant. The last time he'd seen Jasper, he'd given him up for dead.

Jasper nodded.

"Miraculously well." The man said turning away slowly, putting his top hat back on.

Jasper waited a moment and then peeked in through the door. The apothecary had been ransacked. There wasn't a vial left whole. There were puddles and dust everywhere. Jasper was confused. First of all, why would Adler destroy the apothecary? And why wasn't Doctor Brown concerned? He seemed quite at ease about the destruction of his business. Jasper pushed the door open. There wasn't a footprint anywhere. There was no back door.

The real question that ate at him—where was Adler?

He had just scratched a letter from the Hebrew seal on a Golem's chest and watched a little boy fall from the crumbling rocks. Algernon's gun lay at his feet. His chest was being crushed by a second Golem, who had caught him from behind in a bear hug and Algernon was kicking, trying to figure out how to work his way out of his predicament. The seal on the Golem behind him was carved under its eye and Algernon began bashing its face with the back of his head. He could feel the warm trickle of his own blood coming down his neck. He hit it repeatedly until he felt gravel and debris on his shoulders.

The creature let him go, falling to its knees. He'd already fired one shot into the stone chest of a Golem; it stunned the creature, but it kept coming. It was a disaster. They all kept coming. He picked the gun up and turned around, looking down the barrel. He knew he was in trouble. They'd heard him.

The flickering blue cavern grew quiet and the Golems moved away from Algernon, back to their positions along the outside of the big room.

Behind him lay a man in a pile of stones, holding his head. Algernon moved quickly to him, grabbing the back of his head. He looked at the blood on his hand. "How are we feeling?" he asked the man.

The confused looking man finally looked up, "They're coming for you now."

"I know," Algernon answered. "It's all part of a plan."

"Plan?" the man asked. He rubbed his head. "What plan?"

"I don't know yet," he replied, "but for now, you should act dead." There was a sudden sharp pain inside Algernon's head and he could hear nothing. A depression washed over him like a black wave. His thoughts went blank and a shrill whistling penetrated his mind. He dropped the gun and fell boneless to the ground. His agonizing subsided and Algernon opened his eyes to see the room filling with Vampyres. The slender, beautiful creatures seemed to materialize from thin air.

He only had a moment to look around and he saw a tall Vampyre, beautiful in appearance with a most wicked smile. It was the one he'd seen before pushing Kat on the gurney and talking to himself. The one called Ilya. Next to him was a younger-looking one, the only female in their group that he could see. There stood another one, whose face seemed to shrink to the center of his face into a squinted wrinkle; he looked much older. He did not see the rest, but they kept appearing. Some hovered above high above him and others stood on the ground. They were all alien and strange, beautiful in their refined appearance. Whatever aging had happened in their lives, it had softened into a perfected state. Even the one with the wrinkled face looked sad like a child, his eyes bright and emotionless. They all had a childlike-quality in their smiles and their shining eyes. It was eerie.

Algernon had dealt with Vampyres before. He could do it again.

He fell to the ground. "Oh the pain!" he screamed.

Ilya, the Vampyre, stretched a hand out and seemed to turn something inside Algernon's head. He collapsed onto his side and cried out. There was an awful sound coming from cells.

The prisoners banged on the bars. They clamored and howled. The large hall echoed with shrieking and the clanging of fists on metal.

Ilya looked around at the mess. A lantern had been shot out. There lay two dead Druid bodies and a very interesting-looking adventurer.

The Algernon Elliott. He laughed. *Foremost expert in the preternatural.* He walked up to Algernon, who lay on his side, moaning. *Premier exorcist and killer of Vampyres in Europe. In truth, no more than a meddling amateur.* He leaned in toward Algernon and whispered, *This will be so much fun.*

Dusk set with sweeping clouds like a billowing sheet thrown hastily across a bed. The quiet town seemed more eerily silent than usual while Edwin kept look out. Thomas moved ahead into an alley. The boys were vigilant. They tried to put their emotions aside, but inside Thomas was crumbling. Mister Smith was dead and gone and they were guilty of failing to save him as they had done for Mister Williams.

The townsfolk were still under the spell. The medallions, the pendants, the seals on the doors; the curse was everywhere. The thought of the world as magical scared Thomas. For Edwin, that would not be a problem. What was magic? All things were magical in his opinion. Somewhere between curses and Vampyres and disappearing people, somewhere among the thoughts of monsters and strange, misplaced memories and dreams, Breton really was a magical place for him.

"Ned!" Thomas whispered. His eyes narrowed in on another alley. He looked down the alley next to the inn where Kat had so often found them hiding, looking to eat.

Edwin looked across the way and his heart sank. She was gone.

"Look!" Thomas pointed. Something very strange was moving. There were bodies moving up and down the walls. Thomas made a break across the square to the big tree. Edwin followed him closely. They climbed the well-known tree as though they were running up the stairs of their own home.

There they were; the Vampyres hid in the shadows of the twilight and one of them laid a body at the side entrance of the Crow's Nest. It was the perch where they would wait on Kat, where just days ago, Mister Williams had fallen asleep as they waited to pickpocket him again.

"Who is that?" Edwin wondered aloud.

"I don't know, but just look at them!" Thomas whispered. Vampyres scaled the walls like they were ascending underwater . They treated the walls like it was solid ground. They shifted in and out of sight.

The Vampyres disappeared as quickly as they had come and the body lay there unmoving and dead to the world. A brawny arm rolled out from under the body and Thomas could see locks of blonde hair from the tree.

The worst thoughts began to fill his mind. It was easy to avoid thinking about what could have happened to Kat when there was no evidence of her pain, but his eyes were welling with tears. He was already half way down the tree before Edwin could even see the body in the distance.

Thomas bolted across the square; despite any Vampyres, he stumbled, winded, up to the body that lay there, blinded by his own tears, *Kat!*

Edwin came up behind him, looking around for any witnesses, but no one was around.

She looked serene, peaceful and asleep, as if she had laid herself there to take a rest from her work. A strong arm lay out, palm up and her head rested on the other arm like a pillow.

Thomas fell to his knees sobbing. Edwin put his hand on his friend's shoulder to console him, but his own heart was broken. Edwin hurt too, but he swallowed it. Thomas didn't want to be touched and he shrugged Edwin's hand away.

Thomas crawled on his hands and lifted Kat's head. She was heavy, but he lifted her to his chest and wept. He swore she was sleeping; she had to just be sleeping.

Edwin wiped his eyes and then he felt a chill. Something was wrong. He was overwhelmed with a bad feeling. "Tom..." he stuttered. From a dark corner of the alley, he saw small lanterns appear, two eyes from the shadows that lit up a shadowy head until it became a body that stepped into the alley.

The Vampyre laughed and showed his fangs to the boy. Edwin turned on his heels, "Thomas!" He began to cry when he found himself in the shadow of another figure that came from the mouth of the alley. Edwin looked up to see an old man smoking a cigarette.

The old man pulled back the hood of his cloak.

The Vampyre smiled. *Now we have ourselves some fun, old man.*

The man replied quietly. "Old?" He laughed. "I resent that remark." He took one last drag against his cigarette and threw it to the ground. Thomas heard the small cherry sizzle in a puddle near the old man's boot. Edwin was frozen in his place. The man stepped by and put his hand on Edwin's chest. "*Niños*, get behind me."

Thomas held Kat tight, unable to contain his tears.

The Vampyre stepped forward, grinning. The silence was pregnant with the Vampyre's smug smile and the smoke that Gallegos exhaled.

"What is your name, demon?" the old man asked quietly.

No. The Vampyre laughed. *You won't have me so easily, ancient one.*

The Vampyre begin to move forward and then suddenly disappeared into a haze with a sound like the hiss of steam. The old man didn't flinch. He adjusted his old ruffled shirt and closed his eyes.

Edwin grabbed at the door handle behind Thomas, but it was locked. He wanted to find Glenn. He poked his head around the corner, but two of the sheriff's men stood at the front door of the Crow's Nest.

Without a sound, the man ground his foot into the cobblestone street and turned slightly. The Vampyre reappeared, but it was too late. The man was ready and struck him with an open palm in the center of his chest. The Vampyre grunted; the sound echoed hollowly like a bone falling into an empty barrel. He grabbed his chest and disappeared into a haze again.

The old man waited.

The second time, the Vampyre appeared from behind him, but the old man turned just as quickly and with two fingers struck the Vampyre at the neck. The Vampyre grabbed at his own throat as if choking but the look of surprise slowly gave way to a wicked grin.

Thomas swallowed and wiped the tears from his eyes with his dirty sleeve as Edwin bent down behind him. "You have to let her go." His eyes darted around the alleyway. There was nowhere to run without being seen.

"I won't ask again." The old man began. "But what happens next will hurt very much." He turned to face the Vampyre directly.

The Vampyre's face lost its smile. He put his arms back down to his. The Vampyre showed his fear and rage. His amber eyes began to glow bright red. He didn't know what was about to come, but he understood that the man in front of him was capable of killing him. The Vampyre turned toward the boys as the man spoke quietly. The Vampyre began to sob. *No!* The creature ran toward the boys, enraged.

Edwin pulled at Thomas's collar, but he wouldn't move. He stared directly into the eyes of the Vampyre as he came at them. The Vampyre looked sad and, with each step, more and more pathetic.

Thomas never looked away.

The man put his fingertips together in prayer and with his final words, the creature exploded with a flash of light and wet ash that covered Edwin and Thomas.

The smell of sulfur and burnt skin rose from the alley.

The man walked up to the boys. "You must leave her with me."

"No." Thomas replied quietly, hardened and cold.

The old man smiled. It was warm and genuine. "I understand." He paused as he got down on one knee. "But I know that you have started something cannot be undone."

The boys looked at him intently.

"You now have war on your hands and the smell of *Vampiro's* death on you." He sighed, looking for another cigarette in his pants pockets. He huffed. "You are great warriors," he smiled confidently. "You must stay to your task. You have freed many people this day."

Edwin interrupted impatiently, "Why did they set this trap for us here?"

"Trap?" the man mused. "No trap. Was a message." Then under his breath, "But what that message is, I still am not knowing." He looked out to the square. "Now is good time for you to hide again in the darkness."

Edwin looked out the alleyway and had heard enough. He trusted the man. He had saved his life. That was enough, but Thomas needed more. "What did you say to him?" he asked the old man.

"A Prayer. Believe in the prayer that they be blessed with light of faith and they will ultimately die. Light is light," he explained enigmatically. "*Vade Retro Satana.*"

"Pavl," Thomas said. "The Vampyre told me—in my mind..." He paused. "His name was Pavl."

"You have done him more justice than he was worthy," replied the old man. "The *Vampiro* fears being forgotten more than he fears death. You now carry him with you— some part of him at least." He looked down at the large girl in the little boy's arms with some concern and great interest. She was the missing piece of the puzzle. "Leave the girl with me and I will see to it that she is taken care of."

G enevieve Moreau woke up running. She had already been running and, in her dreams, she had been running through fire. Tears were streaming down her face and she let out a hoarse, yet horrid, shriek. She could barely lift her arms and the sensation of pins and needles filled her weighty hands. She felt like she was still inside the nightmare, but suddenly everything was hurting. Her ears rang. She screeched again.

They were somewhere in a corridor behind her, laughing and clawing at her.

Genevieve looked ahead through the sea of her own tears to see a thread of light. It was coming from up above somewhere. It looked like heaven. It was the orange, low burning glow of dusk. She put her head down and despite how much it hurt her feet and legs, she ran harder. She didn't know where she was, but she ran. She could hear them coming. The light grew closer and closer. She wiped her eyes and began running the way she always had. She could outrun anyone in town. She heard them clamoring around the corner.

They were going to kill her.

The hallway opened into an open passage that rose up into what would have once been a well. It was bone dry and the creek that had fed it had been closed off with stones. She dove into the single thread of light.

Clawed hands reached at her.

There was a sudden sound of hissing and she could smell burned flesh. She looked behind her to see them, dark creatures wanting to devour her. Their eyes glowed in the half-light.

You made me burn myself! one hissed, angrily.

Genevieve didn't take the time to answer; a ladder was at her back and she began climbing. They screamed and whistled to her.

The voice of another came, *You'll have no time to save yourself!* It hissed like a snake, angry and smiling. *Darkness is coming!*

She climbed up the ladder, reached over the wall and forced herself over onto the cold, damp grass. She knew exactly where she was. She had made it to the old well near the center of town.

B ernadette Allen stood with her back to the door of the tailor's shop. The silence and the darkness of night were eating at her. It hadn't sounded that quiet in decades. She looked down at her hands and frowned at how small and weak they looked with her bony fingers wrapped around the butt and barrel of the scattergun. She wasn't the young lady she had once been and the truth was that aside from the visitors she'd had earlier, the last years had been very lonely.

She could almost hear her fiancé calling across decades, across the tea fields, "Bernadette!" She was such a romantic. The memory of him had kept her sane that long, but this night particularly was going to be hard on her. She felt the paranoia like spindly fingers creeping up the back of her neck from under her blouse. The hairs on her thin arms were raised.

She thought she could hear scuffling in the distance. Her mind was probably tricking her. Then she listened again. There were horse's hooves and feet coming down the road. Miss Allen listened for the wheels on Mister Desmond's carriage but she didn't hear them. Desmond terrified her. He was the complete embodiment of evil. She didn't fear violent men. She didn't even fear the Vampyres as much as she feared Desmond's indifference to life.

That man was responsible for much more than the deaths in the town. He was responsible for her solitude.

As Thomas rounded the corner, on their way back to their hideout, he saw horses reared. Two men had their guns drawn on Alexander and Albert near the tailor's small house. Albert sat on the ground, where he had tripped, dropping some of the food they had stolen and Alexander stood defiant between the men and his friend.

Thomas was so angry he could spit.

"We have to do something," whispered Edwin.

There was nothing that Thomas could imagine them doing, but he calculated the scene as quickly as he could. He heard one of the men cocking back the hammer on his revolver.

They began to panic. "Tom," Edwin whimpered. "Anything. We have to do something." His eyes scrambled along the ground.

The door to the small house opened slowly and with a creak. The men looked up and laughed. There stood old Miss Allen, the tailor; the lunatic was smiling and leaning on her cane.

"Go back inside, Miss Allen." One of the men condescended.

"Now, you young men ought to know better than to pick on these boys," she started. "They ain't got no family."

"Miss Allen, you shouldn't be out after dark." The man shook his head as he stepped over some of the stolen goods that the boys had been carrying. "You just let us take care of these here orphans."

"Yes. It is quite dangerous in the dark," she replied dryly.

The man ignored her reply. He looked down at the boy, who sat scattered at the foot of the porch stairs. Something caught the man's attention. The old lady had not gone in and from the feel of the cold steel pressed up against his cheek, she was not planning on it.

"Drop the gun, boy," she whispered with a smile, pressing the large, single-barrel gun into his face.

"There's no need for this, Miss Allen." The second man, large with a gravelly voice, said calmly as he turned his gun slowly on her.

She commanded, "Find your feet, child." She spoke without taking her eyes off of the second man who had his gun on her. She thought about the guns and how her situation was changing. She did not regret her decision to make this her moment to fight, but she hated that the scattergun only left her with a single shot. However deadly the spray of the gun, one of the men would be left alive.

"You don't want to do this," the second man said. Her gun did not shake. She was not scared. He didn't break eye contact.

The old woman stared directly at him while she pushed the gun into his partner's head. She noticed that his eyes were a graying blue but that they had the yellow of a man that drank too much. She didn't look away. "Now, Scut. You best git." She knew the names of every one of the sheriff's men and counted them each as her enemies.

Alexander took a step back but the men had their eyes on him.

One of the horses whinnied and then there came a scream from across the street. The horses reared back on their hind legs, spooked and the men ducked. The man in front turned his gun on Miss Allen. Gunfire exploded.

Both Miss Allen and the man fell to the ground.

The screaming was coming from all sides and the second man turned to find his bearings. Edwin brought down a large branch on his gun arm. The man yelped in pain. His screaming added to the cacophony. The horses screamed in panic and there were moans under the horrible echo of gunfire.

Alexander quickly picked up the gun that had fallen to the ground and pulled the hammer back on the revolver, turning the gun on the man. His yellowed eyes looked sad.

Edwin held the stick out at the man, who gritted his teeth.

"I'm going to kill every one of you," the man grimaced.

Thomas spoke very quietly from behind him and the sound of the spooked horses galloping away subsided. "That's unlikely."

The man turned slowly.

He continued. "Tell the sheriff or whoever you run to." He walked up to the man, quiet and angry. "The day of our captivity is passed and war now beats at your door." His voice rang with authority. It sounded like something someone much older might say, like the boy had read it from a book. In reality, it had been a speech that Algernon had spoken years earlier. Spencer had told the story to Edwin and Thomas many times.

The man smiled at the little boy, his yellowed teeth exposed.

"You can go now, Mister Scut," Thomas replied.

As the man walked away, holding his arm, Thomas turned to the boys with a thankful smile and he cast his eyes to the lady who had not moved. He shook his head, solemnly. "Albert," he instructed quietly.

Albert walked up the stairs to their fallen ally and then quickly flashed a smile at the boys. He reached down to help the old woman up and she was quietly laughing. She was bleeding from her collarbone but she was smiling. Miss Allen grunted as she used the large gun to get up. "He winged me." She winced.

Thomas and Edwin shared a look and Alexander picked up the other gun and then stepped over the body of the dead man to gather their food. Everything was covered in blood and some sort of human matter.

"Well, quit standing around," she called, "You've got work to do!"

The mayor's house was cold. To Ernest, it felt colder inside than outside. The streetlamps were burning and they cast their sad, yellow glow along shadows through the broken windows. The drapes moved ghostly and slow.

He limped alone through the large house against the requests of the children back at the abandoned farm, but he felt compelled to move forward. It wasn't every day that a man was hanged and survived. He carried the burden of guilt, knowing that Spencer Mayhew should have lived and that he should have died.

"I'm just a fat old man." He mumbled to himself. What good could he be to anyone?

In some ways, he knew the house better than his own home, though there was always one room that he had avoided at the command of the mayor. He pushed his sore body up the stairs and contemplated what all he would have done in his life had he not been so committed to the work of the town.

How could he have been so wrong?

He paused at the middle of the stairs.

He felt a heavy weight, a guilt in his stomach that he could not break. He felt responsible for the deaths, the orphans and the miserable lives of those still trapped in the town. No amount of knowledge gained could ease his pain. He felt like a murderer.

He put his hand to his throat where the rope had burned its mark on him. It burned like a brand and he thought, *I deserved to die up there*.

The mayor's private study was lit and exposed. The lanterns flickered with a breeze from a broken window down the hall and some pages fluttered.

Ernest had an immense love of books and learning and his head cleared of the evil spell that had kept his thoughts so foggy. He began remembering his youth and his love of books. At one time, he had been a New Yorker and during the time of the War Between the States, he would steal books from windowsills or markets so he could read them and return them quietly. He was much thinner then, only a college student when he had been brought to Breton.

He went over the notes he'd taken from the day he'd been arrested. Someone else had added to them. The maps that lay delineated in front of him told him a very strange story, one that had already been validated through his conversations with Spencer Mayhew. Breton did not exist at all, nor had it ever. The fictitious township was not in Virginia. He looked out the window, attempting to fathom with a perplexed grin how he could have lived the whole of his adult life some thousand miles north of Virginia.

"Breton" was in Canada. He flipped through the pages of the books and cross-referenced them furiously; like a student of the word, he found the truth. The township, if he could call it that, was a government project approved by the American and Canadian governments to "rehabilitate" the Vampyre population.

There were signatures from representatives of various European governments as well, including an English Prime Minister named Sir Edward Smith-Stanley and Napoleon III on behalf of the French. There were signatures for Austrian, German and even some African and Oriental representatives. The project had been approved by many governments looking to diminish violent populations of Vampyres within their borders. Even representatives of the Vatican had signed.

If Breton was a secret, it was a very large one.

Using something that was referred to in the paperwork's shorthand as "B-Heart," the "LORDS" would be able to maintain a small town as support for their project. It was to be located somewhere in New Brunswick, Canada, directly north of Maine.

The Virginia fishing economy was a farce. There was simply a group of brainwashed villagers running around preparing the way for "culpable parties" or "convicts," depending on the record. The projections were bleak. The controlling mechanism for the whole project was some sort of "biomechanical device" that acted as an amplifier for "telepathic" energy. Unfortunately for those involved, the device seemed to have been losing its strength. *That would explain all of the strange behavior around town and all the running around,* he thought. *The sheriff and Desmond must have been adjusting for the weakness of their device.*

The records all pointed to the long-term maintenance of a feeding system for Breton's Vampyre population, who was housed in an extensive system of caverns below them. It sent shivers down his back and into his legs. He knew all the names. Especially Heath, Adler and Burroughs.

Everyone was in on it.

The entire history of the town was written in the journals. He assumed that the only reason they weren't in code was because Heath had such bad handwriting that it wasn't necessary. Luckily, he had made a living out of reading and interpreting the man's words. He began tearing sheets out of the journals and stacking information he thought would be relevant. Ernest scribbled down names and dates. He kept the inkwell close and the quill to paper. He looked across the large desk and observed the blueprints spread in front of him, trying to fathom how it was all so much bigger than he had originally thought. It had only been a few minutes, but he was absorbing everything there was to know about Breton, New Brunswick, Canada, as quickly as he could.

The fire burned low at the stable and the group sat gathered quietly around its warmth. The devastation of their failure hung on them like a heavy, wet blanket. Shoulders were drooped and the quiet sobbing had given way to sniffles and to the silent thoughts of children faced with no home and bound to no leadership. Their adventurous mood had fallen to fear and doubt.

The farm did little to shelter them from the cold, but it held up: a hardened orphanage home to hardening orphans.

Patrick kept the twilight watch and aside from the rustle of the grass and leaves, it was silent. There was nothing. It unnerved him. The sheriff's men should have come already. He had killed people. There had to be consequences. *Marcus. Marcus?* He contemplated. Patrick's stomach turned with a dark sickness. *What did the Sheriff mean?*

Patrick still didn't trust the silence and he watched between the blades of grass and among the trees for any shadow that moved like a man or a beast.

He was ready for a fight.

When the Vampyre Michael appeared behind him with a soft gust, Patrick turned his gun hard enough on the man that they both heard the gun cut the air. Michael leaned back to avoid having the barrel of the boy's pistol directly in his face. "I don't think that thing'll kill me, but I'd rather not risk it." He smiled softly. Michael didn't let the boy know that he felt something dark welling inside Patrick's heart.

Patrick lowered the pistol slowly, untrusting of the Vampyre, with his jaw locked in grief and anger.

Michael too had suffered loss. For what little he had come to know of himself, mostly he felt bereaved. He was still unaware of what had happened earlier that day. He had lain on Ernest's couch for the rest of the evening contemplating the death of a friend, compounded upon the disappearance of Kat. He felt responsible for both.

He could no longer feel Kat throughout the town and he no longer feared the worst. He accepted that there was nothing left to be done. Her blue eyes however, as he'd remembered them in the lamplight of the cramped room, continued to haunt him with their sadness. She had been trapped. Something deep inside of him wanted her to be free of it all.

He sighed as Patrick told him what had happened. Mister Smith was lost, Ernest was gone and the sheriff's men were everywhere. There was no victory in sight.

It wrenched Michael's heart and he put an uncomfortable hand on the boy's shoulder. Patrick did not pull away nor did he cry, he simply hung his head and the two of them shared the silence. Michael had seen the sheriff's men on the road, preparing Desmond's carriage. He knew they weren't coming to the farm. "Let's go back for a moment," he told Patrick, who nodded his head, confused, slumped and worn. Michael didn't trust the boy, but he made sure to keep him close.

They returned quietly to the flicker and crackle of the small fire.

"Are you not at war with these men?" Michael asked the children, allowing his voice to continue filling the small barn.

"What war?" asked Newt Bullington. "We're just kids."

"Yesterday, you waged absolute war with the sheriff, with those Vampyres and with the world, with not much more than your wits!" Michael replied. "Children, maybe. But you've put fear in the hearts of people. You've made enemies of bad men." He paused. "You're the good ones."

His words rang into the chests of the children just as four of them walked up. Alexander and Albert carried food and guns and Thomas and Edwin came up behind them.

Michael continued. "No matter how many die, no matter how many of us don't survive, we push forward now."

"That is easy to say when you are a Vampyre and nothing can kill you," replied Emily Hughes, who helped Alexander with the burlap sack of stolen goods.

Michael looked down, almost ashamed of what he was. Before he could answer, it was Edwin that replied to her. "But they can be killed!"

Everyone turned to him.

"There was an old man." Edwin entered the room. "And he made one of them disappear completely. A Vampyre exploded right in front of us tonight." He could tell that no one wanted to believe him. He held his arms out. "Smell me! Smell us! Look at us!" He looked at Thomas, whose dirty face was streaked with tears. "He even told me how—"

"He's right," Thomas interrupted.

Michael walked over with a confused look on his face. "I suppose that settles the question of one's mortality," he replied, pensively.

"But I know how to..." Edwin tried again.

"BANG!" cried Oliver Whipple from behind. "You are exploded, Vampyre!" He ran to Michael. "BANG!"

The room grew very tense. No one knew what the men had done to Ollie while they had him and it was the first time he'd spoken since they had rescued him from the Sheriff's men.

Penny tried to apologize for Ollie and force the child to sit but Michael stopped her quietly.

"BANG! Explode the Vampyre!" he cried and then strangely, he whispered in an eerie singsong, "They are going to kill you all."

"He's possessed," Emily observed.

"No," Michael replied. "He is graveled. Thoroughly confused."

"What can we do?" Newton asked. His voice changed to one of hope.

Michael smiled at him and asked quietly, "Newton, can we be friends?" It was a strange question, but it was sincere.

"Yes."

"Good." Michael smiled. "I need you to believe in me."

Everyone shared a strange glance.

Michael continued. "Because what comes next, I cannot imagine being pretty." He kneeled in front of Ollie but avoided touching him. Something felt off.

Patrick interrupted. "What do you plan to do to him, Vampyre?"

"Well," Michael replied, "I am not sure, but I feel I can remove this confusion from him."

"Do it," answered Thomas quietly, looking at Patrick.

"Do whatever it takes." Patrick left the farmhouse and marched back to his post. Whatever trust Michael was building with him, the boy shrugged off, disappearing into the dark woods.

B lood covered everything. Even its smell permeated the room. Bernadette felt like a wounded dog and she chuckled. She thought that someone should put her out of her misery. *It seems he tried, but missed.* The laughter caused her to cough and though she expected to see blood, she tasted nothing.

The bullet had torn through her shoulder and her right arm was losing feeling. She sat naked from the waist up, old and wrinkled and bleeding from the small hole just below the bone. She attempted to cauterize the wound as quickly as she could manage. The immense pain was debilitating and she cringed each time she tried to pick pieces of her blouse from the small hole.

It caused her to go short of breath. She gathered a piece of thick leather used for sharpening blades and laid it with her needles where she had cleared her worktable. The scattergun sat quiet and reloaded next to her on her left side, pointed at the door.

She had already dragged off the dead, headless body around the side of the house. *With one good arm, no less,* she thought. She knew they'd be coming soon. There was no time to lose.

She had searched for some bit of liquor to numb the sensations, but ended up just boiling a pot of tea instead to calm her nerves. The pain was dizzying and she'd only pressed bits of fabric against the wound to slow the bleeding. She had no intentions of dying and she grabbed needle and thread, just as she'd done thousands of times before.

She put the leather between her teeth. The prick of the needle against the flesh under her collarbone was uncomfortable, but it was the throbbing pain of the wound that caused her to clench and bite down on the rolled leather.

In the pain, she flashed through memory. Her bony hands, bathed in blood, shook as she handled the needle. The pain caused her to remember. She remembered her lover and the plantation nights. She remembered her youth and the smell of the fields of black tea leaves, an ocean of green and black and the sticky Southern summers. She remembered Desmond's carriage. She remembered the full moon on the night when Desmond's men killed her husband so long ago. She also remembered trying to fix his wounds before waking up some years later in Breton.

For the first time, she felt she could make a change. The pain she felt was his pain. It was their pain. She sewed the wound with thick thread and snipped off the end of the thread skillfully. As for the exit wound, she would not have so much luck. She looked at the fire and the poker that sat in the flame and coal, almost red. Then she looked at the pool of blood below her. She knew what she had to do.

The sound of sizzling flesh was barely broken by a scream muffled by gritting teeth in leather.

Alonzo Gallegos pulled the window closed in the cellar of the Crow's Nest. He was contemplative and worried. The stout body of the blonde girl, Kat, lay across his makeshift table of ale barrels, crates and wooden planks. She was dead. What Gallegos knew that others would not know or could not possibly know was that there would be much more to her death than the simple vessel strewn across the table.

There was a sad beauty in her, laid out, hands crossed on her chest. She looked like a renaissance painting. She was round and strong, though her features were delicate. She had the corseted, supple curves of a French farmer's daughter and the strength in her arms of an old German bar wench. In his old age, he could see it.

He had seen men call many things beautiful over the years. With the turning of the twentieth century, beautiful women were thinner and thinner. The young woman in front of him would not have been among them. Her classic elegance was from another time and place. There was sophistication to Kat's beauty. The candlelit room could not contain that beauty and he thought that there was a tragedy in knowing that the girl died without knowing love or a larger purpose. He saw that sadness in her when she greeted him at the door on his first day. She knew what most people did not know and lived like they did not live. *Perhaps*, he thought as he sat on a crate near her deathbed, *she had lived some less-restricted version of life in the strange and unfortunate town.* That was a comforting thing.

He considered whether or not to tell her father right then or to wait. Gallegos knew already what was coming, or could approximate an idea and it was both bloody and ugly. He lit a cigarette to clear his mind and contemplated how to tell her father what he considered to be the strangest news the innkeeper would ever hear.

That would have to wait. He sensed a change in the air because something, some breath of magic, was stirring around him.

He could hear the scuffling and screaming just outside the cellar window. Things were not going so well for Desmond's men. Gallegos heard the Sheriff yelling at one group to clean up the mess near the tailor's house and a group calling out that some townsfolk were having "episodes."

The sheriff simply yelled, "Fix it!" to each of them. "Fix it!"

Gunshots were fired and then a moment of silence followed by more scuffling. *It would seem*, thought Gallegos, *that this spell has lost its flavor*.

The girl still lay in front of him and he made his final decision. There was no use in telling her father about her "condition." Over the next few days, the town would be rioting and in flames, so the cellar would be a tomb and that would be fine for her.

As for his own safety, Gallegos would return to his room only long enough to claim his few worldly possessions before disappearing into the woods.

ΠΊΠΕ

Glenn sat at the window of the Crow's Nest and watched the men running through the town cleaning the mess they'd made. There were people wandering around confused, like sleepwalkers and police officers forcing them back into their homes. There was the hissing, horrible sound of the Vampyres up in the trees. It was a sound Glenn hadn't heard in years. At least he could not remember it.

He could not cry anymore; he was dried and hollow. He put his head in his hands and closed his eyes. He just hoped it would be over soon.

The hiss got louder and Glenn looked up. The courier girl, Genevieve Moreau, was running toward the Crow's Nest. Her head was down and she dug each step into the ground as if it would make her burst forward. She grunted, in a dead sprint toward them. Glenn looked to the door, where one of the girls, a young barmaid named Alexandria, was locking the door.

"No!" he yelled. "Don't!" The chair fell from behind him where he stood.

The girl just looked at him, startled and confused.

Glenn pushed his way between tables. "Open it! Open it!"

Before the girl could even move, Glenn had pulled the heavy door open to see Genevieve running, head down across the street. "Come on, child!"

She looked up and he could see the streams of muddied tears on her face. Glenn calmly stepped out of her way, allowing her to collapse in the doorway. He could see the hand of a creature reaching at her ankle. Glenn stood tall in the doorway and the Vampyre stopped cold.

"You don't plan on coming in do you?" he growled at it. His gravelly voice rattled.

Oh. You don't mind, do you, love? the voice asked with the charm of an old soul and the voice of a child. It slinked forward, standing face to face with Glenn.

"I do mind," he replied quietly.

Oh. She replied, pitiful and feigning sadness. *That's so sad.*

The Vampyre was astonishingly beautiful. Glenn knew her. Her eyes glowed in the dark like sunlight through stained glass.

He looked past the Vampyre that had once been his wife, Zoya. A death certificate ended their marriage. As far as Glenn was concerned, she was dead.

Oh, don't be so hurt, Glenn. You always do this. He missed her voice. It hit him in a very deep place and he was emotionally raw. She hadn't changed at all since they were young. He missed her soft Russian accent and her smile. It pierced him like a dagger. He thought about his daughter. He remembered them together.

Glenn hated her accent. Any time he heard Russian or Cossack workers talking in the inn, he thought of her. It was nothing but sadness.

"I want my daughter back," he demanded, staring somewhere beyond her.

Our daughter, Glenn, she answered.

She was our daughter. Then he pulled his eyes in on her. He looked at her cold in the face. "She is *my* daughter now. Her mother died when she was young."

She looked at him knowingly and sighed. *You'll never learn, love.*

"There's nothing to learn," he replied. He seemed to grow in front of her and he clenched his fists.

Genevieve crawled away from the door toward the bar and Zoya just looked at her. *You're lucky little one. The wolves lost interest in you.*

"Listen to me," Glenn threatened. "When I find out what you had to do with Kat's disappearance, I swear I'll find you and I'll rip your heart out myself."

Zoya looked up at him. She looked hurt. For a split second, Glenn could see something real in her.

I would never do anything to hurt her.

"Get out," he replied with a slam of the door.

Through the door, he heard it. *I protected her.*

He turned to Genevieve and for the first time in a long time, he didn't seem so angry. He looked like Glenn the innkeeper, the kind-hearted Mister Lamphere. He reached down and picked up the exhausted girl, who looked pale and sick. She was in shock.

"I bet you've plenty to talk about," he said softly as she raised a hand to say something. "But it'll wait until tomorrow." He picked her up effortlessly and turned to the girl who'd said nothing. "Prepare a bed and bath for her." He felt the girl falling from consciousness in his arms. *And now the children begin returning from Hell.*

He carried her up the stairs and laid her on a bed, thinking of the daughter that was gone.

When Jasper Markov peered into the small room in the rear of the church that had been home to Adler and his nephew for so many years, he did not expect to find the parson sitting on the floor with his legs crossed. The old man was mediating.

Jasper tried to shake off his nerves. Outside, the police were gathering people and walking them home. Many of the townsfolk were wandering around talking to themselves; it seemed that they were all going crazy. Ironically, the Vampyres stood in shadows laughing and taunting them. He had no intention of hunting any of those terrifying things. If anything, he would have loved to capture one for a freak show. He always loved freak shows as a kid—it had led him to his profession in the circus.

"Come in and don't make a sound." Parson Adler spoke gravely and quietly.

The confused Jasper raised an eyebrow but obeyed.

Candles were lit throughout the room. It looked like a very dark, strange ceremony. Light came in from the hallway, creating the illusion of warmth in the old church, but Jasper sensed that it was devoid of faith or empathy. Only the old man's bitterness and anger filled the room.

Jasper began to think, *How did the old man get back—*

"Don't think," Adler commanded.

"Wha...?"

"And don't speak," Adler continued. "It puts me off."

Jasper Markov was more confused than ever and he didn't want to anger the man, so he just stared at the wall. A cold gust of wind sighed through the open doorway and blew out one of the candles with a small plume of dancing smoke. Jasper could feel something changing in the air, as if the room were filling with people. He felt claustrophobic.

Parson Adler let out a deep breath and then spoke quietly, "Yes, it has been done." There was no reply. Adler sat listening. "Yes, they were hung. Desmond's work is going perfectly according to plan."

Jasper knew that was a lie. He looked around. Adler must have been losing his mind. He was just speaking into the air.

"We await the arrival of Ruthven's lantern on the next train." He sat quietly again. The old man must have been very powerful; he had brought Jasper back from the edge of the grave and then seemed to disappear in a room with no doors only to be found talking to someone who Jasper could not see.

"Yes, my Lords. I understand. There will be no need to disrupt you any further." He listened. "Yes. Thank you, my Lords." Adler bowed his head and then spoke more quietly, "May you find in darkness what the light cannot reveal."

And just as quickly as the gust of wind came, the room aired out.

Adler struggled to get up and Jasper jumped to help him.

"No!" he whispered. "Stay back." Steam curled off of his outstretched arm and Jasper gasped quietly. His surprise was evident in his wide eyes.

"Just get me my cane," the old man replied softly.

Jasper grabbed the cane from its position leaning against Stephen's bed. He handed Adler his cane, asking, "A séance?"

Adler raised an eyebrow and smiled. "That would suggest that we were communing with the dead, my young friend." He looked back at the circle of candles. "No. Not in this case. I just told Desmond Burroughs' bosses in New York and Washington that his 'plan' would be a success." He was exhausted, but the old man finally smiled and the smoke and steam just rolled off of his skin. "They won't be fooled for long, but it has bought us another few days."

The human mind knows no bounds. Michael opened the front door of a little cottage outside of Breton. *What imagination could have breathed life into man who has such unlimited capacity for thought?* The house was empty. There was no air and the silence closed in on him. It felt much like the "other world" that he had begun to get used to. What he was experiencing was much more elementary. There was no horizon and just beyond the trees, the world disappeared into a white, milky haze.

There was a flickering light inside the house. No candles or lanterns were lit but everything had a soft glow. "Ollie," Michael called softly. He stepped into the first room of the house, which split into a kitchen and a sleeping area.

A voice came quietly from near the beds. "Oliver, darling, love." It whimpered. "Don't make a sound, baby." The voice belonged to a small, round girl with large, wet eyes. Her lip quivered with fear and she pulled the baby to her chest. Beyond her, he saw through a window a young man, large and brawny, wielding an axe.

"Stay away from here!" the man cried.

A small man stood in front of him, emotionless and cold. "The child now belongs to us."

The girl looked up at Michael and sobbed quietly.

As he kneeled down to her, Michael reassured her. "I am not one of them."

She nodded. "Yes you are," and then said, quietly, "That's why you have to stop them." She looked lovingly into the bundle in her arms. "You have to take him. You have to get him away from here."

Outside, Michael could hear the horrible chatter and hissing of the taunting Vampyres. He felt the presence of another man standing next to him but saw no one.

He heard a voice. "You can help him."

Michael looked outside to see the man raising the axe slowly. The small, emotionless man froze, with condescending eyes on him. The Vampyres came out of the darkness, tearing the man apart. Blood splattered on the glass in the window. Everything moved slowly, each sound echoed and layered over the sounds before.

Michael reached down to grab the woman. "Come on, we have to go."

She sobbed and nodded. "It's too late for me," she moaned, "but he still has a chance." She handed the baby to Michael. He took the child in one arm and tried to lift the woman.

Michael blinked and he was standing at the door again. From next to the beds he heard her again. "Oliver, darling, love. Don't make a sound, baby." She whimpered quietly. Everything was exactly the same, except that Oliver looked eleven or twelve, as Michael knew him, sitting on the bed watching. The scene was repeating, exactly as it had. The memories were coming to life.

"Stay away from here!" the man cried out.

"The child now belongs to us," replied the emotionless man.

"You have to help him, Michael." The quiet voice stated again. It came with a British accent. It sounded caring. It was Mister Smith.

"Oliver. Are you ready to go?"

He was silent. Michael saw that the boy had no mouth; just his mother's big, wet eyes.

"I won't let them hurt you, Ollie." Michael swore and reached out to him. As the boy's hand came to him, he found himself standing in a jail. It was the jail in Breton where the boy had sat quietly for days.

The hissing of Vampyres was gone. The jail filled with Oliver's screams. The building filled with his screams and in turn, Michael's head filled with the overlapping sounds of crying and screaming. The child had spent almost two days unable to speak. He had screamed and cried, but no sound came out. He stared emotionless at the wall in the jail and his body would not reflect all of his internal screaming. All of those sounds were filling the space.

Michael grabbed his head. The sound began enervating him and a thought pierced the sound. "Relax." A quiet voice came. Mister Smith was standing with him. "It's not your torture, is it?"

"There's nothing more tempting for a Vampyre than a broken mind." A voice rang out from outside the jail. It was a voice Michael didn't recognize. He sensed that it belonged to the sheriff. Ollie knew the voice and Michael sensed it. The voice continued. "Bang!" it laughed. "The spell that brought Oliver Whipple here screaming was not for him, sir Vampyre, but for you."

Michael straightened his back and listened.

"Desmond might want to protect you, but it won't last for long."

"Who is Desmond?" Michael asked. "Protect me why?"

"Soon it will all be over."

The screaming stopped. Mister Smith looked outside.

The voice came from outside the building. The sheriff was ten feet tall in the bright daylight, casting a long shadow over Oliver Whipple with a gun to the child's head.

A child should never be made to feel so small, Michael thought.

"Bang, sir Vampyre." The sheriff smiled. "Either you come out here and destroy yourself, or you let me kill him."

Michael didn't move. He watched the man's hand.

"There's no riddle here," Mister Smith observed.

"How are you here?" Michael asked.

"I'm not," Smith whispered. "Ollie just thinks I am. Part of him just needs to be safe."

"Oh, I suppose I didn't explain why this is interesting for you," the large sheriff called out. "You see—if you come out here and stop me, of course you'll die and he'll live, but he'll forget you. And we know that Vampyres need to be remembered. Or," he stated theatrically, "I kill him and you both die."

"There's no winning here," Michael stated through the door.

"That's where you're wrong, sir," the sheriff replied. "It is too late for you, but it's not too late for him." He smiled. "How corrupt are you? How terrible a thing is a Vampyre?" He laughed. "Would you die for the righteous? Would you die for an *innocent*? Or are you past your duty?"

Michael's heart stopped. He could feel the importance of what the man was saying. He had sensed it in Isaac. Isaac had obsessed over the thought of righteousness. It was in everything Isaac had said to Michael. It permeated his thoughts. Michael could not kill Jared for the same reason—he was righteous.

Mister Smith glared out the door. Michael could sense that the imprint that was left in Ollie's mind, whatever it was, was going to poison him. It could drive him mad. The imprint of safety that Smith had left was looking out the door like a guard dog. The sheriff pulled the hammer back on his large gun with a echoing click.

Michael dove out as quickly as he could into the sun. He felt the burning skin, the fire rising up from inside him. He wanted to die. He was dying. He grabbed Ollie and pulled him up as the hammer came down on the gun.

Oliver was gone.

Ollie woke up holding the Vampyre, who had collapsed. Everyone was surrounding him.

Michael was on his back and he wasn't breathing.

"Mister Michael?" Ollie asked immediately. He had just seen him die inside a dream world only to find him dead in the barn. Ollie panicked. The Vampyre that lay there— that man had come to save him. He was the only one that could. Suddenly tears fell across Michael's lapel as Ollie tried to hold in the sobbing.

The children were incredulous.

Penny began swallowing, trying not to cry. Emily gasped and Thomas and Edwin were both astonished. They couldn't believe it. Newt fell to his knees. "Are you alright, Ollie?"

He looked up and nodded quietly, sobbing.

"Is he dead?" Thomas asked quietly.

No one broke the sound of the circle of breathing and sobbing.

"No," Michael answered finally. He opened his eyes with a weary smile. "No more than I was."

The cheer that rippled through the children was quiet, but the relief was obvious. Ollie hugged him tightly. "You saved me, Mister Michael!"

Michael smiled quietly. He looked at the child to see his mother's big wet eyes.

Edwin sighed, "Just glad you're alive."

"That makes two of us." The voice came from behind them. It was a very waterlogged Jared, smiling, bloody and scraped. "So. What's next?" he asked.

The children helped the exhausted Vampyre to his feet. Michael sighed, "Well, I have a plan."

Michael ran as quickly as he could. He sped through the forests from the old farm, flying past Patrick in inarticulate silence, moving down the road and back toward Breton. Michael had been glad to see Jared in the doorframe of the barn. It was a genuine relief. He trusted him. As Jared explained his situation with the shape-shifting Sheriff, Michael realized that Jared was quite a warrior.

Everyone was discussing his or her part in the plan when Thomas began asking why Mister Smith could not have been saved. Ernest had been set free, which was news to Michael who assumed all had failed and both men were lost.

The tension filled the room. Thomas asked angrily why the sharpshooter chose Ernest over Mister Smith. The younger boy, however, seemed hurt and agitated, but Jared kept his calm. "My choice was in simply pulling the trigger," he stated. "I didn't choose one man's life over the other. I just took a shot." It amazed him that he'd made the first shot. It was an impossible chance. It had been the best he could do.

"Where is Ernest now?" Michael interrupted.

"He has a covert at the Mayor's place, I think," replied Edwin.

"Well, sort this out," he answered. "I will return."

With a step out the door, he heard them arguing about Jared's allegiance to the group. Michael laughed as Jared spoke quietly and with confidence, silencing the children around him. "Where would you all be without me now?"

Michael stood in the woods outside of Breton and looked at the rear of the Mayor's house grinning, but as he made his way into the home, his heart dropped. *Kat.*

He sped up the stairs to the room where he had first placed the girl to hide her. He stopped cold in the hallway. Michael was struck with guilt. He was seized by an unbearable sorrow. He couldn't save her. He hadn't saved her. He paused outside the room, trying to grasp the overwhelming grief. He had already lost her. He calmed himself with a breath. The broken window where he had gone out of the hallway was behind him and he felt the cool breeze at his back.

The door to the private study opened quietly and Ernest looked up. He saw the gas-lantern eyes of his Vampyre friend. There was a smile in their amber gleam. Michael saw that Ernest wasn't the same man he had met sitting drunk on a foul-smelling crate. He had been so full of sadness and alcohol, if he could have been called full at all. He had lived an empty shell of a life and his sad eyes, like those of a beagle, were large, round and drooped with a weight of despondency. Those heavy lines of worry were replaced with keen eyes of determination. He even looked younger; his face was lit with the soft lamplight of the room and a smile created new lines around his cheeks.

The smile grew into exuberant laughter. "Look at that suit!" Ernest exclaimed.

Michael looked down at the gray cloth and felt relieved. The first time he'd seen the red vest in its box, he had been sure Ernest was a dead man. "It looks great. It's a gift from a friend."

Ernest stood at the desk and looked over Michael's shoulder, knowingly worried about what was going on outside of the mansion.

"I took care of them," Michael answered. A stack of dead men in police uniforms lay near the police station.

"Good." Ernest crossed the room and hugged the young Vampyre. "It's good to see a friend."

Michael smiled. "It's good to see you too, Ernest."

"Breton is a rouse." With a sigh, Ernest turned to the desk. "If we had suspected it earlier, I am most certain of it now. Heath, Adler, Matheson, the whole lot of them out there are working with the Vampyres— who they call," he adjusted his glasses and looked for the notes in front of him, "simply, The Brethren."

Ernest sat down at the stacks of paperwork. Aside from the obvious work in front of him, Ernest was trying to figure out another mystery. He scratched the stubble on his chin and his glasses sat low on his nose; he furrowed his brow in thought, "Michael, do you have any idea why you were coming here? Any clues as to what was bringing you to this place?"

"No," Michael stated clinically. He sat down and adjusted himself, putting together the thoughts, a jumbled mess in his mind where he had still failed to find a through line. "My name, which I am now fairly certain is Michael, though I am unsure I ever had a surname, was not in the register of the ship. I can put a name to each face on the ship. They are all accounted for. And dead." He sighed. "But they knew I was there." He leaned forward; it was coming together for him. "They weren't pirates either." His eyes burned golden. "I was bringing them here. I was bringing mercenaries here."

"Cloak and dagger," Ernest thought aloud. It seemed to him that The Brethren had found enemies. "If they—that is, if you knew that Breton existed, then surely you knew about the Vampyres, so you couldn't have considered taking them on."

"No. They attacked us long before we even made it to shore."

"Which means that your goal would have been the town, not what was below it." He looked at the blueprints. "Or what was coming toward it."

Michael sat quietly but was intrigued.

"An attack during the day by a group that knew what they were doing would easily have dismantled the town." Ernest continued.

"But there were no weapons on the ship."

Ernest smiled, saying, "Why would you need them?" His knowing eyes connected with Michael's. "The weapons were all here. I believe that this 'device' that is being used, something called 'B-heart,' is losing its strength and the town, as you see outside, is quickly falling into chaos. If I have understood the correspondence between Heath and the others involved with these 'LORDS,' or "the Alliance," another device was—is— coming: 'R-heart,' a more powerful device. That's what all of this is about. That's why you were here, that's why Mayhew and Elliott were here—to intercept this. You have powerful friends somewhere." Ernest clenched his fist. "I have no idea why the Vampyres didn't kill you, my dear friend—but they made a mistake in it." He smiled.

"So what's the plan?"

Ernest pushed his glasses up the bridge of his nose. "Apart from a few more miracles, I would say a hopeless gambit and a lot of work."

"I think that's my favorite kind."

Isaac Constantine opened his hand, sore and aching. He closed it into a clenched fist and his eyes flashed gold with the pain. He opened it and closed it again. He cursed. Michael, the mysterious Vampyre, had damaged him in a way that had never happened before. He felt his senses numbed except for the physical pain that pulsed throughout his body.

He heard something coming from within the heart of the complex. It surprised him that he heard anything at all. There was the sound of extreme pain and madness. It was the sound of torture.

It was a common thing for torture to be employed and Isaac held a great disdain for it, but Desmond kept the practice in high regard. Desmond particularly liked the way Vampyres could get inside the mind of a person and change their perception. It made mining for information very easy.

In Isaac's mind, however, there was no reason for someone to be tortured. He was already full of doubt and was suspicious of some of the other Vampyres. Ilya was young and foolish but most of all reckless. He would bring the entire complex down on them if he thought it would be fun. Isaac hated Zoya and Letsya and the others that followed Ilya around.

Ilya was Isaac's estranged son. Since coming to Breton, they had tried working together, but something had always been different with Ilya. Something was wrong with him. Before Breton, he had been sent to study among the Black Council. He had returned dejected and angry. Ilya rejected the covenant's ways. He rebelled in every way he could. Isaac no longer knew his son. Few, outside of a small circle of friends, even made a connection between the two men. They were nothing alike. Isaac wanted control and healing for his people, while Ilya wanted nothing more than pleasure.

Isaac forced himself up with an arm and made it through the door. He limped along the corridor with a hand on the wall, sensing for the tortured individual. *Elliott?* he asked. The thought scared him. Algernon Elliott could have been captured. It had been reported that he had been seen nearby. If that was true, then Isaac should have been notified. Elliott had already killed more Vampyres than any other single person in recent history. His techniques were the thing of legend.

Algernon Elliott was a horrifying adversary: unpredictable, dangerous and nearly undetectable to Vampyres. Even if Isaac wanted the man captured, he would not have wanted him brought into the complex. The Englishman had a way of being critically devastating. He could bring thirty years of Isaac's work to a halt. He could bring the whole place to the ground.

There were two young Vampyres talking in the corridor and Isaac feigned some strength as he passed them. Shortly after he turned the corner, he exhaled and the pain pulsed in his chest. It was the longest walk of his life and it had been excruciating.

He put his hand on the plain wooden door of a room in the heart of the complex. He entered the room that been converted into Desmond Burroughs' torture chamber.

Algernon Elliott.

The man lay on a small iron-framed bed, strapped down by the arms and legs. There were no physical marks of torture, but the man had a flashing aura of pain. He pulled at the straps, unconscious and feverish. Minutes were passing like days inside Algernon Elliott's mind.

Isaac entered the room and pulled a wooden chair up next to the bed. The walls were carved directly out of the stone and the light from the candles flickered.

So docile yet so dangerous.

He felt lucky that they had made it that far without Elliott and his cohort destroying everything. Suddenly, Isaac was hit was a sense of dread. *The other one, Mayhew, might still be nearby.*

He was completely unaware of the hangings and the dread lingered. Isaac knew no one would interrupt him. Obviously, whoever had brought Elliott in didn't want Isaac to know about it and much less would they want to be in the room when he had found them out.

Isaac leaned into the man, who moaned and mumbled in pain.

We are murderous monstrosities, you and I, Mister Elliott. Guilty. He gritted his teeth. *This should be interesting.*

Isaac opened his eyes, looking around a street. Cobblestone roads led in each direction and the houses all sat together, claustrophobic.

"England." Isaac observed. "How dreary and dreadful." He focused and found himself in the train station loft behind the clock. "Ah, this is better." With another thought, he began flashing through Elliott's memories. The man had an obsession with death. Twenty-seven Vampyres died at his hand. *Impressive.* More recent thoughts flooded through: an anonymous letter, confusion on a train, Elliott and his cohort, Mister Mayhew, lying to Neville Smith.

The scene flashed to the face of a young girl and was accompanied by very strong feelings. Those feelings led him into the complex. She was kidnapped. Things became much more clear. Algernon's thoughts and memories over the last days were very educational. Isaac saw the Shifter guardians and the bullet to the Golem's head.

Clever.

Algernon had moved unnoticed throughout the complex.

How could an entire city of Vampyres not see this man? It intrigued him. Almost two days he had been there and Elliott had to reveal himself before anyone noticed. Isaac could see everything from Algernon's perspective as he fought the golems in the prison chamber. He worked to remove the symbols even as they pummeled him physically.

What are you up to, Mister Elliott? There is no chance of freeing this love of yours if you're risking your life on Druid Golems.

It stopped. Moments later, Algernon sat on the floor facing the Vampyres that surrounded and mocked him. He feigned hurt to throw off their senses and Ilya stood over him talking. "*The* Algernon Elliott." Ilya laughed.

You fool! Isaac knew the danger that the man posed.

"The foremost expert in the preternatural." Ilya laughed. Algernon looked past the Vampyre as two Druids lay on the floor, one male and one female and watched as they cast sidelong glances into the cells.

Oh no. This cannot be.

The premier exorcist and killer of Vampyres in Europe. Ilya smiled.

You terrible fool, Isaac chided. *This is the end for all of us.*

Ilya leaned in as Isaac watched from Algernon's memory. *This will be so much fun.*

I knew this was coming, sighed Isaac.

Algernon moved quickly and held up a fist to the young Vampyre's face. "Do you like magic tricks, Vampyre?"

Ilya jumped back, but Algernon had already grabbed him by the back of the head. The other Vampyres gasped.

You idiot! exclaimed Isaac, unheard by either of the men in the memory.

"I love a good magic trick," Algernon whispered with a knowing half-smile.

Let me go, you fool, Ilya replied abruptly.

"Obviously, you see the problem." Algernon smiled. "In my right hand I hold a small vial full of holy water." There was an audible gasp, but no one moved. "It has been prayed over by numerous priests." He looked past Ilya to watch the other Vampyres. "I don't know if it changes aught, but I know it doesn't hurt." Then he smiled again with a dark gleam in his eye. "I misspoke. It really hurts."

Ilya interrupted. *What do you want from me?*

"Let her go."

Her? Ilya smiled.

Algernon tightened his grasp on the Vampyre's head.

You don't think you can both get out alive do you?

Isaac could sense that Elliott trusted that Ilya's vanity was important to him. It was a plague among Vampyres, Isaac thought. Elliott knew that might be the case. He'd killed and tortured almost thirty Vampyres in the previous two years. For the first time, Isaac felt a sense of dread and real doubt inside of Algernon Elliott's thoughts. The fear flashed and disappeared.

"No." Algernon sighed plainly.

Ilya raised an eyebrow.

Now everything makes sense.

"You give me your word and let her go and I will trade myself in without having to smash this in your ear," Elliott said with such calm it was troubling even to Isaac.

It's getting late. What if she doesn't make it out? Ilya replied snidely.

"Give her until nightfall," Algernon whispered.

Ilya couldn't resist the offer. *It's done.* Ilya smiled. *We'll set her off running toward the center of town.*

Algernon smiled sarcastically and answered, "I'm so glad we could come to this agreement." He knew he wouldn't get a better deal than that. He looked at the other Vampyres, who were beginning to show their teeth. "Aren't you lot glad?" He let go of Ilya's hair.

Ilya stood up in front of the gathering and hissed, *Do it.* He clenched his jaw and began to walk away.

"Your word, Vampyre," Algernon answered.

Ilya waved a hand and two brawny Vampyres lifted Algernon from the ground.

"I can walk," Algernon replied.

One of the Vampyres laughed. The glass vial crashed into the side of his head as Algernon pulled his arm out of the reach of the other Vampyre. Algernon fell to his feet and the tall Vampyre collapsed on the ground, skin sizzling.

The Vampyre screamed in agony.

No, you fools! The Druids! Isaac scolded. *Look at the Druids!*

"I can walk," Algernon stated to the other taller Vampyre.

The Vampyre just raised his hands to show he understood.

Algernon looked back down to see the face and head of the Vampyre disintegrating, leaving the remnants of the body on the ground.

As Isaac unfocused his mind and came back out of Algernon's memories, he could hear the man's screams and the agony within his own head. The echo of it could have driven Isaac mad.

All for a girl, Isaac whispered. *You will have been the destruction of everything I've built.* He paused. *And you did it all for love.*

Khalil Sayid held his face in his hands, writhing with frustration. *It is one thing*, he posed, *to be cursed with such conspicuous longevity. It is another thing altogether to be made responsible for the misery of those who surround me.*

It had never occurred to him.

How unfortunate to come upon goodness in such a way. What a burden it is to be honest.

Most called him Chandler; the false identity afforded him some luxuries in town. The pseudonym had been Adler's idea originally. The people in town would not remember their own lives and it gave those involved in Breton's construction the opportunity to be someone else. Mister Robert Chandler would be just that: a Christian name—a white man's name, an opportunity for the cursed man to step away from his life—that of an immortal murderer of women, children and soldiers.

Some fifty years earlier, Khalil Sayid had become Adler's assistant in a small Austrian town, where they had been asked to perform experiments exploring the paranormal and supernatural by the local government. Money was being sent in from American-based benefactors inside the government. Because of Sayid's past, he was a wanted man, but he was not squeamish and could tolerate the horrible work that Adler was doing. It was a great job for an international fugitive.

Sayid considered that day: two Vampyres had been wheeled in, strapped to gurneys, weakened by unknown prayers. Adler and his assistant were to figure out the regenerative nature of Vampyres. The two Vampyres were very different; a control and a variable. One was very weak and had dry, scabbing skin. He did not regenerate as the other did. There was something sick about him. He was already very old and he had been damaged from a battle with a Vampyre hunter near Spain. Sayid thought about the Spanish Vampyre hunter and shook his head. Everything in his life was coming back to him.

The other Vampyre, he remembered, was a beautiful, perfected specimen of demon. After many months of research, the Vampyre called Ruthven, an English Lord who had angered many in his covenant, finally got into Sayid's mind. While controlling him, he killed numerous nurses and doctors in the Austrian hospital. From deep within, Sayid was able to control himself enough to run his small, brass blade into his own heart, forcing the Vampyre out. He woke up days later with Adler staring at him, disappointed.

He despised Ruthven and did not pity him. Adler and Sayid worked for weeks building a rotating chamber in one of the hospital's towers that allowed sunlight in at different angles. They would dissect the Vampyres by cutting through them with the only thing that could—light. Scalpels would barely draw blood and the cut healed too quickly to matter. They worked first on the weaker Vampyre, Tomás Betancourt, a Spanish property owner that had drawn the attention of the Salamanca University's rogue Vampyre killer.

The light chamber, which was filled with mirrors and prisms, was called the "menagerie of the sun." Sayid had tortured both of the Vampyres for weeks with the idea of it. He took pleasure in building it.

When Betancourt was placed inside the chamber, he cursed and screamed but fell eerily silent as the light cut him across the legs and chest, allowing his blood to pour across the floor. He just stared at Sayid. His look would haunt him for years. Sayid felt guilty for it. He wasn't sure why, but there was a twinge of pity in his heart for the pathetic soul. They removed organs and placed them in separate jars, watching how long it would take for the tissue to die or regenerate. At night, Sayid would observe the jars and watch the organs pickling.

Except for the heart.

The Vampyre heart kept beating and if one got too close to it, it would communicate thought and memory at random with no control. The Vampyre heart would not die.

Adler even began working on some method to communicate with it. Through electrical charges and diodes, they were able to communicate through it, but not with it. It acted as an amplifier of thoughts. They would not remove it from the jar because the tissue around it would regenerate as it found space.

They built a small housing inside of a lantern with gears that rotated while a crank from the outside sent an electrical charge into the diodes. The device amplified the words of the person holding the lantern into immense waves of thought that infested the minds of those around it. It functioned as a sort of mind-control megaphone. They further revealed that they could even convince people nearby that they were having the thoughts themselves. Without the filter of the Vampyre mind, the heart would simply pulse telepathic energy, just memories and flashing pain.

The benefactors were pleased. So much so that a man named Desmond Burroughs arrived in the coming weeks to see that the newly designed "weapons" were put into the right hands.

Khalil had thought that would be the end of their work. He had been right. Shortly after, he was detained and carried away to a place where similar experiments and torture would be performed on him. He thought about how much he hated Desmond and his Lords.

He heard the train from a distance. "Time for a family reunion," he said with an arching eyebrow as he saw men filling the train station to await the arrival.

†EΠ

⊷───◆───⊶

T hings are getting worse in town, sir." One of Desmond's guards whispered into the window of Desmond's carriage. "Hold," he replied, nonchalant.

Desmond's carriage was a beautiful dark cherry with red velvet interior. The carriage came to a halt half a mile outside of town. The driver blew out the ornate lanterns that hung from its front posts and the little orange glow that surrounded the carriage disappeared into long shadows broken only by the soft white glow of moonlight.

"Sir?"

"Let the sheriff and his goons take the brunt of the force in town. We are still hours away from our expected arrival time. Wait until you see the front lights on the train. Do not disturb me until then."

Desmond was unconcerned. He put his hands behind his head, interlocking his fingers in his white hair. He wanted to rest his eyes. The sound of men outside of the carriage grew quiet and he could only hear the sound of the wind in the trees rustling. His breathing slowed as he relaxed. No more worrying about the Vampyres and their lanterns for a few more moments. He had cleared a desk of paperwork in the afternoon and it had cut into his nap.

Desmond hated paperwork, but the great majority of politics was what was on the paper in front of you, he had often told people. He had lost count of how many times a pesky appeal or proof of a man's innocence had come from New York or Washington.

No one was ever innocent.

He didn't even bother to send men out into the camps to find the fools. If they weren't already food for the Vampyres in the fields, they would be soon enough. It was all a bloody mess.

He concerned himself with how to properly reply to such appeals and queries: pneumonia, tuberculosis, or heart attack, depending on the age of the convict. Desmond did not worry on details very often.

He found that the idea of Breton was far more interesting than his desk post working for the Federal Government. He kept the letter he had received "In Conjunction with The British North America Act and the Office of the President of the United States of America" and hung it framed above his desk. He kept the picture of President Andrew Johnson next to his desk for decades after, despite his impeachment just a short two years later.

As far as he was concerned, the War Between the States would never end and Andrew Johnson could be president forever. The outside world rarely affected Breton. Desmond preferred things that way.

"Does Isaac know you're here?" Desmond asked to a dark corner in his carriage without opening his eyes.

"Not yet, he doesn't," the unknown voice answered.

"That comes as no surprise. He has no control over the covenant anymore." He stretched his neck. "It really is quite a pity that he couldn't get the Brethren under his wing after all this time. But I can fix that. With the arrival of Ruthven's lantern, your little covenant'll fall in line, just like everyone else."

Desmond felt the Vampyre lean forward.

"Say your piece then, Vampyre. I would much like to rest before we make the exchange."

There was silence.

"Oh, so you're offended?" He opened his eyes. "Does Adler's experiment bother you so?"

The Vampyre in front of him dressed like a gentleman. He had black hair that sat just above his shoulders. His eyes glowed like candles. He sat with his arms on his knees, listening.

"Well," Desmond smiled, "you shouldn't worry with such unpleasant cogitations. The torture of two Vampyres has fed you and your kindred for thirty years now."

The Vampyre listened.

"Ah, but I've done all the work." He cracked his knuckles. "Spent my twilight years reminding Breton's cretinous populous not to worry about the fact that you and yours might very well devour them every night and that they should go indoors simply to return the next morning for work. All so you can engorge yourselves. All so Isaac's vision could be realized." He leaned forward. "All so you could have your happy Vampyre family."

The Vampyre did not smile and Desmond did not appreciate the fact that he did not thank him.

"So get out of my carriage before I have you torn apart and put in a lantern."

The silence lingered.

Desmond expected one of the men to come to the window but nothing happened.

The Vampyre stayed quiet.

"Who are you?" Desmond asked through his teeth.

"My name is Michael." He leaned back in the carriage. He crossed his legs, making himself more comfortable. "I was a man a week ago."

"None of my concern," Desmond began.

"It is now, Desmond Burroughs," Michael accused quietly. "I have found it in my heart that you are guilty of a multitude of sins."

"You can't do that to me." Desmond stated disbelieving. His voice was dry and panicked.

Michael said nothing.

"You can't do this to me!" Desmond finally cried. "The Lords will have your head!" He reached for the door of the carriage, casting a glance outside into the darkness.

Michael grabbed the man by the wrist. "There is no fear in this place that is not married to your name." He squeezed the man's arm. "Look at me!"

Desmond fell to his knees inside the carriage and his eyes grew wet. "Please don't." He stuttered.

Michael's voice lost its human tone and Desmond felt an unearthly presence. He shivered. The old man looked up and saw Michael in full. The candlelight flames in his eyes grew into tongues of fire and Michael turned dark, with a blazing halo around his head.

The old man pulled away and fell through the carriage door onto the ground. He grunted with the fall. The land was soft and he looked down to find the empty, horrified look of one of his men. He was dead. He looked to have been dead for days.

In all his many years in Breton, he had never seen what the Vampyres did first hand. He always rolled his eyes when the men around the ranch house spoke about it. "Some might rip a man in half," they would say, "and drink the blood from the victim like a man drinking the last draught of beer from his upturned glass."

But they always told him, "The scariest of all is the Vampyre who without touch can drain the life by just looking at you. Just breathe in your very essence and soul."

He scrambled away from the corpse on the dirt road. He saw the dead bodies of his soldiers scattered along the path. He looked across the shadow of the carriage to see the body of another caught running. Their bodies looked deformed and their skeletal faces looked contorted in terrible expressions of horror.

He had not heard a sound.

"You misjudge me, sir," he stammered.

The Vampyre had no reply.

"I am just a man. I am not something to be feared!" he yelled.

The Vampyre's feet did not touch the ground as large wings of darkness spread out above him, blocking the night sky. The wings moved like pyres but did not create any light. They danced like black fire. His charcoal suit disappeared. The attractive young man disappeared. Nothing was there but a monstrous and vacuous darkness, highlighted by the two red flames smoldering in its face.

"What about the people?" he begged.

The creature stopped for a moment. Desmond took the opportunity to explain himself as he stood up. "The people. They've had nothing but this town their whole lives. With a world of horrors out there, why subject them to going out in it? They are safe where they are." His voice calmed. "The truth, sir," he stuttered, with tears running down his face, "is that I am the only barrier between order and absolute chaos."

A voice quietly resonated inside of the man's head. It was something like the Vampyre's voice. *If this is order, they may prefer chaos.*

There was a pause.

"What would you have me do?"

Is it so easy? A threat to your life and now you cry and repent and bend to my will? The voice phased in and out of Desmond's head as he, wide-eyed, listened and bargained for his life. With each word the black flames pulsed. *Only moments ago, you would have put me in a lantern. Moments ago, I fed from your hand. Only moments ago, you were puffed up with pride.*

"No." He wept and shook his head. "Not pride."

Do not! the voice exclaimed. *Do not lie to me! I see your heart, Desmond Burroughs. You do not care for anything. You were puffed up with pride and now it is only pride diluted with tears.*

The black demon faded into a cloud and the young, attractive Vampyre stood before him. "I would that you were dead."

Desmond turned to run, but Michael stretched out his hand and grabbed his arm.

The older man cried out, "Help me! Someone!"

Michael continued in silence.

"Anyone, please!" The tears flooded down his face. He spit through the tears uncontrollably. Fear gripped him and he felt completely powerless. The horror ran throughout his body.

Michael turned the man by his arm but did not open his mouth.

His eyes glowed the deep red of coal.

Desmond felt it resonate inside of him; the voice came again. *Guilty.*

Desmond felt an agonizing pain. His muscles burned and ached. His blood was boiling under his skin. Everything hurt. The torment was crippling. His bones were giving way and he sat at the verge of unconsciousness, but he remained awake, tortured.

The Vampyre opened his mouth and a red and yellow haze began to sizzle off of Desmond's skin. Desmond screamed, collapsing on the ground. He writhed in pain. Michael breathed in the haze fully.

The man disintegrated violently, exploding into nothingness.

Michael was covered in the blood. There was a ring of blood and entrails that spread for ten feet in every direction. His mind was clear. *Guilty.*

Plans had changed. The children were on the move again. Patrick ran ahead of the others, illuminating only a few steps ahead of him with a small oil lantern. Scatterguns and rifles rattled, strapped on his back.

The only other light was the small, flickering cloth torch that Newton carried above his head. Everyone watched the perimeter of light against the envelope of darkness around them. The light forced elongated shadows to dance from the tall trees in the forest. Emily held Penny close and Alexander helped Thomas and Edwin carry supplies, while Ollie, Albert and the other boys watched the rear.

Vampyres were coming.

They skittered and screeched in the far distance.

They were just on the other side of any shadow. Michael had sensed the Vampyres and that was enough for them to know it was true. The pale light of lantern and torch had become a coffin, as oppressive as the dark around it.

A hiss came from within the woods.

Patrick turned with the lantern near his face, causing him to look like a shadowed monster. "We've got to move!"

Newt swung the torch around to the boys in the back, "Come on!"

Ollie ran out toward Patrick, while Thomas herded everyone in together. "Stay close," he whispered. Thomas handed off his supplies to Archie, one of the twins and held back to make sure no one was getting lost.

Edwin stayed close to the middle of the group as they tightened up. "We'll be fine," he whispered to Penny, who had begun to whimper. He wasn't so sure anymore.

The hissing began again, but the second time, it was accompanied with laughter.

Edwin handed off his supplies to Albert and whispered, "Stay in the group," while watching out into the darkness.

Patrick slowed. His feet fell heavier until he stopped.

"What are you doing?" scolded Thomas.

"We..." he tried. "We... we're surrounded."

When Thomas looked around, he could see them in the darkness outside the perimeter of light. There was a horrible sense of fear that finally ran through the group.

"What do we do now?" Ollie asked.

There was no reply for only a split second. Edwin stepped forward and announced, "You will be murdered here, Vampyre."

Simultaneously, the group gasped and laughter burst from all around in the forest. The laughter rippled.

There were even more in the darkness. Patrick ran his eyes along the horizon of darkness and guessed twenty. *Twenty Vampyres,* he thought. *It is hopeless now. These children are all going to die.*

"Murder?" A Vampyre laughed, stepping out of the darkness. "You?" he smirked. The Vampyre looked old and grim, but the lines on his face were missing. There was something odd and alien about him. Other Vampyres stepped into the light, perfect, strange creatures as well. Even their clothes looked old but perfectly clean.

Patrick stepped back quietly. Edwin was crazy. *Why would he do that? Why would he try to bluff the Vampyres?*

Penny began to cry openly and Emily pulled her to her chest. They fell into a blanket of their dresses along the ground. Patrick did not move, but the lantern seemed to shake in his hand.

Newt kept the torch out ahead of him. He had to see them. He used the torch like a weapon, swinging it at the Vampyres, but they just jeered and laughed at him.

"What is your name, Vampyre?" Thomas asked, following Edwin's lead.

There was laughter throughout the woods again.

The Vampyre did not answer.

"Are you afraid to answer?" Thomas asked to uproarious laughter.

The Vampyre stepped forward angrily and slapped Thomas across the face. He fell to his knees. Patrick and Edwin moved to him. Edwin picked his friend up and the group of children tightened up around them. The Vampyres moved in closer, laughing and jeering. Thomas looked up, red-faced, with his eyes watering.

Patrick was getting nervous, but the anxiety caused him to remember what happened before the orphanage. He remembered the night his parents were killed. He remembered the police coming. He remembered meeting Adler and Desmond Burroughs.

Edwin was angry. "Are you so afraid of a child that you must watch your words so carefully?"

"That was your answer?" Thomas asked. "Have you no name?" He hoped that Michael or Jared would show up. He hoped anyone could help. He couldn't stall forever but couldn't give up on his friends.

I smell death here, the Vampyre replied.

"Surely not," Thomas answered. "Unlike you, we are very much alive."

No. The angry Vampyre pointed. *I smell a Vampyre's death. I smell the undying blood.*

"Oh. Did I not wash that off?" Thomas asked. He looked to the edges of the darkness and to the Vampyres that stood over the children. "You come here looking for easy prey," he said. "You prey on weak, innocent children."

You speak boldly. You have all been left because of the mercy of The Brethren. A second Vampyre smiled.

"Fear makes you silent. You made a mistake by leaving us," Thomas countered.

The first Vampyre raised its hand again but was interrupted by a beautiful female Vampyre. *The child calls you a coward and you strike him.* She laughed. *Are you a coward?* She was careful not to give away his name.

The other Vampyres were restless and some had begun clawing at the children. *Let's just have at them*, one yelled to cheers. *We'll skin them for their bittersweet blood!*

I am no coward, the Vampyre said. *But I smell them.*

"His name was Pavl," Thomas answered quietly.

What did you say? the Vampyre asked intently. His eyes filled with surprise.

Thomas looked at him and answered, *His name was Pavl and he was scared like you are now.*

The Vampyre looked to the group of those that appeared with him. *I am not afraid. I simply find it odd that you should need my name.* He didn't look at the child. His eyes wandered past the other Vampyres.

Coward! one yelled, laughing.

Then coward I will be. The Vampyre began walking away.

What? the female asked, following him.

A small Vampyre clawed at Ollie. They all began closing in, except for the two who walked away, talking quietly.

What do you mean, that's what you'll be? Zoya asked.

They're not lying, Letsya replied.

HA!

Pavl never came back from taking the girl to the inn. He looked pale and nervous. *Pavl would have killed that little brat had he been given the chance. Impetuous.*

So?

So he's dead! Letsya continued. *Otherwise he would not have revealed himself to them. Is he to be forgotten?*

Zoya shook her head while she gritted her teeth. *He isn't dead, Letsya. That is foolish.*

I will prove it, he replied. He turned to the crowd, where one weaker Vampyre was disturbing the children.

What's your name, little boy? The weak Vampyre poked, looking like a bald cat. He was small and he had no hair on his face or head. His eyes were large and black and though he smiled, he seemed emotionless. All of his teeth were fangs.

He was terrifying to everyone except Ollie, who replied without hesitation. "My name is Oliver Whipple." Ollie stood up taller than the impish creature.

The Vampyre laughed. He looked ancient and deformed. *Oliver Whipple*, it hissed, reaching out at him. The Vampyre laid its hand on Ollie's shoulder and then collapsed on the ground with a thud. It was dead.

There was a shriek and then hissing. Emily and Penny looked up. The Vampyres were in the trees and all along the forest. They began screaming, *Guilty! Guilty! Guilty!*

Stand back! Letsya yelled at them. *What did you do?* he asked the boy.

"We're Vampyre killers," announced Edwin proudly.

Guilty! the Vampyres replied.

Alexander, Albert, Henry and Archibald got a sense for what Edwin was doing and one by one stood up from the bunch and moved toward the edge of the light. Emily wanted to follow, but she could not bear to leave her little sister, who was still terrified.

Letsya looked at the dead body.

Zoya stood behind him, trying to get a sense for what the children were up to. She couldn't read them. They smelled of Vampyre death. Letsya was right about that. She tried to listen to their thoughts, but they were jumbled and they heard the voices of men, numerous men and the voices of helpless, crying children.

It's a trap, Letsya.

Aye. Something is absolutely wrong here.

"Who is next?" Edwin prodded. "Is it you, nameless Vampyre?"

No, Letsya replied. *Not I.*

A terrifyingly large Vampyre came out of one of the trees. *I am no coward!* she screamed, grabbing Archie, one of the twins and she raised a large, clawed hand to cut Archie's throat. His brother, Henry, jumped at the Vampyre, screaming.

The Vampyre exploded. Her dress billowed like a parachute and the body within it disappeared. Henry tackled Archie but they were both blinded and covered in wet film, mucus and ash. A scream erupted throughout the group of Vampyres.

Edwin turned around with hands steepled, as in prayer. "Who's next?" He asked, masking his own surprise that it actually worked. He prayed just like the old man had and he believed in it.

Eighteen. Confused, Patrick watched the Vampyres running away into the darkness, shrieking and hissing, *Guilty!* What had just happened? He looked at the other children. *You should all be dead by now.*

The children collapsed in a gross, foul-smelling huddle around Penny and Emily. The lanterns collapsed on the ground. They hugged each other's necks, amazed. The collective sigh was audible.

Emily grabbed Edwin and hugged him tight. "You saved us all, Edwin."

Despite the hundreds of things running through Thomas's mind, he suddenly had a twinge of jealousy in his stomach. "Come on, everyone," he huffed quietly. "Let's go."

E rnest grew more impatient with every passing second. He had made his way, limping, from the Mayor's mansion to a broom closet in the train station without being seen. He was thankful for the unrest in the street. It kept the sheriff and his men busy. A thread of light came in through the keyhole and he used it to look at the gold pocket watch that he kept in the front pocket of his vest. He squatted to look through the keyhole and saw the large face of the train station clock and compared the time to his pocket watch.

What is taking them so long?

The late train would be arriving soon and Ernest knew that it would be the only chance to get the children out of Breton. He also felt that there was a great chance that the new device, the "R-heart," could be coming on the same train. A hunting rifle lay docile across his leg. It was the mayor's rifle and Ernest had to break the glass in the cabinet since he could not find the key. He had felt silly looking for the key. *It's the end of the world, Ernest and you're worried about breaking the glass in a dead man's house*, he had scolded.

Michael trusted Chandler the trainman to help them execute their plan, though Ernest couldn't understand why. The strange, little man with the dull, black eyes had always given him such a terrible feeling. Through the keyhole, he watched the sheriff and some of his men entering the train station.

Alright. He began to fret. *Here we go*.

The sheriff instructed his men to get into position. Chandler stepped out of the office.

"You won't be needed for this transaction, Monsieur Chandler," the sheriff said, pointing back to the office.

"I did not ask you, sir. Did I?" the older man replied. "Anything that happens in this station will occur only with my supervision and subsequent signature of approval. Everything that happens in this building is under my absolute jurisdiction." Chandler's voice was cold and stern.

"Do what you will," the sheriff replied. He didn't hide his disdain for Chandler, who stood in the middle of the station watching the men. The sheriff rolled his eyes at the little old man then quickly made his way back out the heavy doors onto the street.

Michael, Ernest thought, *you've gotten us into something terrible now*.

M ichael walked patiently down the road, followed by the horses pulling Desmond's carriage. Its lamps sparked with blue light. He was clean. Whatever blood had permeated his gray suit earlier, his body had soaked up. Even his hair was back in place. Something about him had changed. His mind was clear and he sensed everything around him.

He smiled.

He hid his precious cargo inside of the carriage and he would get it to Breton without fail. There were other, more evil presences out in the world, but they would not notice the disjointed rhythm of what he had begun to call "the town that never was."

From the edge of the forest, Michael watched a dark figure emerge.

You fool, Michael thought.

So much had arisen in Michael's heart during his days in Breton. He had been a blank slate. He had forgotten all he had known about himself. After finding Ernest and ultimately finding Kat and the children, he had lost all hope of looking for the person he had once been. It didn't matter to him. What mattered was that the Vampyres had, in their selfishness, destroyed the lives of the people in Breton and that he was finding out each night that he had the power to change that.

He looked to the figure that stood in the middle of the road. *It's been a tough week for you, Isaac.*

He did not respond.

No quip? No wit?

Isaac spoke aloud as Michael brought the carriage to a halt. *I have to stop you, Michael.*

Michael stepped forward from the horses into the dark road, outside of the lantern's ethereal glow and spoke quietly. *No. You don't, Isaac. Nor can you stop me.*

Anger. You are so angry, he observed. *Anger will destroy you.*

"Strange that you keep speaking on the subject of my anger, Isaac. You are so nervous. It would seem the entire world is collapsing around you. Have you nothing better to think on?"

Isaac smiled. *Perhaps you're right.* He didn't move. Isaac looked at Michael and stroked his scratchy chin. *What is in the carriage?* He looked tired, even haggard.

"Can you not see, Isaac? When I was confused and looking for help, you taunted me, chased me and tortured me. You saw through me, a hopeless fool and you threw me into the sunlight to die. Now, you can't even see what is here in front of you?"

Michael seemed taller. Isaac knew he would have to be careful with his words. *Is there no better way to do this? Killing men and Vampyres for no reason? It doesn't seem like you, Michael.*

Like me? Michael smiled. *What would be like me?* Michael stepped toward Isaac. A cloud of energy hovered around him.

Listen to me, Michael. There is still a chance for you.

Is there, Isaac?

Vampyrism is not an end.

Michael clenched his teeth and his amber eyes flashed with fire. *Yes it is. Your son made a mistake when he did this to me, Isaac.*

Isaac's eyes opened with surprise. *No one knows that.*

I do. Michael continued moving forward toward him. Michael could hear clamoring in the distance. Other Vampyres were nearing them. They hid in the trees. Michael could almost see them in the darkness. Isaac seemed to sense them too. *It would seem we have an audience, Isaac. Is this how you would choose to die?*

Why is it a matter of death, Michael?

You choose now to be diplomatic? Fear moves you.

Perhaps, but in truth, I am trying to come to some resolution with you.

Go on.

I understand that you are angry for what has happened to you and I regret what I did to you to make it worse.

Michael rolled his eyes. "You regret it because of the pain it's caused you. Not because of what it did to me."

Isaac sensed the emerging cloud of energy that floated around Michael. It crossed his mind that Michael was something like an anchor dragging the seafloor. All of Breton was stirring up around him. There wasn't a drop of blood on Michael, but Isaac could see the death all over him. He still shined purely within it, even through his anger. It was justified. Purity had once been the strength of the Vampyres.

Michael, you have to understand that when I brought the covenant here it was to bring them back to something good. His voice changed. There was a sense of humanity in it. *We had endured centuries of corruption and we weren't dying, we were simply getting darker—losing whatever sense for justice we once had. I cannot blame you for your indignation, but I beg that you stop, whatever you have with you, whatever you plan to do—please stop.*

Silence pressed in on them. The natural and organic world around them was transforming as each concentrated and began holding his ground. Michael got closer to Isaac and he sensed the immense force of the older Vampyre in front of him.

"Isaac, I plan to kill you— and your covenant. And every Vampyre that stands," Michael said.

Why do you protect Desmond Burroughs then? Isaac looked at the carriage. He understood that the younger Vampyre would pull strength from each righteous kill. Breton was a good place for that.

Michael did not answer.

Michael was planning something and it added to Isaac's anxiety. He gritted his teeth. He didn't want to say it. *Michael...* he sighed, *I have to stop whatever you are doing. I am bound to it.*

235

Michael's face melted into a bit of a childish smile and he shook his head. He looked into the woods around them and he could count the heads of each Vampyre there. "What happens," Michael wondered, "when one Vampyre kills another?"

Before he could formulate the words, Michael grabbed Isaac by the throat in the way that a man goes to swat a fly. Isaac gasped with surprise. A sudden jeer came from the trees and Michael looked up. "You're all going to die," Michael informed them quietly.

The jeering subsided as Isaac began clawing at Michael, who held him at arm's length. His arm was like a steel pole and Isaac was imprisoned by it. Isaac had not felt so weak in hundreds of years. He was faced with his own demise at the hand of some anomalous boy who had found his vampyric powers only days before.

Michael, please.

There is nothing to be said.

We are just pawns in this, he pleaded as the pain pulsed through his body. *Can't you see that? Please don't do this.* He felt violated and confused. He could not fathom the failure of his own kind. No one was coming to help. They watched morbidly.

Michael's eyes flashed once brightly and then turned completely black and Isaac could see him transforming. It terrified him. He hadn't seen something that powerful in hundreds of years. He closed his eyes and transferred his energy, trying to shift his weight. He opened his eyes in the æther, still gripped in pain by Michael. He couldn't shake him like he had the last time. One by one, the other Vampyres began appearing in the æther.

Isaac gasped for help, his power leaving him. His voice was gone. He reached to the others, hoping they would intervene. The terrifying figure towered over him. The blue energies of the æther were sucked up into a black hazy void that lined the dark silhouette over him. Large, flaming wings reached out, causing leaves from nearby trees to wither and burn away.

The hesitant Vampyres saw that Isaac had no power over the Vampyre. Letsya watched from a distance but after only a moment, without remorse, left quietly. Zoya followed. Ilya appeared nearby. Word had reached him and arrogantly, he walked up through a group of weaker ones. He motioned to the Vampyres near him to surround Isaac and the larger demon. Isaac's eyes showed gratitude, but the larger thing, growing and pulling life out of the submissive Vampyre, took no notice.

Ilya noted something strange. Even though the terrible creature was pulling energy from Isaac, whom he didn't even care for, it was growing too quickly. There were foreign energies around it. It was intriguing. The energies were coming from somewhere else. Isaac must have seen it. Why fall into this trap?

He was pulling energies from every Vampyre near him, and more from within the æther.

It was too late. Ilya watched the first Vampyres encircling the monstrous black creature. *No!* he yelled, outstretching a hand to stop them. It was too late. The first Vampyre, a young arrogant one called Nik, reached out to grab Michael and his arm exploded, throwing bones and meat in every direction. The explosion culminated at his shoulder, where blood gushed from the ruptured joint. Nik screamed and fell down onto his back, clutching the shoulder where an arm had previously hung.

A strange yellowish energy began pulsing in a stringy haze and it rose up from the blood, connecting the shattered appendage to the monster's arm. It looked like the creature was unraveling Nik from the shoulder. He screamed with pain.

While Nik reached from one side, another older, more powerful Vampyre named Joseph moved to tackle the monster and break its grip on Isaac. Ilya was crying out, but Joseph put his head down and barreled toward the creature. Another Vampyre came from behind. Joseph and the third Vampyre, Mahir, simultaneously exploded into Michael who still did not lose his grip on Isaac. The cloud of stringy yellow energy whirled around Michael.

Michael! Ilya's voice felt small in comparison to the creature before them. *You want me!* The void and blackness that sucked up his friend's lifeblood pulsed. Ilya could see that there was more than just the power of a Vampyre. There was some sort of spell around him, something very powerful.

Have you forgotten the night I created you? Ilya said to him. *The night I fed of your friends. That fateful night that you wandered into my life*, he smiled. If Ilya feared for his own life, he didn't show it. The Vampyres surrounding him stepped back, yet no one helped Nik, who continued to scream in pain. One by one they disappeared from the æther and when Michael reappeared on the road in Breton, there lay Nik, bleeding from the shoulder in a pool of dark blood. He and Isaac were both bathed in ash and blood and the smell of death permeated the air. Ilya paced but did not come any closer to Michael. He let Isaac collapse on the ground in the mud in front of him. Everything else was dry.

Michael looked up at Ilya but did not speak.

You intrigued me, Michael, Ilya divulged, as if he'd been embarrassed about something silly. There was a sly smile that Michael could hear in his voice.

Isaac clawed the ground, still trying to pull himself away from the terrifying Vampyre above him.

Look at how beautiful and powerful you are, Ilya continued, *So pure and so strong. The night you were reborn this— this beautiful thing, I was bored.*

Michael listened, the sparks of memory illuminating his thought.

One by one, we boarded your ship of mercenaries and spies and I should have told Desmond or Isaac, let them know. Their enemies were so near. He smirked as he saw Isaac lying there, powerless. *But how much more fun if we just killed you all?* Ilya laughed almost maniacally. *So we did. But then I found you, hiding in the foot of the boat and what could I do with you, Michael?*

Michael had no answer. He was absolutely silent. He began picturing it.

You see, your friends had good intentions. 'We'll kill all the wicked, evil, naughty Vampyres in Breton.' Good intentions, but bad men—like all soldiers, he observed, shaking his head. *All except for one, the one that hid: you. How intriguing.*

You were nothing. Just a haunted husk of a human. There was no guilt in you. Something was already feeding on you! Even if I had wanted to kill you, it would have tasked me to get through it. Just like children that fill orphanages. It's quite difficult to really murder a child. It hurts. And if you're not into that, then you're just not into it. "

Ilya's confession was troubling, but he spoke like it meant nothing to him. *As a child, I was quite a powerful Vampyre. I am much more powerful than my father, though he thinks me foolish.* He smiled at the dying Vampyre at Michael's feet. *Isn't that right, papa?*

And one day, my father slept comfortably. And I crawled around in his dreams, learning the ways of the ancient Vampyres. Over several visits into my father's perverse dreams, I saw the ancient symbols and I acquired a vast wealth of knowledge, including, he boasted, *the ability to convert a man into a Vampyre.* He paused. *And poof! Here you are: the purest, most beautiful Vampyre in the world. It took six of us to do it and there you sat,* he smirked again, *crying, begging us to show mercy while we stacked the bodies in front of you in the sacred shapes, those from whom you would draw life. You see with their eyes, remember their fear. Part of them will always be with you.*

I told him to do all of this, Michael thought. *I remember instructing him to give me a body.* Michael was absorbed in sudden memories. He had run into the belly of the ship, looking for a weapon. He was not a pirate; he was a stowaway. He was no one. All of the indignation, the desire to do right, was the desire of other men.

In a terrorizing séance, the Vampyres surrounded Michael, cutting him with their fingernails, as he screamed in pain, fighting them. They threw him on the pile of dead bodies in the hull of the ship and gathered his blood for Ilya to write the ancient Vampyric symbols on the walls. They chanted over him and the blood ran from his wounds, soaking the bodies below him. He screamed for help and no one came. He cried out and no one listened. Michael remembered falling against the strong arms of the Vampyres and being lifted onto the pile of dead men.

Michael remembered dying.

Michael remembered Ilya.

We could have just killed you.

"No," Michael replied quietly. "You should have killed me." His eyes were cold and even when he wasn't looking at any of the surrounding Vampyres directly, they seemed to penetrate each of them.

But Michael, you were nothing. You were no one. Now you're special. Listen to your voice, your beautiful voice. You are special now. You are of the Blood now.

Michael contemplated his words and in the distance he heard the train whistle. *You and I have nothing in common. I must go now, Ilya, unless you aim to stop me.*

Ilya said nothing.

I will return tomorrow night. He paused. *Prepare for death. Prepare for your judgment.* Michael stared directly into him but did not move. The horses behind him began walking forward and Ilya could sense life inside the carriage but could not feel who it was.

Michael was hiding something.

Michael stepped over Isaac and walked forward. The horses followed. After a few moments, they whinnied quietly as the carriage wheels thumped and cracked over Nik's dead body. The mud sloshed around the carriage wheels. Ilya did not dare look inside the carriage, nor did the others around him, for fear that Michael had a trap for them inside. The strange and quiet procession passed them and they looked down, hoping not to attract the attention of the horrible monster that walked through their presence.

He terrified them.

Ilya now saw what he had unleashed. It was more than a Vampyre. And its voice, its beautiful voice. He knew that voice. He had heard it in his head for years, ever since he had gone east to study in the Black Council. He laughed. If he didn't, he thought he might weep. The voice had been silent since the day they climbed aboard that ship. His thoughts had been fully his own since he birthed that monstrosity. He had brought something back with him. Some psychic parasite that had abandoned him and now used this boy as a vessel.

Ilya had brought destruction down on them all. He felt a twinge of guilt for the first time in years. It was a relief to feel anything at all. The guilt gave way as a quiet thought surfaced.

At long last, chaos.

PART iii

ΟΠΕ

By a route obscure and lonely,
Haunted by ill angels only,
Where an Eidolon, named NIGHT,
On a black throne reigns upright,
I have wandered home but newly
From this ultimate dim Thule.
- Edgar Allen Poe, *Dream-Land (1844)*

The ground was packed tightly. It gave way little by little. Then it gave a bit more. Lines began to form in the shovel-packed soil. A fist punched up through the cold, packed ground. First only a hand clawing at the surface, which quickly disappeared back into the hole. The dirt began shifting around and the hand reached through a second time. As it clawed for life and air, another inch came through and then again until the forearm was exposed. The ground shook and the small cross on the unmarked grave fell over. With another shift, a shoulder appeared as the arm flailed then disappeared into the hole it had created.

Hacking and coughing, Spencer Mayhew emerged from the grave intact. He pulled a second arm from the hole and sat up chest high in the dirt. He was still very much alive and thankful for it. That was the plan all along, but there were too many close calls even for his adventurous taste. When the boys delivered the life-saving envelope, he barely had time to retrieve what was inside. He was fatigued and covered in packs of dirt. It hung from his eyebrows and lips, an uprooted weed still clinging to the clumps of sandy colored dust and grit.

The sheriff had bought the "swallowed letter" gag but the truth was there was more in the envelope than just a quick goodbye from Algernon. The boys delivered the envelope with a short toss onto the floor of his prison cell. A small piece of thin pipe had been neatly tucked inside with a small note. "They have Jenny. Love's a tricky thing, isn't it?" it read. Algernon knew the story of the pipe and it signified his way of saying, "You're on your own," which Spencer appreciated. Algernon usually stayed clear of trouble with women, but Spencer knew that this was different. The bit of pipe was a good guess on Algernon's part too. Spencer's theatrics on the hanging platform gave him enough time to swallow the pipe and suffer his own death again.

What Spencer had not foreseen was the bravery of his kids; the orphans had relived a strange moment in his own adventures, a story he had once told them about his time in Paris when he had gotten Algernon in trouble with a covenant of French Vampyres. He had hidden under a broken wagon for an entire evening waiting for them to bring Algernon out into a cavernous sewer and as they hanged him ceremoniously, Spencer had shot the pulley above Algernon's head, severing the rope. His favorite part was that he'd placed a large wooden barrel full of holy water below the trap door and as Algernon came crashing through, it splashed and spilled all over the entire front row of Vampyres. He remembered that they went scurrying in every direction. "Like cockroaches," he murmured.

The thin pipe that Spencer gripped tightly in his left hand had once been the barrel of a small handgun. It was going to make for part of a flute, a project that Spencer wanted to undertake while in South Africa—a statement to his friend Algernon back at Oxford that though some things were designed for death, they could still create great beauty. It never got that far. As a soldier in her Majesty's Service, Spencer was hanged for treason, which was a just an overblown mix-up as far as Spencer was concerned.

Everything you ever did in her Majesty's service, you did as a lie. They should have killed you ten times over for what you are. They certainly tried the once. He grinned and shook his head. *Shallow grave*, he thought. He didn't think that there were enough people dying to require such shallow digging. The men that dug it were not in any sort of rush. *Strange.*

Then it occurred to him; the sun was long below the horizon.

He cursed.

The shallow grave meant less work for coming Vampyres. He could hear their hissing, like incessant and angry bugs in the distance. They would surely be coming soon.

He quickly dug his way out and let go of the small pipe that had now saved his life twice, allowing it to roll across the broken dirt against the grass. He wriggled his legs and broke free of the packed dirt, noting that the coffin had no top. It seemed lucky at first, but it all pointed to a more stressful demise. The Vampyres were coming.

He cursed again.

His hands slipped and his legs wouldn't break free fast enough. *Spencer Mayhew*, he thought, *survives numerous bullet wounds, curses and two hangings, only to be devoured by Vampyres while crawling out of his own grave.* He chuckled, pushing the ground away. "Now there's a headline."

He grunted loudly and lifted himself onto his knees. He stood and brushed off his pants. It was a waste of time. They were ruined. He touched his finger to his blackened left eye and chuckled and then grabbed the small pipe from the ground and began running. He knew they were coming.

And they were close.

The Vampyre Rurk arrived at the Breton cemetery with the intention of doing away with a body. The anticipation had him feverish. One do-gooder had been hanged earlier and the body would barely have cooled. Rurk had a hardened temperament and enjoyed the thrill of ingesting the meat and the energy of "good" people. There was always a horrible feeling of free-fall. Something about it hurt and felt wrong, but the pain was very much what he had grown to love. There were times when Rurk would toy with the idea of reaching his hand into the slivers of light in the shallower parts of the complex just to feel the flame.

He arrived alone and in silence. The clear night pushed back the last orange glow of dusk. Only scattered clouds moved above him. The cemetery was serene. The other Vampyres wouldn't want any part of it. They partook of the bodies of the brainwashed soldiers and some even claimed that they felt much of the darkness being lifted. Rurk, like others, knew that was a lie. The darkness was what they were. It was what he was and would always be.

He approached the fresh grave, dug out and empty. He stared into the hole made up of broken mud and dirt clumps. The man had climbed out.

Rurk! A voice came from the distance.

He looked up to see Letsya, bounding from the forest. The old bastard had flown from the complex straight to the cemetery and he was almost winded. Letsya was panicked.

Rurk was quiet but he raised an eyebrow.

The schoolmaster, Letsya panted. *He was another—*

Old man, Rurk interrupted. *Gather your thoughts.*

Yes, right.

Letsya was below contempt. Rurk couldn't imagine what stock would become this pathetic bastard of a Vampyre. *You were saying?*

No. Rurk. You must listen to me, the old man answered.

Rurk hated the old slob. Couldn't he just say what he meant?

Your brother, Letsya stammered. *He's dead.*

How?

The Spaniard. He's here, Letsya panted, growing more panicked. *He and two children killed Pavl.*

Two children?

That's the other thing, Letsya announced grimly. He looked down in the grave. *Ilya saw into the mind of Elliott.* He swallowed. *His partner was here.* He pointed into the empty grave. *The partner was Smith, the children's headmaster.*

Before Letsya could even tell him to be careful, Rurk was gone. The wind from his jump pulled at Letsya's coat tails. *Please be careful.*

The leaves and branches whipped past him. Some caught his clothing and others ripped into his skin and hair. Rurk ran through the brambles. There was no path in the thick brush. Branches, twigs and underbrush broke and gave way to his heavy footfall. Angry tears streamed away from his face.

Any Brethren that can hear me, find the headmaster.

T he black carriage arrived at the train station under the light of the bright moon. The low-lying clouds moved quickly, casting scurrying shadows on the ground. Michael looked toward the door and sensed hostility. He put his hand on the door to the carriage while he kept his eye on the road. One of the horses bucked. No one was near. Michael felt a shift in the air.

"*Bonjour, Vampyr.*" A voice with a French accent came from directly behind Michael.

He turned quickly to see Chandler standing close and whispering. "Hello, old man," Michael replied without showing his surprise. Michael neglected to note that he sensed nothing in the man. There was a void where the man should have been.

"Old?" Chandler laughed, "Many are old..."

Michael smiled, cordially. "And you are ancient."

"Ancient, indeed."

"Is it safe?" Michael asked, his voice betraying a sense of worry.

"Absolutely not." Chandler said. "We've the slightest window and I have a distraction just for it." He looked at the carriage, allowing the moment to wash over him. "So you really killed Desmond."

Michael stayed silent.

The old man smiled.

"Tell me they'll be safe," Michael commanded quietly.

"If the next few moments play out correctly, there is no reason to worry."

"Then why do you worry?"

"It is indeed a strange world, Michael." The old man's head tilted with an even more crooked smile.

The sheriff entered the train station with men on either side of him. "Check the perimeter," he muttered. He looked up past the big clock where a small room sat, a possible location for a gunman and the hiding place of one Algernon Elliott who, according to sources, had been detained and was hopefully dead by now.

His men had been disappearing and Matheson knew he couldn't attribute it to the children. Even with a complete arsenal and an army of children, there was no reason they would be able to overwhelm his band of psychopaths. There was some exterior force; there was something or someone that was hindering his plan.

None of it mattered. Within the next moments, he felt he would be able to walk away from his horrible assignment. He could hear the train whistle in the distance as his men jostled bags and opened doors, securing the train area.

The front door to the train station was constructed from a heavy wood and creaked when opened. Parson Adler was heavy-hearted, the antique Austrian lantern in his hands. He'd found the thing abandoned in Desmond's carriage like refuse, its brass greened and glass windows charred after many decades of holding in its evil.

This should get interesting, Tomás, he thought.

Matheson stood in the center of the room, with his fists closed, knuckles against his hips. The barrel of a long rifle pressed against Adler's temple and the squeaky, heavy door shut behind him. Adler turned to see a young officer, in the gray uniform assigned by Matheson to all his "soldiers," staring down the barrel with a smile. The boy nudged Adler's head and indicated that he should move forward. "Slowly."

"There's no need for violence, my boy," Adler assured him quietly. He smiled to himself, *I'm sure you wouldn't even know where to start.*

"Parson!" Matheson smiled. "Glad you could make it."

"I doubt that thoroughly, Matheson," he stated without tone.

The sheriff's false smile melted away. He looked down at the lantern in Adler's hand. "Are you holding onto that for Desmond?"

"In a manner of speaking. He's unwell."

246

Matheson nodded, his cold eyes calculating.

The far door was opening near the platform. Two large young men passed through the door, one after the other, carrying a small chest. They were very careful with it, holding it in their outstretched hands. Whatever it was looked very heavy.

Adler looked at the lantern he held in his own hand and then nervously glanced at the boys. They crossed the room with Chandler following. Just as Adler had, Chandler turned to see a uniformed man behind him, holding a rifle. He waved the rifle at him and Chandler understood. He looked straight ahead.

They stopped in the center of the room. The sheriff looked past the young men, watching Chandler, who had an officer behind him with rifle in hand. Behind Matheson stood Adler, another rifle and a man behind it.

"Put the chest on the ground, boys," The sheriff commanded, removing the large, silver revolver from its holster.

They obeyed, slowly setting the thing on the tiled floor with a light tap. Gunfire filled the big train station and echoed in a resounding cacophony.

One of the boys carrying the chest collapsed. A puddle of blood spread out from his body.

The second shot fired in the train station was not from the sheriff's gun and everyone looked around. The sheriff knew. He looked down at the gaping hole in his chest. It hurt. "Inconvenient," he murmured as the hole closed up quickly.

He turned his gun toward the man standing behind him, Ernest Williams, who looked at him down the long barrel of a hunting rifle. The sheriff only began to think, *Yes, he returns*, before pulling the trigger on his large revolver.

Everyone in the room watched Ernest fall, gut-shot. He was coughing up blood before he hit the ground.

Thomas looked into the train station window near the platform side as the children snuck quietly past the building and filed onto the train. The path had been cleared. There was one train station attendant who lay dead on the platform. Monsieur Chandler had done that. Emily and Penny were already on the train and finding places to hide the twins when everyone heard the gunshots. Thomas drew his hands to his mouth and gasped quietly while a rush of tears flooded his eyes. He wiped them away quickly. "He's dying!" he muttered.

Edwin looked over Thomas's shoulder and saw Mister Williams lying there gasping for air. He looked down and panicked. *Michael*, he thought, *there is nothing in the world as important to me as you being here right now*. Thomas felt guilty for not having been happier about Mister Williams's return; he didn't want to see him die. He could only hope that the mind-reading Vampyre was near.

Matheson turned around, quickly finding himself in a frustrating predicament. With the old man bleeding on the floor behind him, he saw that the Parson was staring at him from behind the young uniformed soldier. "Pretty spry, old man." Matheson said.

Chandler, on the other hand, had run the other soldier through with a long blade and was using the dead body as a shield. He looked at Matheson down the barrel of another "inconvenient" revolver.

"Abandon the lanterns," Adler commanded.

"I think not." He had to get his hands on the lantern. He was so close to his goal. To set free his old master, Ruthven, who'd sent him to Breton alongside his men.

Chandler would be a challenge, but there was no way of knowing about Adler. He was old. There would be no reason to worry about him. He was obviously emotional and very likely angry with Desmond.

"Whatever your situation is—"

"Matheson, I am not toying with you," Adler interrupted. "I am here simply to ask you a question."

The sheriff raised an eyebrow and turned to make sure Chandler wasn't moving in on him. The Frenchman just grinned wildly at him.

"Did you have anything," Adler swallowed, "anything at all to do with the death of my nephew?"

Matheson looked the man in the eye. "No."

"I knew you would lie."

"How would you know that?" Matheson asked. His voice was flat.

"Because he was a child." His eyes narrowed in on the man. "And you would have answered with some semblance of guilt or shame were you innocent." He thought for a moment as Matheson turned his body slowly toward him with his gun in hand. "Also, Sheriff, unlike you, I am invincible."

The quiet anger that the sheriff was holding back burst into laughter. He fingered the bullet hole in his shirt. "No, old man. You are dead." Matheson turned the gun on him and fired the large revolver.

The young soldier let out a surprised gasp and fell to his knees in a pool of his own blood. The bullet would have passed clean through.

Adler didn't move.

Adler stared back at Matheson, who was so surprised that he looked almost sheepish.

"Now you die," the old man whispered, stepping over the body of the younger man, who coughed in the blood. His boot splashed in the puddle.

Matheson wasn't sure what had happened. He fired another round and the man kept stepping forward. Unlike earlier, his shirt did not rip. The old man moved toward him slowly and Chandler let out a cackle. He kept pulling the trigger until it just clicked in his hand.

"Oh, sweet irony," Chandler laughed.

"Now you die," he repeated. The old man disappeared into a cloud that smelled of old tobacco.

Matheson panicked and transformed into a sulfuric and dark ashy cloud, trying to get away from him.

Chandler watched the two strange and quickly moving clouds dance through the room. Through the dark haze, he could see a figure appear near the body of Ernest Williams. It was the young Vampyre.

Adler rematerialized with a wicked look in his eye.

A moment later, Matheson reappeared. He fell to his knees, breathing heavily. "How could you be one of us?"

"One of us?" Adler asked. He sighed. "There is no 'us,' you fool." He stepped up to the weakened man. "You and I are cursed. But we have no more in common than that and that alone is why you and I are in this place. One of us." He scoffed. He looked up at the young Vampyre, who was lifting the old man with eyes full of tears. "If your former employer had cared to punish me, he should have sought to kill me, not my nephew," Adler tried to explain calmly. "You worked too faithfully for Desmond. No man is so unflinchingly loyal to one as apathetic as Desmond. I knew you weren't working for Desmond. Your loyalties are deeper— one of Ruthven's."

Chandler allowed the body he used as a shield to drop in front of him. He righted himself and made his way to the door.

The sheriff laughed, "You'll all die." He coughed, spit up blood and exhaled a small cloud of sulfur. "The whole town is a trap now. I've made sure of it. Lord Ruthven will make a home of your charred bodies! Birds will peck out your eyes!"

The charred lantern lay on the floor and Matheson made his move toward it, ashy smoke curling off of him. He lifted the thing, as his flesh dissipated into a cloud of smoke, ash peeling away.

The sobs from the young Vampyre were filling the room.

Adler just shook his head. He untied the decorative incense ball that hung from his belt. The cloud of smoke carried the lantern rolled quickly toward the door. Adler unlatched the ball and threw it into the cloud. The small metal ball crashed into the lantern with a clang and began releasing a small puff of yellowish gas as it fell to the floor.

The lantern crashed just beyond it, releasing a puddle of ooze and blackened blood.

The cloud pulsed. The lantern oozed across the floor.

Adler approached Michael, who held Ernest in his arms. "Hello, Vampyre."

Michael looked up, but said nothing.

Chandler kicked the chest in front of him open and removed a larger lantern from inside. He felt the thing begin stirring when he touched it. He shivered. There was an amber glow coming from within it.

A withered heart beat in the puddle of black ooze that had fallen open. The cloud of sulfuric smoke began floating to the ground, bleeding and shedding as the parson's mustard gas filled it. Flakes of dried skin were falling from it. The sheriff reintegrated and collapsed face down on the floor. His skin was peeling and his eyes were filling with blood. He coughed up blood. Smoke sizzled from all over him. Ash burned away from his skin as he lay there, unable to breathe, poisoned by the mustard gas. His screams came intermittent as he coughed out puffs of putrid gas.

"Hey, Doc?" Chandler asked, staring at the smoke.

"Yes, Khalil?" Adler replied.

"Should I be worried?"

"Oh no, Khalil." Adler looked up. "Though potent, the imperfect mustard compound should only have affected our friend, Matheson. Just stay away from the body."

"And Betancourt?"

Adler looked over his shoulder to see the Vampyre that was once Tomás Betancourt trying to regenerate. The thing had almost forty years of regeneration waiting within it, but the abuse that his heart had taken over the years from brainwashing the citizens of Breton gave him little to fight the compounded gasses. The heart began regenerating and the bloody organ created muscle and pumped blood that spilled across the tile. The sinew and tissue and flesh unfolded from the beating thing.

"You never know with Vampyres," Adler replied.

Michael sobbed quietly. *Edwin, take the children to the train. Now.* There was no reply, but he could feel the children moving slowly away from the station. Ernest was fading. Michael sensed the first aching pain of loneliness. First Kat, who he'd never had a chance to know and now Ernest, who was the only person Michael, in his amnesiac state, had ever known.

"Please don't go, Ernest," he sobbed quietly. "Please don't quit."

The blood gurgled in Ernest's mouth through a tired smile. "You're a good man, Michael. A gentleman." He clenched his teeth from the pain. His teeth were red as blood bubbled around his mouth. "A good friend," he whispered.

Behind them, Tomás began to take shape, sickly and dying.

Chandler unplugged one of the electrodes from the lantern that he had so carefully designed years before.

"Michael, you're an angel," Ernest smiled quietly.

"What?" he asked.

"I see a light," Ernest gasped. "You're haloed in it, like an angel."

Michael let out an exasperated sigh and a tear fell on Ernest's lapel.

"Like an angel," he repeated.

"Don't give up."

Tomás Betancourt flashed his teeth, starving for blood. He saw the collapsed body in front of him; an obvious sacrifice for his regeneration. He hissed and sunk his teeth into the Sheriff's shoulder. Immediately he jumped back, the flesh around his face continuing to form. He gasped for air. The blood around his mouth that had come from the man's shoulder turned to ash. Matheson's shoulder and neck sunk in like a burnt log. The body smoldered with wet ash as the sheriff crumbled. Tomás grasped his throat, vomiting and coughing up blood. The tendons in his arms began unraveling and snapping below the sleeves of the shirt that had begun to appear around his naked body.

He collapsed across the body of the Shifter in a convulsing mess of ash and blood.

Chandler's hands began to sweat as he disconnected each component of the lantern. He was growing more and more anxious. "Doc?"

Adler did not answer. He knew what Chandler planned to do, but did not want to involve himself any further.

Michael turned to him. "Are you a Doctor?"

Adler's eyes fell to the floor. "Not really. I was a chemist once," Adler continued.

"And your guilt? Why are you suddenly filled with guilt?" Michael asked desperately, "Can you help my friend?"

Adler looked around him. The sheriff was dead. "Did you do away with Desmond, young man?" He thought about the beach.

Michael's eyes had a dull red glow. "I did."

Adler's crooked face curled into an unpracticed smile. His sentiment was marred with his own loneliness as he thought about his gentle Stephen. He looked at Chandler, knowing what the man was about to unleash.

"He was supposed to help the children get out of here," Michael muttered, turning his intense gaze to his friend. Ernest's eyes weren't opening.

Adler looked at his hands. He was exhausted. He thought of the little boys that loved Stephen so much. His hands ached. Saving that stupid young man in the inn had left him damaged and he was certain that Williams was too far gone. "Are you a man of faith, Vampyre?"

Michael didn't know how to answer. "I..." he tried. "I think so." He wiped his eyes with his sleeve. "I believe in this man. I have faith in him." He looked up at Adler. "How do I make him whole again? How do I stop this?"

To Adler, Ernest was nothing more than a do-gooder nuisance. He was obtuse and drank too much, but he cared so deeply for the people around him. He should have been some sort of priest. He was a storyteller. Stephen had loved him. A sudden rush of guilt overwhelmed him as he remembered signing the paperwork for Desmond to have the man hanged. Desmond was gone. It seemed so far away.

He knew better. The Lords would be sending a cleanup team and Adler knew anyone left would be gone. That included Ernest.

"Please help me." Michael pleaded.

"Say your goodbyes, if you must," he said reluctantly. "But I will try..." He sighed sadly. "I will try to save him."

Michael whispered something inaudible to his friend and Adler kneeled down by him, his knees protruding from the ceremonial robe. Michael stood up next to him and focused. The old man looked into the gaping wound. The bleeding had slowed. They all dripped with Ernest's blood.

As Adler's hand slowly dematerialized into the aromatic tobacco smoke, he thought to himself, *I hope this is worth it.*

The entire train depot smelled of rich, burning tobacco, like the exhaled breath of a hundred cigar smokers. Michael watched as the white-haired old man's arms and shoulders dissolved into turning tendrils of smoke. Ernest moaned. Michael sensed an unflinching and almost absolute, evil in Parson Adler, but he didn't question the man's state or abilities. He seemed to think that he could save Ernest and Michael believed him.

Ernest was fading. His breathing was normalizing, as Adler breathed in and out. Their breaths were in sync. A blueish glow emanated from the old man. The smoke that poured from Adler's shoulders filled the hole in Ernest's stomach. Both men shook with pain. Ernest groaned. Adler let out a low guttural sound. The skin around the wound was pulling back.

"There is little time," Adler said quietly.

Ernest coughed and gasped and the light tobacco smoke came out of his mouth. Michael focused his mind and stepped into the æther. The train station was gone.

Only the pillars remained there. The place looked like a gateway to some ancient, decadent place, with a large broken arch where the railroad cars had been. It was dilapidated and dark. There were no apparitions and the place seemed abandoned and devoid of movement. He kneeled near Ernest who phased in and out slowly, like breathing. He was blue then clear then blue again. There was a large liquid cloud moving around him.

"Ernest?" Michael tried, "Can you hear me?"

"Yes," he replied. "Where am I?" He paused and looked at Michael and though he tried, he could not get up. "Where are we?"

"I don't know," Michael answered. "I come here sometimes. I think people come here when they die."

"Like purgatory?"

Michael was quiet. "I don't know."

"The world is a many-layered cake." A voice came, booming and eloquent. It sounded young but confident. It came with an accent of gentry and was theatrically British. Michael turned around to see where it came from. Small sparks flew up and down, leaving trails in the shape of a slender body. The silhouette glimmered and the trails of light it left looked like a small black galaxy. "And though some of us have perhaps, let's say, taken a knife to it once or twice, it is still a beautiful, dark and undiscovered world."

"Who are you?"

"Ruthven, Lord, Earl of something or other. It matters little." Michael could hear a smile in the voice. "Ruthven is fine."

When Michael looked down again, the cloud was completely gone and Ernest had disappeared. He gasped.

"Michael, is it?" Ruthven asked.

Michael looked up, searching for a pair of eyes.

"It would appear your kith survived a narrow scrape." Ruthven's silhouetted face had the twist of a frown. "Newly regenerated. Might taste nice."

Michael had a sudden pit in his stomach when he should have felt relieved.

"A yes, you should be quite afraid, but," the smiling voice paused, "be done with it haste forth, for you and I shall have a clever game!"

Michael looked up at him with an arched eyebrow.

"I'm going to murder all of you."

Michael stood and faced the fluctuating thing. It was nebulous and cloudy. Every few moments one of the sparks would reveal a bit of flesh. He shook his head.

"Ah, yes, you'll be quite a lot of fun."

"Why are you here?"

"Captured. Years ago. Boring story, really. I was powerful and beautiful. That's not the boring part. That would be the jealousy of others. It's always so tedious," he began. "One day, during my torture, a scientist, a detestable man named Adler, uncovered what he called 'vampyric telepathy.' Since that day, my heart has been quite literally broken and used as a weapon."

"Who would do such a thing?" Michael asked.

"I certainly would have," Ruthven smiled. "Unfortunately, I was the one captured. It's been arduous and boring having to listen to these fools and their constant commands. So imperative. Never interesting." He sighed. "But it would seem that some bit of sabotage should have me free soon enough."

"How do you know that?" Michael asked again.

There was a silence. "Why would I not know? I am more powerful now than I have ever been. I sense that Adler is dying nearby, which is wonderful. Sayid's obviously setting me free and whatever comes next will be up to me. And that, my newfound companion," he said dramatically, "is why you have a pit in your stomach." With those eerie words, he disappeared into a haze.

Michael looked down and Ernest was still gone. He searched the darkness frantically and emerged in the train station. Time had passed. Ernest was trying to crawl along the ground. There was a distant voice. Michael phased back to find Chandler pulling him up from his knees. "Let's go!" Chandler yelled over the deafening sound of whirling wind.

two

＊———◆———＊

*Knowledge comes, but wisdom lingers, and I linger on
the shore, And the individual withers, and the world
is more and more.*

- Alfred, Lord Tennyson, *Locksley Hall (1835)*

Deep in the underground complex, Isaac fought against his weakened body. It would only be a few more moments. He had to find a safe place. With a hand on the wall, he breathed heavily and made his way back to his quarters. Ilya had brazenly allowed the darkest of the Vampyres to be released. *Idiot,* he thought. There was battling in the holds where the Druids should have been working. Fiends were getting free.

There was a rumble at his feet. A crack moved along the floor toward him just before he felt the explosion of two Golems crashing through a stone wall into the hallway. They tumbled loudly as they fought, maddened with the chaos of what was happening in the holds. The rock ceilings were beginning to collapse as the cursed stone creatures crashed into each other. Isaac quietly and painfully tucked himself into a small, cramped room to avoid being seen.

With his back against the door, he heard the crash outside and felt the small breath of cinder that seemed to sigh under the doorway. It was sealed shut. There was a sudden familiar claustrophobic feeling in his stomach. He grunted a painful laugh as he looked across the dark room. "Hello Mister Elliott. I suppose we're both trapped now."

"Move, Vampyre!" Chandler turned to the door and yelled. Michael moved to his feet and reached for Ernest. "Leave him!"

The air was leaving the room. The aromatic smoke was gone and Adler's body was lying on the floor, just a shell. It expelled dark, charred smoke from its eyes and mouth, spinning up in whirlwinds and dispersing into the darkness of the room. The sheriff's ashes broke up and created a dust cloud, whipping violently through the space.

Michael lifted Ernest gingerly. He groaned in pain. He carried him quickly toward the platform where Chandler held the door. "Get him on the train."

The room filled with bright light that pierced the swirling eruption of smoke channeling into the open lantern that lay on the floor. Chandler was panicking, pulling on the door, trying to shut it, but it would not close. The suction was too strong.

Michael stepped onto the train and found Ernest a place to lie down. Edwin appeared behind him, followed by Thomas and Patrick. Michael could hear the other orphans looking for supplies and places to hide. There was a moment of relief, though he felt like there was something wrong inside the train. He didn't have time to focus on it.

"Are you coming with us, Michael?" Thomas asked.

"No." Michael said, distracted. "I feel I...I have to see this through." He looked at Ernest, who was fighting to stay awake. "Please watch him." He took a last long look at his friend before turning for the door. He glanced through the train windows and saw Chandler running across the platform to the locomotive. Someone would have to get them out.

Beyond Chandler, the cloud of light that devoured Adler was being sucked into the lantern. He could see a man step forward through the open door. He was well-dressed and cavalier. He ran his fingers through his short, ruddy hair and turned his neck in a stretch.

Ruthven stretched his arms, making his way to the door that led to the street. *So close, Matheson. But indeed, so far away. Being dead and all.*

How inconvenient.

The Breton southbound express had been moving at a steady pace for nearly fifteen minutes. Everyone had stayed hidden, but there was a certain sense of escape and magical sense of newness. Oliver felt like he was going to vomit. None of the children had ever been on a train before, or at least as far as any of them could remember.

Newton didn't feel great either, but he was excited. He was alive and he felt successful. "Don't worry, Ollie. We'll be out of this soon." He stood up and looked around the storage car where many of the orphans had hidden.

Penny and Emily sat quietly behind sacks of grain with their legs pressed to their chests. Oliver looked sick and he sat on top of a small, unmarked crate. The twins seemed nervous, but talkative.

Newton stood, worried. Something was wrong.

"Where are you going, Newt?" asked Oliver.

"To the front."

"Oh," Ollie sighed. "I think I'll stay right here if you don't mind."
He made his way forward quickly. Newt worried. "Thomas!" he
called out from the back
of the dining car where Michael had laid Ernest. Thomas
sat by the old man. Alexander and Albert sat across the aisle
ready to do whatever Thomas instructed.
"Yes?" Thomas turned around. His face was tight and
agitated. "Have you seen Ned?"
Thomas saw the worry in Newton's eyes and thought
about it. "Well, yes. He was here just a moment ago." Thomas
groaned. "But a moment ago, we were at the train station."
"But why would he want to stay behind?" Alexander
asked.
There was a moment of silence filled with the noise of the fast-
moving train.
Thomas got up quickly. "Search the train."
Albert spoke up. "I haven't seen Patrick either."
"Or Jimmy." Newton added.
Thomas searched his thoughts and looked back down to Ernest.
"Albert, stay here with Mister Williams. You two: let's find
them."
Breton was in chaos. Michael could hear the sounds of
their thoughts filling the air. There was no single voice anymore.
There was yelling all over town and the hissing sound of large
droves of Vampyres on the edges of the forest. He watched the
train depart from the station and heard Desmond's black carriage
pulling away. Ruthven must have treated himself to it. The
brainwashed haven was about to become a bloodbath. Where
there was blood, there would be Vampyres.
There was a sense of hope for Michael. Jared had gone to
get help. Ernest was on the train with the children. He tried to
hone in on Ernest's thoughts, but where there had been the loud
drone of a singular voice, hundreds of voices flooded over him.
The streets were filling with people who were just waking up
from a very long dream and who were attempting to fill the void
of thought. From a distance, Michael could see a fire piercing
through the roof of a building and the cracks of gunfire filled the
moments of silence as the sheriff's men ran through the streets.
It felt like the beginning of the dream that had haunted him
for so long. Fire. Blood. Death. He could feel the dark presence
within him getting ever closer. Michael was at home.

Edwin hid under the train platform. He kept his eyes closed.
The chatter of the Vampyres had infiltrated the town. They
had never done that before. They always snuck around the town.
Maybe it was because Desmond was dead or maybe they sensed

that the children were gone. He didn't know. He sat nervously next to a pile of men's clothing, suitcases and a typewriter while he heard someone walking above him across the platform.

"Ned," came a whisper.

Without looking to see who it was, Edwin raised a fist instinctively and made contact with something in the dark.

"OW!" The whispered exclamation was James McLaughlin's.

"Jimmy! Are you alright?" Edwin whispered.

"Well, I'm alright. I did just get punched in the face, though," he replied, gleaming. "I'm sorry. What are you doing here?" Edwin asked.

Another voice came from the darkness and once again Edwin's fists came flying up.

"We're here to help." The second voice was Patrick's, but he was too far out of reach for Edwin. "Would you quit surprising me?" Edwin commanded in a whisper. "At this rate, one of us is going to get killed!"

"Sorry, Ned." James looked like a puppy and Patrick let out a soft chuckle. Edwin sighed and after a quiet moment, they all laughed softly with the relief of being together—though for Edwin something deep down was missing. He looked up through the slats, but whoever had been there was gone.

Newton met with the engineer. He was an incredibly tall man with big steady hands, an experienced engineer named John Jones. He told Newt to call him "Casey." Casey already had the train at a breakneck pace but warned that they wouldn't be able to hold out because of rain clouds out ahead. The brakeman and the fireman didn't speak. They were sooty-dark men who worked tirelessly. Only their eyes showed in the night, outside in the engine compartment.

Newt and the other children turned the train inside out. They had a stock of supplies and everything they would need, but it turned out Patrick, Edwin and James were missing. The storage car was the third rail car, following the passenger dining car and the locomotive engine. Behind it came a small caboose. Ollie and Newton continued to snoop around each connected train car. They found the storage car to be the most interesting. They pulled gray and blue uniforms from crates, unused. There were guns but no ammunition and more medallions in some smaller chests. Newt looked under the white blanket that stretched out over something tall while Ollie began opening crates. "I've got nothing, Newt. Just milk bottles!" Ollie cried, disappointed.

"What do you figure someone would hunt with this?" Newt pulled the blanket back to reveal a machine gun sitting on a tripod. It had a large cartridge in the left side and the barrel was long.

"Vampyres," Ollie observed quietly.

"Or bears." Newton replied.

"Yeah, bears too." Ollie echoed.

Thomas stood on the back of the caboose watching the distant town quickly getting smaller; he felt a sudden emptiness. *Why, Edwin?* The wind whipped around him on that lonely moving platform, quickly getting farther away from his friend.

A small pack of Vampyres ran alongside Rurk.

All the fun is in town, Rurk. Why are we going away from it all? a Vampyre named Borys asked.

Rurk's pace slowed. *A group of CHILDREN killed my brother. They were with a man, their headmaster.*

Oh! the other Vampyre answered. *The headmaster was the detective's partner.*

Yes, Rurk replied. *And he is still alive as well.*

A third Vampyre, a beautiful slender female called Natasya sang, *Oh, tonight, tonight we soil our souls with the blood of children!*

The view from behind the train station clock was horrific. Khalil looked down across the floor. The mangled bodies of two soldiers were drained of life, their heads pulled against the large lantern that had contained Ruthven's still-beating heart. Deep down, Khalil felt that releasing him was a mistake, but he ignored that part of himself as he'd done time and time again. He tried to wipe the glass clean as he glared down across the large train station. It was dirty on the other side. The ashes of Matheson and Adler covered the entire room with thin soot.

He felt a strange kinship to the train depot. During his abnormally long life, Khalil Sayid had never held a position of power or a real job of any sort. The last thirty years he had had both. He was sad to see it go.

The one thing he did not ignore was the flaming sensation of rage that seemed to press on the insides of his temples. He looked on the bed where he had allowed Algernon Elliott to hide for so long. A large smile stretched his wicked face as he slid the large, empty trunk at the end of the bed to the side. He pulled loose planks back and looked at the beautiful arsenal of weapons and torture devices that he had devised over the past decades. There lay guns, knives and swords, even chemicals and strange paraphernalia, all designed to maim, hurt and kill. Ernest Williams had always encouraged "Monsieur Chandler" to get a hobby. He didn't know that Khalil Sayid, the most perfect killer in history, were you to ask him, had already found one.

Vampyres ran south along the train tracks, jumping, climbing and running along the brush. None of them revealed themselves. They went as unnoticed as a soft gust of wind when they caught up to Spencer Mayhew, who galloped along the railroad tracks on a stolen horse. He had a gun in his hand down by his side. He stood in the stirrups as the wind blew through his mussed brown hair. He looked like a proper bandit with a handkerchief over his nose and mouth. His goal was to catch the train out ahead of him and he was very far behind.

The horse slowed and then it lurched. Spencer dropped the gun as the horse jerked and he grabbed the reigns more tightly, but it was too late. The horse came to a halt before throwing him across the tracks. He landed on his back and struggled to open his eyes. The fall sent sharp pains across his entire body. He arched and writhed.

The horse whinnied and bucked in panic.

Spencer knew he'd been followed. He would have to get to his gun somehow. He rolled over. It pained him incredibly to get back to his feet. There was no chance of it. He felt a swift nick across the cheek, sharp like a razorblade; the warm blood immediately rushed below his eye. He reached up to feel the blood and felt another nick across the back of his neck.

Spencer saw nothing.

He knew how Vampyres worked and he couldn't understand why they were toying with him. Their desire to kill him should have been enough. There was a nick across his arm and then another across his chest.

"What do you want from me?" Spencer asked.

Want, Mister Mayhew? A voice resonated in his head. *What do we want? I want my brother back and I want you to suffer for his death.*

"Brother?" He had no idea what the Vampyre was talking about. But it never really did with Vampyres. "You'll have to do better than that." He grinned. "I've killed so many Vampyres that I can barely remember most of them."

The Vampyre appeared in front of him. He stepped out of a wisp of smoke. *His name, Mister Mayhew, was Pavl. Pavl Gavrilenko. And you did not kill him. Your precious orphans did.*

Spencer knew they would aim to kill the children and this was his opportunity to stop them—or at very least delay their attack. He beamed with pride that his kids had become Vampyre killers. For the first time, it crossed Spencer's mind that he might not survive his predicament, but with Algernon off in the mines and the children safely behind him, he felt he had won.

He had worried that he would make a terrible Headmaster, but somehow, over the last months, he fed, loved and watched over those children with his life. *If only my Father could see me now*, he thought to himself. He felt quite adult.

Those Vampyres would not catch his kids. They began appearing in front of him, flashing their teeth and smiling. They came up like tongues of smoke appearing from the air. *Is he guilty?* Rurk laughed to the small group. They hissed in approval and Rurk kicked Spencer in the stomach. The force of the blow sent him flying across a grassy knoll and into a small tree that cracked with his weight. He could barely breathe, but Spencer worked his way to his feet and let out a sigh. He felt the wind shift as Rurk appeared over his shoulder.

Guilty, Rurk whispered.

"Really, Vampyre?" Spencer finally straightened himself. "Guilty of what? Of protecting children from the likes of you?"

Rurk curled his fist and pounded Spencer in his chest. Spencer's ears popped, but he could still hear the horse crying. He swallowed hard and spoke again. *Who are you to judge me?*

Vampyres were rarely interested in a lecture on ethics, but if he'd spent enough time around Algernon Elliott, a lecture and a pre-fisticuff goading often sounded quite alike.

The frenzied group surrounded him. He had stalled long enough. The train would have been long gone. He smiled, knowing that they were about to tear him apart.

Rurk held the man up by his shirt collar. Spencer's body began to grow limp and Rurk's eyes responded with a smolder. *No. I want you to be awake for this.* He smirked and forced a clawed finger into Spencer's rib. The man quietly winced with pain and the Vampyres laughed. They could smell his blood in the air. As Rurk broke the skin they laughed in a frenzy like dogs over fresh meat. Rurk stopped, suddenly.

The blood rushed down Spencer's side; he slumped in the Vampyre's powerful hand. *Do you hear that?* Rurk asked, panicked. *Do you feel it?*

Feel? asked Borys, smiling and falling on his knees at the pool of fresh warm blood that was gathering at the man's feet. *I'm about to feel...* But before he could finish his thought, Borys jumped to his feet, screaming. *My skin is on fire!*

He grasped at his skin and clothing.

Rurk looked up, overwhelmed with horror. A terrible creature was flying down on them. Two of the Vampyres began running blindly. *Not again!* one cried. He immediately assumed it was the creature that had destroyed Nik and Mahir. The weaker of the two turned and saw his companion burst into black blood and bones.

Natasya looked to Borys, who was thrashing about on the ground. The creature flew past him, dark wings extended, phasing in and out of reality. Natasya fell to the ground hissing, paralyzed in animalistic fear.

The two fleeing Vampyres had no chance. She looked up to see an explosion of orange and yellow plasmatic energy that draped like wet strings, after another Vampyre had been caught mid-step. Natasya gasped through her fingers. The creature landed, ignoring her and the man behind her, who was struggling to his feet. She recoiled into the darkness.

Michael claimed his prey. The plasma energy came down around him like a cloud of snow. He willed Bogdan to slow. He could feel the abject terror bubbling up before he burst into a plasmatic cloud and was absorbed. Michael turned toward Spencer Mayhew.

Spencer had drawn a gun at him.

"What do you plan to do with that?" Michael asked.

"Vampyres are strong. Not invincible."

Michael smiled and looked at the mess around him. "Yes. That much is obvious." Spencer cocked the gun.

"I wouldn't advise that. I'm not your enemy," Michael replied. His voice seemed to resonate inside Spencer's skull.

"Not yet, you're not." Spencer wasn't convinced.

"There's work to be done back in town." Michael stepped forward from the shadow. His dark hair glimmered in the moonlight and his eyes glowed. "The train you are following is full of orphans, Mister Mayhew: your orphans." Michael looked down and saw the blood staining Spencer's shirt. "But they are too far ahead; you need to let them go."

"Yes but—"

"You'll never catch them. They are safe. Sunrise is coming soon." Michael paused and then smiled. "But you, sir, are a soldier and there's a war to be fought back in Breton."

Spencer stared down the train tracks, lowering his gun. The Vampyre was not being charming. He was right. From a short distance, Spencer could hear the sound of a horse's hooves. His horse was returning. Spencer looked back at the Vampyre.

"My name is Michael, Mister Mayhew. I am a friend. You'll have to fix that side, or you'll certainly bleed out before you reach Breton." Michael beckoned to the horse.

Spencer rolled his eyes and cursed under his breath. "You don't happen to know any convenient Vampyre magic to staunch the bleeding, do you?"

"I'm sure you'll understand why Vampyres might not have any interest in that." He said with a wry smile.

"Well then, we do it the hard way."

Michael watched with intrigue as Spencer removed his shirt and took a deep breath. The bleeding was not slowing. Spencer fired the revolver twice. He gritted his teeth. Pinching the skin around the hole in his side, he pressed the smoking barrel to his skin. He roared and his eyes rolled back into his head. The smell of burning flesh overwhelmed him.

It's a very savory smell. Michael thought. The world had obviously had its way with Spencer Mayhew. He was tattooed and scarred all over, a broken warrior who had offered his life to save orphans thousands of miles from his home. As the Vampyre helped him to his feet, Spencer groaned in pain.

"They *are* your children, sir," Michael said quietly, picking up the man's shirt.

"Is it strange, Michael, that I knew they would be on that train?" he asked.

"No," Michael answered. "The same wards that caused the people of Breton to live in a perpetual haze allowed your bed time stories to imprint night after night into the minds of those children. They remember what you told them. Those fairy tails, those secret stories you gave to them—they are their memories, part of their lives now."

Spencer flooded with disappointment. *A curse?* He had hoped that this was part of being a father to them. He kicked the dirt and laughed at the irony.

"You are part of them now and you saved them," Michael said, turning to walk away. Spencer stood by his horse. He looked down the tracks and cocked his gun.

"Those are my kids." Spencer smiled. The Vampyre was already gone.

I dreamed," she remembered. "It felt like I was outside of myself—I was walking about, lost and aimless. No control of where I wandered." Genevieve Moreau spoke quietly to Glenn Lamphere, who dwarfed her. She felt safe in his presence. He was warm and wore a shy smile despite the terrible sadness that was bearing on him. His eyes had a soft twinkle below his bushy eyebrows.

"But you woke up," he said softly.

"I was set free," she replied.

One of the barmaids brought a large cup of tea. "It's quite hot," she warned.

"Thank you, Marie," Glenn smiled, taking the cup from her in his hand. He turned and handed the cup, handle out, to Jenny, who thanked him.

She could feel the steam on her face and it was comforting. As she watched the young girl leave the room, she noticed a large gun in her apron. "Are we going to war?" she asked Glenn, jokingly.

"My child, there is an awfully evil world outside our door right now and it has chosen to bear down on us." His smile left and his eyes darkened. "There's going to be a lot of killing to do."

"Is it strange," she pondered aloud, "that I believe Algernon came for me?"

"Your hidden gentleman suitor." He listened to the gunfire outside the inn. "No. It's not strange. People have done far wilder things for the sake of love."

There was an aching regret resonating deep inside of her like a church bell. She had not been very kind to Algernon when she'd last seen him. She held back tears and let out a sigh that curled in steam above the large cup of tea that she cupped in both hands at her chin. The young girl sipped at the tea and felt a powerful desire to go outside and stop the Vampyres. She didn't move. She just stared through the steam at the mouth of the cup and thought about love and death.

Pardon me." A playful, childlike voice came from within Desmond's ornate black cart, which came to an unguided stop near the town square.

Two officers in blue uniforms looked out over the square, speaking quietly to themselves even as people screamed from the houses and ran through the streets.

"Excuse me, gentlemen," the voice asked again.

The first turned around and noticed Desmond's carriage. "Yes?" he replied with a raised eyebrow, placing a hand on his holster.

Can you direct me to the home of the former director, Desmond Burroughs? The voice rang out inside of his head.

"Stop," the officer commanded as he pulled the gun from the holster. The horses moved forward.

Thank you for the help, the voice smiled.

"What?" The man asked.

His partner turned with a rifle in hand as the horses begin pulling away. They raised their guns toward the carriage. The guns fell to the ground and the men grabbed their heads with both hands. They collapsed dead, each bleeding from the orifices of their faces.

Ruthven smiled in the dark recess of the carriage.

Alonzo Gallegos watched through the cigarette smoke from the shadow of an alleyway as Jasper Markov crossed a side street behind the old flimsy church building. The boy was hiding something. He had the journal. Just as he began to make his move toward Markov, the young man stepped up into a gloomy black carriage.

Desmond was dead from what Gallegos had gathered, ironically killed by a Vampyre; but someone very important had arrived on the train. He sized the boy up and figured that he might align himself with someone more powerful. Gallegos bit his lip and tossed the cigarette to the ground. "*Hijo de...*" he began to curse.

"It's just me; Jared." A voice came from behind him. The startled old man turned and looked at him. The boy was smiling. "You interested in killing any Vampyres?"

Twilight overtook the afternoon and the two small armies cut away at each other, leaving dead remnants along the cobblestone. The gunfire became more sparing. The smoke subsided. The soldiers were aware, as they had always been, that the Vampyres would be out soon. Sergeant Horatio Cornwall and the Seventh Battalion fell back into the town and without a great deal of organization, took to raiding homes, many of which were already empty. The town was a shell and the wind blew through the buildings, rustling old books and curtains.

It was a ghost town. The few hundreds of people that had lived there had done almost no maintenance. The manipulated citizens had existed under a curse, unable to see the world right in front of them and Desmond Burroughs had seen no reason to put any resources into their improvement.

The streets were full of bodies. Cornwall's men, brainwashed criminals, acted as soldiers and raided an enemy encampment. The citizens of Breton, having recently been freed of the curse, fought back in their madness and the hissing and chattering of awakening Vampyres began in the distance, echoing in the alleyways and rumbling underground. Not all the bodies that lay on the roads were dead. Some screamed in agony. A man cried out, "Help me! I know they're coming." There was no response. "Please, someone." The young man turned and pulled his body across the ground, creating a muddy trail of blood. "Anyone." He saw some soldiers gathering food and supplies. As they carried them up stairs into a large building west of the town square, he called to them, "Please! Help me. I can't feel my legs!"

One of the soldiers turned to him and put down the box, "Vogt," he said to the soldier walking ahead of him, "take this box." He made his way down the stairs and the wounded man, sighed, "Thank you, thank you."

When he arrived at the man's side, he reached down and retrieved the man's long rifle and turned around. "No! Please take me with you."

The soldier walked away quietly, toying with the gun, leaving the wounded man weeping.

The Third Brigade fell off into the shadows of the forest under the leadership of J. Lee Blagburn, who marched among the ranks of his men preparing for a long night at the hands of a terrible and unknown enemy. His army had lost much to the Vampyres but had never faced them directly. It had always been in his mind that they could not. The sea of gray uniforms shifted and moved as the men began setting up camp. Two men walked behind him.

"Are you certain this is going to work?" Jared asked, astonished.

"You asked me to come help," the old man replied. "You asked for my help." He mumbled. His mind was elsewhere.

Soldiers carried large torches and touched the ground with the flames every few steps while saying quiet prayers. They walked in line around the perimeter of the camp.

"You're the only person that will make this work," Jared replied quietly.

The cold, distant look melted from the old man's face as he looked at his ally. "Yes," he thought aloud. "This will work."

The tall colonel turned to them, mid-step. "Mister Gallegos," he said.

"Professor," he corrected, smiling.

Blagburn seemed to bite his tongue. Gallegos sensed that, for all his criminality, this man

was a man of order. He loved that in people. It made them easier to feel out. "Yes. Professor Gallegos," he said through his teeth. "How exactly does this work?"

Gallegos looked around at the soldiers, "Are you asking me how prayer works?" "No." The Colonel replied coldly, "I am asking *why* would prayer work?"

"Ah." Gallegos smiled. Jared looked on at the strange power struggle between the two.

Blagburn, who had been deemed criminally insane, was as interested in finding out how to kill the Vampyres as he was in keeping his men alive and he did not trust the old man to either of those ends. Gallegos had little interest in killing Vampyres and he thought all of the wild-eyed men surrounding him should be killed, but the experiment seemed worthwhile. Gallegos loved numbers and the encounter would play out in a worthwhile gamble. "You see, whereas man is a metaphysical creature, a being that is *físico* primarily that is reflected by his soul, *el Vampiro* is metaspiritual. Being *una criatura espiritual* he is, how do you say, a soul or souls that is reflected by a body."

Blagburn did not respond and he did not want to seem as though he did not understand. He grunted in approval and continued walking.

Gallegos continued the thought but turned to Jared. "*Los Vampiros* have *una historia larga.* During the crusades, they worked among the Knight's Templar and worked for the church. During the Inquisition..." He became very quiet and thoughtful, "they were torturers." He looked directly at Jared and for the first time, the old man seemed withdrawn and scary; he didn't seem human. "*Simbolos religiosos.* He does not like them. *El Vampiro* feels greatly betrayed in his soul by the church and you see, prayer, the *conección espiritual* to another part of our world, can be very, let's just say...harmful."

Both Jared and Gallegos stayed quiet until dusk while men drew lines around the camp with torches and blessed canteens of water that they sprinkled over each soldier and along the perimeter of the new camp. Blagburn had a child-like smile on his face.

Murdering Vampyres, he thought, *how absolutely entertaining.*

†HREE

Through me you go into a city of weeping;
through me you go into eternal pain;
through me you go amongst the lost people.
— **Dante Alighieri,** *Inferno, Canto III (1314)*

The door to the tailor's house opened and Miss Allen emerged into the daylight. She had a crooked gleam in her eye that bordered on wildness. She wore a pastel dress that her darling had purchased for her thirty years earlier. Her shoulder was bandaged and she held her gun, hooked in the crook of her arm like a parasol. She had let her hair down from its tight bun and put it in a ribbon, allowing strands of silver to fall around her face.

The sounds of chaos in town had inspired her. She had played mad for years and now the town had been given to its own madness. In a land of lunacy, she would be the moon.

She stood tall with a smile as soldiers walked in large groups by her home.

One large man came to her stoop and removed his cap. "Good morning ma'am."

"Good morning, sir." Bernadette smiled. "Welcome to Breton, Virginia."

His eyes darted around strangely. "Yes ma'am. Good morning to you." He tried to force a smile, but under his gray mustache, it just looked like a twitch. "My name is Cornwall, Sergeant Cornwall, ma'am and I hate to be contrary, but I am under the impression that we are nowhere near the borders of the Commonwealth of Virginia. Am I wrong there?"

"Does it matter?" Bernadette Allen gleamed.

"Ma'am?"

The soldiers continued to walk past without formation, looking into windows. "Sergeant Cornwall." Miss Allen's smile dissipated, realizing that in the same way that she was not a tailor, these men in uniform were very likely not soldiers. "Mister Cornwall," she corrected herself, as his eyes broadened softly, telling her that her assumption was correct, "does it much matter where we are?"

In the distance a man cried. You and your friends have stumbled into Hell."

Patrick's head was throbbing and he hadn't slept at all. He felt a turning sensation in his stomach and the word "Marcus" floated in his thoughts like a poison. Edwin lay on his back staring up at the floor. Jimmy McLaughlin had fallen asleep without a problem. Hours of sneaking and hiding had found them crawling under the front porch of an office building next to the police station. If it had not been abandoned, it certainly looked like it. All night, the sheriff's men ran around looking for each other and taking cover from gunshots and screaming townsfolk who were waking up from the curse.

The town was full of confused people who felt they had woken up in Purgatory or were in a nightmare. The screaming grew less bothersome over time, but Patrick's headache would not subside. He tried to stop grinding his teeth, but gazing out into the street through a crack in the wooden porch, there was something burning inside his head. *Marcus.* He couldn't remember what it was. Whatever it was, it was terrible. He was panicked. Patrick looked back at Edwin, who stared up at the rotting slats that made up the porch and began to say something but he bit his tongue. Something dark was welling up inside of Patrick Foster.

Michael walked around the Captain's quarters; he'd sealed its windows completely. The boarded windows were stuffed with fabrics and pages or whatever miscellaneous objects he had located on the ship. The wooden crypt creaked dark and breathless. His memories were clouded and his thoughts obscured with rage and sorrow. He welcomed the dark tomb where he could heal.

His mind pulsed with dark energy. He could barely rest and every time he closed his eyes, he was transported into the same expanding dream: the burning city, the endless armies in droves, everything enveloped in the black smoke. There were jerking, steaming metal machines moving across the desert wasteland. It was the most familiar thing in his heart, commander of an army, bathed in flame. He could sense a similar pulsing coming from Breton to the west. There was no more curse, there was no more control. There was only madness.

He had brought his nightmare to life in Breton.

Beyond the trees and mountains, the morning sun came through the left side windows and the wooden shutters created an array of dancing light in the passenger car of the southbound train. None of the children had ever been on a train before and, after all the stress of the earlier week, many of them just slept, rocked by the noisy thing in their dreams. Thomas sat, with his head in a hand, across from Ernest, who was painfully staring out the window.

The door toward the locomotive engine slid open, allowing the tall Mister Jones to enter, smelling of soot and sweat.

"We're coming to a stop for a moment while I do some minor repairs." He spoke quietly to Thomas and Ernest who sat in the front of the car. "Also, there's some food..." He noticed Emily coming toward him with a bowl of stew. "Thank you very much, young lady." The tall man almost blushed. He could not imagine the horror that the children had lived through in that terrible place. He only knew the rumors that surrounded it and had signed a confidentiality agreement that he would never speak about it.

The children were spread out through the railcar and he spoke again quietly, "Just let me know if you all are in need of anything else."

The door closed quietly behind him.

"How are you feeling, Mister Williams?" Thomas asked. From his tone, Ernest could tell that Thomas was tired. He knew the boy hadn't slept.

"I am..." Ernest smiled strangely. "I am very much alive, my boy and thankfully indebted to your care."

Thomas held back a smile.

Ernest knew the boy wanted to protect everyone, but with Edwin missing, there was a certain darkness in Thomas. "I don't know why we're here, Thomas. That is to say in the metaphysical sense, but I am quite glad to be here with you."

"Mister Williams," Thomas began softly. "You know how you used to misplace your flask all the time?"

Ernest smiled. "Yes, Thomas."

"You never misplaced it. We pickpocketed you; Edwin and I did." Ernest let out a small laugh and then grabbed his stomach and groaned. "I know, Thomas." His smile was big, despite clenching his teeth for the pain. "Don't you find it strange that I always got it back?"

"Oh." Thomas rose in his seat, confused.

"Kat or Glenn," he paused and grabbed his stomach, "or Genevieve would always give it back to me."

Thomas was amazed, but he stood to help the old man, "Are you alright?" He looked through the window and he felt the train stopping in the early morning light next to a sparkling lake.

It was beautiful. It was like a perfect mirror of the sky.

Ernest smiled and turned his head to look out the window. "Yes, better than I've been in many years."

Columns formed at the northern mouth of Breton, just past the market. Confederate soldiers in gray uniforms flanked quietly into positions. A white-gloved hand went up and rifles pointed out in rows. "Now, your town is here and for that I am quite amazed." The voice of Southern gentry, accented and bearded in a white cotton scruff, sang with a smile. Colonel J. Lee Blagburn looked out across the town. "I cannot disprove you in this matter any further."

"No sir. And I thank you for your faith and patience," responded the younger man that had led Blagburn's brigade as far as the south entrance of the settlement. "Now, if I know Cornwall and his friend, Corporal Vogt," the man paced, pondering aloud, "they'll already be here. It looks like we're in for a three-way fight."

"How so?"

"Well, sir," the young man grinned, "this is Vampyre territory."

Blagburn showed little emotion but a bead of sweat grew against his brow. "Luckily," he continued, "I have a friend who is an expert in these matters." The boy walked out ahead of the rows of long rifle barrels. "Hold this position until early afternoon and then roll back into the wood and stay together." He began running forward into an alleyway.

"Boy!" the colonel called. He stopped mid-step. "What is your name?" "Jared, sir!"

JARED! the Colonel thought, *That sly bastard. The Yankee captain of the seventh led me out here. He's just a boy!* Colonel Blagburn felt like he'd been trapped, but he knew that the man he couldn't kill was smarter than that. *No. It has to be Captain Jared, but I know that would not be his ruse.* The Colonel looked up to one of his lieutenants, who held back a large chocolate mare. "Carter, mount up. Get back to camp and bring the full brigade to this position."

The lieutenant looked at him with wide-eyes. Something dark had hit him. "This is where we make our stand."

So we're just going to avoid it altogether?" Genevieve asked Glenn as she handed him a handful of nails.

"Avoid it?" Glenn asked. "No. But we have to be prepared. This old building is my home, one way or another." He nodded across the room. "That girl there," he motioned to a young, blonde girl who was moving tables and clearing space, "that is Joanna. She was carrying bread from the market and she saw an entire rank of soldiers lining up. I shouldn't have sent her out in the first place, but I didn't realize things had gotten so out of hand."

Genevieve looked at the ground.

"It's not your fault, child." He grunted softly. "I just haven't been seeing the world clearly."

Another girl, Marie Sutton, moved glasses away from the bar while a young man brought in a crate of rifles from upstairs.

"We just have to weather the storm. We must choose our fights wisely." He was trying in some way to admonish himself. He had to choose his own fights wisely. He put his hand on her shoulder and smiled through his bushy beard. "Quickly now, hand me that board and help me get this window secure."

A rock smashed through the glass pane of the window and Genevieve squeaked in fear. Glenn stayed quiet and looked through the broken pane. The situation was getting worse as the day went on and a constant rain of gunfire went on as two armies had met in the square.

"Alright." He forced a smile.

Genevieve had the board in hand. Her eyes were big. "Let's get this done."

The luncheon hours had passed and the afternoon began to set. The children had explored the countryside and enjoyed a wondrous day, but as the shadows began to elongate from the mountains to the west Thomas felt a pit in his stomach.

He walked back to the locomotive engine where John Jones sat wiping his hands of grease with a rag. His legs hung off the side of the train, resting in the sun. Thomas hadn't slept all night and he fought to keep his eyes open.

"Mister Jones," Thomas said, hesitating.

"Thomas, just call me Casey. I ain't nobody's mister," he said wiping his brow. "Ok." Thomas continued. He couldn't stop looking back north.

"Is something troublin' ya, son?" He waved down the brakeman, who was filling a canteen with water from the lake.

"Casey," Thomas asked point blank, "do you know why we are on the run?"

Casey stood up casually. "It's *Breton*," he answered. "There's always a problem and according to company protocol, we move. That town is trouble and we get out quickly. Chandler gave me the paperwork and sent us on our way."

"Yes sir." The brakeman trotted up the hill.

"Grab Bill and tell him we're about to fire up."

"I believe that Vampyres will be close behind us, Casey," Thomas said plainly.

Casey pulled a ladle from a bucket of water that he poured across the back of his neck.

He let out a laugh.

"I don't see what's so funny." Thomas's voice grew strained.

"Is there a problem?" Ernest asked, smiling as he limped deliberately back up from the trail.

"Vampyres, Mister Williams." Casey laughed.

Ernest panicked. He groaned as he headed back down the hill. "Children! Children! The afternoon is waning! We must get going!" Though he struggled with pain, he began running to gather the children down around the lake.

Casey pointed down at the man. "What was that about?" He arched an eyebrow. "Why did he do that?"

Thomas did not reply. He made his way back toward the passenger car. "So we're going now?" Casey called.

Thomas heard the hiss of the steam from the locomotive. *Yes, we're going.* he thought.

How can you be so nonchalant about this? Letsya insisted. *Pavl is gone and now Rurk has gone to avenge him. Should we not be helping him?*

Ilya had been walking casually into the edge of the town but Letsya's questioning finally began driving him crazy. *Let me ask you something, Letsya Todorov.* He gave the old slovenly Vampyre a sharp look. *Are these matters about which I should worry? I don't care if the entire clan is murdered.* His eyes were cold. *I am not a soldier.* He paused. *Nor am I a god. So what use have I, my ancient friend, in immortality.*

Letsya watched confused. *Immortality?* He bit his lip nervously. *We are Vampyres; we are meant to—*

To what, Letsya? He cut him off. *We are meant to what? Be the judges of a terrible world? We are meant to what?* He only paused for a moment before he put a finger in Letsya's face. *We are meant to crawl around in the dark. You and I, Letsya Todorov, we do not get a life under the sun. We get an eternity in darkness.*

Is it sunlight that you want? Letsya asked, still confused.

No. The stern look on Ilya's young, beautiful face melted away for a moment. *I want...* He swallowed. *I just want a life. With an end. I want a romance. I envy the human cycle.*

Letsya nodded. *Yes. I am quite old now and I often feel tired of sitting through it all.*

But Letsya, he sighed, *we aren't human.*

No.

And I shan't have romance.

No, I suppose not.

273

So instead, I will find some fun, Alliance be damned.

Vampyres descended on the town and in the distance they heard the crying and suffering of the townsfolk. Letsya smiled with Ilya in the twilight as he revealed a great secret.

Letsya, my friend, he grinned. *Would you like to know what the plan was?*

Letsya was quiet.

This. He motioned toward the town; the sound of hissing Vampyres echoed through the air. *Sheer chaos.* His eyes shined with a soft twinkle. *There was no plan. Just what you see here, just this moment: mindless chaos.*

Just shoot him, Vogt!" Sergeant Cornwall commanded. "C'mon, Sarge! The way I figure, you need me," the young boy across from Vogt replied. The standoff had worn Cornwell's patience. The child had been hiding in the damp repository when Cornwall assigned the space to his soldiers for cover from the Vampyres. They had set numerous boxes of supplies among the large bales of hay. The boy had appeared with a large revolver pressed against Vogt's cheek before the rest of the soldiers filled the room. Vogt couldn't pull the trigger. "He's just a boy, sir."

"And he almost had you in. If you don't kill him, I will," Cornwall threatened. *If you were a man, you would have shot him already.* He reserved the judgment, knowing that whatever Vogt was, she was crazy. As he stepped forward, the boy turned the gun on him. His hand did not waiver, but he did not take his glare from Vogt's sweating forehead.

The other soldiers had not moved. The sure-footed child mortified them; he was ragged and wild-eyed but knew how to handle the gun in his hand. Aside from running into battle over and over, the men had never been in a standoff like this. One man, Jason Roberts, who had been a campaign adviser for Benjamin Harrison in eighteen eighty-eight, trembled so much that his long Winchester rifle rattled in his hands. The other man stood frozen, watching the confrontation, forgetting the gun in his own hand.

"What are you men doing?" Cornwall bellowed. "A boy puts his gun on me and you all sit trembling? There's only one gun!" Their guns bounced up ahead of them and their barrels fell on the boy.

The boy responded with a smile. "So it's even now?" he asked.

Guns rose from behind the soldiers. Two more boys became visible; they had hidden in the hay. They were quiet, but their guns glistened with the flicker of shaking lanterns.

Cornwall sighed.

"We will kill you all if it comes down to it," the first boy, a dark-haired child, said. Horatio Cornwall conceded. "It won't." He raised a hand and told the soldiers to lower their weapons.

"My name is Ned and I ain't got no last name," the boy stated proudly. "That's Patrick and little Jim over there and we don't want to make any enemies." He paused for a moment. "There are already Vampyres out there."

"Would I be correct in assuming that you boys know your way around here?"

"Aye sir." The boy smiled. "If you're needin' around Breton-town, I'm your man."

Cornwall was embarrassed and grunted through his teeth. "Fine."

The southbound train sped along below a bright, clear moon that shined over the mountains. Thomas tried to watch the trees that whipped past them in a blur. The moon was like a bright scythe hanging above the trees, ready to cut them all down.

Ernest slept soundly, snoring loudly. It was the first time, it seemed, that the aging man had gotten any real rest. Albert and Alexander played a hand game with Ollie while Newton helped Emily straighten up the cabin. Penny looked through a box of brochures but, being unable to read, just examined the pictures.

Thomas stood up and quietly excused himself to visit the loud locomotive, where Casey looked ahead through a large rectangular window. He stepped across the gap onto the locomotive, but there was virtually no space inside the cab. Bill, the fireman, got up and walked back through the cab. The young brakeman, who never spoke, sat to his left. Gauges, levers and valves surrounded them.

They have to be on to us. I just know it, Thomas thought. "Mister Casey!" he called out over the whirring wind, roaring boiler and clanking wheels.

Casey jumped. "You scared me, son!"

Thomas said nothing.

"Alright. What is it?" Casey said, turning his head to hear the boy's reply.

"Is there any way...?" He tried to speak, but he could barely hear his own thoughts. "Is there any way we could go faster?"

Casey smiled. "Why would you want to go...?" His face went pale as he looked up past the boy.

Thomas turned quickly and saw a small, marble-eyed Vampyre grinning down at them from on top of the passenger car with a hand wrapped around the lip of the roof, wind blowing past him and his dark hair blowing out of his face. It climbed down and even as the quiet brakeman looked up, the thing swatted him hard, throwing him completely from the side of the engine.

"You're not welcome here, Vampyre!" Thomas yelled.

"Vampyre," Casey muttered. "I thought it was a damned euphemism!" He reached across and quickly turned a valve. "Faster it is!"

"You came a long way for a fight, Vampyre!" Thomas called. He'd bluffed once before, but this time, he wasn't bluffing. He had seen Vampyres die. They weren't invincible. He pulled Casey's ladle from its bucket on the floor and began saying the Lord's Prayer. He quickly poured the water along the floor and slung some of it at the Vampyre, but it jumped back up on the roof.

A taller, more sinister-looking Vampyre appeared as a shadow behind the smaller creature. Casey pulled one of the levers. Thomas felt the train moving faster. He'd known they'd be coming.

My name is Rurk, the tall one told him. *Since you seem to be so interested in names. You and your friend killed my brother, Pavl.*

"Well, good!" Thomas hissed. "Great! It's just you and me now, Rurk." The boy snarled at the Vampyres and the smaller one laughed. The tall Vampyre said nothing. "You look just like him," the boy muttered. "Casey, keep us moving. I prayed o'er your water. Use it."

Casey looked up at the Vampyres. Four of the creatures stood grinning in the whipping wind. When he looked back ahead of the train, two more were standing atop the locomotive.

Is this even possible? he thought. "Well, Thomas, listen to me, if you want some real speed, we're going to have to unlock from the other cars," he said, turning to Thomas. "If you can do that, we'll really be moving."

Thomas kept an eye on the Vampyres as he stepped over the gap and through the door. "Where's the man that came through here?" Thomas asked.

Newton Bullington pointed toward the back door where the sooty trainman had passed only moments earlier.

Thomas knew he'd be dead. "Everyone, it's time to get to work," he said to the children in the passenger car without emotion. "The Vampyres are on us."

Ernest Williams groaned, struggling to get up from his seat. The children scrambled into position. They moved to the center of the train car and Thomas began calling out instructions. "Stay tight!" They blew out candles and huddled in the dark. Thomas pulled down the shades.

Every child deserves a chance at a real life. Ernest moved slowly toward the back of the train car. He held his stomach tightly.

The train was moving more quickly and Thomas ran to the back of the car. He picked up a glass milk bottle filled with lake water. He pulled the door open to see a Vampyre swat at him. "I knew you would be here." Thomas smiled.The Vampyre hissed.

He threw the water on the creature. It grabbed its face, screaming. Tendrils of smoke ran from between its fingers. Skin bubbled and its hands began sticking to the skin from its face, which pulled from its skull. Thomas charged at the hideous screaming thing, pushing it between the two train cars. In the darkness, the blood splattered up on the floor of the train car as the creature's legs were quickly chopped and crushed. It squealed in pain. Thomas watched it disappear under the train.

"Well done, my boy." Ernest approached Thomas, who was struggling to pull the connecting clip between the two cars. Ernest stuck his head out to look for the Vampyres. From behind him, he heard a window smash. Penny let out a squeal and Emily pulled her in tightly. "Thomas, go grab more water!" Ernest instructed. "I'll get this."

"Yes sir!" He ran back to the crate of glass bottles.

Ernest was in so much pain. He began to pull the clip when a small Vampyre tackled him. He didn't let go. Somewhere in the jumble of curses, Ernest thought, *Everyone deserves a chance.* As they fell back onto the platform of the storage car, the train jerked as the cars began to separate.

The Vampyre was wiry and she crawled over him like a spider. Even before he could move, she sank her sharp fangs into his neck. He let out a wet gurgle of a scream.

"No!" Thomas cried. The monster's dress flitted in the wind as the train car slowed. He ran through the passenger car and flung the bottle of water through the door at the small thing. The glass shattered against her head. His steps stuttered, finding him at the rear platform, watching the other train car quickly separating. The smoke and steam rose from the creature as Ernest tried to throw it from his body. It screeched and arched its back and Ernest kicked it through the front door of the car. It was still moving fast enough that its body just crunched under the iron wheels.

Ernest looked up at Thomas's horrified face, shrinking in the distance. *Every child deserves a chance,* he thought, pushing himself up. There was a sudden sense that the pain he was experiencing was inconsequential. The blood was running down his lapel and his shirt was quickly turning black and red. He was having trouble breathing and his sight was leaving him. He gave a small wave and smiled at Thomas.

"Hey!" he yelled out. "How about a real fight?"

Almost immediately, four other Vampyres jumped nimbly from the roof of the passenger car to the ground. They leapt and with single bounds, came barreling toward the slowing storage car.

Ernest made his way inside the car, leaving a trail of blood. He straightened his lapel and ran his bloody fingers through his hair as a gentleman, preparing himself for death. "Come on in," he grumbled, welcoming the Vampyres into the darkness.

You fools, Rurk cursed. *It's a—*

As the Vampyres crawled into the storage car, Rurk covered his eyes with his arm. The bright flash and explosion of a large gun firing tore through wood and steel.

Ernest sat behind the large machine gun and rattled off round after round. He prayed quietly with an eerie smile. His arm was going numb and it sat limp in his lap as he cut the Vampyres down. The wood splintered and the metal frame of the storage car collapsed on one side as the large bullets sawed through it.

After only a moment, the quiet surrounded him. The storage car was coming to a halt. The Vampyres were dead and he got up before he gave it much thought.

Somebody could have told me there was a damn machine gun back here, he grumbled to himself. He opened the door to the caboose, which was furnished, dry and warm. He sat down on the caboose's small bed and sighed. *Quiet,* he thought. *The quiet is good.* He sighed with a deep satisfaction. He painfully straightened his bloody jacket. He was a mess and he was bleeding everywhere. *Go take your chance, Thomas.* He reached into his jacket and retrieved his small flask. It was his father, though Ernest couldn't even remember the man's face anymore. It was the last connection he had to whatever life he had lived outside of Breton. He gave it a long, hard look, struggling with his focus as it danced in and out. He leaned forward and rested his head against a fist.

Within moments, Ernest's cold stare fell on the dark wall of the caboose as he died sitting in a puddle of dark blood. He looked much like he had on the nights when he sat contemplating his life in the Crow's Nest, with his head in his hand, wondering if he had made a difference in his life, but in that last moment a contented smile curled at the edge of his lips. He kept his eyes open despite the coming darkness while the sound of the train filled the quiet air in the distance.

Y ou can't possibly be considering it, Glenn." Genevieve admonished the bullnecked man who slid the large oak table away from the front door.

"She's not lying," he said. "I know Zoya and I would know, charm or not, if she was lying to me." He took a long bayonet from the oak table and slid the long dull blade down the back of his pants.

"But Glenn." Genevieve placed her hand on his large arm. Her hand was tiny; it made him think of Kat. "Could she not just tell you through the window?"

He ignored her and pulled the large door open. Ahead of him stood his wife: adulteress and Vampyre. Beyond Zoya, the town was in ruins. Fire was billowing from a distant roof and a woman ran across the square chased by blood-drenched Vampyres, screaming. The gunfire was deafening.

"Here I am, Zoya Lamphere!" Glenn mocked her from across the street, where she stood watching and speaking in the direction of the Crow's Nest. "Here I am, ever faithful. Never faltering." He withheld an angry tear. His shoulders were as wide as the doorframe, large enough that even the Vampyres feared him.

She began to cross the street, her face betraying a sense of guilt and her steps lingering.

Ilya took her, she whispered to him in the middle of the cobblestone street. *Ilya took her and now she's gone. There is something wrong with him and I don't know what to do.* Her face fell into her hands. *They say they brought her back here. That she's fine.*

Glenn clenched his teeth and his hands closed into fists. "They're lying." The door behind him shut. *Good girl, Jenny.*

Will you ever forgive me? she wept. *This is my fault. I know it is.*

His eyes creased as he held back his rage. "Read my mind, Vampyre."

She looked up at him through the tears.

"My wife has been dead to me for years. I cannot mourn or move on with my life. Yet here you stand with news that you are the cause of my daughter's death?" Tears began to well around his blue eyes. "And you want my forgiveness?" He thought while he tried to process the flood of new emotions that hit him like a wave. "My daughter is dead! No one gets to be forgiven for that."

Our daughter, Glenn.

Glenn's cold smile never reached his eyes. He reached to embrace Zoya. "Our daughter..." he said. He wrapped his arms around her and plunged the long bayonet he'd hidden in his trousers into her shoulder. It pierced her heart and he pushed through until he felt the bloody tip at his large stomach. He gripped her tightly. The sound she made was not of this world. She clawed at his back, shredding his coat shirt until blood ran. Her skin felt like hot coals. Husband and wife never broke eye contact as death took her. Glenn could hear the Vampyres hissing all around him. She fell limply against him and her arms dropped to her sides. She was gone.

Carry this Testament, my heart. You must remember, my love. Help our Katarina.

Zoya's lifeless gaze fell away from him.

Glenn saw the world again. He had not thought of his wedding day for years and as he remembered, he saw their faces, Adler, Desmond Burroughs and a host of Vampyres. He had always been married to a Vampyre and she was royalty to boot. Glenn's life flashed before his eyes and he was a very small part of it. Something broke in him. His life, whatever had come before had been erased, suppressed, forgotten, hidden from him.

He'd been robbed of his own memories.

The Vampyre died in his arms and deep down he knew what she had done. Something had passed from her to him. He now carried an even greater burden. Glenn laid her down on the ground and wept openly. He was alone in the world. No one could know his sorrow. He rolled her body onto her side and removed the bayonet from her back before he wiped the bloody blade on his pant leg. He wiped his wet eyes on his arm and screamed as the Vampyres rained down around him.

Genevieve didn't know what to do with herself. She stood silently with her back against the heavy door.

"Where's Glenn?" Marie, the barmaid, asked.

"He...went outside," Genevieve said in a cool tone.

Marie hung her head. There was a room full of patrons that sat in the corner trying to figure out who they were. "Well, if he comes back," she replied in the same tone, "tell him I'm pulling his whiskey." She ladled the booze into a bottle with numerous glasses from behind the bar. She walked back into the large communal room. "There's real drinking to be done."

All the while Genevieve listened at the door. The screams never seemed to stop. Explosions were getting closer. People were running for their lives. Someone outside was knocking on the door. The windows glowed with the razing fires.

Khalil Sayid stepped into the street with a smile. The moonlight gleamed over the cobblestone road, but the lanterns did not light. With his Apache knuckleduster in hand, he had every intention of knocking the fangs out of every Vampyre's mouth and cracking the skull of every fool man that stepped in his way. He carried an arsenal of curved blades and wore a silk turban on his head with a jewel set in the middle. Khalil set out to get bloody and his grin grew wider. He felt like he was molting from the identity of Monsieur Chandler and back into himself.

In the darkness behind him, three boys were making their way across the street and into an alley.

Old lady Allen looked down the twin-barrels of a scattergun at him from across the street. He grinned and tipped his turban. She just nodded. Something about it all just felt like home for him. He whistled as he walked along the street, listening to the deafening cacophony of chaos. It was music.

"God bless!" Miss Allen cursed and fired the scattergun before shutting the door behind her. The front porch had been run over. "If y'all haven't any better sense than that, I'll kill you all!" She crawled behind her overturned sewing table. Her home was dark aside from the small smoldering fire in her hearth. The back door was bolted shut and she had boarded the windows after seeing the soldiers marching in.

"Please let us in!" other soldiers cried. Their heavy fists crashed on the door. "You must believe us! We are good men!"

After a moment, there came screams. Silence followed. She did not move and she did not breathe. Then for hours afterward, she only heard the wet sound of chewing and the crunching of bone. Every few hours, a Vampyre would knock on the door and ask her to come out, but she never answered. Hours of chewing and the hissing and the chattering of an unknown language followed until sunrise came.

Markov did not speak in the carriage with Lord Ruthven. There was a strange discomfort about being near him and Markov tried to keep his mind clear. All day long, Ruthven had made condescending remarks that he'd pulled directly from Jasper's subconscious. Now he was being very polite on the carriage ride.

Oh, I do hope they like me. Ruthven smiled at Jasper though he continued to gaze out the window.

"There is certainly no Vampyre as well-dressed as you, sir." Jasper remarked.

Oh yes, thank you for that. Ruthven smiled. *I do think you are right.* A trunk full of fine clothing had been awaiting them at Desmond's house, sent there earlier by Matheson and his men. He had chosen a beautiful brown suit with green accents and a buttoned cravat.

Markov felt belittled. Instead of racing around town preparing for some battle with the mysterious enemy or preparing to steal riches, Ruthven simply made him go shopping for him. He had spent all day picking out linens and silks, pantaloons, waistcoats and jackets. Then there were hats and wines and socks and shoes. He called it shopping, despite the fact that the shops were empty. He was scavenging a ghost town.

For something as powerful as Adler had described, Markov could not believe how incredibly effeminate and vain Ruthven was.

Ah! And here we are! Ruthven announced as the carriage pulled into Breton. He stepped down onto the street and stretched his legs, smiling. The smell of smoke and burning flesh permeated the air.

Hell is empty, he quoted, *and the devils are here.*

Ilya laughed as the family inside the building cursed at him. Charmingly, he asked, *Won't you let me in for dinner?* The windows had been broken out from the building, but Ilya did little to get inside where they were. He could see them hiding behind furniture and in the kitchen.

A man's voice came from inside. "You are not welcome here, Vampyre. Be on your way."

The orange glow of a burning building silhouetted Ilya's tall, slender figure. *No,* he told them. *If I cannot join you inside, then you will come out and visit with me.* He grabbed a large branch from the ground and walked up to the raging fire as the flames billowed out a window. Though he felt the warmth, it did not burn him. The branch caught the flame almost immediately.

It's one way or the other and there's no back door. He began lighting the fabric in the window. *So I will see you in just a minute.* Ilya threw the branch in through a large, broken window and watched the flame began to flicker. A woman panicked in the kitchen as the ground beneath her feet began to rumble.

The Vampyre's grin glowed in the fire. *Hi!*

Spencer slid the boxes away from the bunk beds in a frantic search. The revolver lay cold and dormant, with its barrel toward the door. The supplies and personal effects of each of his kids were gone, but they knew nothing of his journals and his second gun. There were things he would need if the Vampyre infestation were to continue. There was a rumble in the floor but he couldn't distinguish if it was cannon fire or something worse.

The front door came open with a sigh and he noticed the cold gust from under the bunk. He grabbed the pistol and disappeared into the shadows.

"Well, I am just saying that you shouldn't blurt out 'Look at the soldiers!' when we're trying to sneak around town, James," Edwin scolded as they moved into the orphanage.

"He's right," Patrick echoed as he walked through the door.

"No. I was saying, 'Look *out*. There are more soldiers.'"
He pleaded with them.

"But did you have to do it so loudly?" Edwin asked. "I
think they put a bullet hole in my coat." The boys were relaxed
and though Edwin didn't mind them following him, he missed
Thomas's quiet company. He missed his friend terribly.

James shut the door quietly but didn't respond and as it
shut, the sounds of gunfire seemed more distant and the Vampyres
at bay. They were silent in the dark. Patrick lit a lantern with
some flint and the warm orange glow seemed to give them breath
again as they moved into the orphanage that had been their home.

"Ok," Edwin said. "We wait until we can move and then
we need to find a place to hole up until sunrise. The soldiers,
I think we can deal with but not at the same time as..." Before
he could finish the thought, he spoke again. "Did you guys feel
that?"

Patrick looked back at him. "Feel what?"

Edwin looked at the floor, confused. "There it was again."

"I didn't feel anything," James offered.

Edwin bent over and listened to the ground and his eyes
widened. He was growing more and more confused. "It felt like
the ground was moving."

"It's called a tremor or an earthquake." A comforting,
warm voice came from the shadows.

James jumped back against the wall and Patrick raised
a gun pointed at the darkness, but Edwin just smiled. "Mister
Smith?"

"Yes, Edwin. It's me." He stepped from the darkness to
reveal his slender figure and warm smile.

Edwin didn't wait to see if it was a trap or an illusion
or Vampyre's charm. He ran to the man and wrapped his arms
around his ribs. Spencer's arms came down softly around the
young boy. He knew he had been the only father Edwin had ever
known. "It's nice to be remembered."

Edwin looked up at the man and grinned. "Look, we woke
everyone up."

James stepped forward from the wall and the gun fell to
Patrick's side. They stepped in. "Shouldn't you boys be on a train
getting away from here?" he asked as he kneeled down by Edwin.

"Aye," Edwin replied. "But Kat and Jenny and..."Spencer
laughed. "Yes. I know the feeling."

"What about you boys?" He looked to the others.

"How are you not dead?" Patrick asked, though Spencer
could not tell if the boy was excited to see him or not. The
question sounded morbid.

"I followed!" James answered, ignoring Patrick's

question.

Spencer didn't mean to ignore the question himself but the younger and more excited child beckoned his attention. "Well, alright James," Spencer answered. "I suppose we have each other. Let's get to work." Spencer turned to them quietly. "Did you lock the door?" He noticed that James' face looked panicked. "Ok. Let's get upstairs and hidden. Edwin, grab that box. Patrick, get the door open."

They moved silently through the open door onto the roof of the building and Spencer closed it just as he heard the scuffling downstairs. He slid a heavy branch across the door and made sure it wouldn't open.

Edwin was looking out across the townscape. The midnight bell tolled and he remembered the last time he had been on the roof when it was a different, very sleepy town. There were entire parts of the town that were being engulfed in flames and he could feel the earth trembling and growling. Across the square, he could see the bell tower and the Vampyres that were climbing down its sides.

"The midnight bell is a signal to the Vampyres," he observed quietly. Patrick just stared at the rooftop door, waiting for whatever had entered the building to come flying up through it. James sat quietly out of the way, trying not to panic.

Spencer looked up from the box in his hands. "Yes. Quite astute. Algernon thought so too."

"Mister Smith," Edwin began, as he stared off into the distance.

"Yes, Ned, what is it?"

"Do you remember how on the day that Vampyre hunter came, you told Thomas and me to bring everyone up here?"

"Quite vaguely," he admitted.

"Well, look." He pointed out across the square to the large well that had once supplied all the water to the town. "You also told us to show them the world we saw; I never thought it would be like this." Patrick and James came to his side and Spencer got up from his seat on the access door. They looked out to the well, where hundreds of Vampyres were spilling into the woods and into Breton.

"This must have been going on every night," Spencer observed.

"The last time I came up here was when we were hiding from the sheriff," Edwin remembered.

"I remember." Patrick followed, but his face had lost its color as he watched the multitude of Vampyres nimbly pouring from the well like ants.

"Well, while I was up here, I promised Thomas that I would destroy this town somehow."

Spencer looked down at the boy, impressed by his resolve.

"I think I have just figured out how."

The access door started to bang. The person on the other side of the door had a great deal of strength. Spencer looked out at the masses of Vampyres and realized that he could not face them with the children. Being indoors was safer anyway.

"The only thing we can do is fight to hold our place." Spencer instructed. "Patrick, get behind the access door. Ned, pull the branch. Once Patrick pulls it open, I want you to have it in hand."

"But I have a gun," Edwin corrected.

"Right. We all do," Patrick added.

Spencer looked at him quickly. "Save your shots."

They moved quietly across the rooftop and Spencer kept in his mind how he didn't want to give his position away. *Don't shoot unless you have to.* He bore down on the door and gave the boys the signal. "Pull it."

Edwin pulled the branch and Patrick opened the access door. Spencer pointed his gun down on the top of a man's head that did not move.

"Friend or foe?" Spencer asked quietly.

"You have the gun, sir. I would rather choose not to be a foe."

Edwin recognized the voice. "Jared?"

"Edwin!" The voice called from the dark of the hallway. "I knew it was you boys!" Then he looked up and offered, "The gun won't be necessary, sir. We promise."

"We?" Spencer lifted the gun.

"I bring company."

FOUR

Again the devil took him to a very high mountain and showed him all the kingdoms of the world and their splendor.
- Matthew 4:8 (KJV) (1611)
- As noted in the journal of A.G., Profesor Emérita, u de Salamanca (1858)
Translated to the English from the Reina Valera Version (1602)

The morning sun rose to sighs of relief. There were hours after the dawn where nothing made a sound. Even the wind seemed to hold its breath. The Vampyres had withdrawn and the exhaustion of war and fear had caught up with everyone who still breathed.

Soldiers slept in huddled masses where the uninvited Vampyres couldn't go while others kept watch. The stillness wouldn't last long. They crept along the wall of an alleyway, keeping quiet. There was no reason to stir the chaos in that moment. Spencer led the way, with Edwin, James and Patrick following behind him.

They'd spent all night formulating a plan that Edwin had concocted. With Spencer Mayhew's experience and the wisdom of a man who had come with Jared named Alonzo Gallegos, who was also Spencer's friend and who had fought the Vampyres for many years, they felt they could finally destroy the Vampyres, but it would rely on some diplomacy and a lot of fast work.

Edwin knew him. He was the man that took Kat's body. He was the man who could kill Vampyres with prayers.

Jared had headed off into the woods and Gallegos stayed in the orphanage with Glenn the innkeeper who, having fought the Vampyres for hours in a rage, survived and collapsed from exhaustion at the feet of the old Spaniard.

"Can't we look for some food?" James complained.

"No, we don't have time," Edwin scolded. "We have to make this work."

"But I'm hungry," James whined.

Edwin stopped and let Patrick continue on with Spencer. "James," he told the boy as he placed his hands on his shoulders, "if you wanted to eat and be safe, you should have stayed on that train." He looked him directly in the eye. "You made a choice."

Spencer smiled. He approved of the strong-willed Edwin's talk. He had taught him well.

You can't be serious, Jared." Colonel Blagburn laughed, hoarsely. There was a weak crack in his voice.

They stood, overlooking the entire town from the edge of St. Jerome's roof. Jared replied, "I am absolutely serious."

The view made even the hardened Blagburn weak. The orphanage faced the town's square, where small factions had fought all night. There was black smoke billowing from fires that had eaten their fill of wooden homes and buildings. He sat down near the edge, pensive.

Blagburn had spent the entire night holding his position against the onslaught of Vampyres. The prayers and torch perimeter had only done so much to dissuade the attack, but eventually even that broke. Nothing was absolute. The Vampyres would force trees down into the camp, crushing men. Then they would run larger, mutated Vampyres into the camp, tearing soldiers limb from core.

It had gone all night.

His men gathered rounds from crates while other men prayed over them, causing the bullets to penetrate and kill the Vampyres, according to the Spaniard's specifications.

It was a good battle, but deep down, Blagburn was at a loss.

"If I had known it were you, *Jared*, Captain of the Seventh and my enemy, that had come to gather my army, I would have lopped your head off. And now you show me this. We have become nothing but chow for Vampyres, mice to their cats."

Jared turned and stepped toward the seated man, who was covered in blood and seemed all the more haggard for his lack of sleep. "I am not your enemy, Colonel." He took a breath and grew very severe. "Do you even know why you fight?"

"I am a Colonel of the Confederacy! I fight becau—" His voice rang out.

"No," Jared whispered as he loomed over the man. "You are not." His eyes were piercing. "You were brought here to die, to pay for sins or crimes that you've long forgotten, just like every dead man down there."

"How do you know that?" Blagburn asked. "How do you know so much about these goings on?"

"My story is different." His reply was short. "I was a child that went into the camp of the Seventh Battalion years ago, after my family was killed by the Vampyres, where I became cursed, just like you, the day I donned the uniform of the Union."

Blagburn heard the sincerity in the young man's voice.

"Since then, I found my way to this town, where a revolution was rising, a revolution that will mean the death of the Vampyre, a revolution that will give you and your men a real reason to fight, to fight back, to live, or at least to die as your own and not property bought by Vamps." Jared's voice remained calm, but his eyes were bright.

"So why here?" Blagburn spoke quietly. "Why this roof?"

"In a moment, you will know everything." Jared smiled.

The access hatch opened and Glenn, the large innkeeper, rose up through it. "They're here, Jared."

"Good," he replied. "Let's get started."

Spencer listened to the clanking sound of the boys retrieving bottles and buckets from all over town. The smell of the town was worsening, but the boys seemed used to it. Spencer wore a bandana that helped muffle the smell of death, but it did very little. James brought wooden buckets from the market and Patrick wheeled a small cart with small barrels from behind a row of houses. Edwin came with a smile from around the alley alongside the inn, followed by Genevieve, who had a handful of empty bottles and a rifle strapped across her back.

Corporal Vogt exited a small house. "No, Mister Mayhew, it's empty."

Spencer grumbled, "I was sure there'd be something." He turned to Edwin and Genevieve, who had been helping for almost half an hour. Upon seeing him that morning, she hugged his neck and shared a quiet moment. They thought about Algernon. They were coming up quietly. "Are you sure about this idea, Ned?"

"This *is* pretty crazy," Vogt added.

"Why is it crazy?" Edwin responded. "You saw them, the Vampyres. They showed up in the twilight and they looked like us, all charming, but then when night came, they were wild-eyed. Like animals."

"Bloodlust," Spencer iterated.

"Yeah. That," Edwin replied. "What if I left a trail of caramels and toffees all over the place? You'd lose it then, wouldn't you?"

Vogt showed a crooked smile that made Spencer sick. "I guess you're right, lad."

"I'm so hungry." James continued to whine as he walked up.

Genevieve kneeled next to him, "Why don't you let me take you

back to the inn? Marie can fix you something," she whispered. Everyone was hungry and they didn't need a raid of soldiers at the inn.

He obeyed her with a quiet smile.

Vogt called to some men, who were standing near a doorway talking, "Hey! Keep looking!" They were reluctant. "Yeah! Go on!"she cried. As Corporal Vogt, whose real name was Sara, continued to regain her memory, she grew more brazen. Sara Vogt had murdered two men and she had conspicuously dressed as a man herself. Only Sergeant Cornwall was aware of what she was, but she scared him. He wouldn't risk her rage.

Spencer looked up across the street to the rear of the orphanage, where he knew the heads of each faction would be meeting with Jared. He worried for the young man. He seemed a very adept soldier, but diplomacy was a different creature altogether and Jared had revealed that either leader might have reason to distrust him. It bothered Spencer to think that the only people with him were the innkeeper and that old Spaniard kook.

"Ok." He clapped his hands. "Everyone get back to work."

Heavy fists banged on the side door in the inn. Marie nervously held a gun at the door while Genevieve sat with James, who ate cold soup.

"Let us in!" People were gathering at the door, violently aiming to overtake the building. Glenn and Genevieve had boarded everything up tight and there was no way to enter the inn except for the heavy front door and the smaller side entrance, which they left un-boarded for the sake of having an exit.

The number of people in the inn began dwindling during the night. One gentleman, charmed by a Vampyre, tossed himself through an upstairs window. Marie had evicted two women for fighting over some food. They might still have been out there.

Marie had no reason to answer and no reason to open the door.

There was a cold silence that suddenly replaced the banging sound and then a light rap on the door.

Marie didn't move.

"It's me, Marie."

Her face glowed with surprise. "Glenn?"

"Yeah."

She threw the gun on the floor and pulled the door open to see where Glenn stood, haggard and smiling. The crowd stood back and did not move. Soldiers in different uniforms, gray and blue, bore down with rifles on the crowd that had scattered.

Glenn entered the room, followed by two men. "This is Colonel Blagburn." A man in gray entered. "And Sergeant

Cornwall." A short, round man in a different uniform, blue but stained, followed behind him. "Marie, make sure that these men get rest and a hot meal to eat."

Her mouth sat agape with surprise upon the sight of Glenn, but she gestured to the men toward the stairs. "I will draw you each a bath."

Genevieve had been rummaging through crates when she looked up from the larger communal room to see Glenn. She smiled in disbelief. "How?" She ran across the room to embrace the large man, who groaned in pain at her touch. Beyond the superficial pride, there was sadness there. She knew that it had been his loss that had kept him killing throughout the night.

"You were part of the meeting on the roof that Spencer mentioned?" she asked.

"Yes. The old man, Gallegos, saved me. He was working with Jared, who also knew your friend, Spencer—Mister Smith."

She smiled. "He's some sort of wizard isn't he?"

"The old man? I suppose so." He sat next to James and rubbed the little boy's head as he continued eating. "I stood in a pile of dead Vampyres when they finally overtook me. I had fought them for hours until my body gave out. He came down with a flash of light and then he drug me to the orphanage, where I woke up."

She was astonished. "But you didn't have to go out there."

His tired smile disappeared with a troubled look. He began to say something but reserved it. He looked at the little boy next to him and thought about how he would express the thought that troubled him. He looked at her. "I died out there. My wife and my daughter are gone. As far as I'm concerned, that man is gone."

"Good." She smiled, grateful to have him there. "I'm glad that this one is still with us."

They watched the men begrudgingly try to grasp the idea in front of them and Spencer and Jared spoke in whispers. "I watched you hang, Mister Mayhew." Jared spoke earnestly, "And we did everything we could to stop it."

Spencer half-smiled, "Most grateful for that." He sighed. "But to be honest, I wasn't expecting any help. If you spend long enough alone, you find a strange, resolute strength in quiet solitude. That's where you come up with how to stay alive."

That statement rang inside of Jared's heart. It was disarming. He recorded the thought as though it were a truth preached in church.

"So tell me; what did you do after the shooting started?" Spencer continued.

Jared pointed with a finger, "I was followed on horseback by the sheriff, which..." He paused. "I don't know how to describe what happened afterward."

Spencer crossed his arms. He was intrigued. In a place like Breton, what came next was always interesting.

"The sheriff shot the horse out from under me and followed me into the woods." He wasn't sure if Spencer could believe what happened next. "I started to shoot the man but..." He tried to put it into words. "He turned into smoke."

"What!" Spencer exclaimed. "He was a Shifter?"

"A Shifter, sir?"

"A Shifter, yes. Like Vampyres, they're an abomination. They are demons, elemental spirits who look like us, but at their core they are just 'non-corporeal' things." Spencer laughed, "I knew there was something off with that Sheriff Matheson!" He grinned but his smile turned bleak and curious. "How in Heaven did you survive him?"

The surprised Jared thought back on it, "Well, sir...I threw myself from a cliff into the ocean."

"Jared, my friend." Spencer smiled, "I survived a hanging at the hands of these idiots. You survived an entire lifetime of war, Vampyres and death at the hand of a smoke monster. Next time we come across the subject of 'Why aren't you dead, sir?' you take the lead." He threw an arm around the younger soldier, laughing as they oversaw the "harvest."

Men filled bottles and buckets with the blood of the dead all over the town; some commented how strange that there weren't enough buckets, while others thought more blood was needed.

Down the road, more aggressive tactics were being employed. Soldiers all conversed casually as Sara Vogt crawled over an old wooden fence and into the pigsty. "Just grab them, slit the throat and fill the buckets with the blood," one man told her.

Vogt gave him a cool look and continued her conversation with the other men, "Honestly, it's the tremors, not the Vampyres, that make me nervous."

"Oh really?" Elijah Long, the barefooted soldier, replied. "It's not the demon creatures that raise up out of the darkness to devour everyone in the remote mountain town?" He laughed to some other soldiers.

Vogt looked at him without emotion.

"I mean, perhaps that is scarier for someone like you, Vogt!" another man called, leaning against the fence.

Like me? Corporal Vogt held a large knife in one hand and a bucket in the other. "You all laugh at my cowardice, yet I'm the one in the sty doing the work."

"Well, you're also a pushover." Long laughed.

Vogt walked back to the fence where the men were laughing at her, still unaware of her secret. She forced a strange smile. "Be sober and be vigilant, Mister Long." She pointed the large knife at the man's face. "Because your adversary, the devil, as a roaring lion, walketh about, seeking whom he may devour." Her eyebrows furrowed and her jaw shifted.

"Relax, Vogt." Long smiled. He rolled his eyes. "When you grow to be a man, we'll have this conversation again," he joked.

"You think the Vampyres are the devil?" Vogt continued. "But the earth trembles and shakes, ready to swallow us all up. You and I are just— men." She thought about her choice of words. "We are evil folk, but we are nothing when we tumble into the devil's throat."

"I am quite serious, Vogt." Long's voice changed. "Get to work."

Sara Vogt clenched her teeth. "You aren't listening to me." Her eyes began to glaze. "Nobody's listen—" Long began. Vogt put the knife quickly into his throat and the man's eyes grew with surprise. Vogt turned to the other men, who stood stunned. As the blood began to roll across her hand and splash at her feet, Vogt moved the bucket to catch it. She felt the man collapsing at his knees and felt the tremor of the ground at her feet.

Long collapsed against the old wooden fence, destroying it with his body. The other men ran away, but Vogt continued filling the bucket with blood.

"Cowards," she stated quietly. She bent over the man's dying body as the dirt became mud at her feet with warm, splashing blood and she asked Long, "Did you ever consider that you and I are the devils, Mister Long?" The man's open eyes stared off into nothing. Sara Vogt stood up and looked along the way back to Breton. "The earth is trembling at our fall."

Dusk fell and the town of Breton held its breath. Michael walked the quiet streets, breathing in the anguish. The townsfolk peered from their windows. An onslaught of Vampyres throughout the night followed by abuse from soldiers the next morning left the townsfolk demoralized, hiding in any corner of shadow they could.

He looked out over the square and saw trenches dug in the grass. Carts and carriages had been moved into defensive positions in front of buildings. It looked like a soldier's playground.

"HALT!" A voice echoed along the walls of the empty street.

Guilty, Michael thought. The urge to stamp out the man's life came before he even saw him. *What kind of place draws in such terrible men?* He walked along the street. He sighed as he sensed that the men were about to shoot. He disappeared into a haze as the racket and volley of gunfire echoed around him. Glass shattered and the smoke cleared.

"Vampyre!" one man called out.

Jared ran out of the inn, followed by Glenn, who sent a signal, waving his arms, to Spencer across the square, near the church. Spencer shrugged. He hadn't seen anything. Jared had a hunch.

"Men, lower your weapons," Jared commanded as he climbed over the carriage that hid them.

"Lower them!" Glenn's voice boomed among them.

Jared stepped out, tall and unarmed. He looked for the Vampyre in the shadows along the walls of the street.

They're quick on the trigger. Michael looked past Jared to see the men posted with their rifles pointed out into the darkness.

"Well, we're at war," Jared whispered.

With guns?

"It's a start, Michael." He looked out between two buildings as he continued walking. "And they do quite a bit of damage—more than I would have thought."

There is one Vampyre, Ruthven.

"The name's been spreading all day."

Yes. I have to stop him.

"There's a lot going on, Michael. What am I supposed to do? We need your help."

Michael walked up beside Jared and showed himself; his eyes were on the windows in the nearby apartments. "The others will be able to spot the trap."

"It's not about the trap. It's about the trapper."

"Alright." Michael sensed that Jared was confident: a warrior in stride. "This Ruthven, I feel like he is very," he paused, "vain. But he is quite powerful. I am bound to my duty to destroy him."

"Duty?"

Michael looked like a child as his eyes opened and Jared saw him fight the words from coming out. "I am a Vampyre now. Whatever came before is irrelevant. The failures of these Vampyres here are now my responsibility."

"Well, then how can I help?" Jared asked, soldier to soldier.

"Use your men. You'll know him when you see him. Keep him in the square. He is much too powerful for you. Even the others fear him."

"They fear you."

"They should. I aim to see them dead." Jared smiled. "Where will you be?"

"I'll stay up and out of sight."

"Like a guardian angel," Jared muttered.

"Yes. I quite like the sound of that."

As Jared approached the inn again, he heard Cornwall call across the barrier. "Colluding with the enemy, Captain?"

"The difference between you and me, *Sergeant* Cornwall," he pointed across the cart casually, "is that I know what collusion means."

The twilight was otherwise peaceful, but the unease that came with the fear of death hung on the breaths of soldiers and the citizens of a town that never was. Soldiers stared from their posts along the town, hidden from sight.

An old soldier sat with his back against the dirt in a trench. The silence weighed on him heavily; he squirmed with a gun in hand as younger men handed weapons along the trench. He tried to calm his nerves and his queasy stomach. He sang to ease his nerves. "Oh my darlin'. Oh my darlin'..." His voice sounded like gravel and was out of tune.

From the bell tower, Spencer watched the sun cast elongated shadows across the square. He felt a struggle between his own pride for young Edwin, deep sorrow at his loss, acknowledgment that Algernon would not be returning and an anxious fear of what would come next. The ground rumbled and shifted and Spencer closed his eyes to meditate. From the distance, he heard a voice: "Thou art lost and gone forever," mutely rising up from below like soft bellows.

He put his head against a wooden column, trying to clear his mind. He sighed softly and lipped the words of the song with gravelly voice. "Dreadful sorry, Clementine."

FIVE

Cain: Give—
Give way!—thy God loves blood!—then look to it:—
*Give way, ere he hath **more**!*
- Lord Byron, *Cain; A Mystery (1821)*

E dwin stood by the well with James and Patrick. There were
buckets, barrels and bottles of blood all around the well,
even crates that could hold liquid sat filled to their edges.
The liquid had every hue of red, from bright thin stuff to dark and
muddy, some was even black. In places, it sat like a gelatinous
film, coagulating and drying as everyone worked. The stuff
jiggled from the tremors.

James stared into the woods.

Patrick paced. The leaves below his feet crunched softly,
adding to the shaking splash of the blood. *Marcus?* he thought.

Edwin went to James. "Are you ok?"

The younger boy looked up and gave a weak smile. "Yes."

"What's wrong?" Edwin pushed.

"I'm ok, Ned."

It was obvious to Edwin that he wasn't. He realized that
he'd yelled at him for complaining and the little boy was trying
not to continue. "It's ok to tell me what's wrong, Jim." He sighed
and his eyebrows scrunched as he tried not to pout. "The ground
keeps shaking, Ned and it's making my stomach queasy."

"Oh." Edwin stopped to think. "Yeah, that is a strange
feeling." He looked back into the square, which was only a short
walk away. "Why don't you go lie down in the inn?" he told the
boy.

"Do you think it would make me feel better?"

"I think so." Edwin smiled. He stood up and offered the
boy his hand. The earth began to shake harder. Edwin looked at
Patrick, who didn't even seem to notice. Edwin reached down
and helped James to his feet, "Let's move!"

They ran down the road as the earthquake worsened. The
ground cracked and rumbled. The cobblestones began to separate

from the mortar and they heard the glass in windows breaking around them.

A woman screamed in the distance.

The soldiers around the square jumped out of their trenches. The grass began to collapse into darkness. The large tree that reached toward the inn suddenly disappeared into the ground. The noise was unbearable. Shots were fired and Glenn ran out of the inn with Genevieve. Jared sat still, listening to the earthquake and Miss Allen watched out the cracking windows. "Maybe Hell has come to claim its town."

The ground shook and one of the smaller buildings began to crumble alongside the police station, which had caught flame. Their footsteps were quick but unsure and Edwin tried to make sense of the ground disappearing from under them. They ran faster. "Get ahead of me, Jim!" he cried, looking back for Patrick, who had not followed. They made their way toward the square, but it was disappearing.

Edwin grabbed James by the collar of his coat and his foot went out just as the ground disappeared from under him. Edwin pulled him back, collapsing on the shifty cobblestone as they watched half of the town square become a descending gorge that coughed up smoke and massive plumes of dust.

From the window of the inn, Bernadette Allen watched fire rise up from the chasm. "It is hell." She grabbed her scattergun and moved toward the door.

Soldiers ran in every direction. "Head count!" One man yelled and from the bell tower, Spencer tried to keep the bell from making any noise. "Stuart's gone, sir." Another yelled across the hole. "Wilson, Robertson, Emery and Gillespie. All gone!"

The ground settled and there was an eerie quiet.

Then the chatter of voices filled the way. "What was that?"

"Protect the bell tower!"

"McElroy, Wells, Cook and Karales were in trench two! They're all gone!"

There was weeping from a distance and unintelligible screaming followed by the sound of hissing.

"I can hear them!"

"Take new positions!"

"Get cover!"

Edwin pulled James to his feet and looked over into the chasm. A soldier at almost one hundred yards away, across the great hole, tossed a lantern over the edge to see its depth in the darkness. It disappeared into the abyss. They didn't even hear it hit the bottom.

"I remember who I am," came Patrick's voice. "You wanna know, Edwin?" He giggled maniacally. "I killed them all."

"Patrick? Are you ok?"

"My name isn't Patrick," he stammered, taking a step forward. "My name is Marcus Shields."

"Like Mistress Shields, the old Headmistress?" Edwin asked.

"Yeah," he replied. "She was my Mother."

Edwin felt a crushing sensation in his heart for Patrick. He must have just been remembering his mother passing away.

"I killed her." He smiled.

"What?" Edwin stopped him. "No. The Vampyres got her."

"No." His smile grew into laughter. "The sheriff saw me kill her in the street and then followed me home, where I killed my dad."

"But why?"

"I don't know." He laughed. "Boredom? So the old sheriff put me in there with you all. Honestly, I should have stayed on the train and killed them all. That would have been fun." His voice squeaked with maniacal excitement. "Instead, I have you, Edwin."

He ran at Edwin with both hands.

Edwin froze as Patrick loomed over him.

James acted quickly and pushed Edwin out of the way, taking the brunt force of the large boy's weight and disappearing into the darkness of the looming gap. Edwin fell across the cobblestones with a thud.

Patrick turned on him, but Edwin had already pulled a gun from his belt. "Why?" Edwin searched for an answer.

"Because it's fun, Edwin. Now," he grinned, "it's your turn."

Soldiers came running to see what was happening.

"I," Edwin stuttered, "I'll kill you, Patrick." Tears began streaming down his face.

"No, you won't, Ned," Patrick corrected. "Because you're a *good* boy. You'll never do it."

The blast of gunfire was blinding and deafening. Patrick looked surprised, then his eyes were vacant. He fell to his knees in front of Edwin, who looked past him and saw Spencer pulling back his rifle from the bell tower.

The sudden disgust and horror overwhelmed Edwin and he threw the gun to the ground. "Let's go!" A booming soldier's voice shook him.

Soldiers were running in every direction and the sound of the Vampyres grew. "They're here!" Jared cried and he came barreling between men and picked up Edwin from the ground. "Move! Everyone get to your posts!"

As he was dragged away, Edwin wept. *James! I'm sorry, Jim.*

H oratio Cornwall was not a spiritual man but he prayed, firing shots into the dark. The unearthly screeching of hurt Vampyres filled the air. "Our Father, which art in heaven. Hallow-ed be thy..." he pulled the trigger, "name."

The word had spread throughout Breton that if a person prayed with a sincere heart, the bullet would do some damage to the seemingly invincible Vampyres. Some men had even gone as far as filling up small cups for holy water. They would ordain men, who would pray over cups as they dropped bullets into them.

"Thy kingdom come." Cornwall prayed with a rosary wrapped around his knuckles. He'd already pulled the thing off of a dead body and despite it not doing any good for that person, he hoped it would help. "Thy will," *bang*, "be done," *bang*, "on Earth as it is in," *bang*, "Heaven."

The first wave of Vampyres that came up each night would search and scour the town. When it was clear and dark they would ring the bell, usually around midnight, to let the rest of the Vampyres know it was clear. Spencer explained that this safety measure went on every night. If their new small army planned to succeed, they would have to hold the tower.

The bodies of the Vampyres were piling up. The symbols of the church had a great deal of power over the Vampyres. One of them crawled toward Sergeant Cornwall and he aimed the gun down on its head, where it began whimpering. The gun clicked empty and immediately the creature snickered.

The pot-bellied old soldier jumped onto the creature and pressed the rosary into its face. The skin boiled with smoke and it screamed and screeched at him until blood burst from its face.

He could hear something from above him. "Sergeant!" the distant voice called. It was Mister Mayhew, who kept firing down into the Vampyres that were closing in on Cornwall's position. It was too late. They had overcome him and the small Vampyres bit into the big soldier as he let out a horrible scream. Spencer shot among them and they dispersed. There lay the body, alone, surrounded by the Vampyres that he'd killed.

The survivors were retreating.

S ir!" A soldier came running to the inn. Jared was scrambling to organize reinforcements with Colonel Blagburn when he heard the summons. They kept their heads down as bullets crashed into the stone walls. Vampyres threw objects through the windows.

"There are people coming up from the ground!"

Jared angrily put his face in his hands, gritting his teeth in frustration before answering. *What more could be happening?* "People?" he asked calmly through his teeth.

"Out of the hole, sir." He waved toward the door. "They are coming up from the darkness."

Blagburn raised an eyebrow. Jared stood up and bit his lip.

"I'll hold it all down from here." Blagburn quipped.

"The hell you will, Blagburn." Jared stood up, wincing. He massaged his shoulder and then pointed to a soldier and directed him as he walked. "Make sure we have reinforcements near the church and send a group from the alley behind this building to the hole in the square. Whatever is coming up from inside there, you aim to put them back!" He grabbed a gun from the stack of guns near the door and he ran out into the night.

The cart that had been the barrier for the inn had caught fire and two soldiers tried to extinguish it, but the loud crack of a gun resonated around them. Miss Allen fired off another shell and watched a man running toward the cart collapse, screaming as his shoulder exploded. Her face was calm and cold.

She reloaded.

As Jared approached the edge of the chasm, he found Genevieve holding a young girl, who was moaning in pain. Her eyes were yellowed and she shivered violently.

"Moira," Genevieve pleaded, "you have to tell me."

The girl struggled to keep her eyes open.

Jared raised the gun on them, but Genevieve waved him down.

"Moira. That is your name, yes? You said 'Moira.' Who saved you?"

"Saved us." Moira repeated again. The climb from the depths had been grueling and Genevieve sensed the girl was going limp.

Jared stepped forward, but he didn't lower the gun.

"Who?" Genevieve yelled. She shook the girl. "Who saved you?"

"Elliott." She muttered, drifting out of consciousness.

Genevieve's jaw became slack and she let out a breath, looking at Jared, who lowered his gun.

Jared looked down into the hole. "Elliott did all that?" He could not tell if Genevieve was frowning or smiling. The girl's eyes glistened with tears.

As she lifted the unconscious girl from the ground, she whispered, "I have no doubt in my mind he did."

People of every race were crawling out of the hole. From the bell tower, Spencer Mayhew noted that there was something very wrong. *Must be Druids,* he thought. *No way they could climb out of that hole otherwise. Fiends even. On a bad day, maybe.* He knew very little of demons, outside of Vampyres, but he had read some of Algernon's articles. It had all been theory until he watched them making their way out of the void.

The bright orange flicker of burning buildings began to illuminate the depth of the abyss and he knew no normal being would be able to climb out alone, yet they emerged, exhausted and unassuming. *Better them than vamps, reckon.* As he looked down into the void, quietly his heart sank. *Al, you fool.*

The ground had stopped shaking altogether, but along the side of the giant sinkhole, a building collapsed with an incredible sound. It threw up smoke and crumbled. Soldiers surrounded it when another building fell near it. They were imploding, collapsing into themselves. They pointed their guns at the buildings and yelled incoherently over the noise, trying to make sense of it.

After a moment, Spencer saw something moving around in the rubble. One man crawled across a collapsed wall to help whatever it was, but all Spencer could see was the man falling limp. The soldiers began firing down on it.

It rose from the rubble, taller than all the men, who continued firing into it. "A Golem!" he breathed. *There's no way bullets will stop that thing if it's what I think it is. Al, did you find a Golem?*

E dwin! Snap out of it!" Marie, the barmaid yelled.
    "He just pushed him." Edwin's voice was flat and catatonic. "Jim is gone."

"We're all going to be gone if you don't finish this," she pleaded.

"But..." He stared out the window. "I'm..." His jaw quivered from crying. "I'm just a kid."

"Shut up!" Marie scolded. "How are you going to do this to us all?"

He looked at her, but he still seemed distant.

"You told us to fight." She squeezed both of his arms, begging. "A kid told us to fight like this. Two entire armies out there because of a kid. Your idea, remember? You couldn't save everyone, but we have a fighting chance. You have to get back out there and finish this."

He swallowed. He wanted to throw up. The pain in his stomach, the aching and panic rose as bile into his throat as he worked his way to his feet in the inn.

I guess I'm gonna die. He thought. *Maybe I'll see you soon, James.*

His eyes were a glare and he wiped his tears on his sleeve. "I'll need some help."

Genevieve dripped water from a cupped hand into the girl's mouth after laying her behind the bar in the inn.

"I don't trust it!" Jared yelled across the room.

"I'm not asking your trust, am I?" she replied coldly.

Jared heaved a breath and aimed his rifle between two planks across the window, "Someone find me Glenn Lamphere!" he instructed. The sound of the rifle firing filled the room.

The girl jerked from unconsciousness. "Don't hurt the rock people."

"Rock people?" Genevieve asked, confused. "You are dreaming." She comforted the girl.

Jared ran to the bar. "Did she say rock people?" Genevieve looked up. "Yes?"

"I knew she couldn't be trusted," he hissed. "She's one of them!" He turned the rifle on her.

Genevieve raised a hand and threw herself across the girl. "Stop!" she cried at him.

"Jen, get out of the way, or I will kill you both."

Genevieve did not take the threat well. "Jared," she fumed. "Walk away, right now."

"They're out there destroying everything!" He pointed, wincing with the pain of his arm.

The blood was dark and the stain had begun to crust around his shoulder.

"Save them," Moira whispered. "Cursed."

Genevieve looked down at her. Her eyes were open. "How?" she demanded. "How do we save them?"

The sharp part of the axe blade did nothing for Glenn. Chopping into men with it felt cheap. He reversed itm using it like a rounded sledgehammer. The bodies of Vampyres and men lay crushed behind him. He swung into the chest cavity of a man who charged with a rifle's bayonet stretched out before him.

The sound of the man's bones cracking was quite satisfying. He crunched under the weight of the swing and the rifle fell with a docile click to the ground. The man heaved and grabbed his chest, suffocating as he grasped at the ground, crawling. Glenn brought the axe down, smashing his head in a red splash as teeth and fragments exploded.

He looked around and heard nothing but the crackle of the burning wood along the wall next to him. He breathed heavily, embracing his rage, looking for his next victim.

After that last tremor," Corporal Vogt contemplated aloud as the small group ran from the square, "is there any way it hasn't all spilled?" Like many of the other soldiers, she was covered in darkening blood.

"We won't know until we get there, sir." Edwin replied.

The group ran along the cracked cobblestone, staying close to the walls and signaling to each other to move ahead one block at a time until they came up to the place where all the blood containers sat. Some vessels along the edges had spilled, but somehow the tremors had done little to them.

Edwin began smiling uncontrollably. "It's still possible."

Vogt called the men to stop. Of the six soldiers that had followed, only two carried lanterns. Vogt signaled for them to move forward slowly. "Something's not right," she whispered.

Edwin looked around but didn't see anything. The light of the lanterns reflected in the dark blood in each container. The blood looked like a fragmented red ocean spreading out into the dark in front of them. The soldiers moved forward. Edwin waited anxiously. They heard gunfire and yelling off in the distance. The sound of crickets and chirping came from nearer along the quiet forest. Right ahead of them, they could hear splashing. One soldier stepped forward and the light of the lantern blanketed an impish creature with its head submerged in a bucket of blood.

"Take your shot!" Vogt cried, raising her long weapon. A loud round fired. The guns illuminated the edge of the forest with fire and smoke. The Vampyre hissed from a tree and quickly jumped, screaming, "Guilty!" in a shrill inhuman voice.

Silence followed. The men aimed their guns into the darkness. "Is it gone?" one asked.

Vogt knew better. She laid her rifle down on the ground and pulled a long knife from her belt. She stepped gingerly into the darkness and waited.

"Sir?" one man asked, staring off into the dark, waiting on the creature to reappear. He jerked as he saw it move in the distance between two trees. The light from the lantern moved with him and danced, casting dizzying shadows behind the trees.

They heard Vogt's scream, a screeching high register and the hiss of the creature as it came down on her. The men turned with their lanterns and rifles to find Vogt pinned down by the small creature. The soldiers opened fire, but it did nothing. Vogt plunged her knife into its neck over and over but the creature clawed and slashed at her, letting out a shrill scream. The creature forced itself down on Vogt and bit into her face. She began twitching and the knife stayed in the creature's neck. The men continued to fire, yelling to each other.

Edwin saw his chance. He was enraged. He knew what to do. He pushed through the reloading soldiers. He closed his eyes as it turned its hideous face toward him, its mouth full of red teeth, drooling. He jumped. It caught the brunt of his weight and exploded into wet ash and dark blood. Its bones scattered along the dark forest floor.

"What was that?" one man yelled.

Edwin pulled himself from the ground, shaking and covered in entrails. After an uncomfortable moment, listening to Sara Vogt curse and scream in pain, he spoke. "It's called faith," he replied quietly and with terrible disdain.

For the rest of their time there, Edwin was quiet. His hands shook and he didn't make eye contact with the soldiers. They didn't speak to him. They began his "grand rouse," pouring blood down the well, where he knew the Vampyres would appear. The blood disappeared into the darkness but the splashing echoed.

Edwin thought it was loud like a waterfall or one of the fast-moving streams outside of Breton.

Men poured the blood in a trail into town while he and one other soldier let the cold red liquid splash and stain the walls of the well. Edwin was stained up to his elbows in it and he looked like a wet dog with matted hair. He looked and felt awful.

The soldiers carried Vogt, who was screaming in agony, back toward town. "It took my eye! The bastard took my eye!"

Soldiers were leading the new "refugees" to the train station. The people who had crawled out of the abysmal chasm all seemed catatonic, quiet, in shock.

They heard the heavy door of the train station being pulled shut.

"From one prison to another, it would seem," an older, wrinkled woman noted as she wrapped a dingy shawl across her shoulder. Her calloused hands were abnormally large for her small frame and she shook as she pulled the shawl tight.

"Hush, Mother," a young girl scolded. "How can you say that? They're fighting the Vampyres. Just like the young man who came to rescue us."

"What's that smell?" a short, bald man barked. "We might as well have stayed down there."

"You believe that, Darryn?" another man asked.

Their voices grew and echoed throughout the station, bitter and darting, but lacking any real energy.

Soldiers continued to escort more of them in. Some were pushed, others moved at gunpoint. The room filled with people. Some sat in pews but for the most part, everyone sat in a large circle around the decaying bodies that lay on the floor. No one was surprised. No one even seemed disgusted. For the most part, they were largely unresponsive.

"I say we fight them all." One haggard man smiled a toothless grin, licking his dry, broken lips as he adjusted his battered sackcloth coat.

"Just like a Fiend to say that." The fat bald man rolled his eyes.

"Fiend," the haggard one scoffed. "Right, you all just lie down. All you leafbeards do is quit; that's why we're in this situation in the first place. That's alright by me." He stood up and looked for the door.

"Leafbeard." The bald man laughed. "You caged rats will always fight. Go find your fight. As for the rest of us, we'll stay alive."

The door to the station swung open again. It was just two girls. The bald man saw them and called out, "Moira!"

"More twig-eaters," a sick-looking man grumbled, rolling his eyes.

"The Vampyres are coming." Moira looked to Genevieve, who stood behind her with a shotgun in hand. She scanned the room carefully with the gun.

"Coming?" the bald man asked.

"These people are at war with them." She stepped forward. "And they need our help."

The haggard man grinned. Something was calling to him. "Yes," he began to mutter. "A good fight. No more cages."

Genevieve spoke up in a monotone. "We are asking anyone that is willing to side with us to take up arms against the Vampyres."

"They did this to us," Moira continued. "We can fight back now."

The bald man stood up. "But they won't find us in here." He turned to the crowd of huddled people. "If we make it to morning, we can be on our way."

"You stay right 'ere then old timer." The haggard man smiled, standing up. "Just like a twig-eater to give up before the fight 'as started."

Moira called across the station to the man. "Hey!"

He looked at her squarely.

"We won't be havin' that now will we?" She massaged her hand.

"No ma'am," the haggard man conceded, looking at his bare feet.

"We're all in this together. Those that are coming with us, there are guns and bread for you." Then she spoke louder. "As for those of you who choose to stay—good luck and I hope to see you in the morning."

She walked out into the night as men and women began standing to follow her.

Fiends, the bald man thought. *Always chasing a fight.*

I sn't there supposed to be a war goin'?" Blagburn spoke angrily. "Why is it so quiet?"

A group of soldiers were beating an elderly gentleman on the other side of the chasm, but Blagburn didn't notice. He ducked when a gun was fired near his head. The men dispersed as a window near them exploded from the bullet. Blagburn cringed.

"Mister Jared," he announced. "Is that entirely necessary?" He wrung his ear out with a finger.

"Colonel," Jared replied calmly, lowering his weapon, "this moment of reprieve will be short lived. I believe that the old man Gallegos is right. Vampyres do not trust their senses as we do. They will not appear until a clear signal is given to them and that bell there is the only thing that will do it."

"Yes, yes," Blagburn replied. "They don't value time as we do. I understand what the old man was saying, I am just anxious at the whole matter."

A large group of people were walking toward them. Genevieve led them toward the inn. "Where's your friend?" Jared asked.

"Moira?"

"Yes, that one."

Genevieve smiled. "She's gathering more fighters."

Blagburn and Jared shared a look of puzzled amusement.

Glenn emerged from the alley holding a bloody axe and he approached the men, pointing nervously further down the street. He was covered in blood. Jared turned to him. "Where have you ...?"

"That's Desmond's cart," he announced.

"Who?" Blagburn asked.

Glenn pushed between them and walked toward the carriage. The axe slid down in his hand slowly as the carriage came to a halt. His footfall seemed to spook the horses a bit as he moved around to the door.

It swung open gingerly and he raised the axe.

The young, fraudulent Vampyre hunter stepped out with his eye on Glenn. "I wouldn't do that, sir." His tone chilled Glenn. He straightened his coat and stepped aside to allow his companion to exit the carriage.

A frail-looking, beautiful creature stepped out of the black carriage lightly. He wore a long black coat and gray slacks. He was redheaded and had freckles across his nose, giving him an innocent, childlike look. His eyes were a piercing, bright blue that hazed over with a smoky whiteness. He was otherworldly and horrifying, yet docile with a quirky smile. *Good evening Mister Innkeep.*

"Where's Desmond?" Glenn muttered. He looked inside the empty carriage.

That's quite rude, don't you think Jasper?

"Yes. Quite, sir," Jasper answered quietly.

But to answer your question, Innkeep. He is dead. He looked into the trees. *A certain boring Vampyre, who shall go unnamed, went about killing all willy-nilly and now I am with a new carriage and new friends. Isn't it marvelous?* He smiled at Glenn, whose eyes darted, trying to make sense of it all. He had just seen Jared speaking to the rebel Vampyre.

Ruthven stepped forward to him. *I am quite sorry about the death of your daughter.* He put his hand on Glenn's blood-soaked arm. *No parent should ever have to experience the tragedy of outliving a child.*

Glenn felt an odd chill. "Thank you." His voice fell to a whisper.

Jasper began walking away briskly before making a break for the alley. Glenn turned around to see soldiers running his way.

Your indignation is right. Dare I say righteous? I appreciate that, sir. So you are allowed a moment. Ruthven's voice was in his head despite the deafening sound of the gunfire. He fell to the ground and covered his head. The wood on the carriage burst into splinters and a horse collapsed dead next to him. Another horse panicked, pulling the cart forward. Glenn clenched his eyes shut.

The Vampyre disappeared in a mist.

From a rooftop perch above a dilapidated and abandoned old saloon, Khalil Sayid watched the soldiers running to-and-fro. The rot of death was in the air.

"How's the view, Monsieur Chandler?" Came a familiar voice.

"Ah! Professor Morillo," Khalil chuckled, never turning from the view below, "you startled me. I was starting to believe, that for once, I wouldn't be seeing you before this final night of horrors."

"Final, you say?" Gallegos asked as he plucked a cigarette from his pocket.

"How often are we going to meet like this?" Khalil asked.

"On the precipice of the end of the world."

"Or a Tuesday for either of us."

Gallegos sat on the roof and struck a match to light his cigarette. "I would have visited sooner, had I known that Monsieur Chandler was your new *sobrenombre*."

"The Alliance gave that one to me."

Gallegos nodded. "So you've picked a side?"

"It's always about sides with you."

"Isn't it?"

Khalil turned around and faced the old wizard. He held out a hand.

"What?" Gallegos asked.

"Candy. What do you have?"

Gallegos furrowed his brow. "I haven't seen you in what, forty years? And you think I have candy in my pocket."

"I know you do."

Gallegos grunted and reached into his pocket. He handed a handful of toffees and caramels to Khalil, who sat down next to him on the roof.

"Perhaps a game of chance? I have some dice."

Gallegos shook his head with a sardonic smile. "So you met my friend, the circus boy."

"Ah yes, Jasper." Khalil Sayid smiled. "He stole your name. Names matter, old man."

Gallegos raised an eyebrow of disappointed disbelief. "You were helping him."

"I suppose you could say that," Sayid replied. "I was helping him help me."

"And to what end?"

"To see Adler killed." He smiled. "I was tired of him."

"You'll never change, will you, Khalil?"

"Change?" the younger man asked. "How long, Alonzo, have you been a forty-eight- year-old retired professor now?"

He let out a hmph filled with smoke before answering.

"From Tripoli to Canada... I know you," Khalil prodded. "I know you down to the days."

"Four hundred years, this year," he answered, pensively. "Four hundred years since the day I was pushed out of a window in the university and broke my neck. My first encounter with a Vampyre as well."

Khalil laughed. "I turned one hundred and sixty last week. Not including the forty eight *productive* years before that."

"You don't look a day over eighty." Gallegos laughed.

Khalil raised his hand. "Shh."

"It's always gonna be this isn't it?" Gallegos whispered. Both men stood.

"Scout?" Gallegos asked.

Khalil nodded.

Gentlemen. A Vampyre's voice echoed in their minds. It was a deceptively young voice. The body that appeared on the edge of the roof was that a teenage boy.

"How can we help you, Vampyre?" Khalil asked.

Help? The Vampyre laughed. *Look at the mess down there.*

"Well, as you can see, we're just two old men up here staying out of it." Gallegos said as he tossed the cigarette onto the roof and crushed it with the toe of his boot.

I could just have a quick snack before I go back and tell Isaac about what's going on up here.

Gallegos crossed his arms.

Khalil shook his head. "I'm sorry, *mon ami*, but you won't be going anywhere."

The Vampyre's eyes flashed white hot as it jumped forward at the man's threat.

Gallegos let out a sigh and a prayer and the Vampyre collapsed to its knees just feet in front of the two men.

Khalil Sayid kneeled next to the Vampyre who grunted with agony. "My acquaintance here has killed more Vampyres than any man alive or dead."

Gallegos laughed. "Well, I'm not the one who almost ended the Sin Eaters single-handedly."

Khalil looked up. "Those were different times."

The Vampyre looked up into his eyes.

Khalil looked away. "No, I don't want your testimony. You can die with it for all I care."

Gallegos stepped forward. "You can make a choice here, *Vampiro.*

The Vampyre looked up at him.

"We're just two men having a conversation. You can go and be free."

The Vampyre nodded its head vigorously.

Gallegos waved it away.

The Vampyre stood with a hand to its chest. The fear in its eyes glowed like a pale white light. It took a step backward.

"You can just go." Gallegos repeated.

Khalil made a sound in his throat and wiped his brow.

The Vampyre took another step backward.

"You know, we're past that tonight."

The Vampyre locked eyes with him. *I won't tell anyone.*

Khalil shook his eye with a grimace. *You made a mistake, Vampyre.*

It hissed.

He twisted.

It jumped toward him.

Khalil plunged the blade of the Apache into its chest, sending the Vampyre over the edge of the roof. The Vampyre thudded against the cobblestones below.

"You could have let it go." Gallegos said.

"Not tonight." Khalil sighed. "Now, I'm going to have to go down there and get my gun."

Gallegos shook his head.

Khalil gathered his belongings on the roof. "We still don't know why, do we Alonzo? What are we, if anything other than immortals?"

Gallegos was tempted to jump into a lecture, but he knew the other man needed to talk so with a sigh, he let Khalil continue.

"And if immortal, then why not gods? What's the purpose of all of this? Why so painfully human, still alone, still crazy?"

"I am not crazy," Gallegos cut in.

"Well, I am. That's what they tell me." He paused and let out a soft breath. "We are not as the bastard Nephilim, yet we are not as men."

Gallegos just nodded in agreement.

"So what are we?"

"Relics." Gallegos smiled.

"Why did you come here, Gallegos?" he asked very suddenly.

"A man can't come visit with an old friend?"

Khalil looked over the edge of the roof. "We share a kinship, old man, but we will never be friends."

Gallegos sighed. He knew how the conversation would continue. "Why are you here, Sayid? Isn't this messy thing below you? How long have you been here now? Five, ten years?"

There was silence.

"You were here from the onset?"

There was a hint of guilt in his eyes. "I followed Adler. But after a time, he irritated me and I had the boy help me, thinking that if I could get Adler killed, then the Lords would send someone else."

"But you don't have to be here." Gallegos pleaded. "You could be a spy, a socialite in San Francisco or Prague. A man who cannot die can live as anything he wants. Especially one with your particular *skills*."

"So you chose to be an ostracized 'professor?' No. There is no life for me - or you for that matter."

"What happened to you?" Gallegos had known the man for years after his attempted suicide in seventeen thirty nine. As a Barbary assassin, he had a particular way of "killing" himself after he eliminated his targets that brought him some infamy. From Morocco to Tripoli, he was known as "the Ghost's Dagger" and "Allah's Wrath." It had been over a hundred and forty years since Khalil had found Gallegos, looking for answers and finding nothing but frustrations with the man. "I am here to make a change. You should join us."

He changed the subject. "Did you know that I took piano lessons for two years?"

"I did not," Gallegos answered. He lit another cigarette. The sounds of battle were beginning somewhere below. Guns fired and explosions were followed by the screaming voices of people in the distance.

"In Belfast. She was married. But young and beautiful. I am quite good now." There was a glint of a smile in his eye.

"Ok, Khalil, tell me about her," he muttered into a cloud of white smoke.

He looked at Gallegos squarely and without blinking, Khalil admitted, "I murdered her husband in the street. Blamed thugs. She 'couldn't live without him,' she'd said. She was in the river that night. Dead. Suicide. Real shame, to be honest."

Gallegos never ceased to be surprised by the stark madness of the Berber madman.

"There are no lovers for us, old man." He smiled. "There is no caress. They change yet we do not. No. I haven't changed at all. Not in that way."

"Then why here? Why work for Adler? Why let the Lords control you?" Gallegos asked him as he put the cigarette butt out in the wood of the table. "Between us, we could kill all the Vampyres in existence and be done with them."

"It's not that simple." Khalil said. "I've spent the last thirty-something years living the life of Ives-Henri Chandler, train station manager. It was a life. It was a reprieve. Even your friend, Moreau spent time here. We all need it. Even demon hunters rest."

Gallegos raised an eyebrow. "Considering that Jean-Pierre Moreau has been in Paris these last years, I don't know how that could have been."

"What do you mean?"

"Moreau has never been here." Gallegos said. "Whoever raised that lovely young woman and lived in this strange place, he was not the real Moreau."

Khalil gave the old man a sidelong glance and sighed.

"I doubt anyone down there is who they claim to be. I'm afraid nothing has been as it seems, even to us who know the underbelly of it all."

"More Alliance trickery?" Khalil asked, disappointed in himself for not seeing through it.

"I worry that our mutual friend, the Operator, has gotten involved."

"I was hoping we could get out of this conversation without you bring him up again."

"I know." Gallegos said.

"By the end of this, he's going to have us walking into hell itself." Khalil said.

"That's why I'm here, Khalil." Gallegos said. "Come back with me. We will confront the Operator together."

"No. That's not my path. I am no longer that man. They got in here, Alonzo." He pointed to his head. "They tortured me for years. I have no idea how long. It had to have been at least ten, twenty years. The physical pain was one thing; they had me beheaded once, quite unpleasant really. But the mental torture...I feel much older than I am."

"Join us, Khalil. We can fight back."

"I can't. I already did my part. I helped the one Vampyre rescue the children. That was enough. I am no one's soldier anymore." He whispered, "For now, I will take pleasure in death. The only thing that is missing from my life, I now give to others. Once I go down and get my blade out of that Vampyre's chest, that is." Khalil turned for the door. "After centuries, you've seen this night a thousands times." He paused. "You must have found a pattern." Khalil eyed the Spaniard. "What do you do?"

Alonzo Gallegos laughed. "Usually, I decide which side I think should win and offer them some advice." The old man cast his gaze to the roof tiles. "Then I go hide. Death hurts," he chuckled.

Khalil Sayid shook his head. "Not me," he said. "I die every time."

Freedom," Moira whispered to the large Golem.
　　　The cursed creature pointed a finger toward its chest with the delicacy of gravel.

"Yes. Free like me." Moira whispered. "Now, we kill those Vampyres."

The Golem rattled with anger. Its boulder of a fist crashed again harder into its chest, spraying dust.

From across the way, Blagburn noted to Edwin. "That can't be a good thing, can it?"

"Any help we can get, sir," he replied.

"Yeah. I suppose so." The large, obsidian-eyed rock man made him uneasy.

"You're a good man," Moira whispered to the Golem.

Soldiers kept their distance from the girl and the huge creature. They kept their guns pointed at shadows, alleyways and at the trees. There were at least two Vampyres out there that they knew of and more were coming. Some men worked in the old church, where Spencer watched for Vampyres in the tower. Jared stiffly handed out weapons from crates that lay in a row at the alley door of the Crow's Nest. There were familiar faces among the men taking weapons, but Jared was sure they'd disappeared long ago on the battlefield.

Genevieve brought him a piece of bread. "You look like you've seen a ghost."

He said nothing, but he looked at her with wide eyes.

"Follow me," she instructed.

Jared called a soldier over to continue the work.

Genevieve bounded up the stairs and Jared followed her while gnawing on the hard bread. In the hallway of the second floor, she started talking. "Those men out there — they were your soldiers weren't they?"

With a mouthful of bread, he replied, "Yeah, a lot of them. Some were dead." He swallowed. "How could you know that?"

"Moira told me." She answered without looking back. She ran to the end of the hallway and looked out the window. When he caught up to her, Jared looked out to see the pretty girl talking to a group of soldiers as the large rock creature followed her. "She's a 'Druid.'"

Jared was quiet.

"They are like the Vampyres. Ancient things."

"Why did you bring me up here for this?"

Genevieve's eyes lit up and she turned around to look at him. "Follow me." She opened the final door in the hallway, which had been Desmond Burroughs's room. "I've lived here my whole life. Lived in fear of Vampyres. What I should have feared were men like Desmond."

Jared entered Desmond's room. It was a war room and the soldier in him recognized immediately the import of the space. Maps and diagrams lay strewn across the table and on the walls. Aside from the map of Breton, with the extensive and detailed drawings of complex tunneling systems.

"I knew it!" Genevieve said. "It is a grid." Her voice trailed off as she fell into thoughts of Algernon, whom she had not seen in days. Amidst the panic of it all, her heart sank.

Jared attempted to decipher the writing on a chalkboard. A large diagram of a ten pointed star or what appeared to be an upside down star over its upright twin sat at its center, covered in near-indecipherable script in multiple languages. "Do you know how to read it?" Jared asked, turning to Genevieve, who was looking at a stack of maps.

"Get out." Glenn's stony voice startled both Jared and Genevieve.

"Glen, please..." Genevieve said but it was Jared who interrupted, "No, he's right. This is an intrusion."

Genevieve laughed. "An intrusion, Jared?"

"It's not our place," Jared stated.

"Well, Glenn here has housed the enemy for years."

"I'm sure he didn't know," Jared said.

"I can speak for myself," Glenn said, closing the door behind himself.

The room fell silent between the three as gunshots punctuated the dread outside.

"I don't know if it was my anger," Glenn said, "I don't know if it was how close I was to the Vampyres, I don't know if its because the Vampyre heart in that lantern was destroyed, but I remember things now about my life that had been washed from my memory completely, and what I remember is so harrowing, that I asked for it to be hidden from me." His eyes fell to the floor, "I did it to protect my family, to protect my wife and child.

And then I killed Zoya and lost Katarina — I mean Kat."

Genevieve and Jared backed away from the man.

"I'm not the man I was." Glenn sighed. He shrugged, "Look, I wasn't saying get out because I have anything to hide. I am telling you that knowing this," he gestured to the papers all over the room, "can only do more damage than good."

"You were one of them the whole time." Genevieve's cool tone did not go unnoticed.

Jared gave the young woman an apprehensive glance. She drew a pistol on Glenn. The old barkeep didn't even raise his hands. He laughed and shrugged, "What are you talking about? We all were. The people out there?" He pointed to the street. "The ones killing the Vampyres, the soldiers, the down-on-their-luck townsfolk? They're all in on it. Both of you were somehow in on it. We all did the work to feed that coven out there because of agreements that governments made with other governments on behalf of religious institutions as fronts for nefarious shadow agencies representing the rights of ancient peoples and entities that believe the end of the world is right around the corner."

"Why are you talking like that?" Genevieve's voice cracked as tears filled her eyes. She punctuated each word with the barrel of the gun. "You don't talk like that."

"Yeah, I guess I didn't." Glenn sighed. He sat down in a chair. "I remembered today, that I am indeed not a barkeep. I worked as a bureaucrat in eastern Europe. I also remembered that I am married to a Vampyre named Zoya, and then immediately remembered that I just murdered her in cold blood." His eyes filled with tears. "That I brought my daughter here to protect her from assassination attempts by rival Vampyre factions." He shook his head. "Can you believe that? Some Vampyre named Isaac said they'd keep my wife and daughter safe. All they had to do was make me forget all the horrible things I know."

Genevieve had watched the man run that blade through his wife's heart through the window in the tavern downstairs. He hadn't said another word about it.

"Tell us what you know." Jared said.

"Why?" Glenn asked. "Do you think it could be advantageous out there to know?"

"I think I'd like to know why I ended up here."

"Easy." Glenn smiled.

Genevieve pulled back the hammer on the pistol.

"Okay, easy." He held up a hand.

"Captain, you are in a perpetual reenactment of a civil war battle that never even occurred."

"Why?"

"Why?" Glenn mimicked, "Because you or someone you know was so terrible, so socially unacceptable that you or they attracted the attention of very powerful people, who made you into mindless Vampyre fodder." He slowly turned to Genevieve, "Either pull the trigger or put the gun away but you're making me anxious and I have a tendency to act out when I'm anxious."

Genevieve could have put a bullet in the man's chest for all the anger that was washing over her but she felt the weight of Jared's hand on the barrel. She put it down slowly.

"We're all in danger here, Glenn." Jared said.

"More than you know. My daughter is still out there. The Vampyres likely have her. It is unlikely I will ever see her again. As for us, anybody who survives tonight will be put on a train to God knows where and they put us back in the churn of all their machinations."

Jared smiled, "Then if there is no escape, we might as well understand the game we've all been conscripted into."

"It's all military for you, isn't it?" Glenn asked.

"You hear that out there? Gunfire and wailing? Sounds like war to me."

"Fine." Glenn said. "What do you want to know?" He stood and began to pace the room pointing out documents as he passed them.

"Vampyres have a tenuous relationship with the Alliance, so Breton isn't going to play out well. The Sin Eaters are going to have a rough go of it once they're faced with this debacle."

"The what eaters?" Genevieve asked.

"The Sin Eaters are the high priests of the Magistrate of the Black Court. They are the royalty of the Vampyre theocracy."

"These Sin Eaters priests — they have a god?" Genevieve asked.

"I don't know. They were pretty secretive as I remember."

Jared cut in, "But you were married to one."

"I don't remember everything and I wasn't told everything. Some things are a little fuzzy and some things I just don't know." He sighed. "Now this, I do know." Glenn let out an acid chuckle that raised the hairs on the back of Jared's neck. Glenn pointed at the ten pointed star. "As above, so below and as below, so above." He intoned with mock solemnity. "Working the miracles of the fullness of the one."

"What is that?"

"An ancient teaching." Glenn sighed. "Maligned in my opinion, but that's not my business anymore."

"But it was your business?" Genevieve asked.

"A long time ago." Glenn sighed. "How do you think I ended up married to a high class Vampyre?" The smile that crossed Glenn's face was sickly. "The Vampyres are obsessive. They collect the memories and impressions of dying Vampyres. They call it their testimony. Vamps, they don't talk— not like we do anyway. Their minds connect to each other and to other living things. They record each Vampyre's testimony, painting a picture across time."

"A picture of bloodshed?"

Glenn glared at Jared and then at Genevieve.

"I guess they're just boogeymen to you, monsters in the dark." Glenn looked at the chalkboard again. A cannonball hit a building nearby coughing dust from every joint in the room.

"The Vampyres are the result of interbreeding between early humans and beings from another world. Each of these ten points on this chalkboard represents on of those beings, some call them the Empyreans, but over time, they've evolved in the human mind. Now we call them angels, we associate them in our religions, we view them as protectors. They never were. The star is also the symbol of the Alliance, the decadent organization who liaise between the ancient surviving families of Nephilim. That Golem and that girl Moira out there, both called Druids, who are the descendants of an Empyrean called Asbél, a master of the elements."

"The Sheriff." Jared whispered.

"I don't know what you mean." Glenn said.

"The Sheriff tried to kill me. He was half ghost. He would be solid then smoke." Jared shivered at the thought of it.

316

"Shifter." Glenn shook his head. "No one knows where they came from, but some people think it was an Empyrean called Yeqon that spawned them. Then you have all those men crawling out of the ground. We just called them legionnaires— all I know about them is that they thrive in war times. People used to hunt them out during tribal battles. They were like demigods a thousand years ago. They were all the heroes of old and now they're just decadent monsters."

"So for every one of the points on this," Jared counted again, "ten-pointed star, you're going to name off some angel or monster or faction?"

"You're the one who asked." Glenn retorted. "But there are five, if we're being clear; five families of the Nephilim and before you ask, the fifth are simply called Lords but were once known as Chaldeans. No one even knows if any are still alive. They were some sort of ancient astrologers or soothsayers or something."

The inn rumbled again with the violence of cannon fire.

"So," Genevieve finally interjected, "what are we supposed to do?"

"Do?" Glenn chuckled. "I already told you, there is nothing to do, Jenny girl. We stay in here or we go out there and hopefully we see the daybreak."

"Well, I am staying alive." Jared stated determinately

"That's all well and good but you have to understand that there is no normal out there. It will always be Vampyres and Chaldeans and 'The old gods are waking' and 'the Sin-Eaters need to know where Gideon Cardozo is.' You're not going back to anything good. We belong to them now. We beat these Vampyres because it's how we stay alive and the the guys at the top let us live but make no mistake, no one is going home."

Angrily, Jared began tearing sheets of paper off the wall, collecting journals and books. "Help me find a bag."

"If I survive tonight," he glared at Glenn, "I'm getting out of here."

Why do you hide from me? Ruthven asked quietly as he nimbly and silently walked along the treetops just a few feet above the heads of the soldiers who hunted him. *Ever the hunter, Michael. I sense it in you. I, humble tragedian, am only here to serve at your mercy, if you would ever be so grateful as to let me see your face.* He smiled.

There was no response.

Michael meditated, hidden in a dark storeroom. He focused his energies into a deep quiet.

You tell me more in your silence than you do with words, Michael.

Michael did not move. The air around him stopped moving. There was silence. Even the flickering flame that burned in the studs on the other side of the walls extinguished with a deeper, quiet calm. It was void of energy.

Fine. I won't pretend that I am not quite insulted, though. Ruthven pouted. *I suppose we'll do things the right hard way, now won't we?*

He stepped down out of the treeline to the thundering round of gunfire that fell flat around him.

I wish you lot would stop that. It's quite a nuisance. He turned to where he'd come down and looked at the mess around him. *Did one of you shoot that horse?* he asked in odd bemusement. There were soldiers all around him. They stood quietly with their guns still pointed at him.

No, you did not miss me, so do not shoot again. His eyes flared. *Who shot the horse?* he asked. *Who does that?*

Suddenly a man in one group of soldiers dropped dead, grasping his throat as his eyes bulged in his skull. The men around him dispersed in fear. Men began running in every direction.

From the inn, Blagburn observed, "This should get quite colorful."

Ah. That wasn't so hard was it? Lord Ruthven smiled. *Some hiss and cry, 'Guilty!' I simply wait. And it jumps from your chest, the silent confession.* He watched everyone running. *Where are you all going?* He laughed. With a finger he pointed, watching men collapse, some exploded in a red, bloody mist while others just began bleeding from the orifices of their faces. A wicked grin grew slowly across Ruthven's face. *Oh, now this is much more fun.* He leaned in and reached out to a group of men. *Know my voice. My voice is your own.* Within an instant, they were fighting and stabbing each other. He breathed chaos.

From a shadow in the alley, Khalil Sayid watched Jasper Markov run past him. "You're a real coward, you know that?" Sayid said as he passed.

Markov slowed and cast his eyes at the ground. "You don't know what that thing is."

Sayid turned and looked at the Vampyre, inches above the cobblestone street, making his way toward the inn. "Yes, I do." He could hear the clatter of a rifle and the crushing sound of stone tumbling past him. A young woman fired a rifle at the Vampyre.

Oh, finally. Ruthven turned to her, unharmed and with a flick of his wrist knocked her back. *A Druid and her pet rock.*

The Golem continued forward with a grunt, but Ruthven smiled as he lowered himself to the ground, allowing his bare feet to touch the cold cobblestone. As the Golem neared him, Ruthven's eyes opened wide and the large rock-beast began losing traction. Pebbles and stones began chipping away. It let out a horrid, guttural groan. Ruthven focused his attention on the Golem and with his mind, pushed against the force of the monstrosity. With a cold gaze, Ruthven stopped the lumbering thing all together.

"Where is Michael?" Jared screamed. He looked at the clock on the wall in the inn. "This cannot work if there is anything like that out there!"

Moira tried to pick herself up, but the world around her was going black.

Sayid sighed and walked forward.

Ruthven tossed the large Golem like a small toy into the abyss where it went crashing with a terrible noise. *Ah, Sayid! My old friend.* Ruthven smiled with open arms. *I would say I'd missed you, but I'd be lying.*

"I've thought on this day since we locked you away."

Oh, I'm sure you have, Ruthven retorted with a twisted pout. *A killer, a murdering psychopath wandering the world, while I am taken away from my children—*

"Enough," Sayid interrupted. "I heard it last time and I'm no more interested now than I was then."

Ruthven showed his teeth. *But you'll hear me this time.* He stepped up to Sayid, looking quite a bit smaller and frailer than the hardy old man. Sayid swung immediately with his apache blade at the Vampyre's heart, but Ruthven continued smiling with a chilling gleam in his eye. The Vampyre stopped the weapon in the air and held it there without touching him. *This whole business of hearts is quite troubling.* He laughed. *You even stabbed yourself in the heart once to run me off.* He entered the old man's mind. *Three children, born of a concubine. She offered herself up to the covenant instead of being consumed. Someone in my covenant took that word to the Lords. Vampyres could rape, pillage, destroy and consume of the dead and living alike.*

His eyes burned. *But it was my union with a beautiful Vampyre that angered them. He and I were married, you see and looked to raise our three children happily.*

He paused as Khalil Sayid began seeing it all in front of him. *They tortured and set my children alight in the day and they staked my husband in his sleep. All for my "sin."*

Ruthven's Vampyric invaded every corner of Khalil Sayid's mind. Tears began running down Sayid's face. He collapsed to his knees, clenching his jaw; the sensations of grief and complete emptiness took his breath away, engulfed in Ruthven's decades of pain in only seconds.

Sin. Ruthven continued. *Am I really to be relegated to man's law when I am not man? I am Vampyre. Judge. Neither am I subject* to Queen Victoria nor her law. It was not my "sin" at all. It was my heart.

As far as I am concerned, Mister Sayid, I am without a heart and have been since the day I watched them kill my two youngest boys. Only my daughter lives, I believe, but even that hope is tainted with the prejudice of my fellow Lords. I am nothing now but a murderer, he smiled, *quite like you.*

A thought occurred to him in that moment. *You are quite the anomalous creature yourself, aren't you? Cursed to roam the earth, cursed to be alone, man yet no man, living yet dead, so many times over. Have you ever felt what it's like to be without a heart?*

With a single movement, Ruthven punched through the man's chest. Blood gushed over his wrist. The ribcage snapped, ventricles and vessels ripped and burst and he pulled the man's still-beating heart from his chest.

Khalil Sayid twitched and collapsed on the ground with a cold, glazed look in his eye.

Ruthven smelled his heart. *Oh my. That is disgusting. Just awful.* Ruthven stepped back as the blood puddled around his feet. With a flick of his wrist, Ruthven threw the body of Khalil Sayid into the chasm. *Good riddance to French rubbish.*

The street was silent. No one wanted to attract the attention of the Vampyre. A palpable fear spread throughout Breton.

Ruthven looked up with a perk. *You finally made it.*

"Wouldn't miss it for the end of the world," Michael replied sarcastically.

Oh goodie.

"So your friends, er, should I say, colleagues, abandoned you because of your relationship with another man?"

Ruthven straightened himself. *Yes.*

How Oscar Wilde of you. Michael smiled. *I doubt it.*

Ruthven cocked his head, confused.

No. I don't doubt your relationship, Michael told him as he stepped forward. *But I do doubt quite gravely that you were given up for it.*

You know nothing of the matter. Ruthven grinned.

The street had grown silent. People held their breath as they watched the two monsters circle each other. Jared and Blagburn quietly commanded people to move into their final positions. Genevieve ran with Edwin across the square, trying to go unnoticed. They had to get to the church.

Michael was silent.

You know nothing of the sort! Ruthven yelled as he struck Michael across the face with a bloody fist. Michael hurtled along the road from the force. Ruthven chased him with a fist that crashed into the cobblestone.

Michael vanished. He rematerialized behind him.

Ruthven sensed him and Michael sent a fist into thin air.

You are both Lord and Vampyre, Ruthven. Michael put together the pieces of the puzzle. *How many times has that happened?*

Ruthven clawed Michael across the back and disappeared again as he groaned.

Michael collapsed. *Keen and powerful. I understand that. The real question is—what threat did you pose to them?* Michael felt a foot crush his chest, sending him through Desmond's carriage. It exploded into pieces and Michael's limp body fell hard against a rock wall.

I am the most powerful Vampyre ever to have risen. Ruthven stated plainly. *They feared me. I know the names of all the Lords and the Sin Eaters and they had me captured for it. I was blind to it, caring for my children. I didn't see them coming to clean things up.*

Michael stood up. "That's a better answer."

Ruthven appeared with a wisp and Michael's fist crashed into his face with a crushing blow. Ruthven's neck snapped as his entire body flew back, caught by the explosion. He landed near the edge of the chasm and righted himself quickly.

I still know who they are, Michael. I could offer an olive branch. You're powerful too. The Sin Eaters could help you.

Michael did not answer.

No, you're right. I am just going to kill you. He smiled.

Michael leapt at him, but Ruthven stopped him in the air with a look. Michael hung in the air, inches from reaching him. *Unlike you, a simple Vampyre, I have transcended.* Ruthven gave a sheepish, child-like smile. *I am in this world and another, while you can only step through the gate of your mind to see it.* He grabbed Michael by the lapel and lifted him. *I am everything man has ever feared.* Ruthven brought a fist down, smashing Michael's skull into the ground.

Michael felt nothing; he saw nothing. He was outside of his own skin. He could only hear the voices of those around him. Some were dead. Isaac's voice, from deep in the ground. "You and I must work together, Mister Elliott." Michael felt every part of him running in different directions. He saw the blueish apparitions gathering around him. Spencer's voice from just yards away. "Time's up." Then a young girl's voice. "Get him to the train station." Cold hands were pulling at him as the apparitions came near, but he concentrated.

In the void, something pushed forward within him. *You tried, little Michael.* Michael's own voice was laughing at him. *But you weren't strong enough.* Suddenly he felt a warm tingling in his extremities. *Now, you can watch from in here.*

What...? Michael asked. *What are you?*

The laughing filled his head. The voice that flooded his thoughts was his own.

I'm you, Michael. The real you. I am Michæl and this Vampyric body belongs to me and was given to me by Ilya Constantine. You were a mistake, merely a result of his flawed method of birthing my energy into a Vampyre's body.

No! Michael willed his thoughts up that bubbled through the black tar of his nothingness.

Yes. You are quickly dying and as your light is snuffed, I will take this body with my true strength.

No. Michael said. He clung to life. He thought about Ernest, his friend. He thought about Oliver Whipple. Inevitably, he thought of Kat. "No." He said again, this time aloud. His amber eyes flashed with renewed anger.

"Not if I don't die."

Talking to ourselves, are we Michael? Ruthven chuckled.

You have no idea. Michael grunted. Ruthven was too powerful. He stood above Michael with black, perfect skin and red, flame-like hair dancing slowly, plasmatic and full of energy. There was a dark sense of surprise in Ruthven, but he tried to cover it up. His eyes were white flames in the night. Ruthven brought his fist down again, crushing Michael's skull.

"Do not fight him." The girl's voice came again. "He is far too powerful. Get to the train station."

He could sense the cold dreaming of Vampyres beyond him somewhere. He was in a dream state and standing in an empty darkness; the apparitions were gone. *Aside from me, no one has been here in thousands of years.* Ruthven's voice phased like a dancing flame. *Most would be dead already, but you are transcending into another world with me. The Empyreans came here and built the world you and I both know, alongside the world of man.*

And that's where he's wrong little Michael. Michael's own voice came. *What knows he of Empyreans?* He laughed. *I suppose they'll know soon enough. This Ruthven, he stands at the edge of the abyss and calls it home.* The thing that called itself Michæl whispered, *We are the of the abyss. I respect your will to fight, little Michael, but if you want to defeat this Ruthven, you must let me do it or we will both die.*

No. Get behind me Satan. Michael hissed. He felt like he was in free fall.

Ruthven was gone. There was no body, only a spirit that moved around like hundreds of fish made of light dancing. *So, what makes you so powerful that you wake up here with me?*

Michael was losing himself. He was drowning; the world was far above him. He focused everything within himself. Flames engulfed him, draining him of life as though the sun was burning through him, but in his pain and his rage he surpassed the world of apparitions and crashed with a fist into Ruthven's face, sending him back onto the cobblestone street.

Now, we have a challenge! Ruthven smiled with a bloody lip. *What a blessed day!*

Michael stood up and made his move away from the inn and down the cobblestone street.

Genevieve ran to Moira with Edwin. "Are you ok?" she asked.

"Vampyre," Moira sighed as she rolled over. "Where did the Vampyre go?"

Genevieve looked around. "Uh. I don't know. They ran toward the train station."

Moira tried to smile as Edwin helped her from her back, but her face hurt too much. The bell began ringing and he looked up. "Find cover."

The old adage rang in Spencer's head louder than the bell: *The darkest hour comes before the day dawns.* As the horribly loud sound rang out and shook his bones, he took up his post and watched. There was no silence; people ran around the town like mice scattering in the dark and his head throbbed and his ears rang.

He followed the trail of blood from the foot of the tower past the square and off into the darkness. He aimed the gun down the trail and adjusted himself for the worst. *They're coming, you fools. They're coming.*

SIX

"Death twitches my ear;
'Live,' he says...I'm coming."
-Attributed to Virgil, *Copa (the Barmaid) (45BC)*

Michael quickly scaled the charred wall of a house that had been devoured by flames and leapt across to a rooftop. His footsteps could not be heard from inside.

Ruthven never set foot on the ground.

As Michael watched behind him, Ruthven disappeared into the æther. He could sense nothing from behind him. The sensation of leading Ruthven into a trap was suddenly gone. He was being toyed with and chased.

Michael leapt across a wide alleyway and onto the roof of the train station.

It was quiet and he crept. Michael wondered why he had trusted the voice in his head. It no longer made sense standing there, but he had bought himself a few moments and that would have to be enough.

Thomas could no longer contain his anger. "Everyone stand up." They were slow to move as they stuck their heads up. "Everyone get up!" he yelled. The children scrambled to find their footing and Alexander looked down and saw the silhouetted body of a Vampyre standing at the back door. He screamed. Everyone panicked.

"He can't come in here," Newt observed. "It's the rule of being a Vampyre."

The group held on to each other tightly.

"Everyone be quiet!" Thomas screamed.

A bit frustrated, are we? Rurk whispered, tauntingly, to Thomas. *I am going to kill them all.*

Oh, I'm not above killing children. Rurk smiled. *It's actually quite ethereal. Not pleasant but...*

Thomas stopped listening.

"What if he can come inside?" Albert asked. "Seems awful strange that he plain can't." "Well, that's fine. He's welcome to it!" Thomas yelled.

Don't mind if I do. Rurk told him quietly. *That's all the welcome I need.*

Thomas turned with a bottle of blessed water in his hand, but Rurk was already there, grabbing his arm. *No, no. We don't want to do that, do we?* he said condescendingly. He sank his nails into the boy's arm and the bottle fell with a clank. Rurk looked at the other children but none of them moved. Even as the water spilled across Rurk's leg, he didn't flinch. He looked at Thomas again. *You get to watch,* he said. *I am going to kill every one of them first and you get to go last.*

With a flick of his wrist, he threw the boy against a booth and Thomas collapsed on the floor in pain. It felt as though he'd be thrown from the train.

The children cringed and Emily went to help Thomas.

The Vampyre laughed. *So,* he asked, *who goes first?*

The children tried to run and Newton reached for a canteen.

I guess it's you, then. The Vampyre grabbed Newton and lifted him.

"No!" Ollie cried, attacking the Vampyre with his small fists.

He looked down to see the little boy and he laughed. *How is it that you have killed anything at all? You are all so weak!*

Thomas turned to the Vampyre, "Stop that." He spit. "You'll do no such thing!"

"I'll go first." Ollie volunteered as he held onto the Vampyre's vest.

Rurk shrugged and looked at Thomas, who was fading in and out of consciousness. *Very well.* He smiled, throwing down the larger boy. He kneeled next to Ollie.

Oliver looked him in the eyes and Rurk felt oddly compelled to search his mind. He put his hand on the boy's shoulder and was pulled inside.

"There's nothing more tempting for a Vampyre than a broken mind." It was Sheriff Matheson's voice. He was trapped inside. Ollie fell down on the floor simultaneously with the Vampyre. Rurk was dead.

Newton ran to Ollie. "Are you ok?"

Ollie opened his eyes. "Bang, Mister Vampyre." He smiled.

B ut why the train station?" Jared asked in a whisper. He kept his eyes on the window. "We need Michael near." He could barely hold his frustration.

Two soldiers sat Moira in a chair as she explained, "Your fight with the inner covenant of Vampyres has nothing to do with that poor soul out there."

Genevieve ran past. "Edwin?" she called as she ran up the stairs. "He is invaluable to us," Jared growled.

"He cannot survive that creature out there alone." Moira stood up. "Creature? That little man out there?" Jared quipped.

"He is far more horrible than all the armies of Vampyres all over the world," she answered.

"How can you possibly know that?" Jared moved across the room, frustrated. "Because I am not like you..." Moira began, but she stopped. "I..." She went silent. "No." Jared surmised. "You are like that dreadful stone thing out there."

Her nose flared and her eyes flashed; Moira was growing visibly angrier. "Yes," she hissed.

Jared grabbed her by the shoulders with both hands, letting his rifle fall to the ground.

She was small but solid and she clenched her teeth at him. "What are you?" he demanded as she flinched, but his large hands gripped her tighter. "How could you know that?" he cried.

"Trust her." A calm man's voice came from across the bar. Jared looked over the girl's shoulder to see Glenn staring into a bottle of gin. "She has a spiritual connection to the Vampyre, you see."

When Jared looked down, the girl had shifted slightly and he felt the point of a knife at his chin.

"You should probably let her go." Glenn suggested. His calm was off-putting. The man seemed to be struggling with something deeper.

Jared released the girl, whose eyes burned at him.

"Why the train station?" Jared asked quietly, wincing with his own pain. He could feel his fingers going numb in his left arm.

"My people stayed there. We are not like the Vampyres, but we possess strengths they do not, dominion of the natural world...and the unnatural."

"Like witches?" he asked.

"Child's play."

"Then why were they able to hold you down there in the caverns?"

"Caverns?" She smiled. "We carved this ground." The smile quickly disappeared. "We worked with them because we were forced to, not by the Vampyres, but by those who have ruled above us and above you—the Lords."

"How?" Glenn asked, as he pulled the cork from the bottle.

"Political endeavors, often by threat, mostly by pain, curse, fear. Needless to say, most of my kind are gone." Her eyes fell. "We few that remain can no longer fight them."

Jared realized his mistake. He began to mutter.

"There's no need for apologies and no time." Moira began to smile but it faded. "Trust me for a moment." She took the knife and pulled it from his throat, slowly moving it toward his shoulder. He let her go instantly.

"Don't." He gritted his teeth.

She paid no attention, laying the flat side of the blade against his wound. He sighed with an instant relief. His mind rushed with the sense that the pain was gone; looking at his arm, he watched her lay her hand over the blade covering the bullet wound. It grew brown and green. Moss grew from his shoulder very quickly and then it was gone.

He looked at her; her eyes were a blank gray with no pupils.

She blinked and then her eyes normalized.

He began to speak again, moving his fingers freely.

"No. There's no time." She looked up, listening and her eyes grew wide. She turned to the room. "Spread the word! Stampede!"

W hat will you do now, Casey?" Thomas asked. "I'm sure you'll be in a lot of trouble when you get back.

"The witching hour is past." John Jones told Thomas as the train sped along. "I'm not so worried about all that. The truth is, after they make me sign all the paperwork, they'll send me right back to work. Breton is an awful place and my employers know that."

Thomas saw the lights of a city in the distance. "New York City, Mister Thomas." Casey smiled. Thomas was stoic.

"Do you have a last name, Thomas?"

"Sir?" he asked.

"A surname. Is there anything more than 'Thomas?'" Casey asked.

"If there ever was, I'm unawares, sir."

"That's unfortunate." Casey sighed. "A good name is something worth having."

"I suppose so." Thomas pondered quietly. "What about Thomas Williams?"

"Sounds fantastic, I think." Casey smiled. "I have three children, myself. The eldest is about your age."

Thomas looked down near the gasket where Casey held his hand and there sat a crumpled photograph of the very tall Mister Jones with his wife, Mary and their children. He looked very severe in the picture, unlike the smiling man in the engine.

"There are times in our lives, when we feel terrible...and terribly alone." Casey turned to the boy. "Consider me: I am a man that has a loving woman and three children for whom I would do anything, but I'm always out here, along the rails and among the trees."

Thomas turned to listen.

"We are all very alone in this world. That is the world's joke on us." Casey had a strange grin. "But we're all alone together. We share our solitude. The only thing that matters is whether or not we are willing to sacrifice for all the other lonely souls out there." His gaze was on the door behind him. Casey knew that Thomas was the only person those children had to protect them. "Consider yourself a Jones, Thomas."

Thomas smiled. "Thomas Jones-Williams. T.J."
Casey put his hand on the boy's shoulder. "It certainly has a nice ring to it."

D*awn comes.* Michael heard Ruthven's voice in his head. *Which begs the question. Does he die at the hand of his new foe or does he die at the hands of the very natural aggression of a world that hates him?*

Strange that you should ask. Michael stopped and stood still. *I'm not sure if your rhetoric is about me or you. The difference is that I do not fear death.* He smiled.

Fear, Michael? Everyone fears.

Michael became perfectly still. *Not I.*

You lie, because I sense it in you. Ruthven's voice came from within Michael's head. *You are full of it.* His voice was growing listless and anxious but Michael could not locate it. Michael focused and realized that Ruthven was moving between worlds. It was the only way. *I will not die by your hand, Ruthven. Though I might hold you here until you run to the darkness.*

Foolishness. Ruthven replied.

Cowardice.

The comment struck a nerve and Michael sensed Ruthven's sudden appearance in front of him with a crushing blow to the face. Michael crashed along the rooftop and grabbed his head. *I am no coward, Michael, but I am not suicidal.* Ruthven straightened his jacket.

"Well, then you should not have followed after me."

You're not making any sense. Ruthven walked across the roof and stood over Michael's body.

"You made your commitment with death when you so blindly followed me here." Michael grabbed Ruthven by the ankle and pulled him down through the ceiling.

They crashed into the floor between the rotting corpses of Adler and Sheriff Matheson. Michael stood first, followed by Ruthven, who righted himself in the room full of Druid refugees.

They both burned, unwelcome in the room, but the sensation was no more than superficial. Small flames flickered along their skin.

"Let's try this again, shall we?" Michael grinned as he threw a clenched fist into Ruthven's jaw. Ruthven bowed over to Michael's raw vampyric strength and collapsed to one knee, sliding across the marble floor.

Ruthven squinted.

He focused his mind, but failed to see any change. He stood there aching at his jaw. He should have disappeared from Michael's sight. Instead, he stood in the station, unable to move. Bewildered, he looked around to see disgusting and horridly sad men and women with their heads bowed to him. "Druids," he cursed.

If you hadn't been so concerned with killing me, you would have sensed them here. Michael said. *I searched for you. All day, I came for you and you hid. The one place that I could not see was this place. The gateways between this world and the other were impassible here.*

There's too many of them!" Jared cried. "They'll tear the place apart!"

Vampyres flooded the streets. Edwin's plan had worked. All too well, to Jared's mind. Soldiers took cover inside houses and stores that the Vampyres had previously avoided, but it was no use. They were more aggressive and blood-drunk. Hundreds of the Vampyres ran alongside the buildings, crashing into windows. Some attacked the people inside, despite their bodies bursting into flames.

Fire began spreading wildly throughout the town. The Vampyres crawled up the walls of the buildings and over the bodies left in the streets. They climbed trees and fences, covering the town like ants from a destroyed anthill.

Spencer watched them coming toward him and he began firing down among them, praying silently and reloading.

Vulnerable up here, he thought. *Alone and calling for attention.* He smiled. *I'm starting to sound like my mother.* He fired another shot. *Head. Ouch.* He pulled the trigger again, but finally it clicked. "Damn." Looking down among the Vampyres, he saw his opportunity. *I'll even give you bastards the high ground.* He threw the rifle down at the Vampyres climbing the bell tower as they hissed at him. *Come right up.*

He grabbed the ladder and made his way down quickly. Spencer jumped over a pew and made his way through the church building, where Sara Vogt and a few men were making some final preparations.

Vogt stared at Spencer Mayhew with one crystal blue eye and a still-bleeding empty socket. She grunted at the men as they moved pews and cleared the space.

Spencer tried not to make eye contact with the person he thought was a boyish man. She gave him an uneasy feeling. "Time's up boys. We need to get out of here." He made a dash for the front door.

"I like churches." Vogt responded as one of the men started moving out the back of the building. "It's like God and the Devil are always here looking for a fight."

Spencer pulled the heavy front door open. "Come one, come all," he beckoned. "We're all welcome in the house of the Lord!" And with a flourish, he disappeared into the candlelit room followed by Vampyres.

Vogt watched the man run past her. The other soldier at her side asked him. "Do we follow?"

"Instead, let's sweeten the deal." She smiled as she plunged her knife in between the man's ribs with a grunt. He fell, grabbing his side and bleeding out on the ground.

Vogt grinned as she made her way out the back door.

Letsya was confused. *We've been tricked.* He looked at the buckets of blood. He felt dizzy; he put his hands on the ground where the well should have been. It had been filled while they wandered in their madness.

We're all going to die.

The first purple rays of light began to fill the morning sky.

This way! called one Vampyre. *They've beckoned us from the church. There's no time to get back to the well!*

The Church? Ilya laughed. *It doesn't matter anyway, does it?* He waited as Letsya came, hurdling through dead bodies.

The well is shut!

Then we go into the Church. Ilya laughed. They jumped over bodies and ran along the walls of buildings until they found Adler's old church building unoccupied. Ilya felt the light begin to burn as he dove into the dark building.

It was completely empty; it was a trap.

Ruthven snarled, barreling toward one of the praying Druids. Michael stopped his movement flat with a fist that caught him in the stomach. Ruthven gasped in pain. *Bad form, Michael.*

Michael was quiet. *You won't have the time to kill them. Time is up and I'm going to make sure you are dead.*

The bald man watched as the two Vampyres fought each other. He could almost hear their thoughts as long as he stayed in meditation, focused.

The blue figures in the æther, they are ghosts are they not? Michael asked.

In a very elementary way, Ruthven answered. *The apparitions are just residual energy of the dead. They are like walking memories, mere empty shells.*

But they are energy, Michael continued.

Something like that. Ruthven wiped sweat from his brow.

Michael realized that when there were concentrated groups of the apparitions, he could see both worlds at once. "So these Druids have a lot of that energy on this side."

Ruthven replied, *The longer we are here among them, the more difficult it shall be to continue for you to continue speaking aloud like that.* He sighed, growing more exhausted.

Michael closed his eyes. He could sense it. The sun was coming. It was over. He smiled.

No you don't. Ruthven began running toward the door.

Michael could sense a presence from outside the building. Someone was there to help Ruthven. He wasn't going to allow it. He tackled Ruthven, sliding into one of the pews. Ruthven rolled under him and Michael brought a clenched fist down next to Ruthven's head and showed his teeth in a wicked smile. "Now, you die."

He focused all of his energy, trying to absorb Ruthven's essence as he had done to the other Vampyres, but the more he focused the weaker they both got. Without access to the æther, he would damage himself as much as Ruthven.

Ruthven let out a groan of pain and Michael clenched his teeth.

You're suicidal, Ruthven accused.

"And murderous," Michael replied, smiling.

Ruthven gasped at the transformation. Michael's eyes grew aflame and fire burst around his shoulders like demoniac wings. Ruthven's own skin and exterior melted away to show black skin and flaming red hair; his blood red fangs grew, skin and gums peeling back from the bones.

Everything melted away. Ruthven, a skeletal abomination, screamed. Michael clenched his teeth, dissolving them both in the horrible pain.

They began blending into one mind in the struggle. They both saw the colored flames, magenta and purple, blue and red, rising inside their minds. There was desolation and dead solitude as parts of them died away. Despite the memories of murder and hatred, there was a cold, dead silence overcoming them. *It's over,*

Ruthven. Michael sensed a void. Ruthven was completely gone. He was dead.

Michael could barely hear the chanting of the Druids around him. His eyes grew more and more tired. He could hear his dreaming thoughts crowding his mind. He could no longer fight and his limbs shook with the wretched pain. The flames engulfed Michael and the darkness surrounded his mind as he collapsed on the skeleton below him. *Death,* he thought. *Peace, finally.*

"The sun has risen," the bald Druid announced as the chanting dissipated throughout the train station.

Ilya and Letsya looked across the dark room quietly contemplating their demise.   *This could have been avoided,* Letsya told Ilya plainly.

But isn't it beautiful? The chaos, I mean. Isn't it inspiring? Ilya smiled while two young Vampyres filled themselves of a soldier's body that lay in the church. They listened outside as the hissing turned to the sound of crackling and screaming. The bright morning sunlight had caught the blood-drunk Vampyres outside. There were hundreds of them running in every direction, trying to avoid the sunlight. It was no use, even as some jumped into the chasm, they realized that the passage back into the complex had been blocked by stone. They dug and moved the rocks as best as they could, but it was hopeless.

All for a game, Letsya said.

Life is a game, Letsya. All of it. Ilya smiled as he sat down in a pew.

Three more Vampyres came in through the front door, all burning. The flames decreased, and they squealed and moaned in pain, tossing themselves on the floor.

We're saved! one cried.

Ilya laughed.

I didn't want to die, Ilya. I wanted things to continue as they were!

Ilya sighed.

For the first time in forty years, Letsya felt the chill of a tear on his cheek. A group of Vampyres came in through the back door. Other Vampyres helped them onto their feet and patted out the flames on their skin. There was a full congregation of them in the church. They gathered in the darkest corners of the building, holding each other. *Why is it so well-sealed in this building?* a young, handsome Vampyre asked.

That's a good question. Letsya said. *I think they led us here to make sure we didn't escape somewhere else. They plan to kill us here.*

Vampyric voices created a psionic cacophony; abject fear and the desperate loneliness known only to primordial demigods would leave a psychic scar on that place for æons.

Ilya put his hands behind his head and stretched his legs, reclining in the seat. *There's no use in fighting it, Letsya. What a grand experience it will be. Death truly is a beautiful thing.*

The whole village has gone to war, miss," Gallegos explained. "Man versus Vampyre." He spoke comfortingly to the girl hidden in the shadows of the dark cellar below the inn.

Why didn't they come looking for me? she asked.

"You must understand. Until this moment I could not be sure that you were—" Gallegos eyed Edwin, "coming back."

Edwin stood behind the man, whom he had followed into the dark of the cellar against his wishes. "I never gave up."

A pair of sharp blue eyes suddenly shined in the darkness from behind crates and barrels. *How long has passed?*

"Several days. I brought you here, under a terrible assumption that you would awake in a volatile haze. With your father's hatred of the *Vampiros*, I hid you until we could see how rational you might be. And you could have awoken with *un gran odio*. Some come back knowing only the hunger."

I want my father, she responded in a hoarse whisper.

"Yes. A good idea." The old man turned to Edwin.

"I have a very bad feeling. Like I'm going to suddenly catch on fire," she moaned.

"Don't worry, Kat." Edwin smiled. "We're gonna fix this." He couldn't believe it. He was right about Kat. There was a hopeful grin that wouldn't leave his face.

"*Señorita* Kat," Gallegos began. "My intention was not to hurt you."

"That isn't exactly true," she replied.

"Do you blame me?" he answered coldly as he lit a rolled cigarette. "One of two things had happened. *El primero,* you were killed. In which case, I would tell your father. *Y el segundo,* as we see now, you are *Vampiro.* And he would not know what to do as I do."

Are you going to kill me? she asked quietly.

"I do not know," he replied as a cloud of smoke rose into the darkness.

Edwin jumped down the stairs. "No, no." He looked terrified. "There are men out there. Different men. Black uniforms."

"*Carajo*!" Gallegos cursed. "*La Alianza.* They knew this was going to happen. They always knew. They were already on

333

their way here." He moved quickly to the window and turned to Kat. "Please lower your head as to avoid being burnt."

She disappeared, a shade receding into shadows, pierced by her glistening amethyst eyes.

Gallegos removed rags from the cell window and looked into the morning. "They are *La Alianza's* fixers. They will make this entire place disappear by the end of the day."

"Where is everyone?" Edwin asked.

"They got here somehow. Probably by *trén*." He stuffed the rags back into the window. "They've loaded survivors onto it, I am certain."

"Are they going to kill them?" Edwin asked.

"I suppose," he thought, "if they prove useless. I do not know." He turned to Kat, who was hidden in the darkness. "It would appear you and I will be working together."

Kat waited alone as they ran, whispered, reconnoitered and returned with Spencer Mayhew.

"So it's settled then?" Spencer asked, pulling a long black coat over his shoulders. The matching officer's cap gave him a sinister look in the shadows of the Crow's Nest's cellar. There were men marching everywhere in matching black uniforms. *The mythical E.C.A.* He thought. *If they're here, some big to-do knows how bad it is here.* That was a bad sign. They had to get out of there quickly. The Environment Control Agency was a secret branch of the Lords' "Alliance" that consisted mostly of powerful Druids, Fiends and Shifters. He knew of their existence but had never seen them before.

"Jasper Markov," Gallegos answered. "He is the man with the circus cart. He is now our target. He also has a particularly important document."

"And a Vampyre," Spencer filled in.

Kat's voice came from the pitch black. It's *Michael. I can feel him dreaming.*

"Then it's decided," Gallegos replied.

"I owe him my life." Spencer stated quietly. "I'm in."

Edwin stuck his head down the stairwell. "It's clear into the alley now."

Gallegos took the second coat. "My little *amigo*, you are quite good at going unseen, yes?"

Edwin smiled.

"Yes, I thought so. Meet us at the south edge of the wood." Gallegos turned to the girl in the darkness. "Miss Kat." His voice was cool and deliberate. "What I am about to tell you will not be easy."

She stepped from the darkness as if shedding a cloak.

"Within moments, those windows will go black and you will be trapped here, alone. Likely, you will be crushed. Roots will grow around you as the agents above us convert this place in hours into primeval growth."

Her face went pale.

Spencer groaned.

"Whatever you do, do not show your face to these men. They will kill you efficiently and with alacrity.

You must wait until night and if you are quiet, you will know when the moment is right. You will be forced to dig your way out." He moved toward the door as they heard explosions coming closer. "There is no way for us to protect you from here and we do not have the power that you have." The old man stepped forward and took her hand in his. "Trust in your power.

Follow us and we will see you on the other side of twilight."

One by one, they abandoned her in the darkness. She was completely alone. She waited until the room filled with the smell of sulfur, and death as the buildings around her collapsed. Breton was little more than rubble above her. Kat bundled some rags and set them on the floor. She lay across the ground and looked at the ceiling, her torn blue dress billowing below her like a puddle. She hummed the tune that her mother had secretly sung to her each night and with each note, the world was shown to her anew. Colors billowed like clouds and the darkness was peeled back to reveal a world to explore. The song was the key. She heard voices, voices she knew were ringing from deep in the past, singing in multiple parts. She could see through the æther, as men in black coats made earth of buildings and trees from nothing. Through the prismatic clouds she saw them make a forest of her home.

She wanted to cry, but her sadness was washed away to reveal cold rage. *I will find you, Michael.* She rolled over and clenched her teeth as she buried her face in the cloth. It grew damp with her angry tears as she tried to rest and wait for the night to come.

ΕΠD

EPILOGUE

I saac Constantine sat with his legs crossed. Steam danced in curls from the edge of the teacup in his hand. The smell of Earl Grey was refreshing and warmed him through. He could feel the bright morning sunlight against his back and he cherished it.

"Here we are," came a distinct and gentlemanly voice. "Crumpets, butterscotch candies and biscuits. It's been quite a while since I visited Islington, so I couldn't remember where they kept the biscuits." The voice of Algernon Elliott came with a smile. "You know, they hid them on account of my addiction. They never stayed hidden for long. I have a dog's snout when it comes to the location of biscuits."

"Mister Elliott," Isaac was cordial. "I do not mean to be so rude."

"Rude? No. Go right ahead." Algernon smiled as he poured some tea into a second cup.

"Well, I am quite sorry for whatever inconvenience my people have caused you, but you did come to kill us." Isaac stopped and sipped at his cup of tea.

"Quite right." Algernon's smile dissipated slowly.

"Time, Mister Elliott, is of the essence." Isaac let go of the cup of tea and it floated in mid-air. "In only a moment, you will be dead if you do not make your decision."

The beautiful Islington tearoom began to get darker.

"Am I going to die, Mister Constantine?" Algernon asked, letting go of the teapot in his hand. The stream of tea hung still and the teapot sat atop it like a painting of a waterfall.

"Indecision is itself a choice. We are pressed for time." Isaac replied.

Algernon looked up, painfully, gripping his chest.

"There is a rock on your chest, currently," Isaac explained, "and this subconscious projection will only hold out as long as you and I are both in agreement and you are alive." He stepped around the table to Algernon, who wheezed with suffocation,

"Shake my hand. Agree to a truce. I will save your life and for now, you will protect mine."

Algernon's eyes were growing hazy.

Isaac forced his hand out again.

"Do it, man. Don't be a fool."

"Not much of a choice."

"No choice at all."

"How can I..." Algernon wheezed, "trust you?"

"You don't have a choice."

Algernon's eyes searched the room as it grew darker and darker.

"Mister Elliott, I can and will save you, but you must agree to help me in a small matter once we get out of here. I promise that it is indeed to your benefit."

Algernon collapsed to his knees, looking panicked at the Vampyre in front of him.

Isaac held his hand out.

Algernon reached out and took it as everything around him went black.

Two men in long black coats stood looking at the strange contraption in front of them. As the survivors continued to be wrangled and herded toward the train, E.C.A. Junior agents Timms and Ellgen looked at the series of ropes staked down in one spot next to the old church building. The whole building was covered in blood. The ropes were fresher, clean and free of bloodstains. Someone had tied the ropes to something on the inside of the building and run the cords out through broken windows to pulleys hung from tree branches. All the ropes came back to the one spot between them.

"It's a bomb," Timms surmised.

Agent Ellgen chuckled. "No."

"Sure," Timms replied. "I'll go double or nothing on the bet in the train that if we cut this rope, the building explodes."

"I suppose it don't much matter. They'd be doing our work for us, but no. It's not a bomb." He thought on it for a moment. "You're on." Ellgen smiled.

They stood back and looked one last time before Ellgen removed a knife from his boot. Timms winced and covered his head while Ellgen cringed and swung the knife down on the rope. Pulleys rattled as the rope flew. Nothing happened.

"I guess that's a draw," Ellen said.

Suddenly the large crimson curtains that hung in each of the church's windows began dropping, one by one.

A horrible screeching sound came out of the building as Vampyres were exposed in the sunlight. They ran looking for cover. The curtains fell throughout the building into the rear rooms. There was nowhere to hide. The flames rose from the windows; the building caught fire. They screamed and hissed until the sound gave way to an airy crackling and popping made by the bodies alongside the wood of the church floors and walls.

Ellgen stared. "Was there a Vampyre in there smiling?" he asked.

"So, best three out of five." Timms replied.

"Gentlemen." Agent Hastings said. "We have a day. Let's get to work."

Both men saluted as Hastings passed.

Ellgen and Timms turned to the abysmal sinkhole behind them. "What is that, a hundred feet?" Timms asked as he looked over the bloody edge of the chasm in the middle of the square of the large town.

Ellgen answered, "I've done bigger."

"That's what the lady said to the sailor." Timms chuckled.

"We don't have all day." Called Senior Agent Hastings

"Clear!" an agent in the distance called. He leaned on the wired dynamite plunger in front of him. The deafening detonation caused the shoddy old Inn to collapse almost immediately. A sign blew off in the explosion. It read "Crow's Nest."

As the smoke dissipated, Junior Agent Ellgen focused on the large opening in the ground. He gritted his teeth, reaching out over the hole, wrinkling his brow as the ground shifted around his feet. An intricate system of tree roots began to stretch itself out from one side of the breach like arms. The roots broke from the collapsed rock, moving quickly to suture the fissure like threads in a loom; first large roots danced forward, then smaller ones pulled them together.

Timms walked out across the growing root system, surefooted and quiet. Another building collapsed in the distance. He stretched his arms in either direction and pulled gravel and top soil to him like a blanket across a man's sleeping body. The earth shifted and moved. Dust rose and rocks fell between the roots, filling with a coat of mycelium-rich undergrowth.

"Showoff." Ellgen said.

Where buildings had been, trees were sprouting and spreading. A new forest was overtaking the land. In a matter of hours, a town once called Breton would be no more.

Two hours had passed and Glenn Lamphere looked across the passenger car on the clean train. He knew what would come next. *In a few days, you won't remember a thing.* He thought as he wiped a tear from his eye. He looked out the window and watched the men who had come on the train in their long-tailed black overcoats and shined boots. Even as the bodies of the Vampyres crackled and burned in the sunlight, the uniformed men marched in with their polished guns and matching officer's hats. There had to have been fifty of them.

One man, who wore a white armband on his coat's sleeve, had approached Glenn and Genevieve with a smile. "Many felicitations on behalf of the sovereign governments of Canada and the United States of America." He called himself Agent Hastings. "You have vanquished the greatest covenant of the Vampyren-Nephilim in the world." He smiled. "Let us escort you to a more accommodating location."

The man made Glenn uneasy. Across from him sat Raymond Warner, who turned to one of the soldiers as he passed by. "Excuse me sir, will there be food or drink served on this train?"

The soldier had no answer.

"That's quite rude," he muttered. "The least a man could have would be some semblance of service after that horrifying ordeal."

Glenn could see that the man had suffered no inconvenience. His shoes weren't even dirty, while the rest of the train was filled with people that all had the singularly common trait of being covered from head to toe with the smell of death.

Jared sat next to Moira, sweating bullets. He felt trapped on the train. Death he was familiar with, but he had not been so terrified since he was a little boy. After his parents had been murdered, he hid away any emotion. Walking past his only real friend in the world, as she lay dead on the ground, took away any hope of living. He had seen Bernadette, still holding her shotgun, entrenched with soldiers, who had been ambushed by the Vampyres. They should have been inside, but they held their ground. They were surrounded with the smoldering bodies of the Vampyres they'd killed, the bodies of the Vampyres that *she* had killed.

Glenn looked out the window where men unloaded large equipment on carriages. One man sat a small tank on the platform. He fumbled with a box of matches. He turned the knobs and hoses on the tank allowing it to begin spewing flames. *In a couple of days, I won't remember. I won't remember. I won't have to remember.* He repeated over and over. He filled his head with worrisome words, trying not to remember how he'd taken Zoya's life. He tried not to remember that Katarina had been abducted. *In a couple of days, I won't remember.* He filled his head with words so he wouldn't remember the ponderously horrible future revealed to him by the ancient Sin Eaters. He wouldn't remember whathe saw when he looked into the abyss. He wouldn't remember exactly what looked back.

Moira patted Jared on the hand. "The Black Coats are going to erase it all," She whispered, "Trust no one. If you get out alive, no one will ever believe what happened here." She stood with a polite smile and walked toward the back. She turned to him. "You're welcome. I hope you'll be well." She winked.

Jared looked up at her, but before he could thank her, she was leaving the train car. He looked outside again. *Glenn was right. They knew it was happening.* Jared sat uncomfortably on the train, massaging his shoulder, as he watched Sara Vogt bandage her eye with a sleeve. She leaned back in the seat, the union army shirt unbuttoned, exposing the tightly wrapped cotton bandages around her breasts. She exhaled and searched the room with her good eye, testing her ability to register depth and distance.

Genevieve stepped into the passenger car as it begin to move forward. *Algernon?* She couldn't bear the thought. As she looked around the car, she didn't express her fear. *Edwin? Spencer?*

Only moments later, the cold wind was whipping around Jared. The train was moving incredibly fast. It was his first time on a train and he would be getting off. Genevieve slid the rear door in the passenger car open and he looked at her. "Jared!" she cried, muted under the immense sound of the monstrous machine and the swirling wind around them. "What are you doing?"

"Something's not right!" he answered. His eyes darted with paranoia. "Glenn told us! It's happening! They're gonna erase our memories!"

She leaned to hear him. "No! The only way to fight back is to stick together! We have to stay together!" His neck looked like it had been tattooed along the left side. The veins had turned brown and looked like the roots of a tree. *Moira,* she thought.

"The black coats knew all along! They're all in this together!" He gave her one last glance as the train barreled along the track, knifing through the forest.

Genevieve looked down at the sack full of everything Jared had ransacked from Desmond's room. A long rifle lay across it. "Don't do it!" Her eyes welled with tears.

"It was an honor, Miss Moreau!" He said. She could barely read his lips and her eyes began to water as she looked away. He kicked the sack and rifle off the train. She looked back.

He was gone.

Jasper Markov lowered his cap and reined in his horses attached to his old circus wagon. "Iago, Othello, let's go." The carriage had special cargo. He pulled forward to the town limits, when a soldier waved him down with a long rifle that glistened in the sunlight.

"Good day, sir," the soldier replied coldly.

They will aim to kill you, Jasper. No mistakes, he thought. "Good morning, sir." Jasper smiled.

"Can I ask where you are going?" the soldier stated. It wasn't a question and Jasper felt like the man was telling him he'd made a mistake by being there.

The horses shifted.

"Leaving Breton with..." He swallowed. *Nothing special. Tell him it's nothing special.* "Remains..."

"Remains, sir?" The soldier was unimpressed. "I'll have to see that cargo." He allowed the curl of a condescending smile creep. "Please step down and show me."

"Sir, as you know, Lord Ruthven came here." Jasper spoke as he climbed down. "We know."

"But Desmond disappeared and Lord Ruthven was freed by Adler," he continued. "Lord Ruthven is free?" the man asked with fear in his voice.

"No sir." Jasper replied. "After you." He beckoned with his arms. "He has been destroyed."

The man turned around to face Jasper, who was smiling. He pointed toward the back door of the colorful cart and the soldier turned again slowly toward the rear of the carriage. Jasper took the opportunity and hit him hard across the back of the head.

The man went tumbling and his officer's cap flew into the grass. Jasper fell on top of him, beating the man into quiet submission.

He stood up and breathed heavily and brushed himself off. *I'll have that coat and hat now too.*

He left the body in the forest, off the path and came back to the carriage. He pulled the rear door open and the morning light fell on the dark, iron sarcophagus that he had prepared as an escape for Lord Ruthven. He pulled his new cap down and spoke quietly to the man inside. "Michael, my new friend." He sighed. "Let's see how this works."

Michael lay motionless inside the sarcophagus. He had no power. He was charred and dying.

Jasper pulled out a large, ancient journal and set it on top of the metal coffin. He spoke the magic "spell", in broken Spanish, "San Miguel Arcángel, defiéndenos en la batalla. Sé nuestro amparo contra las perversidad y asechanzas del demonio. Reprímale Dios, pedimos suplicantes, y tu príncipe de la milicia celestial, arroja al infierno con el divino poder, a Satanás y a los otros espíritus malignos, que andan dispersos por el mundo, para la perdición de las almas. Amén."

He heard a quiet groan. *Ah yes!* Jasper thought. *You will not be strong enough to tear me apart as long as we keep this up.* He folded the corner of the page, where he had recognized the words, "Vampiro," "exorcismo," and "debilidad."

He crawled out of the carriage and smiled. *All death and anger in Breton.* He let out a heavy sigh. *New York, here we come. Let's make us some money.* Then a new thought occurred to him. "Ladies and gentlemen!" He waved with his arms theatrically. "Children of all ages! Come one, come all to see the Prince of Darkness!"

Yes, a freak show. That would be quite fine.

He climbed back up on the cart and it lurched forward into the bright new day. He heard detonations coming from within the town. "And we're out with a bang!"